VITYAZ

JAKE BARATKA

Vityaz by Jake Baratka

For information, contact BDI Publishers, Atlanta, Georgia, *bdipublishers@gmail.com.*

ISBN 978-1-946637-12-3

Cover Illustration: Ion Baic
Layout: Tudor Maier
Editor: Dennis Ghyst, Ph.D.

BDI Publishers
Atlanta, Georgia

PROLOGUE

The world this book takes place in is distinct from our own in a few key ways. The key one is based around Middle Eastern conflicts and their implications in Europe. In this universe, a Pan-Arab war recently ended, lasting from 2010 to 2016. Iraq, Iran, Syria, Saudi Arabia, Jordan, and to a degree Turkey participated in this war, with Saudi Arabia and Turkey receiving NATO-allied volunteers, while Syria was assisted by CSTO/CIS (Eastern Bloc) volunteers. The war was started by a resurgent Ba'athist Movement in Iraq, and a drastically radicalized government in Iran. Each participant was in it for a reason--Iran to conquer, Iraq on the hunt for oil and economic gain once again, while Saudi Arabia, Syria, and Turkey kept national defense as a goal. The war greatly disrupted the oil trade with their partners, affecting NATO-associated nations more than CSTO nations; Russia in particular got off easy, as it is one of the world's largest producers of petroleum. Many oil fields were burned, and from all combating nations, millions of Arabs, Persians, and Turks died. In the end, borders remained unchanged, but resources were scattered and lost, leaving many economies weaker than they are in our timeline. This created increased tensions between the East and West, as the West struggled with a crisis of resources. In the midst of this, one company marketing the uneasy trade between east and west decided to prepare for the worst... However, the means are not the point of this book.

The ends are.

CONTENTS

CHAPTER 1

Monday, October 2nd

It was dawn in Moscow, the grand capital of the Russian Federation, Home to over 11 million people. Just a few blocks from the Kremlin, a young soldier wakes up in his apartment. This soldier, a part of the Russian GRU, is Boris Vladimirovich Kasyanov.

As far as he is concerned, his life is devoted to one thing, and that is his country. He had made it through school, went through his mandatory military training, and just decided to stay, as it gave him a sense of purpose. He had made that decision many years ago. Now he works at a military base a few miles from Moscow, and he had about 50 minutes to get there.

Boris immediately began preparing, realizing he'd overslept, and threw together a bowl of oatmeal, the tasteless mixture scalding his throat as he raced to get it into his stomach. He ran to take a shower; then finally dashed out the door and started his old car. It coughed and choked, but eventually roared to life, and he began driving to the outpost. He was already in his uniform, though he had missed a button and would have to wait until he arrived to fix it.

A while later, about 10 minutes tardy, Boris arrived at the gate. He only received a light scolding from the guard and figured that it wouldn't be much compared to what he would get in a few minutes from his commanding officer, the infamously stern Captain Senaviyev.

He was given janitor duty in the morning drill before he could sit down to lunch that day. He was the last one to get food by several minutes.

The rest of the day was the same as all the others, going through drills and training exercises. *What's the point? I've been in the military since before some of these guys got out of high school. This is a waste of my time. It almost makes me miss Riyadh.*

Boris struggled through the day, unenthusiastically performing his "duty" marching around a field and shooting at stationary paper targets.

Much later, as Boris was driving back to his apartment, blindly flipping through the radio stations, he found the news channel, and began to listen absentmindedly. There was something about a string of murders in the Arkhangelsk oblast, and another about some sports player complaining about how dangerous his job was. At that, Boris scoffed. The station had caught his attention now, but the next broadcast would keep it.

"CSTO-NATO WAR IGNITES! CHINA DECLARES NUCLEAR WEAPON COUNT NOW ABOVE 400! DPRK DECLARES IT HAS CREATED A FUNCTIONING LONG-RANGE BALLISTIC MISSILE! ARAB LEAGUE PREPARED FOR CONFLICT ONCE AGAIN, UNITED AGAINST THE WORLD!"

Boris got the announcement his country was at war earlier in the day. He'd been told that he would likely be on a counter-espionage operation towards the end of the month, but that for now he was simply to "Ensure the Safety of Moscow"-- in other words, sit still while others did the work.

Wednesday, October 11th

Over the past days there had been much news about the war. In Asia those at war included most of the major powers, including India, (supported by Russia), China, both Koreas, (The North supported by China, the South by NATO), Japan, also supported by NATO, and Pakistan, independent, declared war on India. While no nuclear exchange had occurred, diplomats and politicians were arguing vehemently both for and against it. The massive battles occurring, even without the nuclear element *yet*, were resulting in the deaths of millions throughout the continent. In Europe, despite heavy fighting, the lines of the NATO and CSTO forces had moved very little, the nuclear option being tossed around just as it was in Asia.

Boris, of course, had no desire to witness a nuclear war. There truly couldn't be anything worse. However, it always stayed in his mind during his unfulfilled days away from the fight in Moscow. He saw it as one of those things you often think about but never really believe could happen. *Surely*, he thought, *there isn't a justification for any sovereign nation to decide it's a good idea to end the world.*

And yet…

Friday, October 13th

22:00

Boris is the last one to clock out every time. Every day, he leaves last, aside from another soldier, whose name he thought was something like Mikhail or Nikolai. Maybe Nikita? He wasn't sure. He was talkative, but Boris had never paid him any mind, though there was a strange familiarity about him.

He was watching the TV sitting in the corner of the mess hall while he was cleaning out some of the fridges' old food. It'd been talking about the war, like all of the other channels. But then, it was cut off by static, and a large beeping noise started, followed by an announcement.

"WE ARE FACING A POSSIBLE NUCLEAR ASSAULT. REPEAT, WE ARE FACING A POSSIBLE NUCLEAR ASSAULT. IF WE ARE STRUCK, ELECTRICITY WILL LIKELY SHUT DOWN FOR THE FORESEEABLE FUTURE. COUNTER-BALLISTIC MISSILES WILL

ATTEMPT DEFENSE OF MOST METROPOLITAN AREAS, BUT CITIZENS ARE STILL ADVISED TO SEEK COVER. GATHER ANY SUPPLIES YOU HAVE. STAY AWAY FROM ANY POSSIBLY MALFUNCTIONING ELECTRICAL DEVICES. IF THIS OCCURS, PLEASE PROCEED BY ATTE…"

The television blinked out. All the lights were off. Boris opened the fridge, and the little light inside didn't come on. *There's no reason to panic. The power probably just went out on its own. This has happened before, like once. It must be a coincidence.*

Then a large rumbling sound, almost deafeningly loud, came overhead, from the direction of Moscow.

"HEY! DON'T LOOK AT IT! IT'LL BLIND YOU!" The other soldier shouted toward Boris.

"I HAD NO INTENTION OF DOING THAT!

"DID YOU LOSE POWER, AS WELL?"

"YES!"

The soldier entered the room. "You're Boris, right?"

"Yes. Would I be wrong in saying your name is Nikita?"

"No, you wouldn't be."

"What are we going to do?"

"We need to see if we can get to Moscow… If there still is such a place," Boris replied.

Nikita nodded, and they both began trying to navigate to the exits in the low-light conditions imposed upon them.

They went out to the parking lot and noticed their cars were parked next to each other. Nikita had a nicer, more modern car than Boris. He looked like he was trying to start it, but it wouldn't turn over. Boris, being an amateur mechanic, got out and asked Nikita what was going on.

"It won't start! It ran perfectly this morning."

Let me look at it."

Boris popped the hood.

"It's… it's dead."

"Dead?"

"Dead. It won't start. Probably ever again."

"Why is that?"

"Your car's electrical control units have been knocked out, so the car's dead."

Boris and Nikita got into the old Moskvitch, which still started. They began driving toward Moscow.

They got onto the highway, and it was pitch black. They could only see about 15 feet in front of them.

Out of nowhere, the tail end of a car appeared.

"WATCH OUT!" Nikita shouted.

Boris slammed the brakes, and swerved out of the way, but the new angle revealed a long line of abandoned, dead cars, all empty.

"I think… *everyone's* cars died…" Nikita muttered.

"What now?" he added.

"I guess we'll go back to the military base and wait until morning; it doesn't appear there's anything to be done now. We're no use if we crash into a car or tree," Boris said.

"That is likely to be the only thing we can do right now," Nikita confirmed.

The two got the Muscovitch on the road and made it back to the military base a little after midnight. Boris parked his old car and stepped out into the night. Before he closed the door and made his way into the building, he thought--*So, politicians and by extension sovereign nations really* can *decide it's a good idea to destroy the world. Go figure.*

Boris and Nikita both made their way into the base silently. They then each found a place to sleep in the base. Boris went to the armory, Nikita went to the mess hall, and they both slept--or tried to. In reality, there was no sleep to be had. The old world was gone, and it was never coming back.

When Boris woke up, he wasn't used to the dark, since the armory didn't have any windows, and stumbled into the door. He opened it, and light flooded his vision. It was morning again. Once he'd fully returned to his senses, he heard talking…

It sounded like shouting, as well. It was probably just paranoia, or perhaps just one of the other soldiers who also decided to head back to the outpost.

The problem with that theory is that they couldn't be here, because of the traffic.

Time to grab the gun.

Boris grabbed an AK-74M assault rifle, the great-grandson of the famous AK-47; then grabbed his knife and put on his helmet. At this point he was only wearing the standard blue and white army undershirt and his fatigues, which also held his Tokarev pistol, a family heirloom and the only thing he had left of them now.

He stalked over to the door where the sound of talking seemed to originate. He could tell there were more than one, and he couldn't hear Nikita's voice.

The door itself was slightly ajar, enough to where Boris could look through it, hopefully without drawing attention. All the men he could see were dressed in black and seemed to be speaking Russian. Nikita was sitting in the middle of them, his hands tied up while he sat on his knees.

Now Boris had to make a choice. He could either jump into the room, with his gun at the ready, and try to talk them out of it. Or he could enter the room and either shoot them, or just keep watching from where he was. He started listening to their talking more closely. It was slightly muffled, but he could still make out the last sentence, which made the decision for him.

"That's it... just shoot him already!"

No time for thinking in that case.

Boris crashed through the door and shot the man closest to him, then ran up to who appeared to be their leader and put him in a headlock, his knife blade centimeters from the man's neck.

"SHOOT ME, AND YOU'LL HAVE QUITE A MESS TO DEAL WITH!" Boris shouted, not thinking how he got this sudden burst of courage, or whether it was just stupidity. After taking action, the pistol of the man he'd shot was close enough for him to kick over to Nikita.

The man with his gun to Nikita didn't budge.

"STAND DOWN YOU IMBECILE!" the commandant shouted.

The man with the gun to Nikita reluctantly lowered his weapon, giving Boris the opportunity to kick the gun to Nikita. It was a Makarov, a fairly small gun, and he managed to pick it up and get his finger on the trigger, aiming up and shooting through the jaw of the man who just a second before had held all the power.

The other man turned and ran, dropping his gun on the way.

Nikita raised his weapon and fired once, hitting the man in the bicep of his right arm.

"Don't kill him. He was a coward. He won't be coming back," the commandant said.

"You're awfully calm for someone a centimeter away from repainting our floors a shade of red," Nikita scoffed.

"I already know you won't kill me. You're soldiers. You killed the one because he threatened your comrade... as for you," he said, looking at Nikita- "I'm not so sure. The one with the newly pierced skull disarmed himself… but I suppose that was his own fault. I, at this moment, pose no threat to you. I'll make it even harder for you to kill me by putting my face with a name. I'm Vasiliy. Vasiliy Andreevich Pogodin. So, soldier, are you going to kill me?" the commandant asked.

Boris didn't let it show, but as the commandant turned his head Boris noticed a small tattoo on his lower neck; the Insignia of the KGB, and the year "1988" inscribed below. Realizing the possible usefulness of this Pogodin, his attitude changed slightly.

"You still assume we live in the civilized world. We're soldiers. We'd have the legal high ground against a common bandit any day. Now, nuclear weapons have been fired and martial law has been declared. In this chaos, nobody would stop me from killing you. As for that, I will more than likely end up killing you, but not today. We may have some use of you."

Boris disarmed Vasiliy Andreevich and unloaded his guns. "Now that's settled, *why* should we keep you alive?" Boris inquired.

"I'm offended. Is it not enough to spare the life of an innocent… okay, you're not *that* stupid, so an unarmed man?" Vasiliy feigned a look of benevolence.

"You're still nothing more than a common criminal. Give us a reason or I'll throw you out with a bullet in your leg," Boris responded, unmoved.

"Am I supposed to give you my college degree? If it wasn't apparent, I got into this base without either of you noticing in time, as well as doing it with the morons I was with. I can steal- -and stealing will keep you alive when there is no law." Vasiliy changed from sarcastic to serious.

"You have no morals and deserve to rot and die. We'll keep you for now, but if it's a bullet that kills you, it will be mine," Boris finished.

"So, now that we're done with this pleasant conversation, what are we going to do next?" Vasiliy asked.

"We should go to Moscow and see what's left of our city. As soldiers, it's our duty. Vasiliy, you're basically a prisoner of war, so you're coming, too. Anyway, I think the best bet for finding people is the Metro. We can figure out what to do from there."

Boris looked at Vasiliy, then back to Nikita, and said, "Fine. But we need to gather any gear we can to lessen the effect of the radiation. We need gas masks and anything else that will protect us from direct exposure."

"We need to stay here for a while, however. There's a rule with radiation--the 7/10 rule. Every 7 hours, the radiation becomes a tenth of what it was. But I'll tell you, even though Moscow wasn't hit directly, it will be a radioactive wasteland for two weeks, when the radioactivity levels will be low enough for us to enter more safely..." he added.

CHAPTER 2

Two weeks later.

It was time for them to arm up. Boris donned his uniform, but also added a balaclava and gloves to eliminate any exposed skin. For weapons, he was armed with his Tokarev, the AK-74M, and the weapon he was assigned to, a Dragunov SVD marksman rifle, which he had on his back, attached to a sling.

Nikita was armed with his Pecheneg Machine gun, and a Makarov pistol, as well as having his military gear on in a similar fashion to Boris.

Vasiliy was armed with a Vikhr "Whirlwind" submachine gun, and a Stechkin automatic pistol. He declined to wear any army garb, choosing instead to remain in his black coat.

The three exited the base, wearing gas masks and having no exposed skin. None of them were experts on radiation, but they knew the less contact, the better. Their goal was undefined, but they knew they had to see what had become of Moscow.

They were heading for the easternmost entrance to the Moscow Metro, called Novokosino. They got into Boris' Moskvitch, and began driving down the side of the road, along the line of broken-down cars. Progress would be slow, but the lower speed would result in better gas mileage, so it may be better in the long run, anyway.

Boris was driving, but his mind wasn't fully on it. It took him until then to realize he had already killed a man. He hadn't once thought about it until now. He never saw his face, he was just a figure in black, that once shot, dropped to the ground and started bleeding. He didn't know whether he would ever kill another person, something he thought he was done with after the Pan-Arab war... but he did know that if the answer was no, that it would be because someone killed him first. He could only assume that Earth would become a kill-or-be-killed world.

Nikita just stared out at the countryside, watching it like he expected something to come out and attack the car. After a while, though, he became drowsy. He closed his eyes for what he could have sworn was a second, and the scenery changed. It deteriorated. It seemed the radiation had affected even the life on the land--with half dead trees missing most of their leaves now making up most of the landscape.

He could only hope the supposed missile interceptors he'd heard of had done some good.

Vasiliy was watching the other side of the road, thinking much more strategically than Nikita. He was looking to see if any cars still had people in them. Most still did, their passengers and drivers slumped to the side, obviously baked by the radiation. Even though Moscow wasn't directly struck by a warhead, non-explosive fragments still got through, and that is what killed so many. While thinking this, he didn't notice the fact that Moscow was within sight, nor that the cloud and ash that was beginning to choke the sun out of the sky.

Another effect of the nuclear apocalypse would be nuclear winter. The ash and soot released from the explosions would drop the planet's temperature drastically, and for at least a while, Earth would be a foggy nightmare. This is what occupied Boris' mind during the drive, up until he got close to their destination.

His plan was to cut the engine, and coast for a bit until the car stopped. Anyone in the area would hear the engine, and possibly try to take the car if he got too close. So, he stopped the car, and pulled it behind a high bush.

"It's time. Get out. Pogodin first," Boris ordered.

Vasiliy stumbled out of the car, obviously not expecting being told to leave first. However, as soon as he regained his composure, he stood behind the bush, in a half-crouched position, looking around for any possible enemy.

Nikita got out next, followed by Boris.

"Stay in front of me at *all times*," Boris said to Vasiliy.

Vasiliy didn't respond but nodded affirmatively without looking toward Boris.

"Advance," was the next order from Boris.

The three of them crept forward toward the outskirts of the city. They had no idea what to expect, as they had no way of knowing how the police had managed the crisis, nor of whether Boris and his group would be seen as hostile.

The entrance to the metro wasn't too far away, but every second felt like an hour. As the group passed the furthest-out buildings of the city, they knew it would only get worse. They had no idea what sort of things could be waiting for them.

As they looked at the city itself, the buildings seemed to be undamaged; obviously the missile interceptors had done an adequate job keeping the city intact; however, it was a ghost town. There wasn't a soul walking the streets of the once very busy city. The devastation wasn't immediately visible, as the real devastation obviously was the result of the radioactive fallout that had draped over the city. In many of the now silent buildings the dead likely rested, while the only ones alive were those below, in the Metro system.

There's a decent chance we'll just be shot by someone before we even get anywhere. These buildings likely aren't totally devoid of life, and every window could house a man with a gun, and our death, Boris thought. Though he'd been in battle before, it was still incomprehensible that at any moment, his life could suddenly end. Or the idea of surviving a shot, and bleeding out in the Moscow streets, likely watching Nikita die as well, and Vasiliy run, only having made it a day through this new, devastated world.

No matter how much he tried to contemplate it, or tell himself it couldn't happen, it just wasn't a thought that would leave his mind and leave him feeling alright, especially since the "couldn't happen" logic had already failed him once in the past month.

He kept watching. All the buildings were quiet. He kept his eyes fixed on windows, rooftops, anywhere he could be ambushed from. Then his foot hit something. He stumbled over the leg of somebody lying face down on the pavement. Boris considered checking to see if they were still alive, but in his heart, he knew that they weren't, so he just continued walking. That was something he would unlikely to get used to.

But he was now more aware of the bodies all around him. There were some on the street, some in cars, none moving. He kept walking. They would reach the metro in less than five minutes now by his estimation. That's when he heard a voice. It was coming from an alleyway. He couldn't make it out.

He then made the third irrational decision since the start of the Apocalypse, rushing past Vasiliy (whose presence was irrational decision two), he charged around the corner, into the alleyway, where a bewildered teenager clutching a knife stood.

"G...Give me your valuables!" he shouted, trying to sound intimidating, but his voice was quaking. He couldn't have been much older than 15, with pale skin and blond hair. He looked like he hadn't slept in ages.

By this time, Nikita and Vasiliy had come to join Boris, and then Boris said, "Kid, put the knife down. Walk away. We don't have many valuables anyway."

"We should just shoot him," Nikita said, somewhat sarcastically.

"I said give me your stuff!" The teenager shouted.

"Here kid," Vasiliy said, tossing him a gas mask. He immediately turned around and kept walking the direction they'd been going.

The teenager was unable to respond, and so Boris, then Nikita, left the alleyway.

"Why'd you do that?" Nikita inquired.

"He reminds me of myself. I'll admit I used to be nothing more than a petty thief. Maybe showing a bit of decency can save him. Granted, it probably won't. Why not try, though? We have extra filters and masks in the car."

Neither Boris nor Nikita knew how to reply. They hadn't seen and never would have expected him to do anything like this. They were at the entrances to the Metro now. Boris went to knock on the gate, but he got no response. He expected this, and decided to advance forward, breaking open the gate. The threesome marched down into the darkness of the Metro.

They only went a few steps before floodlights buzzed on, and a voice over a megaphone shouted at them.

"WHO ARE YOU, AND WHAT IS YOUR BUSINESS?" the man on the other side of the megaphone was balding, but looked strong.

"Lieutenant Boris Kasyanov, accompanied by Sergeant Nikita Gorbunov, and Mr. Vasiliy Pogodin. Seeking entrance to the Metro!" Boris replied, business-like in manner.

"Take their weapons!" the man shouted. A few men in rags with old-looking Kalashnikovs stepped forward, looking as wary as the teenager they'd met earlier.

"You will do no such thing," Boris stated, as calm as before. He raised his weapon, and Nikita and Vasiliy followed suit.

That's when a taunt came from one of the men aiming at them.

"Cowards! You should be off fighting the Yankees!"

"There aren't any Yankees to fight, you idiots! Most places outside the big cities and Moscow are glass!"

That silenced the heckler.

"What did you think was going to happen? You aren't going to return above ground and keep living like normal! This metro is likely one of the largest groups of humans anywhere on the planet now!"

Boris looked to his side, and realized it was Vasiliy who was shouting this. Vasiliy then began walking forward through the crowd. Boris and Nikita just followed behind him, into the Metro.

They ended up stopping toward the end of the station where they decided to sit down and eat some of their rations. For now, the goal was simply to live in the Metro a few days and see how the people were living. Besides, what else could they really do? Surely, there was no more war to fight. The next few days were spent in the Metro. It was very different living without the sun rising every day, without Boris looking over to the Kremlin, to the busy streets, where there were people--humans, living humans, not killed by radiation, going about their lives and doing what they were meant to do. But now… What's the point? What's the point of anything? Like this, the world will slowly starve and die. There can be no future the way things are now. The food here will run out; the limited means of acquiring more will be overtaken by the demand, and across the world this same problem will be repeated.

So, Boris thought, *the politicians and the diplomats decided that nuclear annihilation was a good idea? I wonder. Was it worth it? You will be remembered; you will be in the history books, if history books are written again. And do you know what you've done? Surely you do. You've killed not only millions of civilians, but millions of your own countrymen, and even your own families and yourselves. Even before this all went nuclear, you condemned millions to death,* Boris continued to think to himself, not expressing his thoughts lest others think he'd lost his mind.

One thing he now knew for sure, though, was that he needed a purpose, a prospect. Something to do.

A few more days passed, and he stayed close to Nikita and Vasiliy, and they only made small talk. They mostly intimidated those who threatened to do harm to others, sometimes racking the bolt of their weapon or shifting it in their hands to keep order. However, it wasn't gratifying and every second of it irked Boris, as he was doing almost nothing for these people. They all looked like ghosts as they mechanically trawled through the tunnels seeking to survive, the life in their eyes all but gone.

They went to go eat some "homemade stew" made from very questionable ingredients. They tried to balance between eating what they had and what they could barter for. It seemed that ammunition, which they had in ample supply was going to be a new form of currency. Because of this, they were able to barter quite easily and without much concern, as they could simply return to the base for more supplies if they needed them, assuming no other raiders like Vasiliy came to steal stuff.

Boris sat down on one of the benches in the Metro with his food and began eating. After a few minutes, a relatively young man sat down next to Boris and started talking.

"I need to talk to men who are willing to change something. It may have only been a few weeks, but this Metro will not last like it is." He didn't look directly at Boris, nor at anybody else, but said it with certainty.

"What do you have in mind?" Boris agreed with the last part. He wouldn't watch his countrymen waste away in this Metro any longer. He had no obligations. Why not try to improve things?

"There's a seedbank. A place where the seeds for every known plant on Earth exists."

"I know of the one in St. Petersburg. There is unlikely anything left of it. Looters probably scavenged it and wasted the resources," Boris said, beginning to get discouraged. The idea of going from Moscow to St. Petersburg has likely been discussed by many.

"There is another one. Svalbard. It's on a Norwegian island. I know for a near fact that it wasn't damaged by any bomb, though the villages around it probably were," said.

"How do you propose we go about that, then?" Boris inquired, not sure what he thought of it at this point. Would traveling across Europe be a good idea, for the small chance that bank is still there, and that he'd survive and be able to get most of it back?

"Well, it's really not that complicated. We just need people willing to go with us. After that, we will go to Denmark or northern Germany, wherever we can find a cargo freighter first. We'll clear anything that needs to be cleared off the deck and go to the island. Assuming we make it to the island, we'll first try not to *shipwreck* on the island, and then load up anything we can, sail back, and try to get to Moscow again. Simple," the man said, as if it was a trip to the supermarket.

"That is the stupidest idea I have ever heard and likely ever will hear." Boris restrained a laugh.

"Are you really just going to sit in this Metro for the rest of your life? Why not try to do something useful? As a soldier, it's your job to do whatever you can for the well-being of your country."

"I can't believe I'm about to say this… but if you can get at least twenty men who have enough of a death wish to do this… I'll do it." Boris said this not entirely seriously, though he did have a faint interest.

Vasiliy had been listening, and decided to chime in.

"Both of you are lunatics. If you think that will work, you deserve the horrific death you will likely suffer."

Nikita added, "I also think you're insane, but what the hell else are we going to do? And Vasiliy, you are still our prisoner, so you will go either way."

"…Pizdyets…"

"So, have you made a decision yet? By the way, my name is Józef Sokolowski. Originally from Poland."

Boris stood up, and said "Well… I see no future for me in this place. I joined the Army as a commitment to my country. Now I must help save it. I am going. As for Nikita and Vasiliy, it is up to them."

Vasiliy said, "If this starts going the wrong way… I'm out."

"I agree with Boris. We have a duty. And if Vasiliy leaves I might as well… to find and shoot him as a traitor…" Nikita said, eyeing Vasiliy suspiciously.

"Now we must find any willing to join us. Meet back here, once you have found at least five that will come with us," said Józef.

The group split and went to different areas of the Metro. Boris figured this process could take up to a week, so he figured he had time to make his way down the Metro a few stations, to get to people the others may not find.

CHAPTER 3

After several hours of walking, Boris made his way to the edge of the Circle, or the center of the Metro. That's where he started his hunt. The first man to catch his eye was sitting in the corner of the station, staring blankly at the wall, muttering in something other than Russian.

Boris approached, and said to the man, "You don't seem to be from around here. Maybe I can interest you in something to do."

The man, possessing dark blue eyes and blondish brown hair, followed silently.

The main reason, Boris told himself, that he went to this man first was that he was dressed in military garb and wasn't talking to anybody. He didn't seem to have any connections that would compel him to stay in the Metro, at least not apparently.

The going to get a drink idea was inspired by a shack with a sign that read, "WATER RATIONS HERE". Some government officials were giving out things like water, while others had already started small business ventures, selling things like alcohol and junk food.

They each received a bottle of water and sat down at a bench. Boris gazed into the murky water, beginning to regret his decision. He knew he would indeed have to talk to the man anyway now.

"I'm gathering men. Fighters. Wanderers. The adventurous type. We're going west. If you accept, information will be passed to you as we travel, and you will have an excellent reward if there is success."

"I'm listening. More detail." The man spoke in what seemed to be a Germanic accent. It was obvious he didn't speak Russian very well, but he seemed to understand what was being said.

"We are going with roughly 24 men. We have access to weapons and food to stock our trip. You can back out in the first one-hundred kilometers. After that you stay," Boris said, making up the rules as he went.

"What is reward?" The man gazed into Boris's eyes blankly.

"Glory."

"Elaborate."

"Yes or no. I cannot tell you more without an answer."

The man stood silent for a few minutes, mulling it over in his mind.

"Fine. I will go. I am Otto Freihardt."

"Good. Meet me at Novokosino station in six days."

He nodded.

Boris left the table, surprised he'd managed to get someone. That was one down, four to go.

The second one, Arkady Trubetsky, was around forty, but his age didn't show, and he seemed strong and capable. The real reason Boris took him, however, is because he asked no questions and accepted Boris' offer quickly. He obviously had nothing to lose.

The third one, Zhenya Sudakov, was quite the opposite--he couldn't have been older than 20 and had lots of questions. He wouldn't accept until he was assured he would be well-compensated, as well as knowing further where he was traveling. Boris told him they would be leaving Russian land, but nothing more.

The fourth one was a native Siberian. He was very quiet. He only said about four words in the conversation-- "Petya," "Explain," "Supply," and "Yes"-relative to stating his name, asking about where they were going, if they would be supplied, and his agreeing to go.

By the time Boris found a fifth candidate for his party, five days had passed. At this point, he was tired, as the searching and moving around the Metro didn't leave much time for sleep, but he was nonetheless highly focused. He only had a day left.

As he stumbled into another station, he instantly saw this one was different from the other ones he'd been in. There were red banners with what looked like an Iron Cross hanging from the top of the station, and half-built fortifications stood at the entrance.

He called out to the guards, who looked almost as tired as he was. "Hello! Who are you? I seek entrance!"

The two guards looked at each other. They were either new, or they hadn't had many visitors in this first three weeks of the apocalypse.

One of the guards stood up and walked into the station. The other guard shouted, "WELCOME TO THE REICH. ARE YOU SEEKING TO JOIN THE REICH?"

What is he talking about? Boris thought. "No, I'm just seeking entrance, passage through this station!"

"CERTAINLY, THAT IS UNTRUE!" the man shouted. He didn't even look directly at Boris. He just stared into the empty tunnel, continuing to babble.

After a few minutes of this, Boris decided to turn around. That's when he heard "FREEZE!"

He turned around, and about five armed guards were facing him. Their weapons seemed just as inferior as the ones the residents of Novokosino's had, but they wielded them even more fiercely.

Boris wasn't going to take this. What were these, Fascists?

"What do you want with me now?" Boris snarled at them.

"ARE YOU ONE OF US? A RUSSIAN?" The men droned.

Why does this matter? Does it really only take a few weeks for people to radicalize like this?

"Yes!" Boris shouted back. He didn't expect this would get him the results he wanted, but they obviously wanted him to answer in the affirmative anyway.

"TAKE OFF YOUR BALACLAVA AND HELMET!" The men continued.

Boris complied. He revealed his face, tanned, with dirty blond hair and grey eyes. Boris turned around to place his headgear behind him and drew his pistol on the way up. In that moment, he intended to drop it, to show he was passive, but this was not how it was interpreted.

"YOU DARE RAISE YOUR WEAPON AT US?!" The Fascists shouted, and they readied their weapons.

Boris then turned fully to face them, bringing his pistol up, and at that exact moment a figure ran from behind the five soldiers. One of the soldiers dropped to the ground, having been stabbed in the back. The figure continued running until he was away from the stunned soldiers. Boris got a look at the person, a young Asian man, quite fit in nature.

Boris wasn't going to waste any time and used that distraction to fire on the three other soldiers. Only one managed even to turn to face Boris. By the time he did, he'd already been shot in the chest, and just gave Boris a blank, empty stare as he fell to the ground.

By then, the man with the knife had taken out the last soldier with one quick slash to the man's neck. The Asian man shoved him to the ground, his t-shirt and ragged pants now bloodstained.

The man then turned to Boris, and at that moment Boris thought he would have to kill his savior as well, but instead the man spoke.

"Who are you?" He asked.

"I'm Boris. Boris Kasyanov."

"Jeung. Jeung Kim."

"What happened to you?" Boris asked.

"I was imprisoned. When I wandered in here, they treated me as inferior and as a spy for the communist group that formed a couple stations down. Which isn't true, as I was lost, and simply trying to find my way around. How could I have known that fascist and communist groups even would have existed here? Anyway, their makeshift prison cells, which were just closets and storage rooms, hadn't been cleared out of the stuff in them very well. Mine had an old bottle of water and this knife in it. The doors they used to lock us in were rusty, so I just slowly pried the door off the hinge, sprinted toward this exit, then stabbed those guys. That part was just adrenaline."

"How did you perfect your skill with the blade so well? Are you a military man?"

"I'm not a soldier. I'm from Pusan, in Korea. I spent a lot of my teenage life learning to survive harassment from gangs with a six-inch knife."

"Interesting. Well, I have a proposition for you. How would you like to get out of here?"

"I would, indeed. What are you proposing?"

"Some associates and I are leaving the Metro and going west. That's all I can tell you now, for sake of confidentiality, but after the first 100 kilometers you can either back out, or I will fill you in on the other details. After that, if you defect, you will be shot. We won't look for you if you appear missing; we'll assume you are dead."

"What do I gain from this?"

"Great compensation. Moral and Physical."

"Fine. I'm in. Those Fascists or some other radical group will track me down if I don't go, anyway."

Boris and Jeung then proceeded to loot the ammo and weapons off the soldiers, which included Jeung picking up a Groza assault rifle. At this moment, three more soldiers charged out of the gate and opened fire.

Boris and Jeung turned to face them, and they both returned fire.

Boris shot one of the men in the face, causing his head to jerk backwards, flinging his gun behind him. Before he'd hit the ground, he'd moved on to the second and killed him with a burst to the chest. By this time, Jeung had managed to down the other man, despite having used many more bullets than Boris.

Evidently, Jeung was not at as skilled with guns as he was with melee weapons.

After that engagement, they decided to run back. Boris then began to lead Jeung to the meeting point. It took them a few hours, but they got there relatively undisturbed.

Boris and Jeung were the last to return; the other people were already there. All of those who were recruited were seated on some benches, with Nikita, Vasiliy, and Józef conversing with one another.

Boris glanced over at the men they'd chosen. Along with the men he'd picked, there were some interesting faces, such as a man dressed in a VDV uniform, a woman with a Skorpion submachine gun, and a heavyset man with red hair, who was quite obviously not Russian.

Boris walked over to Vasiliy, Nikita, and Józef and joined the conversation. "We gather any supplies we can now, and we leave at midnight. We stop at our base at 1:00, and then we continue onward. If there is any threat at our base, we will face it before we move on," Nikita explained.

Józef seemed to agree; though he had little knowledge of tactics, he knew that having military gear would greatly aid the expedition.

Most of the group was getting ready to move out, gathering their belongings and either storing them or leaving them behind either for anyone to take or with those in the metro they knew. After about an hour, most of them seemed completely ready.

They waited for the Metro to be "asleep." Though not being able to tell day from night in the Metro meant that some had no set sleep schedule and so could be seen wandering about at any hour, but most stuck to their schedules as before.

The group of Twenty-four then left the Metro, leaving nothing behind.

Boris and Vasiliy led in front, with Nikita and Józef in the back. Their assigned men were behind and in front of them respectively, and they went across the Moscow streets. At this point, most of the people the four had taken with them were lightly armed, only dressed in the clothes they'd had on when the bombs dropped, possessing little more than handguns and civilian-grade rifles. The march to the military base would likely be quite arduous. The Muscovitch could hold five at maximum, so it wouldn't be that useful. Also it was likely nearly out of gas, and though there was an enormous amount of gas to be tapped from the cars on the highway, they had nothing to siphon it with nor to store it in.

As Boris walked past his car for the last time, he muttered "Goodbye" to it, and continued onward. It would be an hour or two before they reached the military base. From there, they could see what other options for transportation they might have.

CHAPTER 4

I t was an uneventful walk.

The group was largely silent the whole time. This was surprising to Boris as he was expecting much more chatter. It also made him acutely aware of how much he disliked standing in front of armed people he didn't know. And he realized that taking these people to a military base and arming them with modern equipment was not going to help the situation, so he was likely to change his position, at least at some point.

After a while, the base became visible from the road. They began to cross through the gridlocked traffic, and Boris said to the group, "Do not go into the open on either side of the road. Weave through, and we will have cover if there are any bandits or other hostile groups."

Nikita followed right behind Boris, and he ordered some troops forward.

"You two, move up next to me," he said to two of the men who were each only a few meters from him.

One of them was a very dull looking man armed with an old Mosin rifle. The other was the female Boris had noticed earlier. She had very light hair and pale skin with a combative look to her.

Those two, accompanied by Nikita, moved to a car next to the front gate. Nothing as of yet.

Boris pulled out his SVD rifle and glanced through the scope to see if there was anybody around. Nothing caught his eye at first, until he saw a glint. It was the glint of a sniper scope.

"GET DOWN!" he shouted, as a shot rang out, striking the man with the Mosin rifle in the bicep. The man grimaced and groaned, but it appeared the hit wasn't going to kill him.

Then Boris stood up to his full height, scoped in his rifle, and fired. The target was standing on the roof of the facility, and he tumbled forward off it. His rifle hit the ground first, followed by a *CRACK*, as the enemy struck the ground. A moment later, a few more men exited the building, wielding some of the weapons from the base. Boris proceeded to shoot another one, and the other members of the group opened fire. Several more men would exit the building, but all of them were shot.

Boris then noticed the uniformity of this group. All were in ballistic masks, wearing black. It could just be a gang of some kind, but it could be anything, including some organization.

At the end of the firefight, Boris advanced first with his AK-74M back in hand. He checked the bodies, and instructed his group to take the weapons on the ground that had been taken from the facility, adding quietly, "Don't worry about the blood… It won't stop the operation of a Kalashnikov…"

He then reached the front entrance and stooped to grab a flash grenade from one of the downed enemies. But, after he grabbed it, the man stirred, and reached for his gun. Before Boris could draw his own, Jeung's knife plunged into the man's throat, killing him instantly. Boris glanced up toward Jeung, muttered a quick "Thanks," and then turned to the door.

He threw the flash grenade into it, and then dashed in, followed by Jeung and Petya. They fanned out to each side of Boris, Jeung with his Groza and Petya with an old SVT-40 rifle that he had kept hung over his heavy coat.

There were two more men in the base, both injured in some way. One of them stood up and attempted to shoot his weapon at Boris and his men. Petya shot the man first, in the direct center of his chest, and with that, the injured man dropped to the ground instantly. The last one was still up against the wall. He was dressed differently from the rest of them. He only seemed half-conscious, and had a large bandage across his stomach, with dry blood staining it. Boris squatted down to reach eye level with the man and shook him to see if he would awaken.

He did and began shouting in German in a panicked voice.

Boris acted accordingly, calling Otto to his side. He told him to try to talk to the man.

They went back and forth for a few minutes, with Otto trying to keep the man calm, succeeding to a certain degree. He seemed to get some information out of him, and then stood up and faced Boris.

"He says that this group of men tortured him, and that there are more. It's some kind of militarist group, formed from members of several countries. He doesn't seem to know where the rest of the group was located, nor how many of them there were, but he did know that there were more of them, and that those men we killed may be missed."

Boris thought for a moment, and said "Well, then, Nikita, Vasiliy, and I will monitor the collecting of weapons and equipment. Arm yourself and gather in the mess hall when you are finished."

Otto relayed this to everyone else, and Boris, Nikita, and Vasiliy stood near the armory, directing people to weapons that suited them, distributing body armor and helmets, as well.

Luckily, there was still plenty of equipment. For the most part, Boris just supervised, and gave information on equipment. He saw several weapons from the armory that he'd never known were there. While most of the people just took a Kalashnikov, there were a few exceptions. Petya took an SVU marksman rifle, the woman Boris had noted earlier took a PP-Bizon, a few others took a Vikhr "Whirlwind" submachine gun, and Jeung took an AN-94 rifle.

Boris explained to Jeung what made that rifle different from most of the rest was that it had a complicated mechanism that allowed it to fire a two-round burst at over 1000 rounds per minute, as well as being quite expensive. This seemed only to make Jeung more interested, as given his lack of skill with firearms, he said, "Twice the chance to hit a target on a trigger pull…" Boris replied "I *really* need to teach you how to shoot…"

In the end, the distribution process took about two hours, and then everyone congregated in the mess hall, talking and examining their new weapons and equipment. Many of them only carried parts of their Russian equipment, making them look more like guerilla fighters than soldiers, as they'd yet to get any uniforms. Boris doubted all of them would take one. Regardless, they looked formidable. Now he needed to teach them how to fight. He walked into the room and got up onto a table.

"Now Nikita and I will teach you how to operate your weapons. We will use the shooting range in here, with five of you at a time. For expedience, my group will go first. Nikita, begin some basic training."

At this, Boris called his men and went into the shooting range. Otto was still using the MP5-type weapon he'd had before but had an extra VSN submachine gun as well. Boris trained him on its use, and then let him be as he seemed to know what he was doing.

Arkady was also fairly adept, largely because he was using a Kalashnikov, known for its simplicity. His hands were somewhat shaky, but he was a surprisingly good shot.

Zhenya was a bit more challenged using a Vikhr submachine gun, and he tended to waste his ammo. Boris had to teach him to fire in bursts, and eventually he began to work like a nearly flawless machine, firing almost exactly three bullets at a time.

Petya was very skilled. He was likely a hunter as a child, and Boris didn't need to help him much, except in the specific operation of his weapon. Boris noted, however, that the only piece of military equipment he was wearing was a ballistic vest; no helmet, gloves, or uniform otherwise.

Jeung had a lot of potential, that was for sure, and he definitely picked the correct weapon. He fired in two round bursts very effectively, at a rate and accuracy surprising given his lack of experience.

Boris let them practice a while longer, eventually calling them out before allowing Nikita's group to go in.

Those who weren't training were doing one of a few things-- eating, sleeping, or exploring the base. Boris and his group were assigned to the latter, staring out into the darkness with some night vision eyewear.

Boris was standing silently next to Petya. It was eerie, staring out into the motionless parking lot, with the bodies of the militarist group still on the ground, though the ones nearest to the door had been moved to make them visible from the road to discourage anyone from entering the base and disrupting this temporary peace.

However, as eerie and silent as it was, it was tense as well, especially considering the base had been taken after Boris shot an unsuspecting man--with his people then storming the base, wiping out the defenders. That was concerning, considering that was during the day and achieved with an ill-equipped militia.

Granted, these militants didn't seem well-equipped, nor trained, but it appeared they would act ruthlessly, as even the wounded man tried to kill one of them before he met his inevitable demise.

That didn't change the fact that it was likely those psychopaths would be coming back, especially since the group they wiped out was probably a scout battalion of some sort. Boris then thought, however, that they should try to injure and capture some of them, to try to get more information about them. This could be important, considering the shaken man they'd found was German, it had coverage in an area at least equivalent from Russia to Germany, if not larger. How an organization this massive activated so quickly was a mystery, despite its growing pains as evidenced by its poorly trained troops.

Boris simply couldn't stop thinking about the situation. He became increasingly tense, clutching his rifle like dropping it would incinerate what remained of the Earth. Boris was staring intensely through his goggles, his gaze darting madly around the scene, desperately searching for an event he didn't want to see, only able to think about the similarities between this and missions of his past.

Apparently Petya noticed this, and he reached out to Boris, putting his strong hand in his shoulder. Boris turned his head to face him, and Petya began talking more than he ever had before to Boris. "Don't focus on how worried you are. Something will happen. Focus on how you will react *if* something does. If a crisis arises on this tiny base, I have my trust in you to guide us to victory. You've led us successfully already. Even though I do not know you well yet, I imagine I will in time, and grow to appreciate you even more." Petya took off his night vision goggles, and Boris, through his, could see Petya's kind eyes.

"Thank you," was all Boris managed to get out before Petya continued.

"Let's go inside... I think Nikita's group is done now." With this, Boris called the rest of his group inside, and Nikita's took their place.

Boris and Petya sat down at one of the tables in the mess hall, each with a bit of rations and some tea.

Boris had never bothered to study Petya. He appeared to be in his late thirties but seemed wise beyond his age. He had dark brown hair, with even darker eyes, but they emitted a calm, knowing aura.

"How did you... get here? And why do you still have your coat?" Boris asked, out of his newfound curiosity.

"Well, I'd been told I should move here. I was a writer, you see, and my family told me I wouldn't get anything accomplished if I lived out where I did, in Baykit. They told me to move to

Moscow, but I refused for many years. Eventually, I gave in, and they allotted me most of the money they had – more than I deserved – told me to go, and that they'd miss me, and then I was off. I still had my coat on as I exited the plane, and a few hours later, before I'd even managed to get to my hotel room, the sirens went off and I dove into the nearest entrance to the Metro. I was able to keep nothing but this rifle a local militiaman dropped (which in my panic I somehow managed to retrieve), this coat, and a notebook I've have carried around for a couple years to record my observations." He stopped for a second, and then added, "So what's your story?"

"Well... I'll start by saying I always liked writing stories as well, but my father told me I was to serve in the military, like he and his father before him. My grandfather was this big war hero from The Great Patriotic war. I think his first name was Konstantin, but I don't remember his last name, as my father told me he changed it to his wife's maiden name to evade some of the attention he was getting after the war. Anyway, my father always wanted another hero, almost giving me his name, but my mother thought otherwise. My parents were often conflicted over what I should do with my life, but after my mother fell ill, my father's plan won out. But he changed. He was a good man, but... well, he just wanted everything to be as he thought it should be." Boris conveniently left out details of his actual military history, something he was not quite ready to share with any of these people yet.

"Well, maybe, one day, you'll be able to have an audience to write to," Petya replied thoughtfully.

Boris and Petya talked a while longer, mostly about how it was like before the war, and their respective lifestyles. They ended up being the last out of the cafeteria; everyone else was asleep. Guards weren't needed anymore, as Nikita stumbled upon some old Soviet landmines left over on the base. Although technically illegal, it really didn't matter now. He had them placed outside the base in any place that made sense, figuring everyone would wake up to the sound of an exploding landmine, so nobody really needed to keep watch.

Boris ordered them to sleep near their weapons, however. This militant group, apparently called The Order based on the writings on their uniforms, could be more numerous and powerful than they imagined.

Boris decided to take the main office, not for his status, but because it was the least crowded, and because he'd been in there before; though usually not for legitimate reasons. He was behind the desk, in the corner, with his sleeping bag, which he'd kept in his car, and put in his backpack. It took up some space, but Boris was skilled in "efficient item rearrangement" and was usually able to fit things where he wanted them to fit, regardless of whether they 'wanted to' or not.

He placed his Kalashnikov on the chair but kept his Tokarev right beside the sleeping bag.

He woke up to an explosion. Though it was so loud that his ears rang for a full minute, he wasn't the least bit surprised. He nearly laughed, out of the sheer predictability of the enemy.

He rose, nonetheless, and picked up his weapon and sidearm, put on his gear, and met with everyone else in the cafeteria. They were scattering about, but for the most part seemed ready. Nikita was trying to organize them, and Boris figured he'd just let him manage it. Boris instead made his way to the roof, so he could see the enemy. They were likely approaching much more slowly now.

He got to the lip of the roof and found Petya was already there. It wasn't until then that he got a good look at the enemy.

This obviously wasn't the rabble they faced yesterday. These men had military-grade equipment and garb.

Those with assault rifles and light-machine guns all wore a black helmet, a ballistic mask, which obscured their entire face, and supposedly could to some degree defend against small-caliber rounds. Given these men all had one, they were more likely for the purpose of intimidation.

The rest of their uniform consisted of a dark-grey camouflage, ceramic armor, and shiny black boots. Boris also took note of the old trucks on the road they had arrived in. They could be useful, if his team survived the assault.

As more entered the area, Boris noticed two distinct groups of these soldiers; in the first group, the men were arranged in rigid formations, and moved robotically. As they approached, Boris could make out the words "The Forgiven" written across their foreheads. The second group was made up of those lacking that identifier, who moved in a much more natural manner. Boris didn't know what to make of this, but the difference was glaring.

Boris changed his focus to see Nikita, Vasiliy, and Józef leading their men to sit behind some cover, to ambush the men once they got a bit closer. Although most of the mines in their path had gone off, it didn't seem to interrupt the ranks of the enemy. Even though the mines had killed some, the gaps were filled nearly instantly, and they continued to advance, unfazed.

Boris figured he would begin firing as soon as he saw one of them make a move.

Nikita acted first by throwing a hand grenade into their lines. It landed right in front of the first rank, and the men spread out, though not in a panicked way. Some didn't get far enough in time, and were killed, but the rest raised their rifles and began firing in Nikita's general direction.

Boris and Petya then stood up and began firing. The lack of responsiveness from the enemy was concerning. He'd shot about five of them, and they hadn't looked up yet. After that, though, he heard a very clear, but stern-sounding voice from the back lines say "Up there. On the roof," in English. Interestingly, the voice had no discernible accent. It wasn't Russian, or Polish, or German, or even British or American. It was very basic.

The one challenging them appeared to be some kind of officer, with a white star on his black helmet. He swiftly directed about 10 men to fire on Boris and Petya. Their accuracy was mediocre, but when their weapons were out of ammo, they would reload them very quickly, in machine-like motions. The discipline was incredible.

The other strange thing was the incredible morale these men had, or the lack of it. They didn't react to the death or injury of any of their comrades… He and Petya had shot five of their men. One of them was bleeding heavily, lying across the boots of one still alive, but there was no reaction from the man in the boots. After that, a man was shot in the stomach, falling, with no cry nor complaint to his own death. Boris then noticed something else. One of their injured was leaning against a box behind the others who had fallen, holding his hand over his wound, and kept jerking his head forward. Boris didn't understand at first, but then realized.

He was trying to scream.

Since he couldn't, he was just lying there, dying, unable even to cry out in pain. Boris almost had pity for this man, when he stopped jerking his head, removed his hand from his stomach, and drew his sidearm. He then attempted to fire at Boris but missed every shot. He then raised the pistol to his own chin and fired.

Boris needed to analyze what that meant, but he couldn't do that now, as ten more men had taken the places of those who'd been shot. The difference between the first and second group of men was even more stark; the majority of those who had stood and died were those with "The Forgiven" marked on them; those without were standing behind cover.

As he stopped to reload, he saw that Petya was firing very confidently, seeming to have no fear of death. Seeing Boris' shock at his lack of fear, Petya remarked, "I'm going to die one day, maybe this day. I have decided to face it with courage."

Boris was amazed at his bravery, and decided to muster some of his own, as he thought about things for a second. Surely, he wasn't to die now, but if he was, why not go out bravely?

At this, he stood up to his full height, and drew his Kalashnikov, dropping his SVD to the ground. He then began to fire into his enemy. They didn't react to his sudden surge of courage, and many were too slow to react. The remainder of the men facing him fell quickly, and by now, the main group's numbers were dwindling.

Once the enemy was down to about twenty men, the officer threw his hand up in a fist, shouted, "Withdraw!" in the same toneless voice, and the remainder fell back, all except the human-seeming among them keeping in stride as they fell back.

Boris noticed that they continued to fire, but then realized they weren't shooting in Nikita's direction anymore. He saw one man, who was bleeding heavily, attempt to follow his comrades out of the battle, when a cloud of blood burst out of his forehead. The shot came from the direction of his retreating comrades from one of the unmarked men. The wounded soldier's head jerked back, his hand twitched, and his head hit the ground, motionless.

The only thing Boris could think was that they weren't going to let him have any living prisoners. This indicated they could be hiding something, which meant that Boris needed to find one of them who was still alive.

CHAPTER 5

Boris then began to make his way downstairs, toward Nikita, to give the order to search for survivors. When he came out to face his men, he saw Józef crouched next to a man lying on the ground with blood all around him.

Boris approached, and saw that it was one of Józef's men, a young man with a round face and a moustache. He was quite obviously dead, as he'd been shot in the center of the chest, and he'd lost too much blood. Józef had an expressionless face. Clearly, he hadn't witnessed death this way before.

Boris had lost soldiers before in battle, and the loss of one, especially, still haunted him. Therefore, he was able to relate. He squatted down next to Józef and said, "He was the first. He may not be the last. Just know that he died for something worth dying for... Our victory avenges him."

Józef still said nothing, but Boris stood up, and went to Nikita.

"We need to search the bodies. Collect ammunition; look for survivors."

Nikita replied, "Yes sir. But why do we need to search for survivors? It would certainly appear that these enemies aren't the type to change sides."

"Because the retreating ones shot the wounded that couldn't fall back with them. It's either a harsh system designed for efficiency in retreat or they don't want us to learn about what they are," Boris replied, and then began walking to the bodies, preventing Nikita from protesting further.

Nikita then gave the order to search for survivors, and seven men fanned out to begin checking the bodies, as well.

It was a very unpleasant process. Most were shot in the chest or head, and much of the concrete around them was bloodstained. Boris searched through them, walking among them, trying to see if anyone had survived. It would be quite ironic if his soldiers and militiamen were a bit *too* deadly.

Boris never took his eyes off the ground, he just kept prodding the bodies with his boot and examining the equipment they used.

Then something grabbed his foot.

Boris spun around and instinctively kicked the perpetrator in the face, knocking him onto his back. This one had been shot in the upper chest, near his shoulder. The man then attempted to pick up his rifle, which was pinned under another soldier. Boris leaned over the guy and kicked him again.

"We've got one!" He shouted over at two of the other men searching. They ran over, and helped Boris get the man into the base, as he was still struggling, where they laid him on a table, and tied him down with duct tape. One of the others started treating his wound, and Boris leered over him, preparing to take off the mask. Boris could see that this survivor was one of those with "The Forgiven" written on his forehead.

The medic, Dmitry, finished bandaging the wound and stepped away. It had taken longer than it should have because the man was still attempting to break free. Boris then reached to the man's face and removed the mask. He instantly stopped moving and became completely motionless. The man was still alive but was completely silent. He was shaved completely bald; no hair, no moustache or stubble, he even lacked eyebrows. He had pale skin, and light blue eyes, with a very average complexion, along with a strange black device on his forehead.

Boris tried speaking to him in Russian, only saying "hello", but he said nothing. His eyes just blankly stared at the ceiling; his mouth closed. He was definitely alive. His chest rose and fell as he breathed, but he was completely unresponsive.

Dmitry removed the man's vest next, and he revealed his once again unexceptional torso, as he was neither overfed nor underfed, though he seemed more fit than most, which made sense considering he was supposed to be a soldier. Regardless, the man continued to be unresponsive. Boris then drew a knife on the man, and made it seem like he would attack him. The man's eyes followed the knife, but there were still no vocalizations or movements.

Boris then started trying to speak to the man in English. "Hello. I am Boris. You are safe here; the fight is over."

The man remained unresponsive but moved his head up to see Boris better. He said nothing.

"What is your name?" Boris continued.

"I am unit 47 of the Forgiven," he said, in a way similar to how people are depicted in movies resisting giving up information during interrogations.

Boris wasn't sure where to go next with this but pressed on.

"I am Boris Kasyanov. I only mean to ask you a few questions. Who and what do you work for?"

"I serve only the Overseer. He leads us, in The Order. We mean to bring peace to the world." His robotic tone persisted, as if he'd been programmed to give these answers.

"What is the Forgiven?" Boris asked next.

"We are forgiven for our past sins by the Overseer. We pay for our sins in blood," he responded.

"What kind of sins?"

"We resisted the Order at first. The Overseer forgives us, he redeems all who seek forgiveness. You have sinned against us, against the Overseer. He will forgive you, if you seek him."

"We have only defended ourselves." - Boris knew technically his side had started the hostilities, but it was clear they would attack anyway - "And maybe we can work out a way for us to be at peace. Here, I'll even let you go. We'll let your guys pick you up."

Boris knew this was a dangerous idea, as he could quickly turn and try to kill them, but he had to investigate his behavior; it was likely tied to the device on his face, but he didn't know if he could remove it without killing 47. He did, however, doubt that if his friends returned, it would be to retrieve him. It would likely just be to burn this place down.

He untied the man, and he stood up and left the room. Boris observed him as he proceeded to wander throughout the base. Boris noticed he didn't seem to have any radio equipment on him, though it was entirely possible some type of signal was being sent out by the device on his head.

At this point, it was fairly late, and Boris and 47 were the only two people left in the mess hall. Some were asleep, others were outside, still more were in the shooting range.

Boris figured he'd probably try to figure out where to put 47, so he stood up, and began to walk toward the door to the barracks to see if any space was open. When he did, he heard a bolt release, and chamber a round. He spun around and saw 47 pointing a Kalashnikov at him.

"47! What are you doing!?" Boris was not surprised by this, but he expected to be more prepared if it happened.

47 spoke and said, "You have committed crimes against the Overseer and his glorious Order. Following protocol #217, you are to be executed!"

47 then fired twice at Boris, both shots missing, but not by much. Boris then decided the only way to survive and not have 47 immediately shot by someone else was to rush at him. Boris did so, running with his head down. Tackling 47, they crashed into to the ground.

He realized he hadn't thought this far ahead and stopped for a second. The device on 47's forehead was pulsing now, and he decided it was now time to do something about it. He grabbed the discarded Kalashnikov and then proceeded to slam the stock of it straight into 47's forehead. 47's head snapped back, and regardless of the condition of that device, he was definitely out cold, though *probably* not dead.

Boris then sat down on the table and looked at 47. The device was definitely smashed, and even though Boris hadn't really thought about it before, he was definitely glad the device was external and wasn't *in* his head, but just attached to it, a bit under the skin. There was, however, an impression of the device on his forehead, and a few small punctures that were bleeding a bit. His nose, on the other hand, was bleeding a *lot*. Boris called over Dmitry, and had him patch 47 up, putting him back on the table they had him on originally, restraining him, again, just in case.

He then told Dmitry not to say anything, and that he'd address everyone in the morning. Then, a very exhausted Boris stumbled over to the office and fell asleep almost instantly.

The next morning, he got up and went to the mess hall. Everyone was there, eating something or just talking, and he got their attention.

He then proceeded to quickly explain what had happened, then ran into the room with 47 in it. Dmitry was there, and Boris proceeded to ask, "How is he?"

"He is alive for sure. He should probably be up in a few minutes…" Dmitry responded. While waiting, Boris explained what had happened, and Dmitry didn't seem as concerned as what he saw in the brief expression he saw on everybody's face before he left the mess hall. Dmitry said, "It's the only obvious thing that was, I guess, not natural, so It'll probably have *some* sort of positive effect."

A few minutes later, 47 woke up, and the positive effect was different from the one they expected.

He was still quite calm, but there seemed to be--though there really isn't a precise word or way to explain it, *life* in his eyes.

"Where am I?" he asked, in English.

"You're in Russia. Do you speak Russian?" Boris asked him.

"Yes," he responded. So that was still true.

Had he just been 'reset' or something?

Boris then answered his original question. "You are in a military installation West of Moscow. We have… recovered you from an unknown entity, to our knowledge called The Order that seemed to have control of a large part of your mind. We do not work for them. We want to help you. What's the last thing you remember before being here?"

"The last thing I remember is being in a dark room, being tied down, and having some sort of device affixed to my forehead after being told that this was 'redemption' for 'resisting the Overseer." There were a few others with me, as well…"

"That sounds accurate," Boris replied, showing whoever Viktor actually was the pile of scrap from the chip.

Boris then asked, "Who are you? Do you know your name, or anything about before you were given that chip?"

"I do know who I am… I think. I'm Daniel. Daniel Reeves. I lived in the U.S. somewhere. I think I was with the military… but I wasn't a regular. I don't know. I can't remember. Everything is a bit foggy."

"That makes sense, I had to smash you in the face with a rifle to get your mind back," Boris said. Daniel looked surprised but said nothing. Boris released Daniel and told him, "Get your guard up. Let's see what you can do."

Boris threw the first punch, which Daniel instinctively blocked. Boris swung a few more times, to make sure that wasn't a fluke. Daniel successfully blocked them all and began to retaliate. Boris' Spetsnaz training was useful here, as he was able to block the blows in turn.

The two of them fist-fought for nearly half an hour, neither landing a significant blow.

At that point, Boris stopped, waited for the right moment, and when Daniel swung again he threw him over his shoulder, and said, "Alright. That's enough."

Daniel was still sprawled on his back, but got up quickly, ready to swing at him again.

"Fine. We'll need to do that again. Then I can beat you." He said, not in an entirely serious voice.

"Now that we've established you could probably kill most of us in our sleep and run off, which I could see you doing since we're technically supposed to be enemies, and since you're American, I'm going to ask you what you remember about the Order."

"Well… I'd imagine I'll remember more than this soon. It'll probably still be a bit before my mind clears up, but I remember that I was somewhere in Poland, I think. Near the border between them and you. I think this was the day or two before the missiles, just when it was still a conventional war. We were in a fairly large base and I just remember these men… dressed all in black. Not like the masked soldiers you've seen, but similar. They rushed into the base and started shooting. We thought they were you- Russians, that is, but they didn't speak at all. Some of us were just shot dead, but there were a few singled out individuals they hit with tranquilizers… I think I was one of those. They didn't seem to feel any pain, either. We were very poorly prepared, just armed with pistols and a few carbines. We'd shoot one, and he'd either go down soundlessly or continue at it like nothing happened. I remember being with them, crouched behind a table I'd knocked over, watching men fall. We weren't the standard soldiers either, as I'd said before, but we were just falling like dominoes. I remember standing up to fire at them some more, and after I fired a shot, which hit one in the face, all of them directed their attention to me and then I blacked out." He stopped for a second, as if asking for a response.

"Go on," Boris said.

"Then I remember a few minutes where we were in a dark facility in god-knows-where, lined up next to other men who were conscious but equally powerless; I couldn't feel my limbs, yet I stood. The men were from all sorts of nations too. Many Americans, some Russians, Poles, Germans, even a decent number of people from different continents; there were African and Asian appearing people as well. We were then split off into groups with movement like we were on an assembly line, and I didn't have control of my own legs... We lined up in a room and were asked many questions. Everyone who answered yes to whatever the questions were went one way, the rest went the way I went. Most of them went the way I didn't go. The way I went seemed to be populated with high-ranking people, and then I saw the device, a few scattered images after that, and then I was here."

"Do you know where the others went?" Boris inquired. He already knew that part of the answer was that a lot of them were now lying dead outside, a thought he was trying to push from his mind.

"I don't. I don't think they got chipped though. They may have been killed, maybe they were already dead, maybe they are just being kept somewhere."

"And what about those scattered images?" Boris asked again.

"There are a few. More come to me every minute. I seem to remember being in a huge crowd of them with that mask on. Somebody was talking. Then I heard a loud 'For the Order! Hurrah!' and everybody's fist went up. Then there's one of being in a truck for days, maybe weeks, then getting out and entering a military base…"

Boris cut in, saying, "Which is where you still are."

"Ah. So, we lost, then?" Daniel replied.

"Indeed. You're the only one left. All of the other survivors... shot themselves. Including those with the devices, like you. We didn't know they weren't... *bad guys*," Boris said.

"Oh. It's unlikely many of them could have been saved anyway... I'm probably a special case all things considered. Why do you think that is?"

"Defective chip?"

"No, or I probably would have gotten the self-control to try to destroy it myself."

"Well... do you think those around you were also chipped?"

"Why don't we check?"

"Alright then." Boris left the room and got a man to help him drag another body in. This one wasn't marked with "The Forgiven." They were piled in a corner, and the smell was unpleasant, to say the least. Boris and the man dragged one of them back and put him on the table where Daniel was. The dead soldier had several bullet wounds in his chest and bled some on the table.

They removed the mask. The man looked similar to Daniel in that he had no hair on his head whatsoever, but with a more Turkic complexion.

He also had no chip whatsoever.

"Check him for anything else to identify him," Boris ordered.

They began removing the man's armor and also removed his tunic, exposing his grisly wounds. However, at that point the marking was obvious. On his chest, just below his collarbone, there was writing that read, "Omnia Per Ordinem". Boris knew it was Latin, but he didn't know what it meant. Dmitry did, however, and spoke its meaning quietly.

"Order above all."

Boris didn't know what to think. Obviously, this was not one of the kidnapped soldiers. Was he a previous member of this organization? Was this man's involvement voluntary? Did it even have anything to do with The Order in general?

"My best guess is this man was a member of them originally. They seem to have been the only ones who fought like actual humans. Either way, we need to move. Soon," Boris said.

Daniel looked up at him.

"And don't think for a second you aren't coming with us," Boris said.

"I won't object. I have to know what this is about, as well. May as well come with the people who have the best chance of actually doing something about it."

Boris nodded to acknowledge, and walked out of the room again, noticing the small trail of blood left by the dead man they had dragged over there. He spent a few minutes gathering everyone and then began his announcement.

He spent a few minutes explaining the situation with Daniel, where he came from, and what they'd discovered from him and the other dead soldier they'd brought in. He finished with, "We're leaving tomorrow. Gather your things. We're burning the dead."

The people took the information at face value and began preparing to head out. Few words were spoken. They began getting their things in order. It was a good thing most of them accepted what they had been told; the march west would make them think otherwise.

CHAPTER 6

Boris didn't know exactly where they were going. He'd have to ask once they were on the road to see if Daniel knew anything. If he didn't, they'd do what they could to find The Order, but they couldn't forget their primary mission: get to the seed bank and use it to save Moscow.

After his announcement and reflecting a bit more on these things, Boris went over to his office for the last time and fell asleep almost instantly.

When he woke up, there was a knock at his door... He instinctively reached for his pistol.

When the door opened, Józef walked in, looking a bit shocked Boris wasn't up yet.

"Nikita says we're about ready to head out."

Boris jumped to his feet and put away his pistol. He then said, "Good. Get some gas cans, as well. We'll give the dead a proper send off, especially now we know most weren't willingly against us."

A few minutes later, Boris was standing in front of the pile of bodies, now drenched with gasoline.

"We'll find out who did this to you...who brainwashed you. We will end them. Goodbye. And to Józef's man...You shall be avenged."

Boris then lit a match and tossed it onto the pile. It caught fire instantly, and a minute the whole mass was lit up.

Boris saluted the blaze and then said, "It's time to go."

He began walking out of the base and gestured for Daniel to follow him.

Daniel caught up quickly, and then Boris asked him, "So, do you have any idea where, in particular, we should be heading?"

He responded, "Well, the best strategy I can think of is to stay near major cities and try to track them down based on where we encounter the heaviest resistance. Besides, we'll need to go through cities for supplies anyway."

"That's what we already were going to do. I guess that works out all right."

Boris then looked back at those following and announced, "We will continue to go on M-1. Our next destination is Minsk. From there we will continue to Warsaw, then to Berlin."

There was some mumbling from those behind him, but Boris paid them no mind.

The next few days were uneventful. As they got further away from the city, there were fewer and fewer cars, soon hardly any could be seen on the road. Here, many kilometers from the city, the countryside looked almost normal again, instead of the dead, grey color it had in Moscow, and what Boris expected it to be like again in Minsk.

After several hours of silent walking, Boris spotted a camper van. It was dusk, around 19:00, and Boris said to everyone, "Stop. This is where we rest for today."

Boris also knew they were close to the 100-kilometer mark. After they'd set up camp properly, those who wanted to leave could leave.

He then organized everyone in and around the camper van. He assigned two volunteers, Petya and one of Vasiliy's men, to stay on top of it and watch for attackers. Boris, Nikita, Vasiliy, and Józef stayed inside the camper van with two others acting as guards, Jeung and the woman with the Skorpion submachine gun, and now an AK-103 rifle, whose name Boris still didn't know.

People began to lay out their items, splitting up into groups depending on which squad they were a part of. Boris observed this out of the camper window and began to discuss the situation with Nikita after inspecting the camper van.

The old camper they were in was somewhat rusted on the outside. There were many pictures and souvenirs from past trips the owners likely went on. It emitted a very melancholy, nostalgic feeling, back to when things were normal, and people weren't killing one another.

"So. We'll be in Minsk after another week or two of walking. We should try to find some other form of transportation there. Walking to Copenhagen isn't a great idea," Boris began.

"You're probably right. If we keep walking for too much longer, winter will set in and we could end up freezing to death. It's already November, isn't it?" replied Nikita.

"I think it is… But I haven't thought about what day it actually is for a while now… Anyway, we'll make the rest of the way to Minsk and do what we can to get some more supplies and a better way to get around."

Boris and Nikita, soon joined by Vasiliy and Józef, continued to talk about strategy, and then old times before the War.

Józef picked up the conversation--"I used to work in an office. It was the same thing, every day. It starved the soul; I needed something different. One day, I left the office and began working as a volunteer for foreign aid organizations, helping the poor of my country and others. My degrees in school were for nothing, but I was satisfied with my life. I'd always wanted a wife, though…I never had the time," Józef told the group.

He went on to explain how he heard about the island with the seed bank from an old drunk he'd been assisting for a while. When he investigated it, he found it was true.

Nikita went next. "I'd always known I would be in the military. My father, and my father before him were in the military. 'You'll grow up to be like me and your hero grandfather, Corporal Alexei Glukhovsky, Hero of the Soviet Union!' My father told me. My grandfather fought in The Great Patriotic War under the famous Yuri Morozov. My father always told me, 'If those Yankees ever decide to come for Moscow, I know you'll prove yourself to be as much a hero as my father was!' So of course I ended up in the military… It's probably for the best that he likely died already; he'd be ashamed to know I'm not out fighting now. At least he got that one story out of the Pan-Arab war, where I saved a comrade's life… but it was no heroism. Enough about him. My mother passed away when I was very young, so the only woman I ever loved was my dear Anya… Miss Sokova, a name I'd heard so many times through school. If a war hadn't started… we would have been married now, just a week after it actually did. I only hope she is still alive."

Boris then told his story: "My grandfather also served in Morozov's unit… his name was Konstantin. My mother spoke of him often, and my father was also a military man. Throughout school the only thing I was good at was writing, telling stories. I did poorly in most of the other subjects, and with that it was hard to get anyone to publish any of my books. I figured instead I'd join the military for a while, and let that idea cool off. Before I knew it, I was a member of the GRU and even managed to be in the last few years of the Pan-Arab war. I myself never found the right person to mentor me. Another reason I decided to join the military." Boris spoke his piece. He had no idea his grandfather had served with Nikita's. Go figure. Now the two families were fighting together again…in the post-apocalypse.

Vasiliy then spoke: "If you expected me before now to say anything, you're an absolute idiot. But here's something, because I'm not going to be some dark, brooding *pidaras*. I'm fifty-three years old, for Christ's sake. I was Soviet Military police. KGB. I did some things, things I do not regret, but I know others would implore. Once the Union fell, Mr. Yeltsin decided to do away with some of the darker elements of his new FSB and I was on the streets in a week. I helped run a bar for a while, and over time connected with some somewhat unsavory characters in case of a war like the one that has happened, simply because I would rather be the bandit than be killed *by* a bandit." Vasiliy finished, then looked off, and out the window, signaling another period of temporary silence until Nikita said, more quietly than usual, "Did you lose anyone, Vasiliy?"

There was nothing but silence. Vasiliy continued staring out the window as if he hadn't heard the question, before quietly saying under his breath, "not because of the war..."

Boris needed a break from the now bleak discussion and left the camper. He walked toward the entrance of the camper van and out onto the side of the road. He looked up into the sky and took in his surroundings. The air was cool and dry. He looked up and saw the stars. If the nuclear winter theories he'd heard about were true, it might be one of the last times he'll see them for a while.

Here, on a highway where the war hadn't reached, there was a beautiful night sky, though somewhat lacking the color and spectacle Boris remembered from his childhood. Maybe he'd changed, maybe the sky had already begun to change. It wasn't the same. Nevertheless, he continued to stare into the cosmos.

If anyone ever discovers this planet, what will they find? Will we even still exist, with even have a trace of us left?

His thoughts were then quite rudely interrupted.

Somebody tackled him, and he was on his back in an instant. He couldn't make out anything about them more than that it was a dark figure dressed in thick clothing, and they drew a knife on him and began trying to drive it into his chest.

Boris was too shocked to vocalize any sort of words; instead, he just struggled to keep the bearded, almost bear-like man's knife off his chest.

Boris then saw another ragged figure run up, this one with a crowbar, and he raised his arm to crash the crowbar down onto Boris's unprotected face; he'd removed his helmet earlier.

Then the man with the crowbar paused, and a loud *BANG!* sounded. The figure dropped the crowbar and raised their right hand to their throat, and he heard choking noises as the figure dropped to the ground.

Boris then took advantage of the figure still trying to stab him having lost their focus with the loss of their comrade, and he drew his pistol and fired point blank into their chest twice. Boris's ears rang loudly, and he couldn't hear anything but the reverberation of the gunshot. He then shoved the man off him and looked to see who'd shot the one with the crowbar.

The woman stood still, with the smoking barrel of the Kalashnikov giving all the evidence needed. Boris stood up and dusted himself off, his ears still ringing.

He then looked and saw his other comrades shooting at several more of the attackers. It was still too dark to see what they looked like, but they were very thin, and all of them were ragged and desperate. This obviously wasn't The Order attacking them.

The assault soon stopped as quickly as it had started, Boris announced they would check the bodies in the morning when they could properly inspect who they had just been shooting. The soldiers all piled back into their tents, each of which had at least one person sitting very anxiously outside their tent, pointing a rifle out in some direction.

Boris then began walking back to the camper van, but then stumbled in making his way up. His hearing had cleared, but it wasn't until now he heard the woman who'd just saved him shouting, "YOU'RE BLEEDING, YOU IDIOT!" At him.

Boris then looked down at his chest. There were some bloodstains from the man he'd shot, but then the stinging set in. As he'd shot the man, he'd gotten the knife about an inch into his side. It didn't look that bad, but it hurt like hell now that he noticed it.

The woman ran into the van and got some bandages, then started patching him up. Boris finally got her name.

"Agh… Thanks. What's your name?" He asked.

"Well, I wasn't going to let that guy kill the CO. I'm Elena."

"Well, that's good to know. What were they, though? They came from nowhere. They didn't have any sort of military equipment or guns, or anything of that sort. The one trying to stab you had a pocket knife and the one you shot had a crowbar."

"I guess we'll have to wait until the morning. I don't think they were part of anything, though. It's unlikely any sort of functional organization would organize a raiding party as poorly equipped and desperate as that one."

After another minute, the bleeding had been contained. Boris thanked her again, and then he went into the camper and passed out in one of the seats.

He was woken up the next morning by Vasiliy punching him in the shoulder, almost knocking him onto the floor, saying "Get up. We gathered the savages that attacked us."

Boris got up immediately and went outside to look at them.

There were four of them, lined up on the side of the road. All of them had been shot, and some of them were still bleeding a bit, as there were small pools of blood under all of them.

They were all wearing leather jackets, which read "Bleeding Soul Riders." They must have been some sort of biker gang. They were all large men, but they were underweight, looking like they'd eaten very little.

So, they'd just killed four people.

Boris didn't know much about bikers, but he assumed they were roaming the land with their bikes to find supplies, but when they ran out of stuff to eat, out of desperation they ended up attacking the first group of people they saw.

How unfortunate, Boris thought. *We probably could have given them something if they hadn't tried to kill us.*

This brought another issue to mind. Would he have helped them? Would everyone else have helped them? While Boris didn't completely know the nationality of everyone in his group, most of them spoke very good Russian, so he had to assume most of them were Russian nationals, or at least eastern European, so what would they have thought of these American bikers?

Sure, they weren't the ones who pressed the button to launch the nukes, but they were very obviously patriotic about their country or at least its people if they were willing to go on an expedition like this.

Granted, Boris thought, *they couldn't have been very smart if they thought it was a good idea to bike across Europe when tensions were so high, and not to have just followed a road into a city, or at least somewhere, rather than just waiting in the middle of nowhere for someone to pass. But I guess we can't know what their motives were.*

Boris then got everyone back together and decided now was the time to give everyone the full truth on what they were doing. He stood on a small stool and began, "Okay, everyone. Our location now is very close to the 100-kilometer mark. Now, I will tell you what exactly we are doing here. I'm not going to sugarcoat it, nor will I waste time. We are going to Denmark. We will then sail north to the island of Svalbard. There we should find a seed bank where almost all plants known to man exist in some form. While it hasn't happened yet, as nuclear winter sets in and the high-level of radiation kills plant life, we will need something to jumpstart the world. We will get some prime specimens of important crops and bring them to the Metro, where hopefully we will be able to cultivate crops, spread out again throughout Russia, and hopefully begin to rebuild what was destroyed. To simplify… continue on with me or walk back to Moscow alone. If anyone will be leaving, do so now, and don't waste my time."

Nobody moved.

"So then, you are all brave enough… excellent. We shall rebuild the world. Onwards!"

Boris then stepped down from the stool and began getting ready to go.

CHAPTER 7

Boris considered checking to see if the camper van would still work, but its terrible gas mileage and large number of people it would have to transport probably wouldn't make good odds, especially considering it could be inoperative from the EMP effect of the warheads...or maybe it was just out of gas anyway.

So, they just walked. It would be more than a week before they were in Minsk, but they had resources to last that long. Resources had been divided between people. Everyone carried their own things, such as clothing and goods, but some people were assigned to things like the tents and cooking equipment, as they were impractical to carry with all of their other items--so there were pairs of people transporting those. These pairs were, reasonably, the strongest members of each group, as some of the other members seemed to be having a hard-enough time just carrying their own stuff.

Boris was still at the front of the group, in the same order as it'd been before. *This next week and a half or so was going to be boring*, he thought. Of course, there was still the off chance The Order or someone else would attack them again at some point.

Several days later...

Boris and his group were nearing Smolensk, which would be a destination on their trip. I'd been a week by now, and nothing had happened in the past few days. Just walking and more walking. Boris did get a bit more acquainted with some of the other people, including Elena, whom he considered himself indebted to.

Smolensk approached, or more accurately, they approached Smolensk.

It was now that they noticed the rumbling sound coming from that direction. It was faint at first, but Boris already had an idea, not even factoring in the sound.

It was gunshots; it had to be. What sort of apocalypse would this be, were that noise not from gunshots?

Is the war still going on? he wondered. It was around 18:30, so they might be able to get in quietly. Given that gunshots are quite loud, it seemed unlikely that it was any sort of large-scale conflict; gunshots would echo across the lifeless buildings and create significant noise. However, this assumption was proven incorrect once they got closer and the noise reached a crescendo.

As the group crested a hill, he found his assumption was incorrect.

He saw an old T-64 tank moving into the city.

What the hell?

Clearly, there weren't enough electronics running through a T-64 tank for it to have been ruined by the EMP effect, but, that begged the question of why it was being driven into Smolensk.

Seeing this, however, Boris got everyone to move off the road and into the brush.

After another hour or so of walking they were upon the city and the pounding, constant noise was only getting louder and louder. It seemed there was some sort of battle going on. They kept advancing through the city, hoping they would be able to pass relatively unnoticed.

This possibility, however, was nearly nonexistent. This was apparent as an anti-tank rocket smashed into a skyscraper to the group's 4 o'clock, throwing pieces of the building onto neighboring structures and the streets below. The rocket hit at about the fourth floor and out of the gap, two survivors were visible dressed in ragged civilian clothes with Mosin rifles and Russian-flag armbands. They must have been part of some kind of militia.

Boris continued to advance, the sound of gunfire right upon them now, with rounds flying over their heads. They then saw the line of men, over the rubble covering their position--Russian Motostrelki, or Motorized Infantry, fighting from behind a row of cars, some of which still contained their deceased occupants. Two were wounded or dead, leaning up against the side of one of the buildings. Boris gestured for the rest to hold back while he went up to try to see what was going on.

"What the hell is happening here!?" He shouted over the gunfire at a man distinguishable as an officer by his holster containing an MP-443 pistol and the parade beret he was still wearing.

"We're fighting an American division! When the warheads were first exchanged, the Belarusian army wasn't prepared, and they lost their land quickly! Several of those men are here now. These NATO troops made it all the way through Belarus quickly, so the battle line here is further east than anywhere else!"

I cannot believe it. Even after so many had died, these men are still fighting each other? Who instigated this!? I have to stop it. This has to stop. This killing is pointless, now that there is a common enemy, The Order!

Boris ran back to his group, shouting "It's the Americans!"

Vasiliy then instantly stood up and took aim with his rifle. Just after he fired a shot, Boris tackled him. However, it was too late. As Boris stood up and looked through the scope of his rifle, he saw a distant figure fall, having been shot in the chest.

"WHAT THE HELL ARE YOU DOING!?" Vasiliy shouted as he threw Boris off him.

"NATO isn't our enemy anymore! The war is over... or it should be! There's no reason for this to be continuing!" Boris retorted.

"Some GRU Operative you are! You're betraying the motherland!"

"I won't betray humankind! This war, whether it had a point before or not, certainly doesn't now! We need to ally with them and face The Order!"

Zhenya, who'd been very quiet for most of their trip, despite his brash personality when he was recruited, finally spoke up.

"Every soldier, Russian, American, whatever, who dies who isn't part of The Order is a dead person who can't help us fight it."

Both Boris and Vasiliy snapped their heads to look at the young Zhenya, and they then stood up and dusted themselves off.

"Fine," Vasiliy muttered coldly.

Jeung spoke up with, "He does have a point. The fact the war is still being fought could be attributed *to* The Order for all we know."

Nikita played off Jeung with, "I love Russia. But I love humanity and life as well."

"So, do you expect us to just march out from behind the cars with our hands up? How do we convey peace to them? It's not like we can tell them when they're shooting at us. Especially considering their government probably told them the same sort of thing our government told us, 'It's not us, but they who started it, or who fired first,'" Vasiliy interjected.

"Maybe this will help." A short figure, one Boris had never really noticed before, stepped forward. An MP3 music player was in his hands.

Boris took a good look at him. He couldn't be older than 16. He couldn't see much of his face as it was obscured by the balaclava they all wore, but his blue eyes were piercing, genuine, and innocent.

"What's your name, kid?" Boris asked. He was young himself, but he knew he was older than this boy.

"My name is Yevgeny, Mr. Kasyanov Sir."

"Yevgeny, I'm not going to ask you to march into certain death based on my crazy plan. I'm doing this."

"And so am I," Said Elena.

Daniel stepped up right after. "I'm American, these are my countrymen, so as am I."

"And I," said Jeung.

"And I," said Nikita.

"I, as well," said Petya.

"Damn it all to hell... I as well," said Vasiliy.

One by one, all of them stepped forward.

Boris finally glanced down at the music player, and selected something, what it was didn't really matter.

"What the hell are you doing you fool!?" the officer shouted.

"Finding a solution..." Boris then shrugged-- "Or quite possibly dying," Boris said.

He took off his helmet, then his balaclava, and marched forward toward the American line. They were sitting behind sandbags and rubble, as war-torn as his Russian comrades. The song continued to blast from his MP3.

"PEACE, AMERICANS!" He shouted as loudly as he possibly could, fully expecting to eat a bullet within the next five seconds.

"COME AND MEET US IN PEACE, AMERICANS!"

He'd nearly reached the midpoint between them. In the wide, destroyed street, not a shot was fired. Not one.

He then said, in a whisper, "Take off your helmets. Show your humanity."

Boris stopped. His comrades removed their helmets. Young and old, male and female, both spirited and jaded.

Boris watched as one American, a dark-skinned man, put down his rifle, and approached. A sergeant shouted at him, but his words went unheeded.

More started to come forward, talking amongst themselves.

The American man approached Boris, now only a meter away.

"The world has ended. We should not fight any longer," Boris stated flatly.

"Nothing truer than that," said the man.

The Russian soldiers who were behind the line of cars began to advance as well, though much more wearily and at a slower pace. They took off their helmets and dropped their weapons to meet their former enemies face to face.

Boris looked beyond the American soldiers who'd come up to face him and saw a man hanging back. This must have been the man Vasiliy shot. He seemed to be of high rank and was in his thirties or forties. He seemed to be unconscious, his eyes closed.

As Boris stepped forward again, the man awoke quickly, and his eyes locked directly onto Boris.

"What are you doing, men!? The enemy is right here!" He shouted.

"It's fine. It's over, "said Boris, in his accented English.

"It's never over… Can't trust a goddamn commie," the man growled.

"There is no good reason for us to fight," Boris stated, realizing it was obvious that this man was not ready to stop fighting.

"It's nothing but a lie. YOU'RE LYING! SHOOT ME ALREADY OR HAVE ONE OF MY TRAITOROUS SOLDIERS DO IT! COME ON!" He shouted.

The man moved his right hand, revealing he had indeed been shot in the stomach. Boris almost stepped forward again to try to calm the man, but the man moved his hand with intent to kill.

The man's pistol was in his hand near-instantly.

"Don't shoot me. I'm not going to harm you," Boris asked the man calmly, not showing any emotion.

"Piss. Off," the officer said. He raised the weapon to aim at Boris's chest.

CRACK!

Boris had not closed his eyes, not even flinched. If there was anything his training and experience taught him, the one shot you won't hear is the one meant for you. He definitely heard this one.

He looked down at the officer, back arched over the rubble he was leaning on, blood beginning to spill onto the concrete, onto the cold, dead road.

He then glanced to his left. He expected to see Vasiliy with the smoking gun, his hand unmoving.

Instead he saw Elena, with the same lack of fear, but presence of determination over cruelty.

"You should have seen that coming," she said to Boris.

"I suppose so…" Boris said. He walked over to the dead man, not a breath of life left in him.

The shot had hit him square in the forehead. At least it was quick.

The man's hazel eyes stared blankly into the sky, the anger in them gone, now in eerie, eternal peace.

"You owe me twice," Elena said.

"I… appreciate it. Hopefully you won't have to do me that favor a third time," said Boris, who moved to close the man's eyes.

Boris then heard motors in the distance. Something was driving towards them.

It was obvious it would have to be The Order. The real challenge was telling their new friends what they were about to face before they got here.

He ran over to the gathering of people, where many, both the Russians and Americans, were talking. Except for the distant sound of motors, the world was silent. Apparently, the ceasefire had spread to all in the near area. Good.

"All of those in the Svalbard Expedition! Over here, now!" Boris commanded.

Most of them separated from the crowd and went to Boris.

"Do you hear that? It's a vehicle. The only people we know to have a large number of functioning vehicles are The Order. Inform them all what's coming. Quickly."

The several conversations and card games that had been going on came to a halt, and different members began to arrange a defense in the rough direction the sound seemed to be coming from, the west.

Boris watched over the preparations. It seemed like there were hundreds, maybe thousands of American and Russian troops in the area. If something was coming, it was going to have be massive to face this mighty force.

Once preparations were completed, the motors got louder. It sounded like there were dozens of them.

Minutes passed like years. The distant roar became louder and louder.

"RPG!" An American voice shouted out into the silence, as a rocket smashed into one of the improvised positions, the blast enveloping three men in flame.

After Boris recovered from the blast, he gazed out into the streets in front of him. A smokescreen had been activated, but the sound of military boots hitting the ground with the approaching vehicles indicated the enemy was right in front of them.

"FIRE!" Boris shouted.

Instantly, the barricades lit up and rounds flew through the smoke, nobody truly knowing if they'd hit their marks. But a distinct metallic pinging sound continued, and Boris knew it was a vehicle making its way through.

As the smokescreen dissipated, Boris saw it. A tank, with resemblance to many of the world's state-of-the art vehicles of war.

That was where the rocket had originated.

The heavy tank turret then aimed toward the area where Boris knew Józef and his men were.

"Watch it Józef!" Boris shouted, though there was no doubt that it fell on deaf ears.

Józef only stood there, like a deer in headlights, as the tank turned its turret to face him. A second after that, a man standing next to him, one of his men, was shot and fell onto Józef, snapping him out of his trance.

Józef attempted to drag the man away, and it was then that the tank fired.

Boris wasn't going to concern himself searching for Józef's remains. It was a shame, though. This was all his idea, anyway. One to save civilization. The idea would live on.

As soon as that shot was fired, several missiles hit the tank at once, locking the turret in place and blowing off one of the treads. Jeung and Zhenya then rushed past Boris, with Nikita and Yevgeny right behind.

Jeung leapt up onto the top of the tank and opened the top hatch. After firing several shots into it, he dropped about four live grenades and ran as Zhenya covered him, before sprinting back himself.

As soon as the five-second fuse was up, the tank burst into flames. This freed up some space on the road, and the foot soldiers of The Order began to advance.

These soldiers were different from the ones Boris had fought before, though. They appeared to be wearing higher-quality armor and advanced not in straight lines, but freely, as normal humans would.

However, even if these soldiers were more human than the ones before, their position was very poor; their only cover was the burning tank.

Because of this, The Order was not advancing very far, and the Russian-American coalition was managing to hold them off.

However, some of them began to show up in the windows of the large buildings around them. Boris had not yet asked himself why these soldiers were fighting on the ground rather than from the buildings. The buildings provided excellent cover.

Then Boris remembered what kind of world he was in right now.

The buildings were almost certainly filled with bodies. Who or whatever lies behind the masks of those they are now fighting are either inhuman or incredibly desensitized.

Boris was still there behind the sandbags, which were not going to protect him from the above Order soldiers.

He and Vasiliy, who'd been standing next to him throughout the battle, noticed this and began firing, as well.

Despite these soldiers being more human-like in motion, their aim was still not very good.

Also, their positions were quickly given away as they bashed open the windows of the buildings before beginning to fire out of them--so surprise wasn't on their side despite the altitude advantage.

As Boris finished off one of the soldiers, who'd tumbled forward off the 9th story of a building onto the pavement below, a booming, accented voice came over a loudspeaker.

"SUBMIT NOW, DOGS! YOUR BUREAUCRACIES AND GOVERNMENTS HAVE ENDED! THE ORDER HAS ALREADY DOMINATED MUCH OF EUROPE! YOU HAVE NO CHANCE! SURRENDER NOW, AND YOU MAY JOIN US UNHARMED!

Then, another explosion shook Boris's attention away from the man over the loudspeaker. It was from behind him, where more trucks were unloading troops behind the lines.

They were surrounded.

"GO NOW! INTO THE SEWERS!" Boris shouted. It wasn't the greatest option, but it was the only one. However, he remained in position. He led these people into this situation, and while stopping the battle between the Russians and Americans saved lives, the whole reason they were there was because of an idea Boris got from a man who was probably dead now.

"GO, GO, GO!" --he shouted as loudly as possible. Many of them had made their way into a sewer. Vasiliy was at one manhole, holding it up, guiding people in, some still firing as they descended into the hole.

Boris knew he was going to have to be the last one in, if he made it at all. He hated owing anyone, and he wasn't going to have anybody die because he wasn't helping them enter. He looked back over to Vasiliy, where he saw Nikita dragging a bleeding Petya into the hole.

What the hell did he do to deserve this!?

As adrenaline rushed through his veins, Boris stood straight up, and fired away at the advancing Order soldiers, killing over seven with his first magazine, before reloading and continuing. Almost everyone was in the sewers now. All except Daniel, who hadn't moved from Boris's side.

"Go, Daniel!" he shouted at him.

"Not a chance! I'm probably the reason they found us!" He shouted back.

The smell of lead intensified as more Order soldiers flooded the area. Boris watched the last person besides him, and Daniel descend into the sewer. It was Vasiliy, pulling a struggling Elena down, as well.

"GET THE HELL DOWN HERE, PLEASE!" she shouted. It wasn't out of desperation, though. It was an order.

Boris reached out to her, but he knew already it was too late.

"DIE YOU BASTARDS!" --he cried out to the nearly 50 soldiers surrounding him and Daniel.

Daniel was silent, but still firing, until five seconds later when he was downed by a hit to the stomach, looking at Boris as he began bleeding onto the pavement.

Boris was then hit right after, in the bicep, and he stumbled backward.

He was hit again, this time in the shoulder of his other arm. He muttered "Blyat…" as he fell to the ground, staring into the sky as The Order soldiers rushed over to him, peering down at him as the world went dark.

CHAPTER 8

The sewer system was dark, incredibly dark, and only a few of those now hiding within had flashlights. Of the couple hundred that were there at the beginning on the surface, about fifty had made it down, with dozens confirmed as lost and even more unaccounted for. Out of the original group, however, only Boris, Daniel, and two others weren't with them. Boris and Daniel were the last ones above ground before the last made it in, and the other two had been killed during the fight.

The group had moved through the sewer to pretty far away from where they had been initially, but several people were posted on each pathway to prevent any sort of surprise attack.

Józef had made it. Arkady and one of Józef's people, Alexandra, had helped to pull him down with them.

He *had* indeed survived, but not without with serious injuries. This was obvious as Elena gazed down at him, illuminated by a single flashlight.

Blood trickled down his face, and one eye was shut, either swollen or lost. On his torso, some blood was visible from the man he's caught, but most was from was his left arm, which had been blown off, not leaving much behind.

Arkady had been quick to act to save him from bleeding out, however. A piece of his shirt, the standard striped blue and white Russian style *Telnyashka*, dirtied by use, was wrapped around the stump of Józef's arm. The one major problem he'd yet to address, however, was the massive piece of shrapnel lodged in his thigh. He knew as well as Józef probably did that if that fragment had hit an artery there wasn't a chance of him surviving, but it was still worth trying.

"Distract him," Arkady said simply to Elena as he kneeled down to inspect the area.

Józef's eyes were unfocused. Adrenaline may have saved him from most of the pain for now, but that wasn't going to count for much with what was coming next. "Józef. Look at me. This needs to be removed. Arkady will do it. I need you to focus on me." Elena looked directly into his eyes. Keeping him distracted was the only way to prevent Józef from going into shock. Were that to happen he would simply have to be left behind as the chances for reviving him would be too low.

Arkady gripped the piece, about the width of his fist, in both hands. He gave it a quick tug to see how far it was embedded.

Józef let out a massive groan.

"Józef. Józef. Look at me. It's fine. Arkady knows what he's doing," Elena said.

She didn't really know this, especially because Dmitry was the designated medic, but he hadn't done anything obviously wrong so far, and some help was better than none.

"I was a medic in my time in the military," Arkady said flatly.

"You see? He knows what he is doing." Elena continued doing everything she could to encourage him.

"Just… do it already," Józef muttered.

"I need to avoid causing any more damage when I remove it. Be patient. While it's still in your leg you won't bleed out. It's after that which concerns me," Arkady explained.

"DO IT!!" --Józef shouted, mustering more energy than even *he* likely thought he could muster.

Arkady stared at him blankly before saying, "As you wish."

"Okay, Józef. Focus on me now. This will sting a little," Elena said, turning Józef's head to face her.

Arkady once again grasped the piece in both hands and began steadily increasing his force on it.

"AGH! KURWA!"--Józef's face contorted in an intense grimace.

"Shut him up. They can't be allowed to hear us," Arkady said, maintaining his monotone.

Arkady released his grip on the piece, which had moved a few centimeters, and tore off another piece of his shirt. "Bite down on this," he said.

Elena took the piece and handed it to Józef. "It'll be over soon," she said.

Arkady once again gripped the piece, and as it gradually moved, both he and Elena could hear Józef suppressing the impulse to scream through the fabric.

"Almost there," Arkady declared.

Finally, the piece came out, and Arkady got out a small needle and a spool of thread.

"It's not finished yet. I need to stitch it up or your chances of bleeding out are highly likely. This shouldn't take as long," Arkady explained.

He then, "Check if any of these men have morphine."

Elena quickly nodded and called out to the nearest group to see if there were any medics nearby. The first one to respond, an American, said, "Our medic, Green, didn't make it down here. But Private Smith here has some he managed to grab on his way out."

From the darkness, a needle was tossed in Elena's direction. She caught it, being careful not to touch the tip of it, as this could give Józef a disease or infection, but he'd still live longer this way than by bleeding out.

She rushed back to Arkady and gave it to him.

Arkady then injected it near Józef's wound, and began stitching it up.

Józef began tensing up again and he bit down on the fabric more, though not as much as the morphine must have been easing the pain at least a bit.

After roughly three more minutes, the job was done, though there was now a small pool of blood under Józef's leg.

"He'll live. If nothing else, he won't bleed out." Arkady finished, and then he stood up and went towards a campfire that had been set up on the side.

Józef had regained his senses, and Elena helped him stand up.

"Where… where is Kasyanov?" he asked, grunting with the effort of standing up on his bad leg and his lost arm.

"I don't know," Elena replied quietly. She knew the best-case scenario was that they left him on the road, alive. He was probably dead or going to be indoctrinated into one of The Order's soldiers.

However, she believed if that was the case, he *would* resist it.

She and Józef began to approach the campfire, where most of Boris, Nikita, Vasiliy, and Józef's people were.

She sat down with Józef and glanced down. The uniform she'd taken from the base was stained by ash, dust, and Józef's blood. Now she was here, sitting in a sewer, the instigator of the journey missing an arm and with a bum leg, and the leader missing.

She sat there, silent, for about half an hour before she saw Nikita running towards the fire with some containers in his hand.

"HEY! SOMEBODY HAD STUFF STASHED HERE!" --he shouted. At least there was some good news, they may be able to last there until they were able to move on.

Nikita got some more people to help bring the supplies to the group, now positioned around several small fires and a few lights.

There may have been more elsewhere in the sewer, but they were as good as lost.

After the group finished eating a small dinner, Nikita stood up.

"Tomorrow, I am going to find Boris, regardless of whether none or all of you are coming with me. He stopped the battle, and his only intention is one of saving humanity, as we know. If there was ever a man worth saving… or burying, it's him."

Most proclaimed their approval, as whether they wanted to get Boris back or not, it was better than remaining in the sewers.

After a bit more talking, Elena noticed Vasiliy and Nikita talking with a couple other people who were still holding their weapons. She went to join in the conversation.

"Ah, Elena, good. Another pair of eyes will be appreciated. We're going out for survivors. Some of The Order's men may still be around, so watch out for that," Nikita said.

A couple minutes later, everyone was prepared, and they went up onto the surface. It was sundown, with a cloudy sky. Come to think of it, there had *only been* cloudy skies for weeks.

The group fanned out and began searching the survivors while inspecting the equipment of the dead Order soldiers. Elena came upon one on the ground in front of a window several stories up who must have fallen. She leaned the figure up against the building and removed their mask. The man appeared to be of Persian ethnicity but looked completely human, no artificial modifications. It seemed what had been done to Daniel was an anomaly; something done only to those who disobeyed.

There was, however, a tattoo with what looked like Latin on his face reading *"Omnia per Ordinem"* in small lettering. She already noticed that there was no computer chip on this one's forehead. Possibly he wasn't indoctrinated, but was instead simply voluntarily working for this organization? It was impossible to know.

Elena then made her way to where she last saw Boris and Daniel. There were several dead Order, Russian, and American soldiers laying all around the area, but none of them was Boris or Daniel.

In the empty space between them all where Boris and Daniel likely were, there was a pistol laying on the ground, an old Tokarev, which looked like the one Boris had been carrying around. There was also the MP3 that Yevgeny had given him. Elena picked them both up and examined them, then put both in her bag.

A few minutes later, Nikita announced, "He's not here! Back to the sewers before it gets much darker."

The group made their way back to the campfires, having gained little from the search.

Vasiliy asked them as they climbed down if anyone had found anything, and Elena mentioned the pistol.

Vasiliy then told her, "There is actually a decent chance that is Boris'. That pistol isn't common anymore. However, that doesn't mean he's alive and we still don't know where he is."

"We'll find him… or he'll find us."

CHAPTER 9

It's dark. Very dark. Am I dead?

Boris was locked in a dark cell of some kind. There were no windows, no obvious door, no light.

The air was musky, humid yet tasteless. Boris could sense movement around him, the world was still, yet he knew there was activity around him.

His head felt fuzzy. He had no idea how long he'd been there. He searched himself for a second to see what he had. He was wearing handcuffs and had a jumpsuit on. As he expected, he was completely unarmed.

He then reached toward his shoulder, and then his bicep, and felt no injury, no bullet hole, and only a slight sting upon touch. The inexplicable lack of the wound baffled Boris, but he had to focus on getting out of there.

The problem is he also had no idea where he was. He could be in a different country, or even a different continent for all he knew.

As the minutes passed, he fully realized how little he knew about his situation. He found his "bed," just a flat piece of metal sticking out of the wall, and he sat down.

Am I going to be executed? Is the rest of the group here? Did they escape? Is Daniel here? Where is everyone else? Where am I? Why am I here?

His thoughts were interrupted by a loud beeping and the same voice he'd heard earlier playing over a loudspeaker.

"ATTENTION NEW PRISONERS! YOU WILL BE BROUGHT INTO OUR GREAT ORDER IF YOU

COOPERATE WITH US! WE WILL RETAKE THE WORLD AND UNITE IT UNDER *THE OVERSEER* AND HIS COUNCIL! PEACE AND PROSPERITY WILL BE RETURNED TO THE WORLD! DO NOT RESIST! *OMNIA PER ORDINEM!*"

The council? Boris thought in as his door opened.

Immediately in front of him he saw two people walk out of nearby cells, both dressed in the same grey jumpsuits as he was.

The first one he saw was a man with the Union Jack tattooed onto his forearm, and the words "As Sāman – Never Forget" next to an S.A.S. tattoo.

If Boris remembered correctly, this was the site of a major battle in the Pan-Arab war. The British were in Southern Iraq, as they, along with the United States and most of the other NATO nations were fighting the Iraqis. As Sāman was a town in southern Iraq that the Iraqis had about 120,000 troops in the face of only 10,000 British forces, which included the elite S.A.S. --Boris was not anywhere near the fight, but from what he'd heard, the town was lost and only about 2,050 British soldiers escaped the battle, the rest killed or captured--with the Iraqis suffering all but 25,000 as casualties. The battle took place in 2012, and it greatly weakened the Iraqis, but the British loss made support for the war quickly dwindle.

During that war, Boris was in Riyadh, the Saudi capital city. The main Russian presence in that war was in Syria, but several members of the GRU were in Saudi Arabia. Russia knew that if Iran deployed any sort of nuclear device against Iraq or Saudi Arabia that the Americans would simply send in more soldiers and resources, and the war would escalate more. While Russia could likely stay out, keeping men unnecessarily in Iran or in Iraq, except the parts nearest to Syria, was pointless.

However, there were those aforementioned GRUs in Saudi Arabia, and in retrospect, it was justified. It was done to keep the higher-ups informed on what the Americans were doing. Boris was one of about seven operatives in Riyadh, his group working around an apartment building that was commandeered by American forces. They must have thought that this would make it less noticeable, but the disgruntled Arabs that used to use the place as a gang hideout gathered around it constantly, giving it away. There was an operational hotel next to it, which Boris and his friend Zakhar had worked in, until Zakhar's… time was up. Several times they would hear rumors of a NATO incursion into Syria, and they would inform their superiors on how to position and posture themselves to discourage an attack, and if an offensive were launched, hopefully to stop it. For the most part this worked and prevented any large-scale confrontation. That, however, was not their only purpose there. Their other directive was studying the tactics and strategies behind their movements against Iraqi and Iranian troops; in one sense, both CSTO and NATO had similar directives against Iraq and Iran, both wanting to contain Iraq and for Iran to destroy any nuclear capabilities. And while there were no official hostilities between Russian and NATO forces, off-the-record the lines did blur, and Zakhar was lost in that fade.

The man in front of Boris then revealed his face, at first obscured by his hands covering his eyes over the intense light, and the memories flooded back into Boris's mind.

And there he was, Ischez. Short for the phrase "Ischeznovenie," roughly meaning "fall out of existence," a description given to him by those Russian observers of his fighting in As Sāman. Allegedly, when he shot enemy fighters, almost always in the head, they dropped instantly, seeming to "fall out of existence".

Of course, in Riyadh, Boris didn't learn this name until Ischez was there himself. Apparently, he'd been taken out of the front lines after several injuries and a risk of getting a stress-related condition like PTSD.

Out of the front lines, however, did not mean out of action.

He became a bodyguard for that apartment building in Riyadh.

Boris and Zakhar made a few of the building's bodyguards, who were at first Saudi soldiers, "disappear" while they set up bugs throughout the building to listen in on communications. These "disappearances" were officially attributed to those gangs who lingered outside the building during the nights. Boris and Zakhar would have occasional encounters with them, generally ending quickly and cleanly, after which the bodies would disappear as with those of the bodyguards. However, after a couple months, the Saudis were replaced with professionals. More often than not, as Boris and Zakhar would enter the building to collect footage and audio from the bugs, they would find dead gang members laying up against the side of the building, all shot in the head.

One night, in the last month of the war, Boris and Zakhar had been told to retrieve the bugs as the war was clearly coming to a close--with 3.5 million dead Iraqi soldiers, 4 million dead Iranians, a couple hundred thousand Syrians and Saudis scattered throughout, and tens of thousands of both documented and undocumented casualties between NATO and CSTO.

The bodyguards, as mentioned, had been professional American and British soldiers for a while by then. They were of decent caliber, but not SEALS or S.A.S. by any stretch.

Boris and Zakhar entered through a side door guarded by one person. They were both wearing dark clothes, with a beanie and jacket to appear as civilians for the sixty seconds it was necessary. Zakhar appeared to the guard as if he was lost and asked for direction to distract him. Boris then emerged silently beside the guard and stabbed him. The memory of the man's face completely losing its color, visible even in the dim light, as his life ebbed away from him is still one of Boris's most vivid.

The man was dragged off, and Zakhar entered the building first. He went upstairs, Boris staying down to collect the bugs. The world was illuminated in acid green light through his night-vision goggles. Another guard stood in a doorway, smoking. This one, too, Boris dealt with, the man going down silently, very quickly.

Boris finished his end of the deal, and the second victim lay near the door as he went upstairs to check on Zakhar, who'd always had the bad habit of waiting too long in situations like these. As Boris's head eclipsed the floor he knew Zakhar was on, the lights flashed on. There stood the Englishman, his form immense over Zakhar, who was lying in a pool of his own blood, a hole in his gut, choking.

Boris froze, completely still, but the man spoke first, saying, "I've found you, Ivan."

Boris said nothing, and stood up to his full form, and spat out, "It took you this long to find us?"

The man responded, "Well, that's quite unfair, is it not? I've not been here for all that long. Of course, this is not important. What's important is I shot your comrade here and have tangible evidence in my hand" - he held up the bugs, - "That you've been doing a little espionage, something I'm sure the Kremlin does not need the world knowing. Not to say we haven't been doing something similar, but, of course, you haven't anything to pin *us* for."

"So then, what do you want *chay-pyet*?"

The Englishman then responded in Russian,

"Why would I want more than I have here? There's no need to be greedy. I just wanted to see what you looked like. You know, being the head-of-security, it's hard to find people to fill in for those guards you keep killing. I wanted to see who the so-called 'Grim Reaper' was…" – he changed to English here, – "And call *him* to the afterlife.

During this conversation, Boris had been slipping a knife into one hand, a smoke grenade in the other.

After the man had finished the word *afterlife*, he threw them both.

A gunshot, a grunt, smoke, darkness, ringing.

Boris first saw the bugs, and knew he wasn't going to be able to grab them in time; he smashed them with his foot. He then went over to Zakhar, hoping to drag him back. He leaned over him, face-to-face.

He'd been shot again in the stomach. He'd turned toward Boris with a proud smile on his face. "Go, Boris. I know you'd outsmart him. I didn't. You can go on, go! I can't die with you on my conscience. GO!" his words echoing through Boris's mind as he sprinted down the stairs and out of the building into the dark street.

It's a shame that bloody knife missed his face, as Boris saw a large scar running down Ischez's forearm. At least he had to pay some blood for Zakhar's life.

The two of them locked eyes, both recognizing each other instantly, but not reacting. They both turned silently to the right where they were herded into somethings like a mess hall.

CHAPTER 10

It had been a week since Boris and Daniel had gone missing. It was confirmed that The Order was not going to be back there soon, so everyone had migrated back up onto the surface. Everything valuable--food, water, weapons, supplies, all of it had been looted from those unfortunates who died in the battle.

Since then, Józef had been learning to manage his bum leg and lost arm while, Petya, who was shot in the side, was relatively unresponsive for the first five days.

When he woke up, the first thing he said was, "Where is Boris?" Dmitry, who'd been watching over him, responded with nothing but a sad expression. Since then Petya had been much less talkative. He'd already been something of an uncle to everyone in the group, but he acted as if he'd lost a son. Physically, however, he was fine; the bullet was only a flesh wound, no major organs had been hit. Nikita and Vasiliy had taken dual positions as leader, with Józef as a moderator between them.

Otto had taken command of Boris's squad, though he insisted it was temporary and that he knew Boris *would* return. Otto hadn't spoken very much throughout the journey, possibly due to his limited knowledge of Russian, but now that more Americans had joined up, English was more commonly used, and he spoke much more often, proving to be quite a decent person and competent leader.

However, Elena thought, he wasn't Boris. He didn't create the same inspiration in people, he didn't have the same vigor, the same enthusiasm to put humanity back together.

That was why she knew she would see him again, one way or another.

The group was scheduled to continue moving west. The plan was that since it appeared The Order came from the west, likely from Germany or France, it was likely that as they made their way through cities on the way to Berlin (or even started in Berlin, a likely candidate considering its central location). If they could make it there it might not be impossible to find Boris again.

So, they set off west. Winter was beginning to set in, and snow was starting to fall. It was dreary, and the sun wasn't visible from beyond the grey sky.

It was like Moscow again, intense gridlock throughout the exits to the city. The group of roughly fifty had fanned out throughout the road, all cold, all hungry, all thirsty, many doubting their purpose.

They were on the border of Belarus. Once they crossed, they'd be out of Russia and begin making their way through Belarus, Poland, and Germany. It would be a while before they left Belarus, so finding a vehicle was a high priority. However, for now, there was no such luck. It would be a long slog to Minsk.

Elena pulled out the MP3 player she'd picked up and looked through it. It still had the song Boris had played on it selected, even though it had been off for a while. She dug through her bag, which had some of her belongings from Moscow and found some questionable earphones that might short circuit when used, but then again maybe not.

So, she played several songs with those earphones in, which luckily did *not* short out. She'd heard some of them before, but she didn't know most of them by the artist or name. Either way, it was a good way to pass the time as the snow piled high around and on the highway, burying the abandoned cars in light-grey snow, infused with the ash thrown into the air from the explosions.

CHAPTER 11

oris was directed to a table by a masked person and took a seat as he assumed that his captors wouldn't take kindly to any form of disrespect or noncooperation. Before the masked person left him, they said, "You're one of our future Prospects... don't eat the food." They left, and the mysterious comment went unanswered as Boris sat quietly. If he announced what he had been told, he'd likely be killed, so he kept it to himself. Once he had sat down, he was face to face with Ischez, who'd also been told something by an attendant. His stare was cold and empty, gazing into an abyss.

They stayed absolutely silent, a decision proven crucial when one unfortunate person about ten meters away started shouting in what sounded like a Scandinavian language and was then beaten and dragged away, never to be seen again.

Boris gazed around, peering at his surroundings. About a hundred people, many looking hungry and weak. There was a woman to one side of him, with light hair, and a man to the other side, stocky with dark hair. Both were silent, and tired looking.

Boris's attention shifted to trays that were set on the tables filled with surprisingly edible-looking food, albeit very simple-- including bread, fruit, some meats, and several other things.

There was silence for a minute before every one of the ravenous, starving people in that room started digging into the food set in front of them. All except Boris, Ischez, a woman several seats down, and likely a couple more.

Boris's first instinct for not digging into the food, aside from the fact he was told not to, was that he was used to rationed food and had eaten nothing when unconscious. He knew that devouring large amounts of food after having none could be dangerous, or even deadly. After another minute, he began realizing another good reason: there was a pretty good chance that this food wasn't all it seemed. It *could* be a trick.

Sure enough, after a couple minutes only Boris, Ischez, the nearby woman and several other people elsewhere in the room were left standing. The rest were loaded onto stretchers and carried off away from where they'd entered. The room was empty within minutes, and the same voice, much quieter now, said "All those who remain, stand up, then stand on the table. Make this easy on yourself. What we are doing here is a good thing, do not worry."

One person, on a far end of the room, ran toward their entrance to the cafeteria, and was gunned down within seconds, one last scream emanating from the unfortunate, foolish man as he crashed into the linoleum floor, his blood quickly staining it. Evidently, here they had soldiers who could actually aim.

"Now, we've rooted out another unworthy one. All of you move to the center table, face each other, then do not move." Boris, despite every instinct screaming for him to disobey, moved to the center table and did as instructed; he wasn't going to get anywhere if he was dead.

Once the five-total people had grouped together, the loudspeaker person said, "See you on the other side."

In that instant a pale blue gas flooded the room from a vial in the ceiling directly above them.

How did I not see this before?... this last thought floated through his mind as he drifted into unconsciousness.

Recent events flashed through his mind--the biker ambush, the fighting in Smolensk, Elena shouting at him right before he was captured, and then being brought here.

Then he was awake. Was he? Was this part of the dream?

My head's spinning. What did they hit me with?

It seemed that he was in a moving truck. He was the only person in it.

Wait, no. Is that Nikita? Boris turned his head and the image vanished.

Józef's face stared over from behind him, but it wasn't clear, very unfocused.

"Józef? What are you doing? Get out of here!"

Boris reached up to try to push him forward, away from this place, but Józef leaned back and faded away before his hand got close.

Then the top of the truck opened up. A beautiful starry sky, like what he remembered from his childhood. All the stars, all the colors and arrangements. So beautiful!

Then he saw something huge start to blot out the stars. Bigger than anything. *What the hell is that!?*

It was a giant cartoon bomb falling to the ground with a huge radioactive symbol on it. It passed behind the back of the truck, and the sky became fire.

Screams echoed quietly from an unknown place.

The fire forms were death incarnate--a skull, bones, headstones.

Then the sky cleared, clouds floating through the newly blue sky.

The sun shined bright over Boris's face, right over him but not hurting his eyes. He heard a kind voice address him.

"Hi Boris! Are you awake?"

He looked over and saw Elena. Her face could be seen clearly.

Saved me again, huh? Boris thinks the words and his mouth moves yet the words do not come. She continues to sit, smiling. She stood, and then began to dance gracefully, as a young girl in a field of flowers would.

Why can I see her so clearly? Boris tries to reach out to catch her hand, but it passed right through.

What is that? Shadows, darkness begin to encroach.

The truck hits a large bump, and the shadows are upon him.

The last thing he'd heard from Elena rang through his ears; "COME BACK FOR ME!"

The darkness was all he could see, the smoke entering his eyes, his ears. All that was left is the maniacal laugh of the Announcer...

The truck hit another bump and Boris struck his head on the side of the cot, unconscious yet again.

CHAPTER 12

Minsk was approaching, but not with any hurry. The group had been trudging through the three-foot snow for several weeks now. Many people have had to resort to hunting animals near the road, meals often made up of the huge ration supplies they had with a few cooked rabbits or birds mixed in.

They'd also lost one already. Nobody seemed to notice, but the group which at the beginning was around 60, was now 59. Maybe the missing one died of frostbite, maybe he slept too late one day, maybe he left, maybe something happened to him that will begin to take more of them. Regardless, he had to be forgotten and the group moved forward.

The sun hadn't been visible during those weeks, either. The world was locked in a perpetual evening, it never seemed to get brighter, only to darken at certain times of the day.

Elena had been doing better than what might be expected, but she'd always hated this sort of weather. Not to say she wasn't used to it, but it always had a way of creating problems.

In particular, the air was always stale and cold through the gas mask. At first, it was negligible, but now it left an unpleasant taste.

Life had become now nothing more than a long march that felt like it would only lead to death or getting lost.

After a couple more days of trudging through nothing, even Nikita's tongue held by the cold and solemnity of their situation.

Every time Elena looked to either side to ensure she was not alone, that everyone had at one point or another not dropped into the snow, out of sight, perhaps out of existence, she'd see nothing but silhouettes, all uniform in their dreariness; All hunched over, in long coats, hands shoved in pockets, gas mask filters jutting out at different angles from their faces, weapons lashed across their backs.

One and the same, yet all were different people who desire different things and have their own reasons for being there, yet all were alike as they march through the snow into nothingness.

Finally, Minsk was in sight as the outskirts of the city became visible.

The intense snow clearly had an effect on some buildings; some that likely had structural damage from the war now collapsed under the weight of the snow, and as they approached, they realized how deep the snow had become when Yevgeny tripped in the snow and found it to be the roof of a sedan.

A couple more hours passed, and they reached the first buildings.

Given the impossibility of telling the time from the environment, they had to trust Vasiliy's watch, which said it was around 7:00 PM, although Dmitry's said 6:30, and Jackson, the man Boris had originally met in the center of the battlefield to stop the war, indicated that it was 20:00, or 8:00 PM.

They decided they were going to rest in an apartment building.

Otto went up to a window of a building and pulled out an ice pick he'd had since the beginning of their travels. He then gave it a tired swing and shattered the window; everybody then entered the building and several desks and other things were moved into it to help keep the heat in.

Elena was one of the last in, and took in the ghostly surroundings;

She walked over to a cubicle and found a chair to sit in. It was, however, occupied by a skeleton, still wearing its business suit. She moved the body, unshaken by this given all else that had happened and sat down to stare at the outside world as the snow continued to pile on.

She watched as several of the others began exploring the building, raiding cabinets, searching break rooms, digging through piles of old propaganda posters. An old man was on them who looked like the President of Belarus. Once a powerful figure in the region, now nothing more than a photograph looking back to a time now past.

After staring out the window for several more minutes, she heard shouting from upstairs. She went to investigate, as surely this would be more interesting than sitting around, doing nothing.

She ran up a few flights of stairs until the shouting was very close by. She reached the floor it was coming from, following a group of people to a closed door, where she saw Vasiliy shouting at it.

"COME OUT OF THERE NOW, OR WE'LL SHOOT YOU FULL OF HOLES!"

BANG!

A shot exited from the enclosed office, presumably from the occupant inside.

Elena decided to try something different to avoid escalating the situation further.

"Who are you?" She asked the door in a calm voice.

"Why should I tell you? You've invaded my hideout!" the occupant of the office replied.

"Because I want to know why you shut yourself in this office and why my friend here is dedicated to getting you out of there," she explained.

Vasiliy interjected, "He's got supplies stockpiled in there, and shot at us when we entered the floor. I don't like the idea of someone hostile to us wandering around the building. All I've asked is that he exit the room. At this point, I'm seriously considering just shooting him through the wall."

"I think we can avoid that," said Elena. "Why won't you leave the room then, sir?" she asked the person in the office.

"Look at it from my angle! I'm the sole survivor from a rich office building in the middle of a not-so rich city! Why should I trust you? I don't even know what the hell happened! You could be bandits, or KGB, or who the hell knows who! Maybe you just want to take my stuff and leave me to starve!"

"I can assure you we aren't KGB. There was a war, this much you should know, and it went nuclear. We are some survivors who set out from Moscow to the west. Our only goals are to find a comrade of ours and to survive."

"Fine. I'll open the door if everyone here, but you, leaves and goes back down onto the first floor."

"Do it Vasiliy," Elena said. If this worked it could save a life, though it was questionable at this point what this person would do with his life in the long run, anyway.

Vasiliy gave her a suspicious glance, but then ordered his men out of the room. They begin to file down the stairs.

Elena then turned around and told the man, "All right. Just you and me now. Please open the door."

There was a lot of movement from behind the door, but after a minute, it swung open and the occupant became visible; he was a short man with bifocals, and a collared shirt with slacks.

Elena entered the room to find piles of both uneaten and eaten supplies, mostly consisting of old, spoiled looking lunches and snack bags. She then turned to face him, and he was holding an old revolver to her face.

"It's nothing personal, but I'm not taking any risks. You aren't staying in this building." There was a wild look in his eyes, like an animal's.

"Now, exit the room. Go to the stairs. Any deviation and you will die."

Elena, infuriated, had no choice but to follow these orders. She marched in front of him, walking past the rows of cubicles. Many were inhabited by skeletons, all of them torn apart, their belongings strewn around them, likely by the man with a revolver to the back of her head.

She saw a bit of movement to her left side but didn't react.

Vasiliy.

Really, she thought, *it isn't surprising.* Of course, he didn't leave. The only question is if he'll –

BANG!

I guess he has.

She turned around and watched the man crumple to a heap on the ground, with Vasiliy staring at him, with the arm holding his Makarov still extended, only a meter from where the man's face was a second ago.

"Next time we're doing something like this, think more before you trust. Otherwise *this* happens," he said, gesturing to the dead man. He then added, "You can't save everyone, and some aren't worth saving."

Elena stayed silent after this and made her way back to the second floor while Vasiliy gathered his men back to collect the dead man's supplies. It was almost sickening, but they had to take it, to survive themselves. It wasn't Vasiliy's fault the man died, it was his own…

Back on the second floor the incident was treated like a great occasion; what luck to have found supplies in this building!

Shame about that guy, though.

It turned out, the man had been living purely off of the meagre things that had been left in this building and the ones around it. The fact all of his coworkers had died, and he'd had to scrounge through everything just to get by would understandably drive one insane.

Still, Elena thought, *did he really have to do that?*

This world was no longer hospitable to those who were undiscerning. His poor decision was the only reason he died. If he hadn't, Vasiliy wouldn't have shot him. Simple as that.

A couple more days, and the group would move on and the man would be forgotten, after months and years reduced to nothing more than bones on the floor of an office building, the only sign there was anything special at all about him or that anything had happened to him being the gunshot in his skull.

Later that day, when everybody ate their meal, many of the people treated themselves to some of the snacks the man had been living on, rather than old cans of beans, rice, Spam, and other such unappetizing things.

Elena didn't, maybe couldn't take any of it and instead thought, *what if I'd done something before? If I'd turned, and risked getting shot? I could have saved his life, disarmed him maybe? He didn't have to get shot. Realistically though, what could I have done? After starving and being alone for months, I doubt he'd have any sympathy for people who came marching into his complex. I have to stop this, forget about it or I'll just be torturing myself.*

Eventually she was able to change the subject in her mind to a conversation going on between two people behind her, a Russian and an American, talking about where they were before the war and how they each got to Smolensk.

She then went back to staring out the window, and after a powerful gust of wind from outside through the shoddily repaired windows, she thought she saw Boris's reflection through the glass, but the image was gone in an instant.

After a couple more minutes of staring outside, as the snow continued to pile on, she fell into a restless sleep.

CHAPTER 13

This room was brighter than the last one he woke up in. There was a bright light shining into his eyes forcing him to turn onto his side while his eyes adjusted to the change in lighting. He thought back to the dream, or hallucination, or whatever it was. Was it supposed to mean something? Or was it just his mind bullshitting him?

He was expecting to be tied down on the bed, but he wasn't. He stood up and checked to make sure he hadn't been altered since he was last awake; he had no idea what he was dealing with. Chances were high he wouldn't be able to do anything but sit and wait for something to happen without immediately facing a likely execution. As soon as he'd verified there was nothing noticeably wrong with him, he began to analyze his situation; some bread sat on a table next to him; it looked like rye. He hadn't had that in a while. He hadn't had *food* in a while.

He stared at it. *Can I really eat this? Surely, they wouldn't be testing us again. There wouldn't be a point in doing that. Of course not. I can eat this.*

Boris reached out to pick up the bread and looked at it.

Doesn't look like there's anything wrong with it.

He brought it to his nose. *Smells like rye… I guess.*

His stomach rumbled, he likely hadn't eaten anything in the past 48 hours, at least, but if they'd taken him this far they couldn't let him starve to death, surely.

He still held it in his hand, contemplating taking a bite.

Screw it.

He brought it to his mouth, and just before he was going to eat it, the door opened suddenly.

"I wouldn't eat that," said the figure standing in the doorway.

It was brighter outside the room Boris was in.

Why the hell is it brighter? How do they even have the power to make a light as bright as the sun in here!?

"Fine," Boris finally replied, and he stood up.

The figure responded, after walking into the room, with "I am Dr. Ward." The figure closed the door, and Boris was able to see the person's face. It turned out to be a woman of average height, tanned skin and darker hair.

After closing the door behind her, she began to explain why Boris was there.

"If you hadn't figured it out already, you are here, and not in the... conversion centers because you passed a test. A very basic, simple test, easily thrown by one's appetite. So, I am here to see if you were actually smart enough to *not* eat the food, or if you just decided not to indulge yourself on the consumables placed in front of you. I feel your chances are not good, considering it looks like you were about to eat that piece of 'bread'. It was the same test, but we usually do it again to be sure. You'd be surprised at how many people who didn't fall for it the first time, do on this second test."

"You explained why *I'm* here. But why is anybody here? Why are you testing people, what happens to the others?" Boris inquired.

"Well, in case you haven't noticed, we had a nuclear war. *Billions* died. So... if we are going to rebuild society we need to separate the intellectuals from the common rabble. Our new society will only be made of those greatest people, the others relegated to menial, although important tasks, such as standard foot soldiers, or factory workers. Those who excel will be the politicians, the scientists, the... military commandos of the world."

The last five words stung like nothing else. She *knows* him, and she's likely never seen him before. She's likely only read reports, words on a paper about him. Yet she also likely knows about every soldier he's killed and every action he's taken from when he fought them at the base until now.

She continued after the short pause.

"Yes, I know you, yes, I know what you've done, who you are, and where your associates are staying. They are in Minsk under several feet of snow. I know you worked for the Russian GRU, that you have a former KGB officer in your ranks, that you have a certain affinity for one of the party members. Maybe you haven't always seen us, but there's always been someone there. Someone..." she leaned forward – "*just like you*. You may even know him, actually. He came back with us to see you." She stepped away from the door, and there he was.

Zakhar.

It had to be him, same face, same physique. He stepped into the room as Dr. Ward stepped out.

"But... you're dead..." is all Boris managed to choke out, his voice shaking, and unsteady.

Zakhar looked down at Boris, an inscrutable expression on his face.

"And yet here I am. Before we go any further, I'll tell you what happened after you left. And no, I do not think you were at fault for leaving. If you'd stayed, there's a good chance we'd both have died. Anyway, I waited you to be gone so you wouldn't try dragging me out; I decided one surviving was better than none. I also wasn't going to let Ischez take me, if at all possible. I crawled downstairs, the smoke grenade you'd thrown covering my exit, leaned up against a wall, and began to wrap my abdomen with a few medical supplies I brought, then stumbled to the exit. I opened the door – "He stopped for a second, mysteriously, as if reminiscing upon a fond moment from childhood – "And Ischez was there, bleeding heavily from one arm, holding his sidearm to my face. 'You really expected to stumble out of here like this? That you'd escape? Ridiculous.' He then led me back inside and tied me to a chair in one of the central rooms. He and his men tried to beat everything I knew out of me, but I never gave them anything... except this."

He'd had his arms clasped behind his back in a business-like manner, but at this moment he revealed his right hand – on which his ring finger was missing.

"I lost my ring with it. I never got it back." He added quietly before continuing.

"They said they would put me on the news, that I would be a war criminal, and that The United States, Britain, and all the other Western countries would cry for war, because, of course, the average citizen didn't know their own people were doing the same thing to us, and that Ischez couldn't be touched legally for anything he did, as he was a mercenary employed by some big company supporting the war, one that provided bodyguards for important officials. Another thing conveniently left out, because nobody cared about mercenaries..." He looked off toward the wall, silent for a few seconds before continuing, now beginning to pace the room. "Fortunately for me, regardless of their own affiliation with the military, they *knew* I was GRU, but that also meant that if they were to expose me I couldn't be beaten too badly, so they patched up my gunshot wound. Two days before the camera crews and news reporters were to arrive, I made my escape. I'd been held in that same chair the whole time, except to deal with pleasantries. Throughout the week I'd been sitting there, I'd been slowly cutting into the ropes holding me with a piece of metal that had been sitting in the corner of the bathroom. I'd worn them down to about an eighth of their original thickness; then, one night, at the edge of midnight, I sawed through it and tackled the man guarding me, who had his back turned. I used a section of rope to strangle the guard, then took his sidearm and knife, and marched out of the building." He stopped once more, gathered his thoughts, and finished the story.

"I searched the building and didn't find you. Your stuff, the radio, all of it, gone. I'd survived, but I was dead to everyone else. You, Russia… Anya. I didn't exist. I was simply a resident of Riyadh, a white resident who stood out yet blended in, didn't draw attention. I worked in a garage as a car mechanic, hoping to eventually get enough money to buy a plane ticket to Moscow. Then, I met Dr. Ward, a native Saudi."

She'd come under the guise of fixing a minor problem with her car, but as I was the only one working that day, her true intention was revealed rather quickly. She knew me, as she knows you. While we watched the Americans, she watched us. I'll spare you the details, but because of her I wasn't working in a garage in Riyadh and was instead in Berlin, training recruits for the Organization to Responding to Drastic Events Readily; a group ready for a day like the one several months ago, ready to rebuild society and put its best parts back together. While you have fought us, we are ready to forgive so that you may find your salvation in rebuilding the world."

It can't be. What am I supposed to think? They attacked me first! And yet they try to justify their actions, try to justify themselves with Zakhar. They kidnap Daniel and me, kill my comrades, and expect me to kiss their ass, singing songs of praise?

But still, how'd they win Zakhar to their side? I guess they found him at the perfect time, a time when he was vulnerable, and he would have accepted anybody's help.

And they'd better not fucking know about Vityaz. I sure hope Zakhar doesn't; he just barely made it out in time. I thought he burned with that cursed building, whether alive or his corpse.

"Zakhar… I could not be more pleased that you are alive, but this organization is not what you think it is." Boris said this just after the doctor had left the room. Sure, there may be cameras but that's not important. If he could get Zakhar on to his side, and find Daniel, he could get out of here.

The doctor entered the room once again. "I hope you appreciate being able to reacquaint yourself with your friend here… but it is time for a few… tests. You have an exactly 50 percent chance of making it through, and the reason why will be explained to you shortly." She stood up, and opened the door – "This way, please."

Boris stood up and followed. He went into a room with opposing glass windows. He was across from a man, about his age, wearing a grey jumpsuit with "The Order" stenciled across his chest. Next to Boris were about 20 people similar to him, dressed in similar jumpsuits to the man across him, however without The "Order" stencil. A very clear, almost robotic voice came in over speakers in the ceiling.

"Look forward, prospects. These are established members of our great Order, who have passed this test. We have found their abilities to be in doubt. You will be directly competing with them over a span of a week, and if in the final competition you reign supreme, you will be an honored member of our order. If your opponent wins, you will die, and they will retain their current position and will be unlikely to be selected again. Keep in mind, if you win this competition, you may be on the other side one day. We like to keep our ranks populated only with the greatest among humanity."

Boris analyzed the face of the man in front of him. He had a dark buzz cut and stubble, a strong face. Likely to be stiff competition.

The glass pane separated each pair. The loudspeaker came on again, with, "Now. Acknowledge your competition, do not befriend them. The first test, is a simple one of whether you can disregard the human impulse to trust, especially in a situation where both members are indeed in distress."

The man in front of Boris reached out his hand. Boris met it and gave his last name.

"Kasyanov," he said.

The man replied with "Centurion 14-B. A pleasure." He had a voice similar to that of the person speaking over the loudspeaker. Likely an American, or possibly a Canadian. But it was unimportant, as he was likely as brainwashed as any of the others.

The glass panes rotated back, and A few figures in masks entered the Prospect side of the room and handed a touchscreen device to each person.

Boris moved it around with his hands, searching for a power button. Once found, he turned it on, and there was a simple light blue screen displayed.

INSERT NAME popped up on to the screen. Boris plugged his name into the system, and it returned with, **WELCOME, PROSPECT KASYANOV.**

The loudspeaker voice came on again with "This is your Personal Electronic Assistant, or P.E.A. It will direct you around the building as you prepare for the Test and assist you in learning vital skills you may need to emerge victorious."

The masked figures who handed out the P.E.A.'s then began to direct everyone out of the room, into a new one. It was set up as one would expect of a luxury hotel, with a comfortable looking bed, a television screen, and a large bathroom and closet. There were no windows. Boris still strongly suspected that they were underground, and if they weren't, these higher-ups wouldn't want to give them any view of the outside that could help them plan an escape.

Just after Boris just sat down in his new quarters, the loudspeaker came on once again, this time with a more pleasant-sounding feminine voice.

"Our Prospects are treated the greatest luxuries; the future of humanity deserves the best! Prospects will have one week to prepare for the Test." The voice changed, to a much deeper, more serious bass: "Failure to comply will result in termination."

Is there any way I can get out of this? It may be better to go through with it. I'll take down a trained Order commando in the process if I do. It's the only way I'll see Elena, or Nikita, and Vasiliy again.

Boris looked back to his P.E.A. There were several icons on the screen, divided by categories, such as *Food, Survival, Fighting,* and *Marksmanship.*

Boris first selected the *food* category, as it was very unlikely he'd eaten anything in the past few days. And surely, this time, the food won't contain a sedative.

He was directed to a cafeteria, where there were already about twelve other Prospects being served food.

It was fairly simple meal with things like steak and rice, but it all looked very edible. Boris only got a bowl of rice and some water, for the same reason he hadn't engorged himself on the food when previously grouped with the other hundreds of people. This was because, of course, eating too much after having no food is generally detrimental to one's health. He sat down on a stool on one side of the room, neither near nor far from the others. He began eating, and it was pretty good; the water was cool, the rice fresh. After about ten minutes, he went back to his room and turned on the television. It had two stations, a radio station with an incredible variation of songs and genres, and one that told the history of The Order on a loop. He decided to watch a couple minutes of it because through all the propaganda there were probably shards of truth he might find useful.

Luckily, he'd caught it towards the beginning of a run, where it showed portraits of three different people, likely key founding members. There were two men, one woman. All looked middle aged and very...professional, for lack of a better word; like politicians, or business executives. The sort of people Boris' family would variably look at with great regard or total disgust, depending on their affiliation. He vaguely recognized one of them, but not very well; it's unlikely any of them were heads of state or other leading politicians.

The broadcast went on to explain each leader's story after the silent view of the paintings.

"The Overseer" - The view zoomed in on the first figure, a man easily in his fifties, possibly scratching the surface of sixty, given these portraits were doubtlessly more pleasant looking than the real people – "Was a valued leader of the New Dawn Company, which helped to preserve peace within the major countries during the Pan-Arab war" – At this point, Boris was hardly surprised. It was quite convenient, wasn't it? Boris was attacking the company which helped originate The Order, so of course once Zakhar was wandering the streets they'd try to contact him. – "He even helped an S.A.S. agent recover after an attack from Russian forces, and through his immense kindness even forgave one of the two people who were involved, bringing him into our great society. The other one, as of yet hasn't been found." *Not true anymore*, Boris thought- "But if he is found we know he will make a valuable contribution to our great Order. Many other leaders wouldn't be willing to forgive as the Overseer does, but he is forgiving, and he is the one who brought the three together."

Boris turned off the TV. He'd seen enough, and now, he had a target, a goal. One he may not reach for a while, or maybe ever, but something to drive him through this.

He dropped the remote, lay down on the bed, and fell asleep almost instantly, exhausted from everything that had happened.

CHAPTER 14

The incident in the office building was now a few days behind them, and they continued moving. They'd searched through at least seven parking garages, looking for any vehicle they could use. Until then, they'd only managed to siphon some petrol, which may have already expired.

After some more wandering, they found a school in one of the suburbs on the western end of the city. It looked…off. It had been reinforced and looked more like a fortress than anything else. It appeared the fortifications had been maintained, at least, to some degree. Unlike the buildings surrounding it, it didn't look like it had been ransacked and looted multiple times over as was so often the case. The building was also drawing the attention of the other members as well, likely all noticing the same thing. With no words spoken, the group began approaching the forbidding building. The yard in front of it was completely empty, just filled with the snow, slightly grey in areas from the ash and soot of nuclear explosions.

In a minute they were upon the front doors, with Jeung and Otto entering first, fanning out through the building. It was dark, and there was no electricity. All of the windows had been painted over black, and members of the group began to smash them open to gain at least a bit of dim light in the somber building.

After a couple minutes of searching, Elena, followed by Nikita and Vasiliy, entered the cafeteria. That's when the first large knocking sound was audible, ringing through the building from the other side of the cafeteria. The three of them approached the hallway it was coming from, and found a large row of rooms, all shut with steel doors, one of which was likely the source of the sound. They each went to different parts of the hallway, searching for which exact door it was, before Vasiliy found the one closest to the origin of the noise. He knocked back on it.

A hoarse voice spoke to him. "Are you with The Order?" Vasiliy replied, "We're about as far from being with The Order as we could be." And he shot open the lock of the door, allowing it to swing open, where a thin woman stood with a piece of stale-looking bread in her hand.

"What happened to you?" he asked her.

She croaked out, "The food. The food before, it was poison. They gave us food, it knocked us out. We've been stuck here for a week now, very little food and water up until two days ago, when most of them left. There was gunfire outside the building. Maybe they were killed. Did you see any bodies on the way in?"

Vasiliy replied with, "Whether they are there or not is a total guess. If they are, they have been covered in snow since then. Its a couple feet deep now. There could be tens, or hundreds under there. Someone who didn't know about that possibility would have no idea."

"Well. If you are not with them, then what are you?" she asked.

"I'm with…" There was no real name for this group, army, whatever it was. "The Kasyanov Expedition." Was the first thing that came into his mind, and out of his mouth. Really, it's what it was, Boris Kasyanov's expedition, minus Boris Kasyanov. Oh, well.

"Who's Kasyanov?" The woman asked.

"He's not me, and he's not anyone here. He's someone, somewhere, who got us out here. Our goal was initially to make it to an island, where we'd find many seedlings to restart agriculture. Now we are trying to find him, hopefully we will somewhere along the way. I am Vasiliy. Behind me are Nikita and Elena," Vasiliy explained.

"Well… At least you are not with The Order. I am Yekaterina. Throughout this building there are a few others. There were around a hundred to begin with. They tempted us with food, it knocked us out. Those who did not eat were taken. Maybe your friend was here. Describe him to me," the woman said.

"He's..." Vasiliy struggles for a second to picture him in his mind, the only real image of him being the last seconds he'd seen him, firing his rifle into Order troops. "Somewhere around 2 meters tall. Sort of blondish-brown hair, sort of long. Sound familiar at all?"

Yekaterina was silent for around a minute. "...Maybe. I think so. I think I remember hearing him speak a bit under his breath. He's Russian, yes? It sounded like he had a Moscow accent."

Vasiliy shrugged and looked to Elena and Nikita.

"Yeah, he's from Moscow. Troparevo district, I think," said Nikita.

"Then I do remember him. When those of us who ate woke up, we were massed together in another room here. Probably a former gymnasium. There were men standing near all entrances and windows in the room. Anyone who tried to run was gunned down instantly. A voice came over, and shouted toward the jostling crowd, 'YOU MAY HAVE BEEN OUR ENEMIES ONCE. YOU CAN REDEEM YOURSELVES IF YOU JOIN US! THOSE WHO ARE WILLING TO BE THE FIST OF OUR GREAT NEW WORLD FOLLOW VANGUARD C-379!' He continued to ramble for a while longer after that. Many people, maybe half of the crowd, went over to become part of their army, likely to be brainwashed. The rest of us were told that we were regressive, fighting change. Standing against the inevitable, against fate. We were locked back up and given meagre rations. We were told we could 'redeem' ourselves at any time..."

She stopped talking for a second, looking down and around the hallway, around the building, as if her memory could be strengthened by visual input, before continuing.

"Maybe it was out of their own *sick*" -She spat the word out like poison – "sense of humor… but they said the last one to break would be set free, off into the world. They told us they fully knew we'd starve on what we were being given and told us to join them or suffer that fate. Of course, the idea they'd set the last one free was likely untrue, but it only demonstrated their… unrestrained sadism." She finished.

"How many do you think are still alive?" Elena asked her.

"Less than twenty is my best guess. Open all the doors, but do not reveal what you do not want to see. Many are weaker than me, many are already gone. But save those you can, for if they've made it this far they are likely strong enough of will to help you," Yekaterina replied.

"Or they've completely lost their minds…" Vasiliy said under his breath.

The next half hour was spent opening doors and unloading the living and dead alike. Some were saved, some couldn't be, some were in their last minutes. However, without a doubt, some lives were saved.

There also was no Daniel. Several of the other prisoners were questioned, but it appeared nobody had seen him.

All in all, seventeen people were pulled from the hellish facility. One of them was likely to die soon of malnourishment, but nobody had the heart to tell them.

As equipment and rations were split among the survivors, Zhenya ran into the building from the back lot. He was panting, out of breath. Nikita rushed over to him and gave him his canteen. After he'd regathered himself, Zhenya managed to spit out, "there's… there's trucks in the lot. At least eight. Abandoned. I started one up. They're filled with supplies. I dug to the bottom of the snow… There's… bodies, mostly Order bodies. Someone killed them."

"And left the supplies?" Nikita inquired.

"I guess so," Zhenya replied.

"And who were the bodies that weren't Order soldiers?" Vasiliy interjected.

"I don't know… There was only one that I found. He was dressed in robes, with no body armor. I can find him again, bring him in. I didn't think to do so before because of the trucks."

Zhenya took Ivan, one of the stronger men from the group, and went outside to retrieve the body.

After a couple minutes, they were seen re-entering the building, dragging a man dressed in white behind them. They lay him upon a table, and Vasiliy, accompanied by Dmitry, began to examine him.

The two most glaringly obvious attributes of the man were his occult-looking mask and the sheer volume of bullet wounds he had sustained. Dmitry commented, "This man was not simply shot. This man was desecrated intentionally during battle. One or two bullets would have killed him, because he is unarmored. Yet here he lays with over thirty in his torso alone."

Dmitry began digging through the man's clothing, searching for any items that could identify him.

Vasiliy removed and tried to read the characters on his mask. They are twisted, and looked scratched in. They were written in English, and read "Death, Famine, Pestilence, War." After a closer examination, he made out a burning bull skull fitted to the shape of the mask.

"This must be the work of a cult of sorts… but how could these fanatics have caused so much damage and yet lost so little?" Vasiliy asked.

Dmitry suddenly pulled a thin book out from the man's thigh area, miraculously undamaged. It had the same bull symbol as there was on the mask, with no title on the cover. Dmitry started scanning the book and scoffed as it was apparently filled with nonsensical rambling.

Elena, who'd been sitting in the back of the room for most of this, moved forward toward the book. She picked it up and began to flip through the pages.

It was, as Dmitry said, filled with nonsense. It almost seemed to be a sort of journal, with spurts of some strange philosopher's words throughout. Shortly after, she announced it would be best if the group left.

Nobody disputed this idea as they began to gather their things, and piled into the trucks, which fortunately had massive snow tires and makeshift plows on their front. *Well, even if The Order has shitty soldiers, they certainly know how to equip vehicles to get through terrible weather,* Elena thought.

One by one, the trucks managed to start up, slowly pushing the snow to the sides as they started down the road, out of Minsk, and hopefully away from the terror that was unleashed upon the former owners of those trucks.

CHAPTER 15

Boris awoke with a shock, his device, which he'd already forgotten the name of, telling him, "Good morning, Prospect Kasyanov! Welcome to day 1 of Preparation for the Test!"

A masked figure entered Boris's room shortly after with a massive dish of food for him. The figure was silent and had very stiff body language. Boris thanked the individual anyway and continued the program he'd started the day before. Despite his anger toward The Order, he still needed to learn as much about it as possible, even if it meant sifting through their propaganda. The program continued from roughly where he was before, and he sat through the babbling of the overly cheery speaker, trying to pick out bits of useful information. While he still had no idea where he was, he deduced he was certainly still in Europe. He also learned the basic profiles of the other two heads of The Order. There was the Overseer, whom he'd heard about the day before, then there was the Imperator, and the Provider. How he figured it, the Overseer was the de facto leader of The Order, and generally ran things, while the Imperator and Provider were two side sides of the coin responsible for The Order's operations.

The Imperator was the head of "Defense and Expansion," as it was called, and simply put was the Commander-in-Chief of anything military related. He was apparently an original underling of the Overseer who, Boris assumed, got where he was more from blind loyalty than anything else. He seemed to be about thirty, and had a buzz cut. He looked like a drill sergeant, a good fit for his role.

The Provider was the person who seemed to manage the majority of civic activities within The Order. When she was featured, there was a view across a city that was apparently being "remodeled" as the capital of the Order. Unfortunately, Boris was unsure what city it was, but it was likely in Central Europe, and it was also quite possibly where he was now.

She also seemed to be the head of industry and agriculture, however that was not revealed in great detail. Boris found it unlikely The Order's grip on their surroundings and their overall power was yet as great as they claimed it to be.

Nonetheless, it was still more than Boris had initially expected, but all things considered, he shouldn't have been surprised, considering the degree of luxury afforded to him the past day. Though, perhaps, this was just a show to make their organization seem much greater than it was. After sitting silently for a couple minutes contemplating this, another figure entered the room, this time it was the doctor he'd spoken to before.

"It's time for the first part of your preparation. I'm sure you'll have an easy time with this, Prospect Kasyanov. Follow me."

Boris sat up and followed her out of the room and into an elevator going down, where he was then led into what appeared to be a shooting range.

"I'd suggest you cooperate, Prospect. For the sake of my job and your life. I get a promotion if you survive," she said coldly, before leaving the room.

A wall panel to Boris' left flipped and revealed an immense array of weapons. He figured that he should attempt to practice with weapons he hadn't seen before because he should not be expecting the convenience of choice when the time for action came.

As he began training with several weapons, his mind strayed, to once again considering the justification for what he was doing. Yes, he was being thrust into a competition to the death against someone he didn't know, yet they were without question a high-profile member of The Order he would take out if he succeeded. Of course, it wouldn't be that simple. This person could be equivalent or greater in skill compared to him, but it seemed they had been chosen to participate for failure in their duties, so it was unlikely he'd be dealing a major blow if he wins.

Then, of course, if he won, it's also highly unlikely they were simply going to let him into The Order, no questions asked, and reveal all kinds of secrets. There would very likely be some form of attempted brainwashing after the whole escapade, or at least a psychological test to ensure his loyalty, which of course they would never gain.

As the not-so-good doctor watched over Boris training with weapons, his skill seeming to improve even as his mind drifted further, as he replaced the blank targets with the face of the Overseer in his mind, beginning to formulate a plan to get out, and to bring down the order from the inside.

Maybe they broke Zakhar. They won't break me. Not until I am cold and dead.

A couple hours later, Boris was sitting in the cafetorium, soon gravitating toward the woman he'd seen before he'd been brought there. Since there would be no direct competition with the other Prospects, he might be able to forge a form of alliance with her and others, maybe something that could grow to help him escape.

He sat across from her. There was no time for pleasantries. He needed information and to know whether she was going to be any help or not.

Before he began, he scanned the room for any cameras.

As abundant with resources as The Order seemed to be, he didn't see any. Either they were hidden, or they weren't there. He had to take the risk; he wasn't getting out alone.

He turned toward the woman.

"I'm not going to waste any time here. I am going to win this test, and then I am getting out of here. Period. Are you with me or against me?" He spoke in English, the language most likely to be universally understood there.

"You must be stupid," she said. She sounded French.

"Yes, I must be stupid. Stupid or not, I'm not staying here. Surely you know this Order does not have positive intentions for the vast majority of people still alive," he said.

"Of course, they don't. But you're Russian, I can tell from your accent. Given the fact I know little about The Order, you could simply be a mole searching for disloyalty among the Prospects. I'd be stupid to trust you immediately, given my lack of knowledge. The Order could easily be your organization--one that gained your allegiance after you survived the war and put a different mask on," she replied.

"Could I not say the same thing? I could. Yet I won't. Why? Because I've lost good men to The Order and have been separated from a large group of my friends, who, for all I know, are all *dead*," Boris exclaimed, nearly shouting the last word.

"Fine then. Say I trust you. How do you expect to get out of here? It's a fortress, likely underground, and God knows what country we're in. We aren't simply going to walk out of here," she countered.

Boris continued, "All of these Prospects are being trained right now. Most of them, as of right now, likely do not have a positive opinion of the Order. Any of us who win will then likely be subjected to brainwashing and other conditioning, so it must be before then, as even if some could withstand the brainwashing, doing so would likely result in execution. Our best chance to escape is likely going to be during whatever ceremony follows our victory. If we get the support of as many people as possible, we'll be able to ensure that at least a few of them will make it through. We may then have the manpower to get out of here, and hopefully lose them. From there, knowing their inner structure, we may be able to topple the giant," Boris explained.

"Well… It's better than nothing. May as well try it. Who are you, though?" she asked him.

"Boris Kasyanov, GRU. You?"

"Olivia Durand, GIGN."

They continued with small talk to ease the tension created by the situation. After a couple more minutes, they were called back from the mess hall to continue training.

Boris was brought to a room elevated off of another level. There were several platforms of varying distances and heights scattered around the room; none of them lower than six meters from the bottom level, enough distance to give a painful, though not dangerous fall if handled correctly.

The voice of the doctor came on over a loudspeaker in the room.

"I feel the objective here should be evident. Go between the platforms at will. This is a test of your agility. Depending on how you do, you may be given a slight advantage at the start of the Test. Actually, that's true for most of these challenges. I probably could have told you that before, but it probably won't matter…"

Boris realized "it probably won't matter" could go both ways.

He also thought that doing this exercise was somewhat demeaning, but this was beside the point.

He tried a roughly 3-meter gap first. Not too much, but he figured he might as well try to wake himself up. And of course, The Order was being very secretive about the contents of this Test, so it could be in any number of settings.

He made it across the first gap with little problem. He felt like a child in a playground, which was equally degrading and fun. On one hand, he was like a rat making its way through a maze, but on the other, this could be beneficial and possibly a hint as to what he should expect in the Test. At least it was somewhat fun to jump across large gaps.

He continued leaping from platform to platform for about thirty minutes, when, as he was in midair, the pillars began to drop, and he botched the landing, but managed not to injure himself. Once the pillars had all reached the ground, he stood up and dusted himself off, and while he was exhausted, he was overall fine.

Of course, he to some extent expected what happened next. Several vents opened up in the walls and water began to pour in, and the pillars began erratically raising and falling at different rates. A ceiling tile shifted to reveal a ladder.

The goal here was quite obvious. He had to make it to the top before the water filled the room. He found it unlikely they'd actually let him drown, or that he could just wait until the water filled the room.

"Don't think you can just wait for the water to fill up the room. We're going to charge it with steadily increasing voltage over the next couple minutes. Not enough to kill you of course, but don't make us have to drag you out of here. Even if you pass out underwater, we'll resuscitate you. We've seen worse," he heard over the loudspeaker. Guess that idea isn't going to work.

Boris first stood on top of a pillar that was rising and falling at a steady rate, was relatively close to another one that was higher.

"Ah, good. You're off the ground. Now we can add the fun part," went the loudspeaker again.

A slight buzz was now audible. It probably wouldn't be too bad if he were to fall in now. Because of this, he made a somewhat hasty jump to the next pillar. He crashed into the front of it but had one hand on the edge. He wasn't sure whether he was supposed to be doing this directly after the last test; it was certainly making it more difficult.

Then the pillar he was on jerked up and he lost his grip, tumbling into the water. He was instantly shocked several times, which made getting up difficult. He managed to scramble up on to the first pillar again and quickly made it to the second one, this time managing to get completely on top of it. The next one was around four meters away. There wasn't much space to build up to the jump, but he waited for the pillar he was on to be at its highest point, the one that was his goal at its lowest point. He leaped across the gap, the water still rising, the humming louder, and he landed on the next pillar, almost tumbling over in front of it and into the water. There were only a few more in his path, and he managed to make it to them. In the final leap, he grasped the bottom rung of the ladder with one hand, before beginning to climb up where he was able to go over and drop into the room in which he started.

These "trials" were starting to become quite annoying. He still had a few days left, and no real information on how things were going for anybody else.

After he ate something, he headed back to his room and put on the propaganda broadcasts to drown out the silence.

I wonder where everyone else is… They could be dead; they could be ten kilometers or a thousand kilometers away. If I do get out of here, what am I supposed to do? Wander off east? Try to find my group? Finding them is going to be near impossible unless they find me first.

Boris, like in the other nights, drifted off into a dreamless sleep in the middle of nowhere, waiting for tomorrow.

CHAPTER 16

After a day of driving, it seemed like they hadn't traveled anywhere. The surroundings were still the same, nothing but grey-white snow and fog everywhere. They were out of the city, but they'd still pass by the top halves of buildings buried by the snow. The snow had mostly stopped at this point, but it wasn't melting; just compacting into the ground.

Sometimes they'd spot things, sometimes a hand sticking out of the snow, frozen, maybe not even attached to its original owner.

Elena was seated in the front of one of the trucks with Nikita and one of his men, Arkady. Arkady had been a mechanic before the war and was driving the truck. In the back was Zhenya, Dmitry, Jeung, Otto, and a few others. There had been boxes of supplies in the trucks, another incredibly lucky strike. There were weapons and other items as well, but they were generally of poor quality; rusted, made of cheap materials, some broken. There were a few that were in decent condition that had been made before the war, and there was plenty of ammo, which was used to supply their new members from the school. Albeit likely not very well. There were other bits and pieces in the mix as well, but nothing of major significance was in the back other than several cans of diesel for each truck to keep them running.

However, in the cabins of the trucks there were functioning GPS's. Luckily, a few were still on when the trucks were found, as those that were turned off required a password for access. No one considered researching what they might have been as that likely would have been a frustrating process. The ones that were on were relatively uncomplicated with simple waypoints--outposts, supply areas, locations of destroyed abodes of "Enemies of The Order" and there was a central one simply named "The Heart" which was in Berlin.

After night fell, Nikita and Elena's truck, which was at the front, stopped. It had been constantly in motion until then, with rotating drivers rotating and only minor stops to refuel. Some people got cocky and tried to refuel the trucks while they were moving, but when they fell off they'd have to catch up to one behind them and explain their stupidity. This was tried a few times but had been given up by then.

Elena stepped out of the truck right after Nikita and Jeung. She looked around at her surroundings, the same as they'd been before. Very foggy, and because of the deep snow, the top halves of trees were visible as were the second floors and above and the roofs of buildings, but not much else was. It was probably the next year by now. It had been very difficult to keep track of the date over the past weeks, but she was sure that there indeed was likely somebody who knew, so it wasn't *really* lost.

As Nikita waved toward the rest of the convoy, the trucks began to stop, and people piled out, several already shivering from the cold.

Then Nikita began talking.

"Comrades, based on the information we have from the enemy GPS systems, we think we know where the main base of operations for The Order may be--Berlin, Germany. We've been heading in that direction for a while anyway, but if there is any place where we can fatally strike The Order, it may be there. If it's well developed, we may even be able to seize its resources and get a better start at beginning to rebuild society. If nothing else, it will likely have supplies we can live on before we decide whether to continue north to the island which Boris originally told us of."

Many in the crowd nodded in approval, but most had their faces wrapped in scarves and clothes, so there was little vocalization. Though the world was still, the wind no longer howling, the snow having ended, nobody wanted to breathe in the cold air more than they needed to.

Nikita signaled for everyone to get back into their vehicles and they began to drive off again. Elena went back to staring out the window, watching the very limited surroundings pass by as day turned to night. She hardly noticed when the trucks stopped, and drivers switched, Arkady replaced by Jeung. It seemed as if the snow might have been becoming shallower, but it was hard to tell, as it may just have been compressing by its own weight. It should hopefully clear out as soon as winter ended, but that wouldn't be for a while.

It's strange, Elena thought. *Even though I've seen a lot of snow before, I've never seen this much, and yet it doesn't seem so out of place. Isn't this the basic dynamic of Nuclear Winter? Whatever. We're just lucky we've got transportation.*

Boris isn't so lucky though. He could have been dead on the ground somewhere along the path we've driven, and we'd have no idea.

She'd given Yevgeniy his MP3 player back, but Elena was begging for something to ease the boredom, and the melancholy of the situation.

"Where are we right now?" she asked. She knew she could have just looked at the GPS, but she wanted somebody to talk.

Jeung, now driving, groggily replied "Somewhere in eastern Poland. We'll be in Warsaw soon. We'll see what the situation is there and continue on into Germany shortly afterwards."

In the dim light that entered the truck cabin from the front floodlights Elena could see Jeung's face. He looked as tired as everybody else, but his eyes were locked on what was in front of him.

I wonder what his reason is for being here. I've been with this group for months and yet I still don't know much of anything about anyone. How did Jeung even end up here? He's Korean. Why would he have any reason to be in Russia, and then why would he accept someone's plan to continue even further away from his home?

She considered for a second asking questions like these,

but Nikita was still in the car, half awake and half asleep. She hadn't seen him sleep through this entire journey even once, and she couldn't imagine Vasiliy had either, considering the two of them had become the de facto leaders of this expedition.

Why are they *still here? Their leader and the person who started this whole thing is gone… I guess this trip was for a great cause, but what about Boris? Is it so important that we forget him? They don't seem to consider him a priority anymore.*

Elena figured this question might be worth asking, as it was a less personal topic. It was a somewhat childish question, but she wanted to see how Nikita would respond.

"Are we ever going to see Boris again?" she asked.

Nikita was silent for about half a minute.

"Honestly, probably not… I'd like to think we will, but he could be anywhere. If he's not in Berlin, or in Warsaw, or in the narrow area we are traveling through, we aren't going to find him. Simple as that. The only hope outside of that is if he ends up back in the Metro, which, considering who captured him, is quite unlikely."

Elena nodded solemnly. She stared at the GPS, watching as the arrow that was the truck's icon advanced forward; roads were marked on the map, and they had been following one, even though it was several meters below. The interface was an electric blue, and there were several functions marked in English. One of them was marked "database".

Elena looked to Nikita, who'd been sitting in the middle, and found he'd nodded off, sleeping silently.

She couldn't blame him, really. He'd been up this whole time, after all. But it was a good opportunity to reach across him to the GPS without arousing his suspicion. Jeung may notice, but he was busy driving, so he shouldn't do anything.

She accessed the "database" section of the GPS. It was likely this existed as a way to introduce new users to the interface. Several of the categories she browsed through within contained survival-type entries, their purpose self-explanatory. Elena found an entry marked "personnel." It would be too convenient for them to be listed by name, and there was no real reason for Boris to be there. However, she found a section of "recent captures" within. This would likely contain lists of those who'd been captured by The Order. But because Elena wasn't aware of the scale of The Order, there could be hundreds or hundreds of thousands of entries on this list.

She began scrolling through the register, a few thousand entries long. There was a brief bio of every entry on the list, the two main categories being shady types or others with lengthy resumes.

The entries were categorized by identification numbers rather than names, so it was unlikely that if Boris was on this list, she was going to find him.

She backed out of that menu and began absentmindedly scrolling through different categories.

She decided to search through one more before giving up on this idea; she couldn't afford to be so distracted by this. The last category was called "Prospects." There was a description under this category, which read: "Those recently acquired members of our Order that have shown great potential are put through our Prospect System. These are our future spec-ops units, our commanders, our best-of-the best. The Prospect System involves a declining member of a position being put up for "re-election." The Prospect and the elector are both given a week to prepare for a Test. The winner of this Test gets the position of their predecessor, selected by the Prospect's strengths."

Elena thought for a second. There was no mention of those who had passed these tests on other lists, so evidently information is wiped when someone passes them. These would be worth looking through to get an idea of what the group could face in the future.

She began analyzing the entries; marked by their last names. Most of the entries were formerly in their respective militaries. She searched through the records of former Navy SEALS, SAS, GIGN, and many other groups, several of which were counterinsurgency-based.

Then she saw an entry she somehow knew was present yet had no place there.

"Prospect Kasyanov."

She opened the file, and there he was. The same Kasyanov.

Most of the entries here had high-quality pictures, of both frontal face shots and side-shots. Boris's frontal shot was blurred, but she could tell it was him in the side shot. Same jaw, same hair, same eyes, same face. It couldn't be anyone else. Under his description, there were several notes. "Spetsnaz, GRU, served in The Pan-Arab war. From Troparevo district, Moscow. Exceptional skills in marksmanship, hand-to-hand combat, leadership, creative strategy. Currently located in Berlin. May have been participant in *Vityaz* project circa 2014."

Vityaz project? This was familiar sounding. It had been in the news once. She struggled to remember. It only aired once, and the broadcast has been wiped from the internet as if it had never existed.

Vityaz. Vityaz. I've heard of this before.

It had something to do with a government conspiracy. Something to do with the Pan-Arab war, as well. It wasn't a pleasant story.

As hard as she tried, she couldn't remember what it was about.

And something else was at the forefront of her mind, anyway.

What is he doing? He surely hadn't thrown in with them, not after what's happened! He must have a plan. Surely. He'd never betray us, never betray our cause, never betray me...

But I don't know him, do I? He's GRU, after all. Secretive. We may not even have originally been on the way to that island. The only thing I could do is… Nikita. He knows Boris. Right?

Time for Nikita to wake up. Elena shook him, and he was jostled awake. Jeung finally looked over at Elena to see her wake him up. She gave him a slight smile before turning to Nikita.

"Nikita."

"Yes, Elena?"

"I need you to tell me what *Vityaz* was."

Nikita's eyes widened, his mouth opened slightly, before he regained his composure.

"No, you do not."

"*Nikita.* You are *going* to tell me what Vityaz was."

"Why is this important all of a sudden?"

"I found Boris. He's with The Order. Some prospect thing. I don't think he's *with* them, but he's alive. In Berlin. The GPS had a database, and when I found Boris' entry, I saw mention of a *Vityaz* operation. I've heard of it. I saw the original broadcast. But I can't remember. If you tell me, I will not share the information with anybody else."

"I've seen how you look at Boris. You like him; I know you do. My Kat was the same with me. If I tell you this, I do not want your view of him distorted by what happened during Vityaz."

"All is fair in love and war. *Tell me.*"

"It was toward the end of the Pan-Arab war. Boris, or Sergeant Kasyanov as he was then, had recently reported back on the loss of his associate, Zakhar, in a building he'd been ghosting for the whole war in Riyadh. It was the headquarters for most of the covert American activity of the war, which he had been ordered to observe, keep tabs on, and attempt to weaken in any way possible. It was a very risky job. He was to be left behind if something went wrong. He never learned the specifics of the information he'd collected, and neither did I, not even in the report after the fact."

Nikita looked off into the distance as he continued the recollection.

"Anyway, as I was saying, he'd lost Zakhar at a crucial time. That was the day he'd brought back definitive reports of American agents in Syria, and some in Russia itself. Clearly, a huge risk to national security. And with them highly occupied with the frontline fighting in the war, they were unlikely to notice a couple of men "poof" towards the end of the conflict, which included some of the most desperate months…"

"So Vityaz was an operation to directly attack American assets?" Elena inquired.

"Exactly. And why the broadcast was deleted soon after it was aired. Operation Vityaz was a collective plan to discreetly prepare to pick off all of the agents we'd identified. About twenty in Syria, around thirty in parts of Russia. To be picked off ten a week, on odd days of the month. Some were given convincing doubles to report back later, who would then disappear more 'publicly' to the Americans to try to conceal any pattern. All of this went very smoothly, as I was told. Near surgical precision. Even though Boris was discovered, they never knew for how long the place had been tapped or that Boris had gotten the reports."

"So then… I'd guess we're getting to Boris' part."

"Indeed, to Boris, the men in that building had hell to pay. The man who'd killed Zakhar wasn't in the building, but the commander and all the other assorted officers were. It was Boris, a couple other guys, and I. To this day I don't think he knows I was there. I don't know any of the guys who were around me, but the whole group of us knew which one Boris was. We gathered at several of the entrances. We'd been told how Boris and Zakhar had entered the building before and were told to proceed carefully. But that is not what happened."

Nikita then turned to face Elena directly.

"Boris kicked open the door and began shouting profanities. He sounded like he'd lost his mind, but that building was his personal hell. It had been his sole focus for a long time and his friend was killed in it. His mind was undoubtedly functioning though, as he surgically cleared several of the rooms in the building. We'd split up into groups of two, and I was with him. We made our way through the bottom floor of the building, clearing out several of the guards. I remember having shot roughly three, all Arabs, who made up most of the staff there, many of the Americans having rotated out, gone home. As soon as we were done with that floor, we moved upstairs to where the third group was. The second group was outside, preventing the encroaching local gangs from looting the place; one had been outside the building for a while, and they'd been antagonized by the inhabitants as much as Boris, but they weren't the reasonable kind. By the time we left, about ten of their bodies were strewn across the streets."

Elena was beginning to grasp the scale of the situation and Nikita's reluctance to explain it.

"The third group had been incapacitated. One of them was dead, the other with a bullet in his leg. Boris began yelling incoherently about something called Ischez, and killed five of the six men in the room, all professional soldiers, with deadly efficiency. I went over to the wounded man and helped him stand as Boris stood over the commander of the building, a balding man in his forties or fifties. Boris spoke to him in a maniacal voice, and what he said went something like 'you thought you could infiltrate my country!? You thought you could get away with killing my friend!? Your journey ends here! And here is a dead end! You will be lost to history. I won't be!' and a few seconds later, as I was carrying the man out of the building, I heard a gunshot, and the sound of a lighter flicking on. Boris, with the dead man over his shoulders, rushed me out of the building. He kept repeating 'it's okay Zakhar. It's okay. I'll get you out of here.' As the building began burning to a husk."

"…Wow."

"I'd heard of the Boris that existed before that day, before Zakhar died. That Boris perished on that day. But I did get to meet the original Boris, though I hadn't known him before. And that day was the one on which you saved him in that camper van. I don't know if you saw it, but Boris is a changed man because of you. He may have done something terrible, but he only did it for his country. Now, he is motivated not only by his desire to help his country, to help mankind, but he is motivated to do good by you. He's a good man because of you. If what you say about him being in Berlin is true, we *will get him back.*"

Elena sat quietly for several minutes, contemplating. Did this make Boris some type of psychopath? Or was this something that should be seen as reasonable? In that situation, wouldn't anybody have done something similar?

But now that wasn't the problem. The problem was that he was in Berlin, possibly working for The Order which he'd been hell-bent on destroying ever since he'd encountered it.

If he was capable of what Nikita said, he could either become the group's most dangerous enemy or the downfall of The Order itself.

Another thing to consider was that Boris may not even know where he was right now. And if he was to try to break out and get away, it would definitely be best if the group was there to retrieve him after his doing so. The next problem would be getting there in time. This entry was likely very recent, and it likely didn't give the group much more than a week to get into Berlin around the time he would be trying to get out.

After a few more hours of thinking and of discussing the situation with Nikita, she eventually drifted off to sleep, having been awake even longer than Jeung, who was still driving as she fell asleep.

CHAPTER 17

B oris woke up with a start for the second day in a row. The darkness in his mind had returned. *Vityaz*. It never should have happened and yet it had to. Leave the past.

He got up and stared at the same TV playing the same propaganda as before. A few minutes afterward the same faceless employee entered his room with a meal, which Boris ate absentmindedly, wishing he had a window. As soon as he was finished with the meal, Dr. Ward walked into the room, informing Boris he had to be present in the cafeteria within ten minutes, so he could begin the day's preparations.

He spent these ten minutes as he'd spent most of his time in this room, trying to find a way out. He could be very high up and fall if he broke open the wall, or he could be underground and get nowhere, he could even be underwater and flood this whole area, though if that were true it's unlikely The Order would be so daft as to construct the walls out of something he could break through by himself.

He arrived at the cafeteria in the designated ten minutes before he was guided to another area which was basically a gym. He spent the next few hours on treadmills, weightlifting, and a singular punching bag that was stiff enough so that his knuckles were bleeding by the end of it. This exercise was largely pointless, as anybody who wasn't already fit enough to compete against the person they are trying to defeat, certainly has no chance. Regardless of this, it was still good to get in some physical activity, so Boris could be more prepared for the Test, though of course he still had no idea what that would be. After this test he was given a few choices for some of the open areas, and he ended back up in the shooting range he'd been in before. Even though he wasn't really gaining anything from this, it was enjoyable and satisfying to know that it was costing The Order something to replace all of the bullets he was shooting at this wall.

After he was done with that, he went back to the cafeteria to eat dinner and ended up talking again with Olivia, the French agent. He was still counting on the fact that they weren't being observed, which was a relatively dangerous assumption, though it probably made little difference. They likely didn't have a much worse chance of getting out now as when they passed the test; they'd have more people with them this time, just less equipment.

Olivia said, "I know you have a history with this guy, but it's best you two try to get along. Englishman! Get over here!"

Ischez sat up from the table he was at silently, before stalking over to the table the two of them were at before sitting down. He eyed Boris for a few seconds before turning to Olivia.

"Why do you want me to talk to the Russian, again?" he asked.

"Because he's the one who had the idea to get out of here. He's as skilled as either of us. We need him."

"Why do we need him? Or at least why do we have to cooperate? I almost killed him the last time we met. And his friend."

Boris finally spoke to him, saying "Yet you didn't kill me, my friend is still alive, and we burned your *Pidarasi* base to the ground. You have no room to speak, Tommy."

"That only happened because I wasn't there. If I were, you wouldn't have been so successful, Ivan."

Olivia declared, "Enough. This is pointless. Shut your mouths. You are like children! There wasn't even a good reason for you to be fighting one another in the first place! We must work together!"

Both Boris and the Englishman grumbled angrily.

"...In the end, when we are out, we shall see who is best, who survives," the Englishman said.

"Fine." Boris stood up and walked out of the room, and into his room. He was exhausted, anyway, and fell asleep quickly.

The next day he was woken up again by the stupid device. He picked it up and threw it against the wall. Surprisingly, it left a chip in the paint on the wall but the tablet was totally undamaged. This only upset Boris more, and he went to pick it back up and throw it again.

What is this thing made of!? I probably could bash through the wall with this if I tried hard enough. However, that's probably a bad idea. I should make sure it still works.

Boris turned over the device and saw that it was still functioning as if it had not just been thrown against a wall. Twice.

As per the usual, a faceless figure entered his room and gave him breakfast. Boris ate as he mentally prepared himself for day four of the test, which was called the "awareness" test. If the one with the platforms was any indicator, it was likely that if he didn't do well, he would be zapped, or something similar. But they probably weren't going to kill him, at least not yet.

And as it was yesterday, Dr. Ward entered his room again, though, unsurprisingly she asked him concerning the banging and the dents in the wall.

"I was... testing the durability of your tablet device here. For experimental purposes. It seems nigh-unkillable."

The doctor gave him a knowing look.

She's actually alright, Boris thought. *Maybe she'll see the light one day. Then again, she's also quite possibly trying to manipulate me, even if only in a small way. No one here can be trusted but the people in the same situation as me.*

Boris was, after the few seconds of silence, guided to the

"awareness test" room. It had a central, circular platform on the end of a catwalk.

"There's no foolishness here. You're standing in the middle of a 360-degree screen. If you don't turn to face one of the entities on the screen, the presence of which will be announced subtly shortly before it appears, we're counting on the natural shock from what it does afterwards to knock you off the platform. Falling off, regardless of whether you are surprised by the effect or not, is not advised. Though you won't die if you do. Also, if you see something before it presents itself, point at it, and that'll remove it, just as looking at one that has already announced itself will."

"Alright then. This shouldn't be that bad," Boris said as the words tumbled directly from his mind to his mouth.

"One more thing. The 'entities' will not always be the same, so if one thing doesn't faze you there is probably something that does."

Dr. Ward stepped out of the room, and the screen lit up. The first setting appeared to be a jungle, with large trees and ferns taking up most of the view.

Boris figured it would start off easy, and quickly spotted poorly camouflaged humanoid figures the first few minutes, before their movements became less obvious, and their appearances less noticeable.

They would come at a rate of about four a minute, spread out sporadically within. Now Boris was having to wait to hear a rustling in the brush, or a throat clearing, before he'd see them; he was so rushed to find them that often he'd miss something directly in front of him. He'd lasted about fifteen minutes before one of them finally got him. It was one he'd skipped right over, searching for the one that he'd seen move a few seconds before.

Dr. Ward, in the instant before it was evident to Boris he'd missed something, said simply, "Too late this time."

A deafening sound rang out in the room as the figure Boris skipped over "shot" at him. The shock was so great that he indeed fell off the platform a couple meters to the ground, landing flat on his back.

He gave himself a second to recover from the shock but then got back up and started climbing the ladder. His heart rate had at least doubled since the activity had started, but he wasn't down for the count yet.

Once he was back up, he got through that stage and the setting changed. The 360-degree screen extended to where it was now like Boris was standing in the middle of a massive globe. The pathway retracted. He was now floating in a simulated ocean.

Shit.

Boris never really had a problem with anything on land, but there was a reason he didn't join the Russian naval corps. And now, here he was in this stupid simulation that could throw literally anything it wanted at him.

He began spinning around frantically, searching for anything in the murky water; the sound was an exact replica from some of his worst nightmares.

I hate the ocean.

Then he turned and saw through the murky waters a massive shark facing him. It didn't even count to the simulation as having "attacked" him yet and Boris almost fell off the platform again. The shark swam away after he looked at it, but Boris knew this was going to be difficult. And while he was relatively close to the surface of the water at the very beginning, he seemed to be slowly drifting down, and it was gradually getting darker.

What did I do to deserve this?

Boris continued allowing his eyes to circle the area, looking up, down, left and right. There were several other things like sharks of several types, and they were big and loud enough to not be a threat. But, they got faster. Bull sharks were replaced with mako sharks, and tigers were replaced by unreasonably fast great whites.

After about another fifteen minutes, once again, he was too slow.

One of the sharks "bit" him and the ocean water turned blood red. Boris didn't jump this time, but his heart rate kept increasing. The entire screen flashed, "ONE ATTEMPT REMAINING" As it faded, Boris looked up and sunlight was barely visible. Now, wherever he looked, there was a light that followed him. There was a lot of nothing again until he spotted a giant red tentacle reaching up toward him. He looked down to see where it was coming from and saw a colossal squid right under him; leagues bigger than he'd ever heard they could become. It was grotesque. Scared, Boris's heart rate climbed ever higher, nearing dangerous levels. Boris now had to spot the tentacles as they reached up to grab him.

Every time one of them did, it would drag him down even further, approaching the awaiting terror.

Though he was moving fast, as soon as he was able to get rid of one, he would get caught by another, and get dragged further down. The span of three minutes between the squid appearing and when it finally enveloped him might as well have been three centuries.

When Boris finally was too close, the water turned red once again and countless bubbles scattered around the screen, as the screen blanked. Once he stepped out of the room, he realized he had been sweating profusely, and his heart rate was insane. He went to the cafeteria to sit down.

"What the hell'd they do to you?" The Englishman asked.

Boris simply glared at him.

"It looks like you came out of that awareness room. Do you not like calamari?" the Englishman gave him a clever, though slightly cruel smile.

"The ocean is… blue hell," is all Boris managed to say while keeping his dignity.

The Englishman laughed for several seconds. "I guess everyone has their weakness."

"Idi nahui," Boris mumbled.

Ischez stood up and left, a few minutes later replaced by Olivia.

The first thing Boris said was "What if the Test is psychological? Because if it has anything to do with what I just did we're screwed."

Olivia replied with, "I'd assume you just went through the awareness test? Very misleading name. Really, I think it's a sort of an empty threat test. It's unlikely they'd be doing anything underwater, or that they'll have other people trying to kill us. Anyway, I got us a new lackey."

She snapped her fingers, and a man with a physique similar to Nikita's walked over to Boris. He had blue eyes and blond hair but looked more Germanic.

"So, who might you be?" he asked the man.

"Werner," he replied.

It seemed he wasn't going to be as talkative as Nikita, but he still wanted to try to get as much information about him as possible.

"Where are you from?" Boris asked him.

"Geneva," Werner responded.

So, he's Swiss. I wonder how he got here. The Swiss weren't a part of the war. Might as well try to ask him about it.

"Why did you leave Switzerland? They weren't part of the war, what reason would you have to leave?"

Werner finally spoke full sentences, saying, "Many refugees from neighboring countries came in; the government couldn't support them. Home became a warzone of its own."

Olivia stepped in to offer a bit more information. "As he said, refugees flooded the country as they knew it was neutral, but the sheer number of them overwhelmed the government, and when they had to start turning down entries, sometimes separating families, people began to attack soldiers and border patrols. Soon after, the government collapsed because of rioting and armed conflict. Switzerland, although a bit less devastated than some countries, is really no better off as a nation."

"I see. The safe haven became no better than the voids around it," said Boris.

Both Olivia and Werner nodded.

Boris had another thought--he had no idea how these two people were captured; it could give him an idea of what they had done to antagonize The Order.

"So, how'd each of you end up here?" he asked.

Olivia began first: "I was, as I said, with GIGN. I was close to Monaco on the coast. It was only two days after war was declared that there was an invasion force on Monaco's shore. It was Iraqi, part of an alliance of Arab nations who wanted payback for our interference in their past conflict. In fighting one another, they united, seeing Europe as their common enemy. The information had been suppressed, but they'd been preparing an invasion uniting many Middle Eastern and North African nations. Their troops simply had to travel north across the Mediterranean to France, Italy, and the Balkans."

Boris was shaking his head. He'd never heard about this, but then again, all of the news reports were based on battles that Russia was actively participating in along with several in Poland and many more on the border with China.

Olivia continued, "Even though I was GIGN, a counter-terrorist organization, I was called to defend the area as soon as the invasion started. There were millions of them, pouring out of landing crafts and dropping out of old transport planes; they wanted revenge for our interference in their conflicts. The soldiers in the landing crafts were young and poorly trained and fed. They were slaughtered in great numbers by my unit and several National Guard units as we waited for help. They outnumbered us at least thirty to one. We didn't have any battlements, just a few buildings near the beach."

She paused a minute before continuing.

"There were five in my building, all of us GIGN. We were only armed for short range conflicts in buildings, so we couldn't risk trying to shoot out the window, but we were at an advantage, shooting out the sides and out the doors at those who passed us. We were doing fine until their Haris Almazaliyiyn, or paratroopers, landed on our roof. There were roughly twenty, I think. They swept the house and killed two of our own before they made their way to us. I was in a room with another man. The Arabs got to and tried entering our room. They only had 16 men left in total, and six came at us. The other man and I killed three of them, but my comrade was killed by the last few remaining, shot more times than any of the invaders. I shot two of the remaining and stabbed the other one. The last person outside my room was shot several times; I heard it from downstairs, and I knew I had to get out of the three-story building. I was on the second floor. So, I first dressed in one of their uniforms. I knew they didn't employ women as paratroopers, but my intention was to blend in just enough to not be shot on sight. I splashed some blood from the dead on my chest, broke the window and fell out, then rolled over onto my face, so my identity was less obvious; but I kept a weapon. I was passed over by the soldiers who exited the building, as nobody exited out the front. I moved periodically until I was able to look out to the beach, and then watched as the invaders continued pouring in, though now it was primarily logistics equipment."

She stopped, once again, to ensure Boris was absorbing the

information.

Boris gestured for her to continue.

"So, when night fell, I got up and made my way out of the city in an abandoned civilian vehicle and drove all the way to Paris. The highways were packed, so I went through the countryside, but it was when I was in Lyon that I finally heard that the bombs fell, that sections of Paris had to be evacuated. As with most cities in Europe, no nuclear missile hit it directly because of the anti-missile defenses, but radiation still coated parts of the city and the country. By contrast, both NATO and Russian nukes hit targets throughout the Middle East, including the bases supplying the Arab League. This meant that those who were already in Europe were driven mad with hunger, as they quickly ran out of supplies. They broke into tribes led by separate leaders and attacked one another as often as they attacked us. I don't blame them for this; it was their only option, but their extreme violence towards anything outside their tribe was greater than any I'd seen or heard of; they'd burn down houses and entire neighborhoods as they searched for food. In the end, before I left Lyon to heard further north, their battle lines had collapsed and most of their armies had dispersed throughout the country to fight as guerillas. Some returned to the port they came from, where a couple hundred French soldiers ambushed them."

"Continue," Boris said. Even though this information wasn't crucial to his survival, it was a good idea to get any information about what lay west of him, assuming he was in fact where he thought he was, in Berlin.

"But then... more bombs fell, and more conflicts started. More people died, some beginning to starve and kill one another, more soldiers were sent to the fronts. I left Lyon and went into the countryside. A few days later I heard that much of it had been destroyed, and that the government was starting to fall apart. And that's when The Order came around. They rose up out of nothing. The last TV broadcast I saw described legions of unidentified soldiers storming ruined cities. Before I knew it, they were everywhere throughout Europe. I'd ended up in a military base near Paris right before I was captured and was brought east by plane. My capture wasn't anything spectacular. There were about fifty of them against me. I hadn't eaten much in days and offered little resistance. That's really it for me."

"Well. That's quite a story. Hopefully it'll have a good ending," said Boris.

"Now for you, Werner," he said.

"I will keep mine shorter," Werner said, before starting.

"I was Swiss Special Forces. Supposed to keep the refugees in order as we had no enemy. Eventually there were too many and riots began to break out. I fought with several rioters and looters and killed a few. As the government fell apart I tried making my way to my home in Geneva. I was on the outskirts when a guard stopped me. I told him my rank and position, but I wasn't allowed into my own city. They said they couldn't afford to feed anyone else. I didn't try any further to get in. My family was as safe as I could hope them to be and I wasn't willing to kill a countryman just to see them. So, I wandered the countryside for a few weeks, trying to help any I saw on the way. I formed a small band with other military men not let into cities. We saved the lives of dozens trying to survive out in the wilderness, Swiss and foreign alike. Sometimes we would try to sneak civilians separated from their families into cities. But it was on one of those missions that we met The Order. When we got into Zurich, The Order had already arrived, and overwhelmed the guards. They were announcing that Zurich was to become a part of their 'great new society.' Then, people began flooding out, but some were trapped. I tried to help them escape, but I was shot several times, and woke up in this building shortly after, somehow not seriously injured."

Boris absorbed this information quickly. For one thing, it was unlikely Switzerland was better off than the rest of Europe any more. But another thing was that everyone here had a story that was quite negative about The Order. Boris figured The Order wasn't naïve enough to think all of these people would simply join them, which likely meant that their only chance to escape would indeed be right after the Test. As planned, as it was likely they would be brainwashed soon after their triumph.

He told this to the two others, and they agreed, before he began his own story. He described his frustration at not being able to serve his country while others did, and about his dream to re-establish civilization, and about all of the people he'd met he'd left behind, who may be dead, or who may still be looking for him.

After the conversation, Boris was more certain of his group's cohesion. The problem was that he would have to get a story out of Ischez as well. That was unlikely going to be fun, but it would be for the best. Getting as complete an idea of the world outside of what Boris had seen was essential.

After eating more of his meal, Boris stood and went to his room to rest, his fourth day in this place done with.

CHAPTER 18

The group was nearly out of Poland. They'd passed Warsaw a while ago, deciding to drive around it; it looked like a warzone, which it probably had been. Soon they would be in Berlin, where, if anywhere, Boris was most likely to be. They weren't sure if they were going to try and rescue him, find him, or kill him. It really could go any of these three ways. Either he hadn't escaped yet, he had and was on the run, or he had betrayed the whole group.

Elena was staunchly in the camp supporting one of the former two possibilities. She knew there was no way he would have betrayed them, especially not for the organization that had tried to kill him multiple times.

Some of the others weren't so confident about this, but all of them were willing to go and fight The Order; almost all of them had a personal vendetta against them by now, anyway.

Nikita was somewhat distant toward Elena now, maybe to let her continue to mull over what he told her, or maybe because he *regretted* telling her the story. But either way, Elena was appreciative. It was certainly better to know than not to.

She still wasn't entirely sure what to think of it, either. She'd already established that anyone probably would have reacted the same way in a situation like that, but not necessarily that it was the right thing to do. It probably wasn't, but it did accomplish the goal, and for one thing it had certainly shut down that command base, even if not entirely necessary.

However, Elena tried to look to the future rather than the past. Boris had changed since then; apparently, he used to be very different from the person she knew. The person she knew *was* good, *was* moral, yet he still had to do what was necessary to survive. And in realizing this she felt confident, though already knew, that he'd be unbreakable. He wouldn't be broken by The Order.

But he could be killed by it.

She looked outside the truck after this dark thought and saw that the snow wasn't nearly as deep as before. By now, the truck was sitting a foot or two above the roads, and it was no longer a total wasteland. She could see most of the buildings they passed now, of the trees and remaining life in these areas.

According to the GPS, they were about three days from Berlin, given where they were and the average speed at which they were traveling.

Jeung had finally rotated out of driving, and Otto replaced him. For the sake of making conversation, Elena decided to try to talk with him, especially since they were nearing his home country.

"Otto?" she asked him, to see if he would even respond.

"Yes?" he replied flatly.

"Care to tell me about yourself a bit? We're nearing your home country, as you know. And I know nothing about you," said Elena.

"Uh… sure. I'm from Berlin. West side. I was born a few weeks before the Wall fell. I don't remember, but I was told by my parents that I cried at seeing all the people shouting and breaking it down, even though it was a happy time. But I've still got a piece of it" -he patted his pocket- "and my best friend growing up was from the east side. He was considerably poorer than I was, but we got along very well. We grew up together doing the same things. Both of our families moved out of Berlin, and coincidentally to the same town. We spent our time hunting with an old family rifle, and both of us were good shots. We ended up in the military as adults. We participated in the Pan-Arab war, like it seems everyone has, but we quit the military afterwards, deciding that war was not our calling. We started a small business, which went pretty well for a good while. I was in Moscow when I was because I'd met someone online who'd offered to help me expand the business. When war was declared, I had no friends there to help me, so I had to stay in a hotel for several days. I was going to take the Metro to the west end of the city to see if I could make my way to NATO lines to get back home. Now that I think about it, it was a foolish plan. It's probably for the best I didn't leave after the bombs fell," Otto finished.

"So… do you know where your friend was when you left?" Elena asked.

"He was still back at home, running the business. It wasn't located in any of the bigger cities, though we did have some offices in them. He likely survived the bombings, but I have no idea where he'd be now," Otto replied.

"Maybe he'll be found one day," Elena said.

"I have a feeling he wouldn't want to be found, however," Otto said, before adding, "and he probably thinks I'm dead anyway."

"Do you have anyone else who may be waiting for you?" Elena asked. She hoped he had others who cared for him.

"My parents passed away a few years ago. As for a girlfriend, I had one, but she left me a few months before I went to Moscow. We had differing views on issues involving the upcoming war. She told me I would have to go and fight, but I told her that I was done with war, and that my joining the military again would only contribute to the rising tensions. So, she up and left. Went to look for a 'hero' or something. The heroes she idealizes always die first," he said.

"I see. Well, the world hasn't ended yet. Maybe you will find someone, and your friend as well." Elena tried to encourage him.

"Maybe," Otto said, unconvinced.

"Also, you told me her view on the war. What was yours?" Elena asked.

"Well… I'd seen war in the Pan-Arab conflict. It was brutal and barbaric. Men killed each other like they were animals. I believed that every measure should have been taken to prevent war. Yet, of course, that didn't happen and this war ended civilization as we know it. Even though she may have been right about the war being inevitable, I feel justified knowing that I'm at least attempting to fix the damage done," Otto replied.

"That's a good way to look at it," Elena said, nodding.

Otto nodded one more time before continuing to drive silently as he had before. Elena noticed that much time had passed and went back to looking out her window. The snow was gradually getting shallower, now only about a half a meter or so, low enough for the trucks to start driving on actual roads again, though ice could become a problem. Regardless, the group was approaching Berlin.

CHAPTER 19

Boris awoke with a start for the fifth time that day. He was beginning to wonder if this was something that happened on purpose. He had been waking up at about the same time every day, though he usually didn't bother to check the time because it didn't really matter. When he looked forward, he noticed that the marks on the wall were gone.

He was only somewhat surprised by this, but it did bother him that someone came into his room at night and he didn't notice. Yet, then again, for all he knew, that person closing the door is what woke him. But it wasn't really important. The usual figure came into his room at the usual time, giving him the usual meal. It was still good, very good, but he was starting to develop a distaste for it, because while he was being treated well, others starved all over the world.

But guilt wasn't going to get him anywhere. So, he stood up and checked his tablet to see what he was going to be doing that day.

"Hand-to-hand Combat," it read.

I feel bad for the unlucky bastard who's going to be stuck in there with me, Boris thought. He'd always been particularly skilled at close range, as he'd developed a good sense of hand-eye coordination and good reflexes from a childhood containing too many video games. People had said he would grow fat from it, or that he'd go blind, but guess who's laughing now?

He went into the room where he was assigned; it was a very simple area. Slightly padded floors, the type that your feet wouldn't sink into, or crack your head on if you fell. After he entered, the Englishman followed him.

It all made sense now. They probably get the two most evenly matched people to face one another. He hoped they'd pull out the loser to keep him from getting killed because neither of them could afford to suffer any severe injuries.

Boris assumed that The Order would normally have to bribe both sides into fighting a bit, as most would end up being future comrades, but that was not the case this time.

Boris and the Englishman were staring each other down as the loudspeaker came on. It was a male voice, likely the person watching Ischez's actions.

"Prospect Macintyre, Prospect Kasyanov. Welcome to hand to hand training. This is as simple as it seems. You will fight until one or both of you goes down. After your match, you will be led into separate rooms to practice with actual weapons against dummies. No real combat with weapons is allowed here, as we certainly don't want to kill off any of our prospects."

Boris cracked his knuckles. He'd been waiting for this ever since he discovered Ischez was still alive. He also knew his name now, at least his surname, Macintyre. However, that was irrelevant as in his mind the beast would always be Ischez.

This was also likely to be a very close match. Both Boris and Ischez were very strong and fit, Boris being a bit taller, with Ischez being slightly stockier. It would come down to the wire, and it was entirely possible they'd both have to get dragged out.

Boris had no desire to *kill* Ischez, but he wanted nothing more than to beat him here.

The loudspeaker started counting down, and Boris and Ischez were circling each other.

"3...2...1..." There was a brief pause--

"FIGHT!"

Ischez swung first, barely missing Boris's head as he ducked. Boris in turn swung at Ischez, hitting him in the stomach. Ischez barely even flinched as he retracted his arm back to guard his face.

Boris swung, in turn, but Ischez caught his arm and threw him over his shoulder. Boris landed flat on his back, and this was his wakeup call. He spun his leg around to meet Ischez's shin, which knocked him down. Boris stood again, but Ischez was already on his way back to a standing position, unfazed.

Ischez swung several times more, but Boris blocked most of the blows. He counter-attacked on one, locking Ischez's arm in place and striking it with his elbow in a desperate attempt to break it. Breaking his arm wouldn't matter in the end. If The Order could heal gunshot wounds it could fix broken arms.

There was a slight crack, maybe a small fracture, but despite the grimace scrawled on Ischez's face, there was no great reaction. Ischez then took the opportunity to swing his other fist into Boris's side, knocking the wind out of him. Boris keeled over, and Ischez hit him again, knocking Boris onto the ground. He rolled out of the way in time to avoid his opponent's foot crashing down onto him. He stood quickly afterwards, but his endurance was starting to wear off; he was almost entirely relying on adrenaline now.

The two were facing each other once again, circling, waiting for one to make the next move, which could decide the bout, as both parties were beginning to wear out.

Both of them moved in nearly the same instant, each hitting the other on the shoulder. They both recoiled a bit at the shock, but the fight was back on.

Ischez swung once more at Boris and he sidestepped, moving behind Ischez. He put his foot out in front of Ischez and shoved him down. The Englishman caught himself almost as soon as he fell, and quickly lunged out towards Boris, tackling him. Boris was bewildered, and Ischez, now on top of him, began bearing down on Boris, trying to hit him in the face as much as possible.

Boris attempted to block as much as he could, but he was still pegged multiple times. With one strike though, Boris caught Ischez's fist, and hit him in his injured arm, Loosening Ischez's grasp as Boris shoved him off.

Boris, standing over Ischez, kicked him in the side, but Ischez then caught his foot and twisted it. There was a cracking noise similar to the one in Ischez's arm, and Boris was spun around.

He tried to get up, but he couldn't. He had no idea how long he'd been in the arena, but he knew the end was near. He did everything he could to try to coax himself up, but the most he could do was drag himself to lean up against a wall, where he sat up, and saw Ischez, up, but on his hands and knees. He tried to get up multiple times before he finally keeled over and collapsed.

The fight was over, finally. Both Dr. Ward and Ischez's mentor came into the room and helped them up. Over the loudspeaker, a new voice shouted "DRAW!"

After Boris took a shower, cleansing himself from the sweat that covered him he began thinking about the outcome. Maybe it was for the best. If he'd won, there was almost no chance that Ischez would support the plan any longer, possibly out of sheer disdain, and if Ischez had won not only would it have been a major blow to Boris' pride, but it also would have undermined his right to be the leader of an escape attempt.

So, he decided a draw was probably the best possible outcome, and, mentally, declared Spetsnaz and the S.A.S. even. Hopefully he could recruit another member from either of those groups at some point, as they were among the very best, after all.

He hadn't noticed the injury in his heel until now that his adrenaline had worn off. He called in a medical officer, who took him into another room blindfolded. Understandably, they wouldn't want him knowing the layout of the place just yet, but he cursed under his breath when it was put on. He tried to keep track of the turns, but it proved futile as he was spun around intentionally several times on the way there.

The blindfold remained on as he received treatment. A needle was stuck into his leg, and he exclaimed, a bit too loud, "*Chyort!*" That's when he heard someone clear their throat next to him.

The person began speaking, in Boris's native tongue. "Ah, a native Russian. I was beginning to think I was the only one," before chuckling.

"Indeed. I'm not from anywhere special though. Moscow, Troparevo District. My name's Boris. Who would you be, friend?"

"Ah, I'm from St. Petersburg. Kirovsky District. I'm Volodya."

"So… why are you here? Who are you?"

"I'm one of the Prospects, as I'd assume you are. Just did the hand-to-hand thing. I cracked one of my ribs. You should see the other guy… heh. I was VDV before the war started."

"Nice, VDV Paratroopers. I'm a Prospect as well. GRU Spetsnaz. Alpha Group. Describe yourself to me since I assume we're both blindfolded."

"Spetsnaz? Huh, aren't you special. Alright. I'm about 1.83 meters tall. Broad shoulders, brown hair. Not too specific, I know, but I'll be sitting around the cafeteria when I'm out. We'll talk then."

"Alright."

After Boris said this the medical officers entered the room again, and sedated Boris. When he woke up, 90 minutes later, he was told, his foot was fine. He had no idea how they did it, but it didn't matter all that much. Soon he was taken back into his room and the blindfold was removed. He checked a clock, and it was evening. It was about time to eat again. So, he went to the cafeteria, and saw who he assumed was Volodya sitting next to another man, who had dark skin and looked quite capable. Volodya was looking around the room, not eating much of his food.

Boris got his food and sat down in front of Volodya, first, of course, making sure it actually *was* him.

"Volodya?" Boris asked, in Russian to be sure Volodya recognized it as him, as Boris never bothered to describe himself.

"You must be Boris, then. Yes, I'm Volodya," he said.

Volodya was true to his word, with a relatively average build and brown hair. Sort of surprising he was VDV, considering that meant he parachuted out of airplanes while being shot at for a living. Didn't seem like something he'd do.

Boris then looked over to Volodya's friend and asked in English, "Now who is this?"

The man responded with a deep voice, in one word, "Safiri."

"So where are you from, Safiri? Tell me your tale." Boris figured this could be an interesting story, as this man seemed like a native African. It could be interesting to see what he had been doing around the time of the war.

"My homeland is Ethiopia. I was born towards the end of the Communist rule there. The government was very... unstable. So, after a term of mandatory military service, I went north, through Sudan and Egypt. I saw many things, and mercy was not one of them. I had to fight and kill, or I would have been killed in turn. After making it to Cairo, I stowed away on a boat to Croatia. Once I was out of port, I was an alien in a foreign land not in much better condition than my own. At that time, the Bosnian war was still being fought, and I was in the conflict. Many saw me as an enemy, as I was foreign, but one day after a particularly rough fight I was picked up by members of your Spetsnaz, who were serving as observers to the conflict. I was told I showed great talent and I would be offered asylum and citizenship in exchange for military service. So, I went to Russia, and was found fit to serve in the VDV, when I met our friend here, Volodya. We were in the same units. He's a good man, I trust him," the man finished.

"That's quite an interesting story, my friend," said Boris. He figured he might as well get some information from Volodya, as well.

"So, Volodya, how did you get here?"

"Well, friend, I'd say it's quite interesting how it happened. Safiri, here, and I were on the frontline of defense for the Motherland. As soon as war was declared, we gathered into planes, and were off within an hour. At the time, people weren't nearly as fearful as would be expected. We were at war with some of the most powerful countries in the world, but none of us reacted as we would have if we'd simply heard it on the news. We were over Poland, which several days earlier had been experiencing serious unrest between the pro-NATO population and the population that supported us. As we approached Warsaw, we heard from our pilot that there was already fighting below between the two. And that's when we realized what was really happening, and what we were going to be jumping into. We didn't even know who we'd be shooting at, who the established army was with, so basically whether we'd be shooting at rebels or soldiers. But by then it was too late. The lights went off, and we dived into the city, which was in flames. There was already an offensive by the army on the edge of the city, which we could see it as if from the eye of a bird…" Volodya trailed off, and Safiri spoke.

"Massive armies, helicopters and planes, tanks and platoons of foot soldiers were running and shooting at each other. We watched as our comrades were ripped apart in the air, as the planes that took us there, regardless of whether the troops had jumped out of them yet or not, were getting shot down and plummeting into the city, knocking down buildings and killing men. And for a brief second, I made eye contact with one of the pilots. His plane had the American star on it, and I saw in that instant the fear on his face, or maybe the confusion. A second later a burst of fire caught his plane and he crashed into the ground, just barely outside the mass of buildings."

Volodya picked up again, continuing his description of the battle.

"Safiri, I, and several other men landed on the top of a skyscraper, and began making our way down, trying to get closer to the ground, so we could shoot from the windows. While we were about half way through the building, I caught sight of three tanks, whose drivers must have seen our parachutes land on top of the building. They then blasted the structure of the already heavily damaged building. If there was ever a time when everything was truly still, it was as the building began to fall out from under us. The tanks began to drive away to avoid the collapsing building, luckily abandoned except for our sorry squad. The building was falling against another, larger one, which wasn't as damaged. If it had been as unsound as the one we were in, we wouldn't be here to tell you this, but it wasn't enough to save everybody... I managed to grab onto the edge of a doorframe a few seconds before our building crashed into the other one. Safiri was above me, and safe, but there was another one, a friend of mine, corporal Fedorov, who was sliding down towards a broken window another man had already fallen through into concrete and debris. I caught his hand as he reached out to me, but then our two buildings collided. The impact was incredible. I hit my head on the wall, and it wasn't until a second later I realized that the Corporal was gone, tumbling towards the ground..."

Safiri picked up once again, "We, just the two of us now, crawled sideways, towards the bottom of our building, before making our way out from the bottom. When we landed, we only had one functioning phone to contact HQ, but all we got was static, for maybe ten minutes. Then, a panicked voice came over the radio, with 'NUCLEAR WARHEAD INCOMING! INTO THE UNDERGROUND, ALL UNITS!'"

Volodya continued, "And so we did. We made it into their metro as quickly as possible, where there was an incredible number of people, both civilians and soldiers. And, God forbid, there was still shooting. Maybe it was down with us, maybe it was above us, but there were still people shooting each other. The entrances were sealed off, and several minutes after that, a blast rang out that was nearly deafening, despite the heavy doors sealing us in. People cried; others stood silent. We got moving. We had to separate ourselves from the crowd and make our way as far east as possible to have a chance of getting back home. We still don't know who hit the city, but I hope if still alive, they regret what they did. Not only where there still soldiers trying to get in, but civilians who'd shut themselves into their buildings and homes. I have no idea how many died that day...Perhaps one day Warsaw can be rebuilt. Anyway, we made our way to the easternmost station of the metro, which took a while, considering we had to pass through huge crowds without losing each other while avoiding the conflicts that dotted throughout the area. It took almost two weeks for us to make it to the easternmost station Thanks to Safiri here--" He gestured over once again to his friend –"We knew that was about the length of time required for much of the radiation in the area to dissipate, and so we left the underground and headed west. From there, the rest of the story is pretty simple. We hid out in the outer city limits, and we saw as The Order stormed the city. We tried to hide out from them for as long as possible. We lasted quite a while, hunting a few animals and scavenging people's houses for at least a few months, before The Order started to realize that houses were being looted and so began searching for us. Clearly, they found us, taking us without incident here. We were simply too exhausted to fight back. Maybe it had something to do with the fact we were still dressed in uniform, since The Order seems to like to recruit from high caliber soldiers. But that's basically it."

"Thanks for your time. Talk to the GIGN woman if you want to know why we are getting so friendly." Boris stood up and walked out. He was tired now and needed some sleep. He was glad, once again, that he got more information about the outside world as that would improve his ability to make good decisions in the future. He went into his room, and then had a horrifying realization. If the group was still going west, regardless of whether it was for him or to continue his mission, they were very likely to go through Warsaw. He wished he had a way to warn them of the impending danger, as while The Order likely hadn't seized cities like Moscow yet, it sounded like Warsaw was likely heavily patrolled, given its proximity to The Order's capital. Boris then deduced with relative certainty that he was indeed in Berlin. He now needed to consider that as he approached the day of the Test, the final parts of the plan had to be put in place and as many Prospects brought in to join them as possible.

CHAPTER 20

"We're nearly in Berlin," was the first thing Elena heard that morning, spoken with a characteristic lack of tone. She looked over and it was exactly who she thought, Dmitry.

Nikita was still passed out in the middle, though he would probably awaken soon, as he'd been sleeping longer than Elena had.

As Elena had been able to learn a lot about the people around her during this expedition, she figured she'd try Dmitry, too. She didn't expect too much, but it could explain how he'd become so stone-faced.

"So, Dmitry. What did you do before the war?" she asked.

Dmitry sighed for a second, before starting in a manner Elena didn't expect.

"You know, the other guys in the back have told me that you've asked them all the same question. I'm sure most of them had better stories."

"Maybe they did. But I'd still like to know how you knew what you did, it saved Józef's life after all."

"Fine. I'll keep it very simple though. The past is over. I was a doctor from Volgograd. I'd been to college, done everything a good student did, everything a good student dreamed of. I became a doctor and made a good deal of money doing so. I liked helping people; it was certainly fulfilling work. But I lost my license. Luckily for me, the Pan-Arab war started, so I joined the military, and became a medic. My losing the license or having had one didn't really affect how I was trained so I was like any other. Anyway, I was in Syria, and I was only involved in one skirmish. Then the war ended, and I came back to Russia. I was on leave until the Great War was about to start, and I got a call and was told to go to Moscow. I went, and I was part of a point guard near the Metro. The alarms went off, and then I went to the Metro. That's all."

He paused for a second, and then added, "And I'm not going to tell you how I lost my license. So, don't try to ask."

This was basically the story she expected, and there was no doubt something about how he lost his license that had affected him, but it was unlikely she would get that information from him.

She nodded and gave up the conversation, looking back towards the road. There was only light snow now, and they were already getting to the main part of the city. Sure, they were *probably* in the right place, but Berlin is a massive city and it would likely take them quite a while to find the place Boris might be, assuming it wasn't revealed by the presence of some spectacularly grim or beautiful structure.

But then Elena thought, *but if they have the capability to do all they've done so far, we're surely being watched already. We should expect something. Like an am-*

Her though was cut off by three radios in the cabin of the vehicle screaming, *"RPG!"*

The next few seconds happened in slow motion. A gleaming rocket crashed into the side of the vehicle, and the world started spinning. Elena was flung out of her seat, having taken her seatbelt off long ago due to the discomfort, and through the windshield onto the street. She landed well and scrambled back against a building as the truck continued to spin out, until it flipped over. She watched a figure tumble out of the cabin, but she couldn't tell who it was.

By the time everything stopped, it seemed that at least the first couple of trucks had been hit, and it was very likely that the last ones had been hit as well to ensure there wouldn't be any escape.

Once the chain of explosions ended, Elena noticed the ringing in her ears taking the place of the noise, but there was no gunfire taking its place, as she expected.

She looked down at herself as she stood up. She had a few cuts along her arms and torso, but there was nothing too major, and adrenaline was likely keeping the pain from seeping in.

Elena looked up, and around the area where the truck lay smoking. There was only one visible figure right now, and she couldn't tell who it was.

She approached the figure, obviously male, laying against the wall of a large apartment building, with his head down.

As Elena got closer she could begin to make out who it was.

Otto.

She was next to him now and sat down on her knees to look into his eyes.

He looked up at her and gave a half smile.

"I guess my time is up, then," he said, as casually as describing the weather.

Elena looked down onto his torso, where he was indeed bleeding heavily. There was a jagged piece of metal sticking out of his chest. Józef may have been saved after shrapnel hit his leg. But this was different.

Elena reached out to him, and Otto met her hand with his own, his hand sweating, but his grip still strong. Elena felt something in his hand. She retracted her own and she knew instantly what it was.

His piece of the wall. She examined it for a second and saw half of a peace sign etched into it.

She looked back up at him, and he coughed slightly, a small trail of blood dripping out from his lower lip.

"I know I'm not getting out of this. I don't need you to lie for me," he said.

"Otto… Where did your friend live?"

"Parchim. North-west of here. You're looking for Marvin. He has dark hair. If people are still there, you should be able to find him. The people in that town were always nice…" His voice drifted off and he made a simple request.

"Please help me move. I want to see the sun one last time," he said. He was under the shadow of the building, and Elena helped him limp over to an area covered with sun, where he looked up into the sky, cloudy, but the sun visible.

While still looking up at the sun with Elena helping to hold him up, he spoke his last.

"I only hope I helped you all to fix the world."

Elena began to gently sit him down as his breathing slowed and his pulse wound down. Tears were streaming down Elena's face as he closed his eyes, and he exhaled his last breath. Elena clenched the piece of concrete in her hand, before placing it in her pocket.

She went behind the truck, where much more of the carnage was visible. Dmitry was against one of the still-functioning trucks working on what looked like Jeung, while everyone else stumbled around, swinging their weapons at every movement, waiting for an attack. Others looked lost, like they'd just been placed on a different planet.

Nikita was at the forefront of it, a large cut across his eye that was still bleeding, ordering the recovery, while she could hear Vasiliy further down doing the same.

She then saw Yevgeny, sitting down away from it all, looking truly terrified.

She walked over to him, and his eyes widened as he saw her.

"Are you okay!?" he asked.

Elena looked down, and aside from now feeling some of her injuries, she realized her uniform was soaked in blood.

Otto's blood.

"I... uh... It's... not my blood..." was all she managed to get out.

The fear plastered on Yevgeny's face didn't fade.

"...Then whose is it?" he asked quietly.

"...Otto. He... didn't make it. He's at peace now," Elena replied, trying to sound as soothing as she could manage.

Yevgeny looked down at his feet.

"Am I going to die too?" he asked.

"Of course not. I won't let you." Elena said. But really, she had no confidence that even she would survive this. Boris could already be dead, and they may have walked into the most devastating trap imaginable. Everyone in this expedition could be dead within a matter of days.

Yevgeny seemed somewhat comforted by Elena's words, and went to fiddling with his MP3 player. Its battery had died a while ago, and they ran out of spares, so he just played with the buttons, pressing them in certain rhythms. There were outlets in the trucks, but they had a plug input that nobody there had ever seen before.

As Elena observed the area, it seemed like only the first two trucks were hit really hard. When she questioned Nikita, he said their truck was hit by two, and that the third truck was targeted but the rocket missed.

Overall, when all was said and done, there were two dead, Otto and one of the Americans. There were about ten wounded, consisting of people like Jeung, Zhenya, and even Dmitry himself. The most heavily wounded was the person who helped Zhenya bring the cultist back to the school, Ivan. He had several pieces of shrapnel and glass in his arm and side.

Much of the food and water was lost, as well with some munitions, but not enough yet to pose a major threat. It was actually a crate of MRE's that saved Dmitry's life; a box was right next to his head. Had it not been there, a piece of metal would have torn into the side of his head, but the box stopped it.

This was the best news from the whole scenario, as aside from Arkady and an American medic, Dmitry was the only person with medical training, his much more advanced than the two aforementioned, though Arkady's quick work with Józef certainly saved his life.

The group continued to piece itself back together, Elena taking part in the action of trying to scavenge anything useful from the destroyed and damaged trucks, and helping guide the others to push those disabled out of the road so they could continue forward. The plan now was for them to travel in groups of two, keeping constant radio contact with the groups nearest to them as they searched for the likely locations of Boris and the HQ of The Order.

That night, most people slept in the trucks. While some members of the party patrolled outside them, others inside the trucks operated the radars of the trucks that had them, trying to locate any suspicious heat signatures or anomalies.

It was a sleepless night. Elena took off the coat of her uniform, down to her undershirt. She was still haunted by the day's events, and her ears were still ringing, though it was down to a bearable volume. Hopefully, this would go away at some point, but something so minor simply could not be the focus of her attention.

So instead, she drifted off to sleep, thinking of finding Boris... and what she was going to do to the people who killed Otto and the American.

CHAPTER 21

B oris awoke once again with an unpleasant start.

Today was the sixth day by his count, and he began his morning routine. He had today and tomorrow, and then the Test began, which he may or may not survive. It didn't matter how close or far his comrades were from him now, he must win that competition.

And now he had more people to help him. Probably. Later, at lunch, he would be able to discuss with Olivia what happened.

However, he first had to get through whatever test he was given today. He already knew what it was, though.

It was melee weapons training. He and Ischez both would likely be participating in that, considering that they both had to be worked on in the infirmary after their bout.

Boris entered the room, which looked like the gym he'd been in earlier, but one of the walls was entirely stocked with weapons--from Scottish claymores and Japanese Katanas to modern military combat knives.

Although Boris had never trained in combat with anything other than a knife, he always had a particular interest in medieval-era type weapons. The expert level of craft present in some of them was astounding, and as a child he always liked to pretend he was one of the nobles who helped St. Alexander free Russia from Mongol rule.

He scanned the wall, looking for a definitive weapon from the time and era he was looking for--a Bardiche, a giant axe that was capable of incredibly powerful strikes while also being effective at defense due to the large size of the head, allowing for more surface area to block a blow.

He stopped marveling at the beautiful weapon and picked it up, while also taking with him a survival knife, similar to the type many members of Spetsnaz had been issued. It was a shame he didn't take one with him, but the thought just never came to mind.

Then he turned around and saw Ischez. They exchanged menacing glares but looked away and went back to focusing on what they were supposed to be doing. As much as they despised each other, they needed to cooperate if they expected to get out, so for the most part they left one another alone.

Boris walked over to the targets, mostly made of ballistic gel meant to simulate how a human body would react to a strike. Boris always found them sort of repellant and had no problem destroying them.

He started with the Bardiche. He first went for a direct overhead strike to see how much power the weapon really had. It was heavy, but not quite as heavy as he expected. He swung it down upon the dummy and the blade cut down past its nose. Quite powerful, indeed. And had a human been sitting there, quite deadly, as well as bloody.

Boris looked back at Ischez, mostly armed with more modern weapons--a machete, and several knives. Ischez was likely expecting more modern weapons to be available for the battle, but Boris wasn't so sure. With access to this many options, it was likely more could be scattered around the place.

He figured it would probably be a good idea to rotate through many different weapons. He swung the bardiche a few more times, leaving deep cuts in the dummy, but eventually turned around and spotted a bow.

He'd never been particularly good with bows, but it was worth a try, as it was possible that he would end up only with that option.

He picked up the bow and several arrows; his knowledge of its use was very limited, but it looked like a formidable weapon. He drew back the bow, which required much more force than he expected, and aimed the arrow at the target.

He fired once, and the arrow cut across the dummy's shoulder, not missing, but not giving a fatal blow, either. However, Boris was beginning to get a feel for it. On the next shot he hit the dummy directly *in* the shoulder, and on the shot after that he hit it in the chest.

So, he wasn't terrible, but he found it unlikely he'd do well at hitting a moving target. His best chance would be to find a gun in the arena; it was as simple as that.

After the bow, he moved on to a Japanese katana for the novelty of using the legendary weapon. He found it to be quite balanced. It hit hard, and was easy to swing, though the durability of the blade was perhaps questionable.

After a while longer testing out many different types of weapons, he was called to exit, and went to eat at the cafeteria. After getting his food, he sat down next to Olivia, who'd been explaining her plan to Safiri and Volodya.

As Boris sat down, he could see by the expressions on their faces that Olivia was indeed convincing them of what they needed to do.

He then tuned into the conversation, hearing the end of something Olivia said.

"--trying to take over what's left. That's why we need you to help our group get out of here."

Both Safiri and Volodya nodded, and they seemed to understand. Then Safiri spoke.

"So how is it you expect us to go about escaping, then?"

Olivia glanced over to Boris, looking for an answer he might give better, which he then attempted.

"It depends on the situation. We have a plan for all probable scenarios. If it's a flat-out deathmatch, where there's us on one side of a field and The Order forces on the other, the plan is for us to group together, armed as well as possible, and kill our designated opponents. Then if we get outside we run; if we're enclosed or inside, we wait to be retrieved and attack whoever attempts to do so, as we make our way through the facility to an exit. If it is a grouping of one-on-one battles in which we are separated, each of us will separately beat our opponent and execute the second part of the former plan, where we then try to meet up. If the situation changes from any of these, improvise. We're all supposed to be the best and brightest, after all."

Boris knew it wasn't a flawless, convincing plan, but it was the best they had at the moment.

Safiri nodded his head, likely thinking the same thing. Then Boris remembered another thing he thought went without saying, but figured it was best to emphasize it.

"And try to kill your designated opponent. A dead Order member is the only one that works in our favor."

Both Volodya and Safiri nodded in agreement.

After the designated eating time was finished, Boris went back to the weapons training room and continued practicing with large variations of weapons, including spears and clubs, all while trying to imagine a realistic outcome in which he survived the Test and actually got out. He went to sleep that day with that thought still in mind.

CHAPTER 22

Elena woke up the next day with the truck already moving. Inside the front with her were Jeung and Nikita. Jeung had a bandage wrapped around his forehead and left arm, with Nikita sporting an improvised eyepatch. Even though she was pretty sure he hadn't lost his eye, he probably wanted to protect it and the area around it from infection, as well as from any blood oozing into his eye.

Elena looked down and realized her arms were bandaged in places, as well, where the worst glass cuts were. They hurt, but the pain was tolerable.

Thank God for Dmitry, was her first thought, as it more than likely was him who did the work.

Nikita, in the center as he was before, was operating the radar on their truck. If they neared The Order HQ at any point, it was quite likely to spot it. They drove for roughly an hour before something started transmitting.

Blip. Blip. Blip…

The dots on the radar were being picked up from an old office building. If this wasn't the Order HQ it was quite likely this was at least some kind of outpost.

As the trucks rolled to a stop, Elena continued to stare out the windows, trying to ensure that nothing was going to pop out of one and kill them.

Nikita, Jeung, and Elena exited the truck and loaded their weapons. They all knew without saying that this could be it. Even if the building itself wasn't, it was possible there was construction in the basement, or something like it.

The three of them surrounded the front doors, painted black from the inside.

Nikita reached to his walkie-talkie and spoke into it.

"Vasiliy. This is Nikita. We may have encountered the base of operations for The Order, or an outpost. Copy?"

A static-filled response came back in with "Copy. Rendezvous imminent. Wait until we have arrived before investigating, over."

Elena nearly laughed. The designation, "The Big Four," as the soldiers called them had mostly died out by the time the American and Russian soldiers joined them, but the four still used the term occasionally, at least between Vasiliy and Nikita.

Nikita looked up at Jeung and Elena and said, "This is it. Boris could be waiting for us right in there, about to die. I'm not waiting for Vasiliy."

He bashed open the door with his rifle and quickly shot a shadowy figure in the main lobby of the building. Several people could be heard above them running down onto the main staircases on either side of the once-magnificent reception desk. As they got to the top and their silhouettes became discernable, the lights flickered on, and they were visible.

It was not The Order. It was a group of tired people dressed in ripped, worn, and faded civilian clothes sporting hunting weapons and old and new weapons of the military.

Everyone stood in silence.

Nikita was the first to break it, but not with a gunshot.

"Who the hell are you!?" he shouted at them, using English.

One marched out from the group of people and walked down to stand in front of the desk. He was unarmed, and middle-aged.

"I am Hans. We are part of the *Deutsche Freiheitskämpfer*. I think your word for our band would be... Partisans. "

Nikita responded, "Partisans? How long have you been here? And is this the headquarters of The Order?"

The man replied with, "Yes, partisans. We've been here since the war started and The Order began to rise up. We've lost many, some were kidnapped, but we've kept harassing the enemy. We even destroyed a few trucks from a convoy they sent out yesterday. I'd be careful."

Nikita, Jeung, and Elena were silent, shocked. *That wasn't The Order who shot at us,* she thought. But then she looked over to Nikita.

"You... didn't... shoot... The Order," he growled, his face contorted in rage.

"What do you mean?" The leader asked.

"THAT WAS US YOU SVOLOCH!" Nikita shouted at him, his voice booming and echoing through the building.

The leader twitched. He looked back at his followers.

"But... you were in their vehicles." A man stepped out of the crowd. A bit stocky with dark hair was the deliverer of that statement.

Nikita whipped out his pistol and centered it on the man's head.

"YOU KILLED ONE OF YOUR OWN COUNTRYMEN!" Nikita thundered.

The man who stepped out looked crushed, but Nikita wasn't finished.

"OTTO WAS A GOOD MAN, AND YOU TOOK HIS LIFE FROM HIM!" Nikita continued.

The man who'd stepped out of line asked in a broken voice, "Otto who?"

"Freihardt" Nikita responded.

Elena had never known Otto's last name, and even though her interpretation was likely incorrect, in English it sounded like "Free Heart." She found it fitting.

The man who'd asked Otto's name fell to his knees, and Elena knew who it was. She didn't know how it was possible, especially since she thought he lived a bit further northwest, but that was him.

"Marvin?" Elena asked.

The man, who she presumed was indeed Marvin, looked up and nodded.

Elena walked up to him and heard him whispering over and over again.

"I fired the shot. I fired the shot. I fired the shot. I fired the shot."

Elena bent down and tried to comfort him, saying, "You couldn't have known. You just did what you needed to survive. It could have been anyone who died there. And Otto was a hero, he helped us get all the way from where we started in Moscow to where we are now. He told me his story, and I think he'd want you to have this."

Elena pulled out the piece of broken wall, with the peace symbol etched on it, and handed it to him. Marvin pulled out his own piece and matched it. A smile spread across his face, and he stood up.

"So, what are you doing here?" he asked Elena.

She responded with, "We started our journey to go to Svalbard, an island with a seedbank we may be able to use to repair the damaged agricultural system, to restart life. Our goal evolved as we discovered The Order, and now our goal is to retrieve the leader of our expedition who was captured by them a while ago."

The leader of the partisans overheard this, saying, "I'm afraid chances for your friend aren't good. None of our people that they've captured have ever come back. We've never seen them again."

Elena shook her head, saying "No. He'll come back. I know it." She was saying it half because she believed it and half because she wanted to deny the possibility it wouldn't happen, and she wouldn't dishonor Otto's last wish. That was the only thing that kept her going.

Hans shrugged, saying "in the meantime, you can stay with us if you need to. You're quite a small party."

Nikita interjected, somewhat irritated at Hans's condescending tone, saying "Actually, we're not a small group at -"Several motors were heard right outside the building, which then quickly stopped. Several of the windows in front of the building were shattered as soldiers poured in, Boris' soldiers.

"GET YOUR HANDS THE FUCK UP!" Vasiliy shouted to the group of Partisans.

Vasiliy had been leading a Mobile Base of Operations, which contained a convoy with the majority of the soldiers. He had several dozen with him right now, all of their guns trained onto the group of fighters.

All of the Partisans rose their weapons, while Nikita and Hans tried to defuse the situation.

"Woah, woah! We're friends here! Don't shoot!" shouted Hans.

"Hold your fire, hold your fire goddammit!" Nikita ordered.

Most of the fighters lowered their weapons, without a shot being fired. They continued to stare each other down, the Russian/ American forces on one side and the German partisans on the other. All of them had been enemies at one time or another, but now they were all united under one cause--to defeat The Order.

Nikita looked over to Vasiliy and saw suspicion written all over his face. He then glanced over to Elena, and they both knew that breaking the news to this group that these were the people that opened fire on them could spark a conflict that would crush their overall chances of being able to take down The Order in the end.

Nikita went over to Elena and confirmed this, saying, "We can't tell Vasiliy what happened, but we can't keep it from him either. Especially if one of these partisans slips up and tells him. That partisan will die. So, we have to tell him."

She responded with, "Well then, who's going to tell him?"

"I'm not sure. Maybe we both should. At least then if he does something we can restrain him."

The two of them approached Vasiliy, and Nikita started.

"Look, I'm just going to tell you this flat-out. These people were the ones who shot at us. They didn't know we weren't The Order, which is something we should have predicted. We were driving their trucks, after all."

Elena continued, with, "And they are sympathetic to our cause! They are willing to help us take down The Order, or at least help us get Boris out. They'll be useful... You can kill them later if you want to."

Vasiliy didn't directly look at either of them. He'd been one of the most unpredictable people in the group. It was equally possible that he'd accept this and move on or that he'd lash out and kill every partisan in this building, in this city.

Vasiliy's truck was not hit, but he'd been friendly with Otto. He was also greatly upset by the fact he allowed the group to be ambushed; though nobody could possibly have held him responsible, he still saw it as his fault that he didn't do more to stop it from happening.

Elena looked at Vasiliy, whose gaze was not on her nor Nikita. He instead gazed over to the partisans, all tired and worn down. There was a glimmer of sympathy in his eyes as he saw their pain; they had not only killed someone who could have helped them, but also a fellow countryman.

Elena, who had her hand on his shoulder, noticed him relax significantly. He had been very tense before. As he relaxed, a tired-sounding sigh exited him.

"Fine. We'll have the Partisans divide into groups and have them ride with us. They are not, for any reason, allowed to travel without one of us. Only under those conditions will I accept help from them."

Nikita nodded enthusiastically, glad he could come to a sound conclusion that didn't include Vasiliy bashing anyone's skull in.

The sun was beginning to set. The Partisans, a few hundred in total, had spread out among the group's trucks; even though they'd lost a few, they still had dozens of trucks.

Elena got back into the front of theirs, with about ten Partisans riding in the back. They included both Hans and Marvin, as well as a few other interesting characters; a middle-aged family consisting of a father, mother, and teenage daughter, a Middle Eastern man, and a former police officer.

The group continued traveling, communicating constantly, until Elena fell asleep in the truck once again around 10:30.

CHAPTER 23

This is it, the last day, was the first thought Boris had as he awoke.

He stood up and was served breakfast soon after. It was as good as it had been before, but he'd been enjoying it less and less as the days passed.

His mind was haunted with images of Elena, Nikita, Józef, and Vasiliy in his mind. What if one of them was dead? What about Jeung, so far from home? Otto, *in* his home? Zhenya, still a child? Dmitry, whose medical expertise had saved lives? They could all have been dead days ago. These thoughts had come to him before, but they wouldn't leave him now.

His thoughts were interrupted when his tablet flashed on, indicating what the final preparation for the Test would be. Simply called "Purpose."

So, this is when they try to brainwash you, thought Boris.

He reluctantly followed his attendant to a different area of the base. He expected to be strapped to a machine or put in front of a screen that would indoctrinate him with nonsense.

Instead, he was in a room with two full walls entirely made of glass. He tried to discern what was behind them, but they were fogged. The outsides seemed gray, but with a tinge of blue.

The room itself was sterile white like the rest of the building. He sat on one side of a table as directed and was told, "He'll be here in a minute."

A minute later, the door opened. In walked Zakhar, which Boris expected, but then a man who must have been the Overseer.

Why are they bringing their leader to a person they just taught to kill?

The Overseer looked like he was portrayed in the propaganda broadcasts, but a bit more tired, a few more wrinkles on his face. It must be difficult running an organization that exterminates insurrectionists and conquers territory.

Then he spoke, with little accent.

"So, you must be Mr. Kasyanov. I'm sure you have several questions. I'll do what I can to answer some of them. Go ahead and ask."

Boris was hesitant, sensing everything he said would likely be used against him in some way, but it was worth trying to get information.

"I feel the obvious question is why you are talking to me. I'm simply a Prospect, not even guaranteed to survive, and I'm sure you have better things to run… like your… 'country'," said Boris, his voice scathing in tone on the last words.

"Well… for one thing my job isn't as involved as you think. I mostly give orders which other people carry out. I sit in an office, the same as I did before the war. Just now my actions affect a greater percentage of people, yet a smaller number at the same time… As for why I'm talking to you, there are several reasons. For one, you are the most promising of the Prospects we've seen so far. For another, Zakhar here" – he gestured over to him - "has told me of your exploits. So, for the sake of interest I decided to come meet you. But that is about 20% of the reason. The rest is because you've killed many of our people, and I would like to know why you did, how you did it, why I shouldn't kill you now, and why you won't try to kill *me* now or later."

The Overseer said this all in a very businesslike tone, which made it all the more condescending, as if he was the CEO looking down upon a lowly employee.

"Fine, then. Why? I killed them because they attacked us. We were in a military base, and they attacked us. How? Your soldiers are of remarkably low quality. Even civilians I'd given very rudimentary training to were able to best them. You *should* kill me. However, you won't, as that would create a sense of paranoia for you as a leader. If you execute a Prospect, the others are less likely to be loyal, and the ones that pass your test will likely have a lower opinion of you, especially since I have made friends with many of them. You could kill us all, but then you are losing a great deal of opportunity; there are some truly skilled people here. I probably will try to kill you later. But this is not something that is unique to me. It's the fate of all dictators. Eventually your reign ends, by natural or man-made means. I will simply expedite the process and begin undoing your damage sooner. If I was capable of killing you now, as I most likely am, I would almost certainly die, which isn't beneficial to my cause. So, my next question to you, is are you going to kill me?"

The Overseer took a long sigh, before starting again.

"No, I am not going to kill you. But if you decide to cross me, I will *break* you. When you win your section of the Test, which you will, I already know that, though, I will do everything in my power to make sure that you don't. You will fully submit to me or I will leave you to suffer for months, maybe even years. Depends on what I feel like. But there is nobody to save you. You have no comrades, no friends, no Russia and no GRU to come help you. There will be nobody to save you, like there was nobody to save Zakhar."

A sly smile crawled across Boris's lips.

"Well then. *Let the best man win.*"

"That we shall," said the Overseer, who stood up, and left the room. The attendant followed, but Zakhar didn't.

"What were you talking about?" he asked.

"What do you mean?" Boris replied.

"About our troops attacking you?" he answered.

"Do you not know how The Order has been operating? It attacks and subjugates innocents. Talk to any of the Prospects, talk to any of the people put under your will, if you don't trust them, trust *me*. They've tried to kill me several times, and they *have* killed several of my friends. There are likely people in this area working to bring down The Order as we speak. You must pick a side."

"Say that's true. What will rebels do to solve anything? They come in, destroy us, then leave the wreckage. Where are we then? We're nowhere, the last establishment resembling a national government is gone, and what's left is anarchy and chaos. There's no plan. The Order puts people to work, but they put them to work to sustain everybody."

"They sustain the few they choose, and they kill the rest. They give you freedom at the cost of the freedom of the commoner. They give to you what they take from others. You have been *duped*. I can only tell you the truth and hope you accept it. *Help us*, Zakhar. The Prospects and I are getting out on the day of the Test. I need you to make sure that we have a clear path to get out, and a path for you to get out. You can help us, Zakhar."

Zakhar stood silently for over a minute.

Boris added another thing, "I won't leave you behind this time."

Zakhar sighed, but then spoke. "I'll do what I can. But I have no intention of coming with you. My life is here now. Maybe if I see myself that The Order needs to be toppled, I'll still be here to help take it down from inside. That's all I can promise you."

Boris nodded, stood up, and before leaving the room, said, "Thanks."

He made his way to the cafeteria, where it was time to eat lunch again. He sat down with Olivia, the Englishman, and a couple others from the group, including Werner, Volodya, and Safiri.

They discussed their final escape plans, as it was likely that except for dinner they wouldn't get a good chance to talk about it again. Apparently, most of the other tributes were in support of the escape. There were several promising people the group mentioned, but Boris never got the time to talk with any of them. He only hoped that if he saw them they would be with, rather than against, him.

After he finished eating, he was informed by his tablet that he was free to go to any of the training rooms that he'd been in before. He decided to go to the simulation response room, as he might get a chance for redemption there.

He entered the room, and as if she already knew he was going to choose this one, Dr. Ward was there, speaking over the telecom when Boris entered the room.

"Up for another attempt, then?" she asked.

Boris nodded. He figured there were cameras and she would see this.

"You know, you were actually quite close last time. If you'd made it another minute or two, you would have passed this. So, we'll see if you can do it this time," she added.

Boris nodded once more before the simulation began. It was in the same order as it had gone before, in the jungle, with poorly camouflaged people showing up first before their cover became increasingly obscure. Boris had little trouble with this, as he was able to see the movements of most of them. Maybe it was a fault in the system, but he didn't have to "see" the person that he caught, he just had to see movement and catch it in time. Before too long, he passed this section.

Then, he was moved to the underwater simulation. It started the same as before, with several sharks attempting to attack him through murky waters. He caught his heart rate increasing again, as it had the first time he'd done this, and it was starting to wear on him.

But then a wave of confidence washed over him.

I'll show them. Even if I die during the Test I'm not going to fail this stupid trial. It's all a simulation, not real. Just get through it.

As he progressed through it, he found it becoming much more routine. There was much less to it now, he just saw the movement in the cloudy depths as he continued to "sink" in the simulation.

Eventually, he made it to the giant squid. This time, as he expected it, the shock effect it had was much reduced. This section of the simulation was actually not much harder than the rest of it, but the tense atmosphere definitely added to the difficulty for someone who let it get to them, as Boris had the first time.

He continued progressing through the simulation, and although he was continuing to approach the squid, he was doing everything possible to keep himself steady, but he was starting to get a bit dizzy. If it went on much longer, he was likely to lose balance and fall over.

However, as his strength was on the verge of giving out, the simulation ended, with the screen taking him out of the water, the squid fading away.

Fuck you, Boris shouted down toward it in his mind.

He stepped out of the room invigorated, ready for the challenges that faced him now. He spent the rest of his day before his final meal reading up through his P.E.A. about The Order and trying to gather any information he could about the Test. However, he couldn't find much, indicating this may have been the first time the Test had been given. But, of course, it could also be that they didn't want him getting more information than they wanted him to have.

After a bit longer of fruitless searching, he sat down on his bed. Thoughts about what he'd said earlier began to flood his mind.

How could I have been so stupid!? I literally told the bastard I was going to try to kill him. Sure, what I said about him not having the flexibility to kill me outright was true, but what was to keep him from making my experience in the Test much less survivable? I guess I will have to make it through, regardless. I still have no idea what the Test will encompass anyway. Anything could happen, and I'll have to take advantage of it.

He let his thoughts mill about his mind for a while longer before he stood up and went to eat what was very possibly his last supper. He was no Jesus, but his situation seemed comparable in a way.

He went to eat and sat next to his comrades.

The tables were grouped up, with Olivia, Ischez, Volodya, Safiri, Werner, and several others who were apparently part of their group taking up the seats. Boris sat down with his food, a simple bowl of soup, before he reflected on his situation.

The first thought he had was, *they could kill us all right now. Storm in and blast us all away. Problem solved; rebellion quelled. But I don't think that would satisfy the Overseer enough. His personal vendetta against me will likely see him try to kill me and my associates during the Test, not during a meal. Where's the honor in that anyway?*

Still, he was uneasy. He got to learn a few things about some of the others joining him, though.

There was Erik Koehler, A member of the German GSG 9; Peter Morris, Navy SEALS; Caio Frangella, of the Italian "Col Moschin". (He learned from Caio that is was similar to the British SAS) and Batu Demriel, of the Turkish Maroon Berets.

If it wasn't clear that The Order drew its Prospects from the greatest military elements available before, it certainly was now.

There were several others, and they likely all had stories of their own, but they would have to wait for later. There was only so long Boris could sit and eat, as he had to make sure he got to sleep before too long; he needed every advantage that he could get.

CHAPTER 24

Elena woke up once again, with the truck in motion as it bad been every day beforehand.

"Found anything yet?" she asked Jeung, who was driving.

"No. But we may be getting close. We've gotten a lot of information from the partisans, as well. They've told us places they have thoroughly searched through, and where The Order is unlikely to be, based on where they have attacked from before. They didn't have the radar technology we have, but it has saved us some time in searching. If the estimates we have are correct, we *should* be able to find them by late tomorrow; now that we have several trucks driving throughout the area, with the support of the Partisans, we should find them soon," he responded.

"Good. The sooner the better," she said. But she didn't mean it. She was secretly, or maybe not so secretly, terrified about this final encounter. What if she didn't want to see what they'd find? As much as she tried to wipe the thought from her mind, there was still a decent chance Boris was dead and had been dead for a long time, not to mention Daniel; his having once been a part of The Order, who knows what he faced?

Elena did as she'd been doing: she stared out the window, watching the empty buildings pass.

There's no way they are just in the basement of some building. They'd probably choose somewhere that's more... pronounced. It seems stupid, but checking places like the Reichstag? It's worth asking.

She asked Jeung, "Hey, have we, or the Partisans, ever been to the Reichstag to check it out?"

Jeung sat silently for a second, thinking.

"I don't think *we* have. I guess it seemed too obvious. Seems like something that would have been bombed out. I'll stop the truck and you can ask them if you like."

Elena got out of the truck just before it came to a complete stop, opened the back doors, and asked her question.

"Have you guys been through the Reichstag before? Like to check to see if there's anything from The Order there?"

The Arab nodded, before beginning to tell his story, in a heavily accented yet clear voice.

"I was there, since the early days. I worked there before the bombs fell. I'd been in the basement, somewhat ironically checking the stock in the basement, recently turned into a bomb shelter, to make sure there were enough supplies. The *Bundestag* was in session, they were even debating about taking nuclear action themselves. Then I heard them. Several massive, spread out explosions. The missile defenses, systems provided to most of Europe by some company, did stop the missiles… but not the radiation… I'm sure you know this story from your own city. But that wasn't it. A few smaller missiles hit the city as well, including one right on top of the Reichstag. In that moment, what was left of the German legislature was gone, with just me down in the bomb shelter at the right time. I waited for a few weeks before I left, then I found my new friends here, the Partisans."

Elena nodded, somewhat shaken at the news. Not only did it cross off another location where the Order could be, but it had another impact. It was such a prestigious symbol, and in the Second World War, her people fought through that building, took it, and destroyed the Nazis, changing the world forever. In this World War, the way the world changed destroyed *it*. It was poetic, but sad at the same time.

She wasn't done though; she needed more information.

"Is there any other influential center in the city?" she asked.

One partisan, sitting next to the Arab, stood up, and responded.

"The New Dawn company Headquarters."

"What?" Elena responded.

"It was the headquarters of a massive foundation, the one that provided the anti-missile systems. I used to work there but I quit a few days before the war. The company was doing some shady stuff, so I stepped out. We've never gone there, figuring it was likely destroyed by the missiles, and it's a bit outside the city. That far out, we lose some of our capability to ambush The Order, so we've never left. But we can go there if you want to check it out."

Something about this connected in Elena's mind, but she couldn't place it. She walked back up to the front of the truck and explained her plan to Nikita and Jeung. They both agreed, replying with responses along the lines of "worth a shot" before they started off in that direction. Considering it was likely to be quite a large complex, they figured they would travel there that day and search the area the next day.

Elena radioed in to Vasiliy's channel explaining what she was doing and asked if anyone was having success on the other fronts.

"No. We have found nothing but several scattered Order patrols which we managed to put down quickly, and more Partisans."

She then explained her plan to him, and he replied positively.

"We'll head in that direction with you and make sure the rest do, as well. It's really the only possible area left in the city where they could be. If it is, you will need support. And besides, we aren't getting much accomplished with our present slow rate of progress." Elena's group turned out to be the closest to it, but it would take some time to get there, as the infrastructure in the city, especially in this area, where thousands had been trying to evacuate west, was not in the best condition.

As she traveled in the direction, she began silently praying, hoping that this could finally bring her back to Boris, or that at least she could know what happened, and help the people of the world fight back against the menace that is The Order.

Jeung stopped their truck roughly half a kilometer from where the complex started, near what looked like a military checkpoint. Later, all of them slept for the night after eating some of their rations, now starting to run a bit low, with more mouths to feed; hopefully this was the right place, otherwise they were going to have to ration more strictly than they'd already been doing for months.

CHAPTER 25

Boris, for the first time in his experience there, was able to wake up gradually, taking his time to get ready to face the day. He was served breakfast as usual, with it being a bit more grand than before. He ate, but not everything, as he didn't want to go from having more than enough to total deprivation. This was an opportunity to ease himself into not eating so much for at least a few days, and he might as well start then. There was a decent chance the Test would be one of endurance, as well as intelligence and skill.

After he was finished, he began mentally preparing himself for any possible situation. Of course, it was ridiculous to think that he could precisely predict what he was going to face, but he might as well try to develop a plan on how to react to whatever he was going to be hit with, especially given his disadvantage of pissing off the leader of the whole damned organization.

At about 10:00, he was called to the preparation area. Dr. Ward was standing outside his room, holding an earpiece in her hand.

"While my life isn't on the line, I do intend to help you win. Take this. It's one way I should be able to assist you out there. But I can't tell you anything more right now. I don't know what awaits you, and if I did, I probably wouldn't be authorized to tell you."

"Thanks. You have been a great help," Boris said. He meant it, as well. While he didn't have any romantic interest in Dr. Ward, she truly had been helpful, and if there was a way he could convince her to leave The Order behind for her own sake, he would.

He followed Dr. Ward into a grand room, where all of the Prospects and the people they were going to attempt to replace were sitting. There was a massive movie-size screen sitting in front of them. This was likely to be an orientation into what they were about to face. As Boris sat down, the presentation started, first with a soothing female voice.

"To our new Prospects, I'm sure you've been wondering where you are for quite a while now. Well, you are all currently outside the beautiful city of Berlin, the home of our new country." The view on the screen was an overhead of the city as it was before the war.

Who do they think they're fooling? Boris thought.

The video continued.

"Because of the wars and conflict of the Old World, this is now what the city looks like." The screen showed a similar overhead to the city as it was then--totally grey, and dead looking. Destroyed buildings, and miles of abandoned, unused vehicles.

Boris nearly chuckled at his foolishness. *Of course. Justification for why they aren't the enemy.*

The narrator continued on with, "Now, one day, under our Order, we may be able to recreate that old Berlin, that old world, but without the strife, without the conflict--one where everyone works and lives in harmony."
The screen then showed representations of both work and life; happy looking people working in a factory next to happy looking people in an old farmhouse.

The narrator went on, "And now YOU get a chance to be a part of it! We have many positions which you may be about to fill; but we must maintain our quota; you must prove yourself better! Your competition consists of those who have been lagging behind; the winner works in their position! It's a great incentive to continue contributing to the collective. You will face many trials, but we are sure the best ones will come out on top!"

Nothing new yet, Boris thought.

Then the voice changed, to a deep, yet clear male voice.

"You are going to be placed in a multiple-square kilometer plot of land we worked hard to preserve before and after the war. All of your fellow Prospects or, if you're a current member of our Order, Associates, will *not* be in the area with you. You will be split up into sectors in this area, each about a square kilometer. You will all start even and have to search for supplies and weaponry to help yourself survive. If you are caught leaving your area, you will be apprehended; cheating is strongly discouraged. Once you have defeated, (Includes killing, incapacitating, overpowering, dismembering, disabling, crippling, critically or mortally injuring) your opponent, you will be directed to an area in your sector where you will be able to leave and take your place in The Order."

The female voice cut back in, cheerily wishing everyone, "Good luck! Per Ordinem."

All of those about to compete were stood up by those watching over them, as they were delivered to a large garage, where they were blindfolded and driven to a flat platform. Boris was placed upon it, the blindfold then removed. Dr. Ward was standing next to him, looking him over. Boris looked down, and realized he wasn't wearing the grey uniform he'd been wearing most of the week. He must not have paid any mind to it but he was wearing a long-sleeved forest green shirt, with khaki-colored cargo pants, and work boots. He was also then given a black metallic watch by Dr. Ward, which he put on without any thought. All in all, the clothing he was given was relatively sensible and, as he looked at his surroundings, he realized they really *were* quite well-preserved. The trees were not as green as trees once were, but more so than those he'd seen in his travels.

Dr. Ward got into the vehicle she'd taken him there in and drove off. She was already beginning to speak to him over his earpiece.

"Your watch, look at it. It will give you updates on the status of people. I'm not the one who manages what comes on through it, but it will provide you with important information. Also, I forgot to tell you there are small cameras implanted in several places on your person, and please don't try to remove them; my goal here is to help you."

Boris nodded, figuring she could detect the motion somehow.

He then began to more closely examine his surroundings; even though he couldn't see it, he heard a river flowing somewhere near him. He was in the middle of a field, with grass up to his knee. There was a large forest filled with high trees fairly close to him. Given his present lack of information, he wasn't sure exactly where weapons and equipment would be. He figured he could scavenge for his own food, but he needed to get some type of firearm before he'd truly be effective. One shot would likely decide this whole thing. He just had to make sure it was his shot.

Placed between the eyes of the Overseer.

He wasn't done until that moment.

He did, however, have to deal with the unfortunate bastard he was tasked with killing now. He'd never bothered to try to learn much about him. There was no point in doing so. There's a saying, "keep your friends close, and your enemies closer," but that phrase implies equality between the competitors. This is almost certainly not the case; he is predator, his competitor prey.

Boris had hunted as a child; His grandparents lived considerably east of Moscow. Because his mother died when he was very young and his father had to work a lot, he lived there for much of his childhood.

When he joined the military, and experienced a few battles, he learned the fundamental difference between hunting an animal and hunting a person.

The animal will usually see a strike coming, but a moment too late. They'll notice something, but not have the time to react.

People don't. If you manage to avoid being seen, you can wait forever for a good shot.

However, in almost every other way, the experience of the hunt was the same. The main difference now wasn't even that significant. In situations before, Boris wouldn't have any idea how many enemies he would be facing. Now he knew he had exactly one; both a comfort and a curse. One would live, and one would die, or no one would live and two would die.

If Boris eliminated his competitor, he would allow nothing to be in the way of him killing the Overseer. Even if it wasn't immediate, it was going to happen.

Boris, after having stood still for some time, finally got the impulse to start moving.

He ran across the field, forgetting stealth. He needed a central area to start from, and to him, that meant he was going to have to elevate himself.

Once he got to the tree line he began slowing down, realizing that it was likely that he could find things laying around here; it was unlikely there would be anything particularly useful, as this was way too obvious a position, but he could probably find something to start him off.

He knew he was looking for the glint of metal, for something to shine.

And he found an object after a few minutes of searching--a slightly rusted spear. Although it didn't look to be of high quality, it was certainly a start.

A few minutes later, he stumbled upon an American M1911 pistol; it was a good, reliable weapon, but had only seven rounds. The gun was also quite loud, so using it to hunt was out of the question; he couldn't risk his competitor hearing him so easily. That left him with the spear for hunting and the pistol for self-defense. He'd really rather not have to kill his opponent with the old pistol, but he wouldn't deny any opportunity granted to him.

Boris continued searching for an appropriate tree. He was a bit leaner and more muscular than the average person but was by no means light. He'd loved climbing trees as a child, but it wasn't a habit he carried into adulthood, especially given that he'd been able to move back in with his father at age fifteen once he got a stable job. So the latter half of his teenage years consisted of him spending time writing and at school, rather than climbing trees.

He kept searching, until he found it--an old spruce tree. His memory flashed back to a similar tree, with his grandfather smiling at him, helping him reach the first branch while his grandmother watched on fretfully.

Boris got on top of the first branch, and his direction was now clear; it was all coming back to him. He made it up the tree, and was soon very close to the top, tens of meters up.

And there, hanging by the strap from the branch of a tree right next to him, was a backpack.

There was no guarantee it would contain anything of much use, but it would be stupid to not check it.

He crept to the edge of the branch he was on and reached out to the backpack. He quickly snatched it off the branch, when he heard a cracking sound.

Shit.

The branch he was on snapped a second later, and Boris barely managed to grab onto a branch of the tree he'd taken the backpack from, but not before his right arm, which had been holding the backpack, scraped up against the tree.

It wasn't especially painful, but it was bleeding. There were a few splinters in his arm as well, which he'd deal with in a minute. First, he needed to check the backpack; it was first priority at the moment, as it might contain something to help treat his arm; blood was already dripping onto his pants.

He tore open the backpack and found several small packs with things like beef jerky, bread, and crackers, as well as two bottles of water. At the bottom, there were also a few bandages. He wasted no time wrapping them around his arm after removing a few of the larger splinters with his fingers.

He sat in the tree for a few hours, waiting for any sudden sound, when Dr. Ward's voice came on over his earpiece.

"Sorry it's been so long. Had to reset some of the equipment and get the signal working. Had to open the connection to it, but nobody else should really be using it. This is the first time the Test has been conducted, so it was of course plausible that there would be a few... bumps."

Boris nodded, and she continued.

"I see you've already equipped yourself with a pistol and spear, as well as suffered a minor injury. I've been able to check in on some of the others, and they are all doing roughly the same, but currently you are only one of two sitting in a tree. Granted, not everyone is even *near* trees. There's one pairing that is taking place entirely on a flat field. The Prospect there is... Ethiopian I think. Looks quite capable. Anyway, you're doing well for yourself so far."

Boris nodded once again, knowing he couldn't communicate back. He was somewhat glad about this, because if he could talk back he could give himself away. Yet, that was a two-way street; his competitor may not have considered this, making him vulnerable to detection and elimination. Boris stayed in the tree for the rest of the day, deciding that he would give his opponent more time to make stupid mistakes, and tomorrow he would work on gathering supplies and better weapons, killing his opponent, then getting out.

And that's when his mind finally became clear on what he had to do.

He first had to kill his competitor, of course, but he was not going to have an opportunity to kill the Overseer here if he had any intention of escaping. He'd have to get away and come back later, hopefully damaging The Order enough in the process to keep them from pursuing him...

But there always was the possibility that Elena, Nikita, Vasiliy, and Józef could find him, however slim it was.

However, as the day drew to a close, around 19:00, a new voice came over the earpiece. It was Zakhar.

"Holy shit, my friend. I'm through. I can get to anyone, since they opened the connection. This is fucking gold. I was granted the ability to monitor what's happening, which gave me special access to data about The Order. Turns out you're right about it. I'm definitely helping you out and will drag myself out of the rubble if possible. And also… your friends are here."

CHAPTER 26

By about noon that day, everybody in the group was assembled near the checkpoint before they advanced towards the New Dawn company buildings, still a kilometer or two out. This was it, or at least it could be. Even Józef was out. He was missing an arm, of course, but he had a pistol and had every intention of going to help save his friend.

The group, now assembled, Partisans and soldiers all, was a couple hundred strong. It was truly grand--Americans, Russians, Germans, even Poles, Arabs, and all sorts of others working together for one goal, with one motto.

Nikita and Vasiliy coined it recently, from a song from around decade ago, from an old Russian metal band.

Smyert e Slava.

Death and Glory.

The phrase was repeated by the crowd. They began marching down the street, in an orderly line, as if on a military march.

Nikita, Elena, Józef, and Vasiliy headed in, closer to where they were likely to face the first resistance.

The crowd began to spread out near the checkpoint. The army then dispersed throughout the area and were told to wait.

The four, Nikita, Józef, Elena, and Vasiliy, were going to go in first to ensure they were in the right place. The plan was to create both a diversion and an ambush in this way.

The four of them marched through the central gates, where two squat buildings stood several meters back. This had to be at least something, as both still looked well maintained. The windows were shaded, though, so it was impossible to tell if they'd been identified or not.

As soon as they stepped across the gate, the gunfire started. The bullets hit the ground several meters in front of the four, and they began to run back as quickly as possible before the bullets reached them.

The four of them all began to return fire, towards the windows, which didn't break. They must have been bulletproofed. At least that meant they couldn't be shot at from them.

Several Order troops advanced upon the four but were all shot down as some of the allied troops began to move up, taking positions behind abandoned vehicles, walls, and outside the lots, trees and bushes.

The Order sent in a second wave, but these were not the same. Dressed differently, they all took cover behind similar surroundings, and the fight became much more drawn out.

Considering this was merely a checkpoint, and the fact that their actual numbers were still unknown, this was likely seen by The Order as just a commonplace attack by the Partisans.

The gunfight dragged on for quite a while longer, and it was clear that those they were fighting now were not the average grunts. At least a few of their own had been killed while only two of their enemies were confirmed down.

However, as time went on, the allied troops began to filter in more, and soon The Order troops were defeated. But, by now, it was late afternoon. The group advanced, some going through the trees and brush outside the road, and some, including the four, went down the road, moving from cover to cover, until the buildings were in sight. They were still several hundred meters away, but they were massive, and attacking at night like this after everyone had been fighting the whole day, even if not in a particularly intense way, was not a good idea. However, they couldn't keep their guard down, as The Order continued to dispatch small groups of soldiers to face them, though, they were obviously not sending their best. They could be massing for a greater attack but making sure to keep their enemies on their feet.

It was at this time Elena noticed Vasiliy's "thousand-yard stare" as she'd heard it called in popular media. When he looked out into the distance, there was something about his eyes that implied he didn't want to be doing this but was accustomed to it. It had prevented more than one ambush, however, as he'd point out something nobody else had seen.

At the end of the day, people began to take "shifts" sleeping, as The Order continued to harass them in small numbers. Elena ended up falling asleep against the piece of concrete she'd been hiding behind for most of the day.

CHAPTER 27

Boris eventually fell asleep in that tree, but he had a hard time at first, because he knew that at least someone from his group had made it there… somehow.

As great as this was, he still had to pass his section of the test. But he needed to communicate with Zakhar, and maybe with Dr. Ward, as well. He knew that whatever he did was going to be seen by both of them, so he had to either trust that Dr. Ward wouldn't do anything or think of a way he could communicate with Zakhar alone.

He needed to ask Zakhar to move the escape beacons to a central area where all of the Prospects would be directed if they passed their test, so that they could all meet up in the end. Then possibly he could prevent The Order from stopping the Prospects grouping together at the end. Because they were told they would be "apprehended," that probably entailed them sending some troops their way, so even a slight delay could be enough. It could give the Prospects, likely to be fairly well-armed at that point, time to prepare a defense before they could breakout and escape the area.

With any luck, they could bring Zakhar with them, and maybe Dr. Ward, as well. Both could be useful in the future, and both were good people, just misguided.

He woke up the next morning, still in the tree, to the sound of rustling in the brush below him. He looked down, and there was a squirrel sitting on the ground. He figured he could kill it, but also that he wasn't going to be there long enough to need to do that.

Instead, he climbed down the tree and continued to scour the area around him for weapons.

He searched several trees, under rocks, and through bushes, for most of two hours, before he actually found something new.

It was laying against a tree, the sun shining on it slightly--a *Mosin-Nagant* Rifle, fitted with a PU 4x-magnification telescopic sight.

The weapon had been used by many of the greatest snipers of all time; people such as Vasiliy Zaitsev, who killed many German officers and snipers during the battle of Stalingrad in the Great Patriotic War, and Ivan Sidorenko, the deadliest sniper of the war, with over five hundred kills of German soldiers.

After he stopped marveling at the famed rifle, he picked it up. Next to it was a small pack, containing about fifteen rounds, a bottle of water, and a few pain pills.

He pulled back the bolt on the weapon, opening the chamber so that he could load it. He put five rounds into the weapon and wanted desperately to test-fire it. The bolt was smooth, and the wood polished. Now, all he had to do was find his enemy. He'd fired a Mosin before, but never one with a scope. The sight in the scope was fairly simple, but effective, with a central post, where the tip was the point of fire.

He first decided to get up into a tree, as glare from the sun would make it nearly impossible to sight in if he had to shoot his target when the target was in a tree, with him on the ground.

He also had to consider that the glass in the scope itself would reflect the sun, which mean that at certain times of the day, it would be very easy to see him scoping in, that is, if his enemy was nearby. But that gave him an idea. He spent half an hour getting into a good position on a tree on the edge of the tree line, with dense branches and leaves, then positioned the rifle out from the tree, with the scope just barely sticking out.

It was a stupid form of bait, and if his combatant detected it, he could simply adjust his sights and shoot Boris in the head; he couldn't really defend himself any better.

Boris continued to rest his hand there, sticking the rifle out, before he tired, then using the weapon's strap to hang it off of a nearby branch. This would slow his reaction time, but it wouldn't change whether the first shot hit him or not.

Dr. Ward communicated with him occasionally with highlights of news about what everyone else was doing.

"The Ethiopian has been following his combatant for about an hour now."

"The French woman is in a tree above her combatant."

"The Swiss guy's been hit in the arm, but his enemy is currently bleeding from a shot to the gut."

"The Finn threw a knife, hitting his enemy in the thigh. His opponent is bleeding out so it's really just waiting for him to officially be 'dead.'"

While Boris had never heard anything from this Finnish person, this was the one who was closest to being done with his test, which meant he had to get Zakhar to act quickly, and he himself needed to respond quickly.

He could try to send a covert code to Zakhar somehow. Perhaps he could just directly write out a message. But then he realized, he was sitting on a tree, and he had a spear.

The blade was probably sharp enough to carve at least a primitive message out to Zakhar, but to be safe, he was going to do it in Russian.

He got to work quickly. It was awkward and difficult to carve the letters in with the spear, so he took the blade off, and held it like a dagger, carving in the characters.

While he knew that Dr. Ward could read Russian, he didn't think she was fluent in it, so it would take her longer to understand what Boris was trying to get across to Zakhar.

The first two words were "tell Ward." He hoped this got across to Zakhar to explain what was happening and what Boris' plan was to Dr. Ward. Zakhar came on over the channel, and asked Boris for confirmation; "You want me to tell her what you're about to do? I can just connect our channels and you'll be able to hear us both talk."

Boris agreed, and Zakhar got into explaining to Dr. Ward why she was in the wrong organization. As he did this, Boris continued carving into the tree's trunk, this time writing "put victory beacon in same place for all."

This one took a while longer, but it coincided with Zakhar finishing the explanation to Dr. Ward. She was silent, likely thinking, on her side, but she responded a few minutes later, with "I'm too stuck in here. If I escaped, they'd track me down and kill me before I got very far. Also, toward the beginning of my initiation years ago, they injected a tracking device into my arm, so they'd always know where I was. I can't leave, but I will do what I can to help you. I've always known there was something off about this organization, anyway."

Zakhar then apparently examined what Boris had just carved into the tree, and said, "So you can all gather once it's over, so you're stronger together? There's probably no better option."

Boris nodded once again, and then went back into his position on the tree branch, with the scope glinting.

Boris waited for nearly an hour, until…

CRACK!

A round was fired, and it whizzed by Boris's ear. He wasn't sure if this was because his enemy knew where he was, or if he just missed.

Boris picked up the rifle, but then deliberately dropped his spear to the ground. It was about the same length and thickness of a rifle, so it could be convincing enough for his enemy to think he'd hit his mark, and that Boris had dropped his weapon.

Boris waited for a few more minutes, when he could hear

movement in the grass a few dozen meters out.

He quickly brought the rifle to his face, peering through the scope, and he saw his enemy, dressed similarly to him, with what looked like a Karabiner 98 rifle, with no scope, creeping in his direction.

But by then Boris had already waited too long.

He saw the glint of Boris's scope once again, and fired off a desperate shot, but it missed entirely, flying off into the woods a few meters to Boris's left.

Boris didn't let this distract him, however, and lined up his enemy in the scope. The man was running but was doing so at a consistent enough pace that Boris could compensate for it and hit him.

Boris had his finger around the trigger, the bullet ready to go into his opponent's heart, and then he squeezed the trigger.

Fire erupted out of the barrel of his rifle, and through the scope he saw his enemy tumble to the ground after a cloud of blood formed where he'd been hit.

Boris couldn't be sure that his enemy was dead, however. He didn't see exactly where the bullet hit. However, the round the Mosin fired was very powerful, and if he hit his enemy in the arm it was unlikely he would have dropped, so his enemy was almost certainly hit in the torso somewhere. His opponent likely didn't have much life left in him.

Nonetheless, Boris had to be sure, as he hadn't yet been notified of the location he was supposed to go to after killing his opponent, which meant his enemy couldn't be dead yet. Boris had to finish him off, so that he could get moving.

Boris climbed out of the tree and started creeping towards the location of his enemy. If he was able to crawl away, the blood trail would certainly lead Boris to where he was now.

Once Boris was close enough to see whether the man was

still there or not, he could tell they'd left already. There was no groaning, nor the sound of labored breathing.

Boris found the place and saw a small pool of blood as well as a backpack sitting in the middle of it; there was a trail leading off into a small grouping of trees.

Boris then went to grab the backpack.

Then he heard beeping, reaching a crescendo.

It only took him a split second for him to process his opponent had left a trap in there for him. Boris flung the backpack towards the trees, in the direction his enemy had gone, and it exploded only a second later. Shrapnel went into the ground all around Boris, but luckily, he wasn't hit too bad; a few small cuts formed on his arms, and one on his leg, but nothing that would slow him down at this point.

It was almost over, but in this situation Boris almost wished he didn't have any comrades to meet with; if he didn't, he could simply wait until the bullet killed his enemy, whether he bled out or went into shock. However, both of them were running on a timer right now. If his opponent wished to survive, he'd have to kill Boris quickly, then manage to get to the rally point to be extracted by The Order. He didn't know if Zakhar shifted the waypoints. Boris has to kill him soon or he'd never reach the waypoint in time to get to his friends and escape.

So, one way or another, somebody was leaving the arena and the other one was going to stay, laying in a pool of blood.

So, Boris followed the trail. His opponent may not be as on-guard as he had been before, as he may expect that Boris had been incapacitated by the explosion. Of course, he would know Boris was still alive, but he may think that he'd outlive Boris.

Boris followed the trail until it led to a tree, which had some blood dripping down it. Boris wasn't sure what plan his combatant had, but it didn't seem to involve any sort of stealth. It was very unlikely he'd have been able to get to another tree, and it was an incredible feat that he got into the tree at all.

Boris first climbed up the tree, getting to a low branch. He started trying to deduce how his opponent would respond to him. Leaving the explosive in the backpack was likely his last *real* chance to kill Boris, and it was likely he had at least one hand occupied trying to hold his guts in, put bluntly. So, he probably wouldn't be able to use his rifle; he perhaps had nothing more than a pistol. Boris scanned above him, thinking that maybe he'd see a leg dangling off of a branch, or some other giveaway, but he didn't; the branches were thick, and his opponent was relatively thin.

Boris sat, silent, for several minutes, until he heard a movement and then a groan.

So, he was up here, of course, but now Boris just had to find exactly where.

However, Boris didn't have the time to do this, as he heard the sound of a gun cocking, and in that instant he knew exactly where his opponent was.

Directly above him.

The first shot grazed Boris's leg, and it started bleeding very quickly. It was painful, but considering it didn't actually *hit* him, he was probably going to be okay.

Boris then had half a second to think of a plan; he could either try to aim around the tree with his pistol, or he could simply try to shoot *through* the tree with his pistol, or the rifle.

He wouldn't have the time to pull out the rifle, so instead he drew his pistol and started firing above him, at the branch. He knew that wood wasn't particularly bulletproof, so the bullets *should* go through. Boris fired seven times, enough to empty the one magazine he had for his 1911, and he saw as a dark figure drop off the branch onto the ground. Boris lay back on the branch he was on and waited for the light ringing in his ears to diminish before he looked down on the ground, where his opponent lay in the dirt, hit with at least five of Boris's bullets, his blood pooled under him.

Looking at the man's wounds, it appeared that Boris's first shot with the Mosin rifle hit the man in the stomach; so, if Boris had waited, the man *would* have died, though it would have been a slow, painful death. So, despite how bloody it was, Boris killing the man with his pistol was an act of mercy, in a way, as he didn't have to sit and bleed out in that tree. Despite the incredible tech The Order possessed, fixing a shot to the stomach is very difficult, and it's unlikely the man would have ever made it to the waypoint, regardless.

Boris then observed the man's weaponry; he left the rifle on the ground, but he also had a pistol of a 1911 design, so Boris took out the magazine and put it in his own weapon. The man had shot it at him only a few times, so it had a few remaining rounds. Relieved that was over, and Dr. Ward called him up shortly.

"Alright, you won, no surprise. Now move to the waypoint. It's in the zone the Finnish man was located. It's in the middle of the arena, so Zakhar likely chose it because it would easy for anyone to make it there. I have plans to inform him, you, and every other winner to proceed where you are headed. All Prospects are dressed the same, The Order's people another way, so they *should* be able to tell you all apart.

Boris went in the direction he was prompted to by his watch. It had registered how many meters away it was, as well--about a kilometer out; Boris was probably near the middle of his "square" and the waypoint was likely towards the middle of the adjacent square.

Boris had a somewhat difficult time making the trek because of his injured leg, but he was able to go on, after bandaging the wound with his remaining supply.

It took him about half an hour, and apparently, he was one of the first people there. He sat under a tree, directly at the location of the marker.

Then he heard a voice, with a Finnish accent.

"Look up, friend," it said.

Boris did so, and he saw a surprisingly well-camouflaged man sitting on one of the branches; he'd coated his face in mud and greenery, as well as his hands, shirt, and pants. He was a dark mix of brown and green, and Boris wouldn't have known where he was if the man wasn't absentmindedly swinging his legs forward and back as he sat on the tree branch.

Boris climbed up the tree and started observing the man before asking questions. He noticed the man was carrying a weapon that looked like an American M16 rifle, one of the earlier models.

Boris looked a bit harder and noticed he also had a bow strung cross his back. A very large one at that. He also had a quiver with around four arrows in it.

Boris then asked who he was, and how he'd beaten his competitor.

"Kakko. My last name. Mine was fairly easy considering I've already won. My competitor was a bumbling idiot, stomping through the woods with a big sword and a shotgun. I heard him coming ten minutes before I'd even seen him from where I was sitting in this tree. I'll admit, he couldn't have done much else, because at any range his shotgun wouldn't have done him too well, but he sounded like he was trying to make all the noise he possibly could. So, when he passed under my branch, I drew this bow I've got here, and shot him in the back. He was a big guy, so I had to hit him again and he went down *hard*. Then I stayed in the area and searched a bit more before I found this rifle--" he said, gesturing to the M4 "-- and then I waited. Your friend, Zakhar, contacted me, telling me not to move too far, and that people would come to me. So here I am. You're the first, though I've been told that some Prospects are currently in pursuit of their opponent, and one of The Order members won their bout, but it was against somebody who wasn't willing to join us, so really it's no loss. There are about three people heading for us right now, all friendly and sympathetic to our cause."

Zakhar's voice cut out, and Boris was left sitting in the tree, but after a few minutes he lay down on a branch and started scanning the surrounding area for anybody who wasn't with them. Though alarms weren't triggered, as would have had Zakhar not changed the waypoints, it was, nonetheless, extremely unlikely that The Order wasn't beginning to realize what was going on. So, hopefully the rest of the Prospects would finish off their opponents soon and be able to stay hidden from The Order.

Boris sat in that tree for another half an hour before the three Zakhar had told him were on the way arrived. Safiri, Werner, and someone Boris didn't recognize were among them. They were all armed with relatively modern rifles. By comparison, the rifle sitting across Boris' lap was a fossil, as it was over a hundred years old. Maybe the weapon itself wasn't, but its design was.

This, however, by no means meant Boris' rifle wasn't deadly. In the right hands, it could even be more so than a modern weapon.

Boris didn't bother to ask how the three who'd just arrived killed their opponents. Considering their armament, they likely had well-won gunfights. He then learned the one he didn't recognize was a former member of the U.S. Green Berets, and was in France when he was captured, maybe even near were Olivia had been.

He then realized he hadn't heard anything about her yet. He hadn't reason to be concerned, and if he fell asleep now, he'd likely wake and find several other Prospects had arrived, quite possibly including her, but it was starting to become a slight concern. Boris fell asleep, though it was a bit more difficult this time; the bark of this tree was rougher than the bark of the tree he'd been in before, and it was still midday, but he wanted to get a bit of rest before he left.

He woke up a few hours later, not having gotten enough sleep, and only having eaten some meagre rations before he slept, he was by no means at his peak, but he was ready to make a breakout if at all possible.

Then, Dr. Ward came on over the radio.

"Your friends have broken into the field. They've extracted a couple of the Prospects and killed several Order troops. From what I'm told, they've taken a few losses but are still at significant strength. Their numbers are over one hundred."

Boris was concerned enough about hearing "a few losses" that he didn't even realize how greatly his party had grown since he'd left it.

Then, one more voice came in over his earpiece. "Mr. Kasyanov. I'm heading to you now. I have some equipment for you and your friends."

It was Dr. Ward.

CHAPTER 28

When Elena awoke, she was still lying against the concrete segment. Her back ached as she tried to stand up, but a hand grabbed her shoulder and kept her down. It was Vasiliy, sitting against the same piece. She realized where she was, and then stopped trying to stand. Vasiliy spoke first, "We're doing alright. We've still got a few asleep but then we're going to rush forward, because like this we could be fighting forever. We will probably lose a few doing this. Be ready and know it's necessary for us to get through before they can mobilize more of their men. And, last thing, as of right now, we've killed about fifty-ish of theirs in the small waves they've sent. We've lost four, three of them Partisans, one of them a Russian soldier, who I think is alive but not well enough to keep at the front. The Charge order is coming in a few minutes, wait for Nikita's voice."

Elena waited, her heart rate steadily increasing, until she heard Nikita's voice ring out over the area.

"CHARGE COMRADES! URA! URA! URA! GET TO THEIR GATES!"

Elena hesitated for more than a second, but nobody else did. Allied fighters flooded in from behind her, rushing forward towards the front gates of The Order's citadel.

She then stood up and started running, too. She was towards the back, but it was still a harrowing experience. Those in front of her fired their rifles and pistols towards the buildings, shattering windows and managing to hit enemies. However, several of them dropped dead. It didn't take much to stop them, any hit to the leg or torso stopped most of them. The person in front of Elena, a larger man, one of the Partisans, was carrying a large machine gun. He was huffing air in and out of his lungs, breathing heavily as he fired blindly in front of him, the sound almost deafening.

They were getting closer to the gates of The Order's main building where they'd be able to take some cover. Several were already hiding behind it. From the windows of the main building, several figures were shooting at them. But when Elena was about fifty meters out from the gates, an entrance to the enclave was opened, and a truck with a large machine gun backed out, and it began to roar to life.

Elena sprinted harder than she'd ever done in her entire life. The bullets scattered from her left to right, so she angled her approach. She looked to her left and watched as several of the slower Partisans, largely those who looked injured or underfed, fell, being hit nearly ten times each before tumbling to the ground, dead or dying.

Elena was now almost to the wall and was preparing to dive as she saw holes appear in the back of the man who was in front of her. He kept going for about three or four steps, but he kept getting hit and blood kept shooting out of his back. He fell to the ground, face first, laying totally still.

Elena, however, had already dove for cover. Dmitry was sitting a meter in front of her, and reached out his hand to pull her in. Elena's arms scraped against the concrete, but she was alive and unharmed... she thought.

She brought her hand down to her side and felt something warm and fluid. She looked down and realized she'd been shot, but she didn't feel anything. Her mouth was gaping open while Dmitry stared at her wound, already considering what to do. Luckily, he had his backpack with medical supplies with him, but there was no guarantee he could do much.

Before he likely even had the chance to think about it, he ripped open his backpack and took out a syringe with morphine and injected it into Elena. He then started talking.

"It looks like it's only a flesh wound. Passed right through. You didn't lose any organs but I'm going to have to stitch you up fast or you're going to die. But you aren't going to die."

Dmitry's voice, as monotone as ever, was still comforting in this situation; there was no fear in his voice. He knew what he was doing, *right?*

So there, behind a large segment of concrete, raked every minute or so with small caliber bullets, Dmitry sewed up Elena's gunshot wound while she did her best to sit still.

On the other side of the front, Nikita and Vasiliy were fighting side-by-side with Jeung and Marvin. By then, they'd shot out most of the windows. Inside were relatively standard looking offices, though they were well maintained and several of the computers on the desks were on; at least before they got shot. Not only were Order soldiers fighting them now, apparently more competent than those encountered in the past, but there were also simple utility workers who'd taken small pistols and were firing out the windows, as well.

Nikita and Vasiliy tried to avoid killing them, aiming simply to disarm them as they were more likely to be convinced to switch sides, considering that The Order's indoctrination was primarily imposed on the soldiers. But the Partisans had no mercy. Despite their likely lack of training and the fact the Partisans had suffered much heavier casualties than the other soldiers, they fought with a grim determination, and Vasiliy was quite surprised as he saw The Order's soldiers getting hit, several falling forward out of the windows.

Then, a voice came in over Vasiliy's radio. It was a female voice, and he'd never heard it before.

"This message is going out to all of those entities assaulting this area right now. I've been informed that you are associated with a certain Boris Kasyanov. I'm not with The Order, not anymore at least. I'm in the building and will try to exit and join you. But that is not the purpose of this message. The purpose is to tell you that your friend, Mr. Kasyanov, is out in the fields to your southwest. There are several other people with him. Those dressed in green shirts and khaki cargo pants are with you. Those in dark grey are your enemies. I cannot explain further. Find them, get them out, and take me as well if you can. I'll be with them. Hopefully".

Nikita heard this and acted fast. He grabbed the megaphone he had still been carrying in his backpack and announced:

"THOSE HOPING TO RETRIEVE BORIS, COME WITH ME! I KNOW WHERE HE IS! PARTISANS, HOLD YOUR GROUND!" Vasiliy nodded at him and said "good luck, comrade. And bring Elena with you, if you can."

Nikita nodded in the affirmative, and then started moving across the concrete barriers, all unfortunately starting to crack from the sheer number of bullets now embedded inside them. He got out into the open, fired a few more shots at the machine gunner, and turned, not even seeing he'd hit the gunner in the neck, not seeing him fall off the truck, choking.

He then made it to the barrier that Elena was behind. He first saw Dmitry hunched over, his back facing him.

He then got around, and saw Elena laying there, white-faced, bleeding from her side. Nikita spoke softly. "We're going to get Boris. Are you in any condition to help us?"

Elena smiled lightly, and then tried to stand. She couldn't, so instead she whispered to Nikita, "Go get him. Bring him back."

Nikita nodded, and waded out into the fields, with about twenty men behind him; including all of those Boris knew best; Jeung, Józef, Zhenya, Arkady, Petya, and several others, including the black American soldier Boris had gone out to meet to break up the fight between the Russians and Americans.

Most of these men, Petya, Arkady, and Zhenya in particular had been subdued after Boris disappeared; Petya most of all. He hadn't spoken to anyone since he was gone, and he mourned as if he'd lost a son. But now he was solid, and steadfast as he'd been in the beginning, walking right beside Nikita as they went to find Boris. The voice that told the group of Boris' location guided them through the brush, heading to where they thought he'd be.

CHAPTER 29

Boris sat in that tree once more, looking through the scope of his rifle more scrupulously than before, waiting for Dr. Ward and the others to show up.

He also didn't rule out the possibility that Dr. Ward was not on their side and was simply sending a large detachment of soldiers to come and kill him.

But no, that was not the case. Dr. Ward came in a truck by herself. She parked under the tree, where a few others had gathered. Out of the truck came most of the other Prospects and some people in Order uniforms, probably those also deciding to defect.

Zakhar was not among them.

Once Dr. Ward was out of the truck, she directed Boris to look at the back, where he saw a box containing his old equipment--his uniform, helmet, AK-74M, and Dragunov. However, his Tokarev pistol was nowhere to be found. It must not have been picked up with him.

Boris looked at the stuff he had now and decided what he was going to do with it all.

First, he left the pistol under the tree. Maybe someday in the future he'd come back there and find it, but he didn't want it with him. As for the Mosin, he gave it to one of The Order defectors, telling them to take care of it, as it *was* an iconic part of history. The defector also was likely best not trusted with an automatic weapon.

By the time most of the equipment had been unloaded and the fighters had armed themselves, soldiers of The Order were already surrounding them.

Boris wondered why they were prioritizing them over the mass of attackers on their doorstep, but he then figured that the way they saw it, it would be easier to take on the well-equipped combatants first. Killing them would be a high priority considering most of the Prospects were members of one of the Special Forces.

This wasn't an encouraging thought, but it did put into perspective what exactly was going on and what Boris would have to survive before he could get out of there. The Order got ever closer, creeping forward in their dark gray uniforms, some of them not even fully outfitted--showing their bare arms, many not even wearing the standard masks of The Order. You could see their faces; human but not. They were all grim and there was very little life in their eyes.

Boris ordered the group of around twenty to hold steady, all of them lying concealed in a tree or bush, all now armed to the teeth.

Once the majority of The Order troops were about fifty meters away, Boris whispered, "Begin."

All around Boris the foliage and trees lit up, tracers flying out of them, into The Order's ranks.

Boris then heard clearly for the first time the voice of one of the soldiers, one of those without a mask.

"Sentinels, defensive formation! Hold fast!" said a voice in an unaccented tone, similar to what Boris remembered Daniel's voice sounded like. As Boris's mind drifted away from the battle for a split second, he thought about Daniel, and about how he still had no idea where he was. Nonetheless, he couldn't dwell on it for too long.

He drew his Dragunov rifle, the polymer it was made of feeling foreign in comparison to the wooden frame of the Mosin rifle. However, its impact would be the same; they fired the same bullet, after all.

By the time Boris was scoped in, several of The Order's Sentinels, as they were apparently called, had fallen, several laying in the long grasses, dead.

Now that many of them were not wearing masks or uniforms, there was much more of a human element to the experience, and they did indeed fight, or at least seemed to fight more like humans now.

Admittedly, they still weren't very good.

However, it was also now more real. Boris could see the facial expressions of the dead and dying in their last moments, yet he still managed to shoot them as efficiently as ever; once a person is used to battle, killing becomes instinctive.

He could intuitively sense his surroundings. Now that he was on the ground, he could feel the dirt see the grass moving gently in the wind, and sense the movement of those in front of him. Conflict, in a way, is peaceful--reminiscent of a shooting gallery of sorts--one pops up, Boris puts it down, the mind dulling awareness that it'd just caused the death of another human being. Yet, Boris knew that his awareness of having killed others would resurface at some point. Just not today.

Boris, after having shot his third magazine empty, stepped behind a tree to reload, and looked around him. While he was in total focus, the rest of his comrades fighting simply hadn't registered. Or it hadn't until he saw a few of his own people laying in the grass in pools of their own blood. He didn't panic or cry out, but he silently acknowledged that they'd died for a good cause. He didn't recognize any of them, however. Hopefully they were at peace.

On the other side of Boris' tree was Werner, who was leaning up against it. It appeared he'd been hit, but considering he was still shooting, likely not incapacitated.

At that point Boris realized he'd been waiting too long and got back around the tree. But now some of the Sentinels were firing off into the direction Boris and his people were firing as well.

Is there something behind them? he thought.

Then a familiar voice which he'd genuinely missed for several months came on over his earpiece.

"Boris. I know you can hear me on this channel. We're currently engaged in a gunfight. We'll be with you shortly."

Nikita!

CHAPTER 30

Nikita tuned his radio channel back to Dr. Ward's, where he quickly thanked her for patching him into Boris's earpiece. He then stepped up to where everybody else was fighting. They seemed to have taken The Order by surprise with this attack; they were scattered throughout the area, several spinning around to shoot at something behind them just to be shot in the back in turn.

Of course, the volume of fire directed at Boris and his comrades was much heavier than it was from Nikita's side, but that wasn't a major issue as they were both somewhat concealed. Nikita couldn't see any of the fighters that were with Boris, much less the man himself, though he did see a couple of Order soldiers in one area drop to single shots, which could have easily been from Boris, though there was no way to be sure. The Order's numbers seemed to be dropping quite quickly, and Nikita already saw a few of them slinking away into the brush from the corner of his eye. It was guaranteed they'd mass another wave to try to attack them, but it seemed for now they'd be in a position from which they could advance in mere minutes.

Nikita moved forward into a larger part of a clearing between the woods and The Order troops and noticed that the majority of soldiers weren't fully in uniform, and most noticeably, that they didn't have the usual masks. Now, they almost seemed human.

Almost.

They were still brainwashed, fighting for an immoral authority. With this in mind, Nikita continued firing at the few who remained. The majority of them had been killed by now, the rest running off, though they could come back to attack later.

Nikita then lowered his weapon, and the field appeared to be clear. He said quietly, "move," and advanced into the open. He heard a familiar voice from the other side of the field shout out, "cease fire, friendlies!"

Nikita, followed by the rest of the group, met in the middle of the field, not unlike how it was, months before, when Boris met with the soldier now alongside Nikita, and ended the previous conflict.

As Nikita approached Boris, he sized him up; he still had his uniform somehow. His balaclava wasn't on, showing Boris's face. Nikita had almost forgot what his friend's face looked like, but there it was. Maybe a new scar or two, and Boris was sporting two bandages, though he still looked the same.

As they approached, now only a few meters away, they both reached out their hand and shook, before pulling it into an embrace. No words were exchanged, but both sighed in relief.

CHAPTER 31

"You look tired, my friend," was the first thing Nikita said.

Boris shrugged, revealing the truth in Nikita's statement. He smiled a bit and asked him how he was.

"As tired as you, probably. I still don't know how the hell we found you," Nikita responded.

"Heh. Fate, comrade. Believe in it," Boris remarked.

Nikita then dug into a compartment in his backpack, retrieving Boris' pistol from it, holding it out towards him.

Boris smiled at him heartily and took his pistol back along with its magazines, and he loaded his pistol quickly, examining it. "This scratch was not here before, Nikita." He feigned a concerned expression and Nikita shrugged, somewhat surprised, and said "I didn't do it." Boris laughed and patted his shoulder.

Boris then looked over Nikita's shoulder, and saw Petya. Petya looked elated, and there was a large, genuine smile over his bearded face. Boris patted Nikita's shoulder again before he moved past him to meet Petya.

"Hey, uncle Petya," he said.

Petya didn't say anything immediately, but he pulled Boris into a bear hug.

"How've you been?" Boris asked.

"Boris, I wish I had the honor of being your blood uncle. You're a brave soul. Worry not about me, I'm continuing on alright. Anyway, you need to see how the group you've founded has grown. What you've created has continued to become greater,"

Petya said.

"I certainly intend to see it, once we're out of here," Boris responded. He noticed that Petya didn't look quite as healthy as he had before, but it was probably just due to the stresses of the journey.

He then went to Józef and looked him over.

"Good to see you are still alive, my friend. Any regrets about our quest yet?" Boris asked him, chuckling a little bit at the end.

Józef replied, "I have no regrets, not yet anyway. Damage to my person are a small price to pay."

"Good man," Boris replied.

He nodded at the American soldier and shook his hand once again. "Good to see we're both alive to meet in the middle once again," he said.

The American nodded, and Boris went to Arkady and Zhenya.

"How've you two been?" he asked them. He noticed immediately that Zhenya looked much older.

"We're alive," said Arkady.

"And where is Otto?" asked Boris.

Arkady and Zhenya looked at each other for a second, before Zhenya spoke. "He didn't make it. Died a few days ago. Killed in an explosion. Nothing too spectacular, really, but he went out bravely. Didn't complain or nothing."

Boris nodded grimly. He knew that not everybody was still going to be alive when he finally made it back to the group, but it wasn't something he was prepared for and, out of everyone, Otto…

He then returned to Nikita and asked what the plan was.

"Well, we've been fighting outside this compound for a while now, but now that we've found you and some of your new friends we're ready to get out of here if we can. We've probably done enough damage, or at least we've definitely shot up their building a lot," he said.

Boris nodded and went over to the Prospects and announced the plan. All of them seemed to accept it, considering it was better than staying outside the Order HQ and fighting a guerilla war in the forest.

Then Dr. Ward turned to Boris, and said what he'd been expecting, if not what he'd hoped she'd say. "Now that I've helped you all out and brought you together, I'm going to return and say I only found one or two of you. Then I'm going to stay there. If you return, I'll try to contact you and help you again, but I'm not going with you. Zakhar is going to stay for now, as well, as we discussed before. He hasn't been in contact with you for a while because he was without doubt under suspicion. He's going to have a very difficult time staying out of trouble in our ranks… but he still will be here to help you when you return."

Boris nodded. He'd been hoping Zakhar and Dr. Ward would be coming with them, but he knew it likely wouldn't happen. Their help was still invaluable throughout this process, which quite obviously would not have turned out well had it not been for their support.

So, rather than argue for why they should go with the group, Boris simply said, "Thank you. Good luck, Dr. Ward."

Dr. Ward nodded and got into her truck, and then drove off back towards the HQ, which was full of holes from gunshots and light explosives.

Boris got to the center of the group, where Nikita's people and his people were talking offhandedly about who they were, while watching the horizon.

"Okay, we're going now. Follow Nikita," Boris said, not exerting himself to get the message across.

Now that they were walking and most of the group was

preoccupied with the patrol, Boris asked Nikita quietly, "and about Elena?"

Nikita sighed, and Boris's heart rate jumped, though he tried not to let it show.

"She was shot once. I think she's okay. Dmitry's treating her right now. He's probably going to need help to get her out of here."

Boris didn't respond, he simply looked at the ground. Regardless of what happened to Elena, he really couldn't risk it all now because of his personal feelings. The mission would go on, especially now that he was a part of it again.

They were approaching where the group of friendly fighters were, still shooting into the windows. Most of them had been shattered and several of the offices were basically destroyed. Whether they had really been in use was debatable, especially because Boris was almost certainly underground for most of his experience, but there was likely a lot of logistics and communication equipment that had been destroyed in the offices. This could provide an element of surprise if there was an Order presence in Denmark, where the group was headed now.

The volume of the fire was at a decrescendo, and it seemed that most of the friendlies were beginning to back off now that Nikita and Boris were visible again.

Then Boris saw Elena, being carried by two men, Jeung and Dmitry. He didn't bother to call out to her as the main focus really had to be getting out of the area now, as they couldn't afford to try to stall The Order for much longer.

Boris got into a truck that apparently had once belonged to The Order, and Arkady was in the front, driving. In a few minutes they were in Berlin, and they stopped near the Bundestag and everyone got out. Boris had noticed the Partisan fighters, and that they must have been Germans; likely to remain there and continue to harass The Order.

Indeed, that was the case, and he exited the truck and stood next to Nikita and Vasiliy.

"We've got our man now and gave The Order a blow they won't soon forget, despite taking some losses," said Nikita. There was a slight lack of confidence in his last few words, as most of the casualties, based on the bodies Boris had seen, were members of the Partisans, though this was likely no fault of anybody but The Order.

As motors were heard in the distance, large ones at that, Boris and his group gathered back into their trucks, but this time Boris sat in the back of the one with Elena, Dmitry, and Jeung.

Elena was unconscious, but Dmitry said she was not dead nor dying, though she probably wouldn't be up for a while.

Boris then had Jeung explain what had been happening for the past weeks, though they'd felt like years. He heard about them experiencing the incredible power of the winter in the European Plain, which apparently had been caused by the nuclear fallout, although it seemed somewhat limited in how far it extended. He also heard about their finding the building in Belarus, which of course Boris didn't know was in Belarus, where he'd been kept, and the first trial was held, and also about how they'd met the Partisans and lost Otto only to find that his best friend had been the one who killed him.

In the chaos of the situation, Boris had never even spoken to Marvin; he didn't even know he existed. But maybe, if they return to Berlin, he'd find him again, and tell him Otto's story as Boris knew it.

At the end of Jeung telling his side of life for the past while, Boris explained his situation to them. Being captured, losing Daniel, the fever dreams, waking up without the slightest idea of where he was, and being thrust into a deathmatch in which he'd be indoctrinated into the military of his worst enemy. It was certainly a fantastical sounding story, and what astounded Boris still was that it was true. However, once he explained to the others what The Order was--a group of some of the richest people in the world who prepared for this type of war to create their own state, it made more sense how they'd managed to take power from the crumbling governments of Europe so efficiently.

After finishing his story, Boris ate a few rations and fell asleep. Even though he fell asleep in a moving truck sitting down, it was the best rest he'd had in weeks.

Once he'd woken up, he called to the front of the truck, and asked where they were and how long it would be before they made it into Denmark.

Arkady called back, and said that they were in northeastern Germany, and that they'd be in Denmark by the end of the week.

It took Boris a second to process how out of touch with the world he'd been. "By the end of the week?" he asked. He didn't know what day it was. "Yeah." Arkady said. "It's Thursday. We'll cross the line on Saturday, probably."

Boris responded in the affirmative before leaning back in his chair. In the back with him, he finally noticed, were the Finnish man and two more former Prospects he didn't know, who'd fallen asleep as soon as they entered the truck. He guessed they didn't have the luxury of sleeping in their part of the competition. Boris felt somewhat guilty, as he hadn't been worried about his competition as much; he knew they wouldn't be serious. Because of the Overseer's sense of honor, he wouldn't have one of his underlings kill Boris, so Boris knew, whether subconsciously or not, that it was probably safe enough for him to sleep in that tree.

Boris shrugged off the feeling as he examined his weapons. Even though he'd already used them in the past, he hadn't been able to accustom himself to them again. The Tokarev pistol had a spot that didn't shine as brightly as it once had, but other than that it looked fine. The other weapons, his Kalashnikov and his Dragunov, being made of polymers, both looked to be in good condition. It was evident the items had been stored rather well, even if not with much care. Boris' uniform, though it felt clean, hadn't been ironed and had some wrinkles. It really wasn't an issue of course, but was something he noticed in the idle time he spent waiting for something else to happen.

Boris spent much of the rest of his day daydreaming and trying to plan ahead for what he'd be facing in both the near and distant future. In Denmark, the group was going to have to find some kind of large ship, ideally a container ship, and sail it to Svalbard. This would, of course, require fuel, a ship in decent condition, and a good amount of luck. It was unlikely that many people would have a mind to try to escape in a container ship, though, at the back of his mind, Boris imagined groups of people trawling the seas in large ships, living off of fish and only returning to land occasionally. It didn't sound like a bad idea, really. Radiation in places it still existed would be limited, and as long as the tides weren't any different now, it was likely one of the safest ways to live.

But humanity wasn't going to rebuild this way. It's good for those that choose that life, but Boris intended to try to restore what had been lost. It would be years, decades, maybe centuries, but it would happen, if he had anything to say about it. One day those in the sea will return to land and find civilization has returned, hopefully better than it was before their ancestors left it.

After another hour or so, the convoy of trucks stopped, and drivers rotated. Boris offered to drive the truck he was in, simply to occupy himself. He was up front with Zhenya and Józef, now, who was quietly looking out the window.

Boris' truck was one of the first few, but since he wasn't in front, his view was mostly limited to the back of the truck in front of him and the surroundings to his sides. He tried to stay at a reasonable distance from the truck in front of him, but in the mirror, he could see the truck behind him was quite close, so trying to brake at all would likely create a significant accident, not a good thing to have happen.

So, Boris was stuck squeezed in between these large trucks all carrying people, which was somewhat nerve-wracking. It was unlikely that any raiders would try to attack such a large convoy, an advantage Boris and his group have always had, given their large numbers, but it wouldn't be impossible for a group of very brave, stupid, or desperate people to try to attack them. It just would be impossible for them to win.

Boris also heard a faint voice in his mind tell him that if the convoy was ever to be attacked, it would be while he was driving. This was almost certain. The world often has a way of things like that coming true. Though anything would be preferable to being captured again by The Order, they could be attacked by some bloodthirsty group of cannibals or other crazed group. A person never really knows… He remembered for a second that cult that he'd been told the group had encountered after he'd been captured. It would be far-fetched to imagine that same group ending up in the area around Denmark, but something like it probably existed somewhere in the area.

Groups like that always find their way into existence. Boris would be glad to wipe them out of their reality t, but he'd definitely prefer it not have to happen while he was driving as closely packed as a sardine in its tin.

Boris continued to let his thoughts wander far outside the cabin of the truck as the hours passed, and the sun set without his noticing. The headlights flicked on, and he stared once again into the matte gray of the back of the truck he'd been driving behind for hours now. He'd already counted all of the visible scratches, bullet holes, and other imperfections across the back of it. Some of the bullet holes went through into the back of the truck, but there were very few and considering he was driving, a few meters back, looking into a truck that was also moving at night, he wasn't going to be seeing much through them. Even if he could, there wouldn't be much to look at. The back of all the trucks weren't illuminated, except for a slight dim glow from cheap lights. Most of the people back there were probably asleep by now anyway.

Yet Boris felt no fatigue. It felt like he'd been driving for days, but maybe the fact he wasn't constantly expecting to die or wake up in some new location against his will, his body was resetting itself somehow, in a way he'd never really understand.

The group soon stopped to rotate drivers, but Boris refused Jeung's request to drive, even though Jeung said he'd driven for long periods of time himself on the way to Berlin, Boris refused and told him to rest. Jeung had likely been working himself to death anyway. Jeung shrugged and went back to the back, muttering something in Korean before he was out of earshot.

Boris ignored this and went back to driving as soon as the truck in front of him started up. He gave himself a bit more space this time and found the truck behind him had done something similar, now not riding up on his bumper, but instead holding a few meters behind. Boris was more able to relax with this safer position and continued driving into the dark of the night.

Another few hours passed by, it seemed that the night was coming to an end. Boris was starting to notice a bit of fatigue, but still probably not as much as he should have by that point. He took a small shot of Vodka from his flask and continued driving. He wasn't going to drink much. He hadn't been drinking much before, and decided he needed something to keep him going. Since he'd mostly been driving in the same direction, a small amount wouldn't harm him, though he still somewhat regretted giving up any of his decisiveness or brainpower to the alcohol, despite the minor difference it was likely to make.

Józef, now was the only person who riding with him, as Arkady had switched over to the back recently, finally woke up, as he'd been sleeping for several hours by now.

"So. Really. How have things been throughout the company, Józef?" Boris asked

"Well... I'll admit there were definitely those who were beginning to lose hope considering that our leader had been stolen right out from under us, but I'd say the majority of us were willing to fight to the bitter end. Especially now that you're back, I'd say morale is at a high. Assuming we actually find a way to get to Svalbard, we should be in the clear. All we'll have to do then is make our way back to Moscow and start... rebuilding. Maybe if we find some other groups of civilized people on our way we could provide to them. We definitely owe the Partisans something when we return to Berlin. There could be some military equipment in Svalbard, as well... maybe we'll have the power to bring down The Order while they are weak, and we are strong. If we give them too much longer they will simply grow back, stronger than ever, and whatever we build they will eventually destroy. So, what's your plan in that regard?"

Boris thought for a few minutes, before a plan started to come together.

"Priority number one is still delivering the supplies and resources we get from Svalbard to Moscow, so we can get civilization running again. But bringing down The Order is just as, if not more important for everyone. So... maybe the best hope is that we send most of the trucks with those who are less able or willing to fight to Moscow, assuming we can trust that they will actually bring the vital cargo to Moscow and that they won't simply keep it for themselves. For those who are willing to help us fight, we will keep a few of the trucks and fight The Order with the Partisans. Whether we win or lose, the supplies will reach Moscow, and The Order will hopefully get destroyed. It's the best plan I have."

Although Józef felt that he already knew what the answer to this question would be, he asked anyway. "And where do I fit in this plan?"

"Józef.... I believe you are an adult and can make your own decision on this. The Order took your arm and much of your blood. I wouldn't dare stop you from trying to help bring down The Order. I'm not sure whether you can drive or not, but I'd trust that with you in the caravan of trucks going to Moscow, they'd all get there. I'll let you decide for yourself."

Józef nodded and smiled. "I'll think about it and try to do what's best for both me and the group. I wouldn't jeopardize the mission for my simple desire for revenge against The Order. But I wouldn't want to run while you fight."

Boris sighed, and laughed a bit, before saying, "Well, I know your mind is in the right place comrade. Whatever decision you make will contribute to our success regardless."

Boris handed Józef his flask of Vodka, partly because he didn't want to tempt himself to drink any more, but also to toast the man who was willing to fight when he was debilitated and had a clear way out, with no loss of the high respect of his fellow comrades. *All men should strive to be like Józef,* thought Boris.

With this, Boris' mood lightened a bit further, and the monotony of driving was becoming an afterthought as he instead began thinking about what he'd do once he returned to Moscow. Whether he would or wouldn't be hailed as a hero, he would return as a man who fought and bled for humanity and wouldn't give up until he'd rebuilt it, even if he had to do it piece by piece. Only then would he *truly* rest, and he could get on with whatever his life could be then. …He still had his situation with Elena.

Of course, there were still many questions remaining about what would become of things. Would the Moscow region become some sort of country? Would he be called to leave it? Would things, centuries in the future, go back to how they were before the war, with countries so often in conflict? Or would there be true peace? Would the destruction of the civilized world really teach humanity the lesson it needed for so long?

Boris shook his head to clear his mind and kept driving.

CHAPTER 32

After another half hour of driving, a radio came on in the truck that he didn't even know was there.

"Vasiliy here. Be advised, there is a roadblock ahead. It doesn't look like something that was up before the war. This could be the work of The Order or some other group. We will stop soon." This meant they were likely going to have to negotiate with somebody, though Boris had no idea what group that might be.

"Hey Józef, are we in Denmark yet?" asked Boris. "Józef, where are we right now?" asked Boris.

Józef looked at the GPS in the truck before responding, "We're just on the border of Denmark. However, I highly doubt that these are Danish soldiers holding us up."

The trucks began to slow to a stop, some pulling off the road. Boris stopped his truck and saw the ones behind him starting to slow as well. As he opened the door of the truck and began to step out, he readied his weapon, turning off the safety as he heard a voice come on over a megaphone.

"Attention. Turn back now. We do not accept visitors in our new society. If you don't return to whence you came, we will expel you with force, by the power of The Atom!" the voice spoke English in an accent that didn't sound Danish.

Boris laughed, and called out to everyone in Russian, "This isn't worth dealing with. Vasiliy, negotiate. Everyone else prepare to start shooting at them. If they don't accept our terms, then you are free to fire at your discretion."

Vasiliy began speaking to them. "We have the power to crush you a thousand times. We are on a benevolent mission for the benefit of humanity. Let us through or we will destroy you *utterly*. Don't say I didn't warn you." It was quite an aggressive form of negotiation, but it was probably the only sort of thing that would work against a group as prideful as this one seemed to be.

"FOOLS!" the voice shouted at over the megaphone.

Boris didn't waste a second.

"Fire!" He shouted.

From the trucks and those group around them fire erupted into the roadblock, mostly made up of a central two-story building, with a side building across from it. By the end of the minute, the windows on each of the buildings were shattered and the whole area was silent. Boris called out, shouting, "Anybody hit?"

One or two people called out saying they had minor injuries, but nothing severe. "I'm going to search through these buildings. You two, on me," said Vasiliy. Two larger men followed him into the building, and a few minutes later they came out with a few bodies and a prisoner, who still had the megaphone with him. They were all wearing robes, but unlike the masked cultists in Belarus they showed their faces and appeared less... Satanic, for lack of a better word.

However, they still didn't seem remotely rational.

The robes they wore were ragged, and all had a jagged symbol that looked like an ancient rune painted on them.

Boris walked up to the person that one of Vasiliy's men was restraining. "Who are you, who are you with, and why did you think you stood a chance against a so obviously better armed opponent?" he asked the prisoner.

The man in robes stood silent, and Vasiliy's other man hit him in the head with the butt of his rifle. "Talk," the rough man said to the robed figure.

The man in robes shrugged and spat down onto the ground. The interrogator turned the safety off of his weapon and pulled the bolt back. "*Talk,*" he said again, more severely this time.

The man in robes burst out, "You cannot hold me like this, heathens! You reject the power of The Weapon! I will tell you nothing!"

The interrogator shrugged and chuckled slightly. "Fair enough." He said. He fired once into the man's foot. The soldier holding the man in robes dropped him to the ground, clutching his foot and groaning. "Heal me! By the power of the Atom!"

"I will aim for your knee, then your thigh, then your stomach, and I will leave you to die until you give us information," said the interrogator.

Boris had never given this man much thought, but he was quite brutal with his interrogation. He figured that Vasiliy may have taught him considering this interrogator is obviously much more of a physical threat, which likely makes the whole process go much smoother, for fear that the interrogator could break an arm if need be.

The robed man continued to groan and cursed at the interrogator once again. "I won't tell you anything!" he shouted out afterwards.

"Your choice," said the interrogator. He fired again and hit the robed man in the knee as he said he would. The robed man wasn't relenting, however, and managed to go another ten minutes before he started to say anything.

"We worship the true power of The Weapon! It has recreated our world and cleared out many of those who plagued it! It is our job to cleanse the world of those who are left…" he said, his eyes unfocused.

"Where are the rest of your compatriots?" the interrogator asked.

"We reside around The Weapon! In the middle of the Broken Field it lays for us to repair it!" the man shouted out incredulously.

The interrogator shoved the robed man down violently and Vasiliy summarized what was said. "So, we face a cult that worships nuclear weapons. They've probably built huts around a field where some undetonated bomb lays. We could pass it by but getting rid of them and being sure the bomb is actually defused would probably be a good idea, as this bomb would be a great way for The Order to kill us on our way back."

Boris nodded in agreement and spoke in the affirmative. "He's probably right. Eventually we'll get our people this far west, once we've started rebuilding, to try to help them, and we don't need to deal with a cult while doing it. Might as well get rid of them now, or at least see if we can pacify them."

Nikita, who'd finished circling the area, searching for anyone else, then spoke. "So, is that the plan? Drive around a bit and try to find them? We don't really know what they are capable of. Try to get a better location out of that guy before we do this."

Vasiliy nodded at Nikita, and spoke to the Interrogator, who finally gave his name, Roman. "You know what to do. Aim for the shoulder next."

Roman nodded, and then walked over to the cultist who was still laying on the ground clutching his knee. "Location. Exact. Now. Or I break you," he said.

The robed man looked up with a scowl. "I won't tell you anything else, I will not betray The Atom!"

Roman waited for a second, thinking, then said, "We only wish to talk. Now you will tell me."

"No!" the cultist roared.

"Bad decision," said Roman, who then shot the man in the bicep. He was starting to run out of nonfatal locations at this point, but what else could be done, really?

Though the groaning from the man, he could be heard. "Not long from here. Before the first building, turn left. Then go forward. It's there"

Roman grinned and hoisted the man up. He dragged him over

to Dmitry and told him to give the cultist "temporary" fixes to his injuries.

Boris got back into his truck as everyone was rounded up and they began driving while on the lookout. They didn't gain very specific information, and they weren't diverging that far off course, but it was good that they now had an idea where to go.

After about fifteen minutes of driving, there was indeed an open field with several huts and improvised shelters built around it. Boris ordered everyone to search through the compartments in the back of the trucks for radiation suits, as a still-active bomb, even if undetonated, would almost certainly have made the entire area radioactive. The group already had two raincoats--yellow ones from earlier in their travels, but two people could be lost easily.

They later found about four more stark gray ones that seemed to be in good enough condition to use. Boris took one, Vasiliy took another, followed by Roman, Jeung, Arkady, and the man who'd originally held the cultist, Grigori Voroshilov.

The radiation suits were made of plastic and weren't easy to breathe in nor very flexible, so everyone could only carry a bit of their equipment. Boris carried only his Kalashnikov with a single spare magazine that fit well enough in the suit that he could get at it without losing it. This only left him with 60 rounds, but if he preserved his ammo carefully, it would be enough.

The group also took the man in robes, but didn't outfit him, as it seemed that he was averse to radiation suits and because he wasn't worth being put in one.

Grigori held onto the robed man, dragging him forward, as the shots to his leg significantly hampered his movement. However, his being present could provide some leverage in any negotiation, so the potential benefit in keeping him nearby was too great to leave him with the convoy.

As the squad of six plus their prisoner made their way to

the center of all the huts, the bomb became more noticeable. It was a large warhead imbedded into the ground. Small groups of ragged people began to quietly surround the group, all dressed in strange suits on an overcast day.

Boris approached the warhead, and the whispering from the crowd began to grow louder; several pointed at them. A few of them were armed, but none risked firing; even if the cult worshipped the warhead, they did seem to know it was fully capable of killing them.

As Boris looked at the warhead and analyzed some of the writings imprinted on to it, expecting that he'd see Russian, maybe Korean or Chinese written on it. But when he looked closer, his heart sank to the bottom of his stomach.

Ordis Ordinem.

This wasn't a Russian missile. Nor was it North Korean, or Chinese.

The Order launched this missile.

Boris's heart began to pound rapidly. He couldn't say anything now. He'd have to make his way back and confirm what the rest of the group probably just saw. He couldn't see his face through the visor of his mask, but when Boris looked at Vasiliy, something was conveyed through the toxic air that signaled they both understood what had happened.

Boris was about ready to turn around, leave, and never return to that place ever again, take it off any maps he could find, but he was approached by an older looking man wearing robes similar to the one the cultist he'd captured was wearing.

The bearded elder spoke, and said, "Come closer, creature. Who are you to approach The Atom?" he boomed.

Boris turned around, and in the split second he had to think, considered shooting the man down and burning the field to the ground. While he could easily kill the man there *were* people here, people who might return to sanity one day.

Boris blandly responded to the question with "Just passing through. We mean no harm, but one of your followers attacked us as we tried to get near."

"Is this true?" inquired the old man to his follower.

The injured man nodded his head solemnly.

"We greatly appreciate that you didn't repeat his… courtesy," Vasiliy said through the mask.

The elder turned to him and said, "We do not attack… guests. We only wish to exist with The Weapon and revel in its glory."

Now that the whispering had stopped, likely in reverence for this elder, Boris could hear the quiet ticking of his Geiger counter. The levels of radiation weren't as high as he thought they'd be, but at this level anybody left here was going to die within a few weeks, especially considering, how sickly the majority of them looked. He wished he could do something to save them, but they all likely had severe radiation poisoning at this point, so it was probably just best to leave them with what they were doing and wait for them to die off.

In this situation, I should at least try to keep The Order away from this place. If they ever did reunite the world under their rule, a bomb with their motto on it wouldn't look too good for them.

"Sir, we have full intention on returning your follower to you. Hand him off, Grigori." Grigori dropped the man onto the ground, who coughed up a small bit of blood.

"In exchange for sparing his life, we expect that you will let us pass, and that If you ever see a group dressed in gray donning masks, do not trust them, for they seek only to destroy," Boris said, hoping this negotiation would work.

The elder stopped to think for a second. He appeared to be contemplating the question, but the quality of his thinking was questionable, at best, considering the type of group he was heading.   However, after another minute of reflection, he simply said, "Yes. Go now."

Boris didn't skip a beat and turned around and left the area. The Geiger counter's clicking was starting to become maddening, anyway. Once he got back to the convoy, he removed the suit and he and Vasiliy looked at each other.

Vasiliy nodded, indicating for Boris to speak, and he did, since most of the members of the group were there, probably wondering why they hadn't heard any gunshots and what had happened.

"That bomb they worship...had The Order's motto written on it," Boris said, and he paused for a second, letting his words sink in. "While there is no way to know if it was among the first missiles fired, nor that The Order started the war, but they did fire it. I told the people at the bomb site to keep The Order from getting to it, in exchange for us returning their lackey."

Somebody in the group called out, "but what about the possibility their group could grow?"

Boris answered quickly, as he already had planned to respond to this question. "The bomb was still technically active, and radiation was leaking out of it at a pretty good rate. Everyone in that camp is likely to be dead in a month or less, for better or worse."

"So, with that in mind, we are going to continue north. We should be far enough in about two more days. Everyone, get back in to your vehicles," commanded Vasiliy.

Boris attempted to get back into the driver's cabin, but when he stumbled, he finally realized he hadn't slept in nearly a full day, so, instead made his way to the back, the full effects of his fatigue starting to weigh in. As soon as he got into the truck, he fell asleep on one of the seats.

CHAPTER 33

B oris woke up several hours later, almost at dawn. It was still dark. His eyes fluttered open, and he sat up. Once up, he felt the presence of someone next to him. He whispered, "Hello?" into the darkness. The dim light that usually was in the back of these trucks wasn't functioning, so he couldn't see much of anything.

"Hello," responded a voice. Even though Boris hadn't heard it for quite a while now, he knew it was Elena.

"How are you doing?" he asked her.

"I'm fine. I woke up not too long ago, how long was I asleep?" She asked.

"I'm not sure. It's been a few days at least. It's been hard for me to keep track of time given how I was for a while."

"I'm glad you're okay. Where are we right now?" she inquired.

"We are currently somewhere in Denmark. Once we're on the northern coast we're going to look for a container ship to take us to Svalbard."

"That's good. Can you tell me what happened to you? I can't begin to describe how different it was without you."

Boris proceeded to tell his story to Elena, not skipping any of the important details. Everything from when he was first captured to when he fought in their trials with the other Prospects and escaped. However, he left out the strange visions he'd had in transit to The Order HQ in Berlin.

Elena then described what had happened to her recently, and

Boris learned about the man who'd barricaded himself in that office building, the endless drive, the incredible amount of snow, the Partisan attack, and Otto's death…

The last months had been dark for all of them. However, Boris thought, *we are nearing the end. One way or another, this will all be over soon. Whether it ends in Svalbard, Berlin, or Moscow, it will end.*

Boris then began to conjecture that The Order could have known about Svalbard. It was a relatively well-known location, and it seemed like something that an organization like The Order could have something to do with… Perhaps it explained, in part, how they've thrived. If so, Boris could only hope that they hadn't sucked it dry, and that if they got there, it wouldn't be much before them, so they could at least fight for the area.

Then what about the logistics? Most of the people's uniforms were now black with soot and dust, badly in need of laundering. And it seemed they weren't well prepared for the cold, either, in terms of camouflage or actual equipment. --However, according to Elena, most of them did have winter gear they were able to wear while walking, and most of it was okay, but it didn't seem like it would be practical for combat. Hopefully it wouldn't come to that, though.

The sun soon rose, and Boris was beginning to tire once again from sitting so long in the back of the truck. He figured he'd wait through two more driver rotations, then he'd drive into the port, help them search, and sleep again once they were on the ships they'd hopefully find. In the meantime, he went back to resting, though he couldn't fall asleep. So, instead he continued talking to Elena and some of the others in the back of the truck until he eventually drifted off. Apparently, he still had some sleep to make up

He spent the rest of his idle time daydreaming, as he'd done on boring days before the war, usually spent with him staring out of his apartment window onto the busy streets of Moscow, Red

Square barely visible…

Eventually, the second driver shift came, and Arkady went into the back while Boris went into the front. Looking at his surroundings, it definitely still looked like Denmark. It was beautiful country, though still somewhat gray as everything was now. That was so familiar he barely thought about it.

He began driving, maintaining a reasonable distance between him and the truck in front of him, as he continued north. The goal was Aalborg, and according to the GPS it was not far, or at least not for Boris. In a few hours they'd be there and then they'd find a ship and take off…ideally.

The longer time passed, and the closer Boris got to Svalbard, the more pride Boris felt about what he was doing. He'd organized this. It was Józef's idea, of course, he thought as he looked to his right and saw Józef still in the front, asleep.

With his eyes back on the road, the weight of what he'd achieved really hit him. He'd gotten a group of random people to follow him to what seemed like certain death only a few weeks after the deadliest war in human history, crossing still-irradiated land, fighting a malevolent force, uniting two nations that were still fighting, in one area, then getting captured by the malevolent force, working his way through it, and making his way out thanks to the group of fighters *he'd* created. He didn't want to be some sort of Messiah, but even he couldn't deny that he was proud of what he was doing. When he returned to Moscow, the normal people of the world would again stand a chance to survive, and maybe what once had been normal *life* could return.

Then Boris's thoughts shifted perspective. He'd done bad things as well. For the first 100 kilometers, the people he was with didn't know where they were going. Some of those very people were dead now, including some he'd grown close to. Otto, in particular, as well as several of the Russian and American soldiers. Then there was Józef, who first had the idea, losing his arm, still not having full use of his leg.

The price had undeniably been heavy, but surely it was worth it? It would have to be. If it wasn't for this expedition, the original followers would likely have starved, the soldiers would have killed each other, and the other Prospects would have been indoctrinated into The Order, and added to their ranks.

After several more hours of driving contemplating these mixed bright and dark thoughts, the group arrived at Aalborg. It was in the late afternoon, but Boris still felt completely awake. The city wasn't as large as most of the other ones they'd been through, and they made it across the urban landscape completely undisturbed. There was absolutely no activity whatsoever in the city, or so it seemed. When they arrived at the commercial port, Boris was delighted to see several container ships. Most of the containers in them had probably been looted or only contained spoiled goods but searching a few couldn't hurt for the voyage ahead. The trucks pulled to a stop, and Boris got out of his truck, the first person to do so; he was very eager to begin.

He first decided to literally scope out the area, using the scope of his Dragunov rifle to scan the ships, and he didn't see anything… at least until he did.

A lone figure standing on the top of a container. He was swinging something down on to the top of it. Maybe trying to break it open?

He looked closer and saw that the person was not wearing an Order uniform, just some shabby looking clothes. Shortly after, someone else, smaller in stature, approached and tugged on the taller one's pant leg.

It's some sort of family, Boris thought. *Maybe we could help them? But depending on how aware of the news they were, they might not be happy to see several armed Russians around here. They probably haven't survived this long unarmed, so they might shoot at us on sight. Or at least the taller one would.* Boris waited for everyone to get out of the trucks, and miraculously remembered the names of the two people he was looking for: Jackson, the man Boris met in the middle of the Belarus battlefield long ago, and Gramza, the second to follow--two of the American soldiers. The two people on the ship would probably respond more positively to American soldiers.

"You two," he said.

"Yeah, Kasyanov?" said Gramza.

"On the third container ship, there are two people. They look like civilians. Maybe we can help them, but they probably wouldn't respond well to Russians. I need you two to go over to them and try to bring them over here, so we can talk to them. We'll follow behind you but stay out of sight. If something goes wrong, we'll do what we can to help you. You good with that?" he asked them.

Both of them looked at one another, then nodded. Boris waited for a minute before beginning to follow, gesturing for Vasiliy and Petya to join them. One pleasant person, and one not-so-pleasant person.

After a few minutes, Boris could see Gramza and Jackson through his scope, right next to the ship.

"Hey! You guys! We've got some supplies for you if you need it! We are soldiers!" shouted Gramza.

Boris didn't hear anything in response. A few minutes later, however, the two ragged figures appeared from behind the ship. The taller one was holding a pistol. The smaller one was following close behind but was unarmed. It was probably the child or younger sibling of the taller person.

The two groups engaged in a verbal exchange for a few minutes, but it was too far away and too faint for Boris to hear. Some of the things said made the taller of the two appear confused. This was likely the part of the very abbreviated story they were being told where the Russians and Americans started working together, or maybe it's about why they were actually at the port. Either way, the taller one, who Boris now was able to focus on appeared to be a late-teenage-year male. The smaller one looked like it was probably his younger sister.

After a few more minutes, Jackson gestured to the two to follow him. The taller one hesitated before agreeing. Boris then stood up, slung his rifle across his back, and dusted himself off. If he was going to be presented as the leader of this group, he'd have to look at least somewhat professional. He also removed his helmet and balaclava, revealing his uncut hair and beard. This actually looked *less* professional, now that he thought about it, but there wasn't much to be done about it.

After another minute, the two civilians were close enough for Boris to see. He was right, it appeared to be an older brother with his kid sister. Once the two of them were close enough to Boris so that he could make a somewhat long reach to shake the older one's hand, he spoke quietly to them.

"I'm not sure what they told you two, but I am Boris. We have no intent to hurt you and can help you."

Jackson walked over to Boris' side and quickly summarized what was said. Apparently, he'd told them that the war between Russia and America was over, and that the whole group was working to go to an island where a seed bank would be, so they could begin to rebuild.

Boris nodded his head and turned back to the two standing in front of him. The boy was about as thin as would be expected for someone living in these conditions; he probably hadn't eaten a full meal in a long time. The younger child seemed a bit more well-fed.

"How do we know you are who these two say you are?" the boy asked.

Safiri, who Boris hadn't noticed was relatively close by, said, "Because this man got several people, including myself and Americans, who should have been his enemies, out of the clutches of a truly evil force."

Gramza spoke, as well. "The whole reason that we're *here* is because of that. He and I were on opposite sides of the battlefield at first, but he brought us together, and even ended up sacrificing himself to get captured just to save us."

Several other people spoke briefly about how the group was indeed benevolent, but Boris started to tune it out. It was old news now, anyway. His sole focus was figuring out what he could do for these two and then heading off to Svalbard as soon as he could.

So, he stood quietly, waiting for a response from the older brother. "We don't need your help. We've been surviving on our own for months now, anyway." Boris shrugged, and said "Do you see yourself kid? You're starving, even though you are alive, you can't live like this for much longer. Everyone around here is *gone*. The closest inhabited place we've seen is Berlin, and even there it's only Partisans fighting The Order."

The brother stood for a few seconds, processing the information, probably wanting to make sure he said the right thing. He was, after all, surrounded by fighters with guns, and he only had a small sidearm for self-defense.

"Who is This Order you are talking about? Are they the ones in the grey masks?" he asked.

Boris looked over at Vasiliy, who had a grim expression on his face. Boris nodded at him, as Vasiliy seemed to want to describe them. "The Order indeed does have a fancy for grey masks, and grey uniforms. Grey everything, really. They kill people and captured our friend here" -he gestured to Boris- "and have done some serious shit. If you know who they are, when and where did you see them?"

The boy then spoke without hesitation, "Yesterday. They came through yesterday. They loaded up one of the container ships and sailed off. They shot at something earlier, and they certainly didn't look trustworthy, so when they were too far to be able to see where I was, I took a few... how do you say, potshots at them? A few hit them under the water line, but I probably didn't do anything."

Vasiliy responded quickly, "Excellent. We are chasing after them. We know where they are going, to the place *we* were initially going ourselves. When we get back, we'll bring you some stuff. Stick around this port and wait for our return. If you ever see any of their kind again, get out."

Vasiliy looked over to Boris and both of them knew they had no time to waste. Vasiliy called to Safiri, who began gathering everybody into groups. Boris asked which of the container ships the boy had been through that looked to be in the best condition, and soon after they began boarding the ship, with Boris directing the loading of supplies onto the ship. They arranged a few more logistics, like establishing where everyone was to sleep, and then Boris made his way to the captain's bridge. He looked down onto the deck, where dozens of his men sat on the containers, talking. Boris had never captained, or even been in a vehicle so large in his entire life. Soon, they were off.

CHAPTER 34

He was soon joined by Petya, who climbed up to the Captain's bridge about half an hour after they'd begun sailing into the seas.

"Notice how the further out we go, the bluer it gets?" he asked. The water was indeed somewhat grey at the port, but now it was starting to look like the ocean. It was still overcast, as it had been for months now.

"Yeah, you have a point, Petya. Have you ever been sailing?" Boris asked.

Petya chuckled a bit. "Only a few times, and never on something as large as this. I served in the navy for a few years when I was a young man. Never fought in any war, but I did sail the Baltic seas. It was beautiful, but never quite open ocean like this. I'm not an old angler or anything of the sort, but I've always had… an appreciation, I'd say, for the sea.

Boris nodded, and turned back toward Petya to speak. "This is actually my first time sailing. I've been through lakes and rivers a few times, but I'd never been out into the ocean… I was never a fan of it. Though sailing on this large a ship and seeing it from up here makes it much more pleasant."

Petya nodded. "Every man has their poison," he said.

Boris considered elaborating a bit more, when something hit Boris out of nowhere. *Ischez*. Boris hadn't seen him since they escaped the Order. It could be sheer coincidence of Boris simply not having seen him, but it did seem somewhat concerning.

"Petya, have you seen Ischez… err, Macintyre, the S.A.S. person?" Boris asked.

"I'm not sure I even know who that is. But there are two or three I heard who sounded British," Petya responded. He looked out into the containers, and pointed one out, a man looking over the edge of the ship. "That's one of them. Maybe he'd know. He sounded interesting, in any event."

Boris thanked Petya and left him at the helm. "I don't know what to expect, I doubt Ischez would seriously try to jeopardize this expedition, without trying to recruit others, except for Józef, Elena, Nikita, or Vasiliy." Petya nodded quietly, before locking the helm behind Boris.

Boris made his way down onto the deck. He descended the stairs to where the Brit was, still leaning over the rail.

Boris stood next to him and leaned over the rail, as well, trying, though somewhat distracted, to think of what to say first. The ocean was sucking away his focus, as he watched the gentle waves ride past the ship.

"So, what's our glorious leader doin' 'ere?" the man asked. His accent was strong, stronger than most of the others, and despite the variety of accents he'd heard from the people around him, he found it hardest to understand the British.

"I could come up with some bullshit, but I'm only here to ask if you know the whereabouts of McIntyre."

"That wanker? Scary. I know 'e was with us at the port. It was 'e, I, and Henderson I think. But no, I 'aven't seen 'im."

"Thanks, comrade. What are you doing here, though? Not a fan of boozing with everyone else?" Boris kept his face straight, but sort of wanted to laugh.

"Nah. Not a… people person, y'know. That, and, well, I do have a slight tendency to get seasick. But watching it 'elps a bit."

Boris allowed himself to laugh a bit at that one. "I thought you Tommies were known for ruling the waves?"

"That was before they put those really big-ass guns on the boats.

Then the Yanks started overtaking us. Like a son that outdoes you and gets all the stuff you wanted at 'is age. An' while I don't fancy the ocean much, you should talk to Henderson… though he's Welsh. Watch him, you might catch something from 'im." The man laughed a bit.

"I'll keep that in mind. What's your name, Tommy?"

"I'm Gill. Like the fish. Bruce Gill. Honestly, my last name is really just the universe taunting me, y'know. It knows I get seasick. Bloody hates me it does."

"Good to meet you Mr. Gill. Where's your Welshman?"

"Said 'e was gonna 'explore' below decks. 'e's probably wanderin' around lookin' for food and such. I wouldn't be surprised if 'e cracks open a two-year old can of tuna and eats it like birthday cake."

Boris chuckled slightly, and thanked Bruce for the instruction.

Boris then began to head towards the decks below, but before descending he waved up to Petya on the bridge, who gave a short wave in return.

The bottom of the ship was quite dark. Boris, luckily, had found some night vision goggles. He couldn't remember whether they were originally his, or if they were just with his stuff Dr. Ward returned when she brought the truck back, but they were useful, nonetheless.

Boris every minute or so, would call out Henderson's name in a speaking tone. After about ten minutes of searching he established that he wasn't on the deck right below the top, and he began working his way down. He figured that Henderson would be on the bottom deck, a good bit below the water line. As Boris crossed onto the bottom deck, only running quick searches through the ones before it, he could sense somehow that he was then below the water line.

He took a minute, mentally, to appreciate that. He was moving forward under water, with people tens of meters above him. It wasn't the sort of thing anyone would usually stop to think about, but Boris was sometimes fascinated with the little things, and this was one of those times. Once he snapped out of it, he began calling Henderson's name again, this time a bit louder. He had a good bit of ground to cover, but he didn't expect to be there too long.

Then, after about fifteen minutes of searching, he found Henderson, passed out against one of the walls with a large, empty bottle of beer next to a broken crate, packed with more alcohol.

Boris walked over to him and squatted down. He turned on the flashlight that Henderson had lying next to him and shined it in his face. He forgot to take off the goggles, so was temporarily blinded, but once he removed them he looked at Henderson, who had snapped awake and looked like a deer in headlights. There was only one empty bottle, so he may not have been completely drunk, but he definitely wasn't all there.

"'o're you? What are you doin' 'ere?" He asked Boris.

I'm the leader of this expedition, and I wasn't hoping to find one of my men passed out on the bottom deck of some rusty container ship. I need to know about McIntyre, and where he is. What can you tell me?"

"Well, I'm not supposed ta tell you," Henderson replied.

"Yes, you are. It's just that I need to… verify that was he already told me is true. He's up on the deck, waiting for you."

"Wot are you talkin' about? 'e isn't on the deck, e's not even on the ship, 'e's… bugger. You got me, sneaky bastard you."

"Where is that you said he was again?" Boris asked snidely.

"Fine. 'e's in Germany. Once we got ta port, 'e said 'e was gonna drive back to Germany and keep fighting The Order. Thought you guys were insane with your plan. 'e took one of the trucks and supplies, that's all."

"And why did you stay, Mr. Henderson?" Boris inquired, his face struggling to not curl into a grin.

"Welp, bein' 'onest, I liked 'avin' a steady supply of food," he said.

Boris was beginning to question who this Henderson was. He couldn't be a part of the S.A.S., that was for sure.

"Mr. Henderson, what is it that you do that got you into The Order's Prospect system?"

"wot 're you askin' for?" He asked.

"Curious," said Boris.

"I was a *physicist*," said Henderson, who then gave a stupid smile.

Boris laughed for a second, but then realized it was possible. After all, The Order wouldn't only have kidnapped military personnel to run their operation. This physicist, however, did seem to be a lightweight. Boris probably wouldn't have gotten this information out of him if he hadn't he been inebriated.

"Alright then, *physicist*, I'm going to take you back up onto the deck, and you're not going to drink anymore. If I find you down here again I'll put a hole in the ship and use your ass to fill it," Boris said. He then dragged Henderson up the stairs, who was incomprehensibly protesting the entire way up.

Once Boris got him back onto the deck, he found Gill waiting, and laughing at the top of the stairway.

"I'll take care of 'im from 'ere, mate. Just drop 'im off," he said.

Boris nodded, and then headed back to the bridge. He realized there really wasn't much that he could do about Ischez, and that he was probably just going to have to try to find his corpse when he returned to Germany. He *was* S.A.S., but there was no way any single man could do any real, significant damage to The Order.

So, Boris shrugged it off. Really, out of everybody in the party, he was probably the one Boris minded losing the least. Though, for all he knew, Ischez could stay alive and they'd end up finding him standing on top of the rubble of one of The Order buildings.

Boris made his way back to the bridge where he found Petya looking out over the deck like an old captain, manning his ship after a long period of time on the land.

"You're a natural captain, Petya," Boris said.

"Aye, Captain Boris," Petya responded, and he laughed his bear-like laugh.

Boris laughed in turn and sat down in one of the chairs. The sun was beginning to set now, and he looked out onto the deck once more. Some people were beginning to clear out of it and go below decks. He then leisurely looked out into the distance, cloudy, but calm.

He then discussed with Petya how to divide up the captaining. Petya decided he'd take the night shifts, as Boris being awake, during the day would allow him to better keep order.

Boris found the captain's quarters after looking around a few minutes, and went to sleep relatively quickly, as the sea caused the ship to rock, creating a gentle sensation of constant, pleasant movement.

CHAPTER 35

B oris woke up early the next morning, and relieved Petya of his duty, allowing him to sleep. Boris left the bridge soon after and went down into the lower decks of the ship to get some food he could eat throughout the day. It was all relatively simple, but what he got would be enough to last him. They'd be sailing today and probably two more days after. They were, of course, still a day behind The Order, but if they ended up getting to Svalbard, a day wouldn't be enough for them to gather everything from the seed bank... but it would be enough to destroy it, though hopefully that wasn't what would happen.

That, and technically speaking, it was not guaranteed that The Order was even going to Svalbard, though it wouldn't make any sense for them to be going due north with any goal *but* that.

Boris continued to stare into the waves, not looking at anything in particular. As it turned out, captaining a ship this large in a linear direction wasn't very demanding, though he definitely had to make some changes as time passed--but, fortunately, so far he wasn't having to battle rough seas.

He'd look down onto the decks occasionally, and saw that most people were talking, generally grouped up based on what country they were from or some other group identity. There were, for example, the Russian soldiers, the American soldiers, and the Prospects. However, they weren't divided into competing camps, but just socializing with their comrades.   Boris   continued at the helm the rest of the day, fell asleep at the same time as yesterday, and woke up the next day to repeat it once again. Now, the air was becoming noticeably colder, and some people decided to stay below deck, while those who chose to stay above did so with improvised winter gear.

Boris continued on with his day, eating breakfast and lunch as he'd done the day before, but then he saw something brewing in the distance that was beginning to worry him, just as the sun was beginning to set once again.

Is that a storm!?

This can't be good.

It was a storm. Massive cumulonimbus clouds were drifting towards the ship, and the waves on the high seas were increasingly rough, crashing up against the hull. Boris quickly activated the ship's intercom from the bridge. "Attention all personnel. We are sailing into a storm. It is unavoidable. Close all entrances to the bottom decks and take everything with you. Stay under until further notice. I repeat, clear the deck!"

All of the people above deck quickly gathered their things and rushed down below. Within minutes, the deck was cleared and now it was just Boris who had visibility of what was happening; everyone else could only hear the sounds--the creaking of the ship, the waves crashing onto its sides.

Petya was up within five minutes, and despite not having gotten his full rest, seemed alert and awake. He first asked a single question in a calm voice, "Is everyone below deck?"

Boris nodded, but didn't take his eyes off of the ocean around him, nor did his hands leave the wheel. He didn't know what to expect, as the environmental impact of the war could certainly have affected the tides. Though impossible to prove, this could mean he could be facing something that nobody before him had.

Within the next half an hour, the water began to swirl around, crashing not only into, but entirely over the deck of the ship. When one of the waves nearly got high enough to reach the bridge, Boris began to lose his nerve. His heart had already been racing for the past hour, but now the sweat was starting to drip down his face, locked in a grimace.

The ship creaked with every impact, and Boris had to fight the wheel to keep going in the right direction. A compass embedded into the panel in front of him stayed true, pointing north, but the needle jerked violently at every wave.

Boris couldn't imagine what those below decks were experiencing. The top deck was covered in the water of both the sea and rain, as both crashed into the metal beast, the thundering impacts never ceasing. It was maddening.

Boris tore his eyes off of the bow of the ship for one second, to glance over at Petya, his fingers locked onto a bar on the wall like fish hooks, his face unmoved.

"I've said it once months ago, I'll say it once more, Petra said. Today isn't my day. I can feel it in my bones. I'll die before letting anybody in this party drown, so fate must be on our side!" he shouted over the roar.

"Sir yes sir!" Boris shouted in response, not having the time nor stoic calmness of Petya to think of a better reply. He was holding the wheel for dear life, fighting its every urge to curve the ship into the waves hitting it, surely capsizing the whole vessel.

The storm seemed to be never ending, drenching everything in sight; Boris had never seen this much water in his entire life. His world was water, and he was fighting the water. He was at war with the world.

Boris looked on beyond the port side of the ship, and there it was. Like something out of a movie, or a video game; a monster of a wave, immense in size.

If this catches us, it's going to drag our wreck to the Norwegian coast! Boris thought. He was starting to panic. If this wave hit the ship at this angle, the ship would capsize instantly and the whole thing would be plunged into the ocean, at least four dozen kilometers from any land.

"Sail into the wave!" Petya shouted.

"What!?" Boris shouted back, bewildered.

"SAIL INTO THE WAVE! TURN NOW OR WE WON'T MAKE IT!" Petya said, his voice booming over the crashing of the wind and waves.

Boris couldn't think of any other idea. There was no option. He looked over to Petya, his face still unshaken. Boris wished he could have the bravery of this man one day.

Boris used all of his might to turn the wheel to the left, and the massive ship began to turn. The wave was getting ever closer, and it was unlikely to be aligned perfectly to the wave by the time it passed. It was, however, the only option available.

The wheel was fighting him. Boris couldn't hold it for much longer; it was going to have to hit soon, or he was going to lose it all. The wave got closer and closer, and was now almost in front of them.

It was so close, almost on the edge of the ship. Boris slapped the intercom button and shouted with all the energy he had, "BRACE YOURSELVES!"

Then the wave hit, and the force ripped Boris off of the wheel and into a wall, and everything went dark.

CHAPTER 36

"BORIS! BORIS! BORIS!" Boris heard his name shouted by a familiar voice. He was dizzy, and thirsty. He felt dehydrated as well.

Boris shook his head in an attempt to clear it and opened his eyes. He was against a wall, presumably the one he'd been thrown against. Petya helped him up quickly and told him he'd only been out for ten minutes, but that he was bleeding a bit. Boris reached up to his head and felt a bandage. The spinning in his vision was starting to wind down, but his head ached.

Boris stood, finding he could do so without falling back down and stumbled over to the wheel. He was astounded to see that the sky was clear. He told Petya to continue the ship north, and he rushed down below to check on everyone.

There were several who had small bruises and cuts, a few had been thrown against something and were still unconscious. However, it seemed nobody had died. Boris continued searching through the people until he found Elena, alive and unharmed, as well. They rushed into a hug and she quickly kissed him on the cheek.

"Glad to see that you're still alive," Boris said, not bothering to think of anything more eloquent.

Elena nodded, but stayed silent. After another few seconds of embrace, they separated and Boris made his way back to the bridge. There would only be one more day of sailing, and from here he would have to be ready to face The Order whenever he found them.

Given that Boris' "shift" as captain was almost up, he released the wheel within an hour of his taking it up again and fell asleep, the eventful and chaotic day finally coming to an end.

When he awoke the next day, it was to Petya shaking him. "You slept a bit late, but it's no matter. What does matter is that there is a trail of oil coming from a large container ship like ours due north."

Boris, having just woken up, took a second to process the information, but then realized that it might have been The Order's ship. The closest thing to a possible explanation he could come up with was that the bullet-holes below the water line in the ship triggered by that the kid at the port and had grown larger after the storm. What was clear is that they were approaching The Order and would reach them before they got to Svalbard.

Boris was able to confirm with certainty that the other ship was going slower as theirs continued to approach it. The Order's ship wasn't dead in the water by any means, but it was definitely moving slower than they were.

Several hours later, The Order's ship came into view. Boris was going to have to be there for any conflict. Even though he enjoyed captaining the ship, his first duty was still to command his forces in a situations like these.

The bow of his ship and the stern of the other ship were now only about 150 meters apart at most, and Boris used the loudspeaker to announce to the group what he was sure they had already seen themselves.

"Attention all personnel. We are approaching a container ship that we are relatively certain belongs to The Order. The plan is to begin shooting at them to try to damage them as much as possible. We cannot hope to sink a ship as large as that, but if we can damage it enough we may be able to both weaken them and beat them to Svalbard. Petya will be taking over as captain for the time being."

As soon as he finished his announcement, he ran down the stairs to make it onto the main deck, where those in condition to fight were preparing to do so, including Olivia, who was already prepared, and walking over to the bow to begin taking potshots at the other ship.

"I feel like one of those Caribbean pirates, going to raid some merchants on the high seas," she said.

Boris laughed, and said, "I'm relatively certain pirates didn't have rifles like this, or giant container ships, but it does have that feel, I'll admit."

By now a large number of their people had their weapons over the rails of the ship, crouched low, and ready to fire upon Boris' order. Boris pulled out his Dragunov rifle and looked through the scope to try to identify his first target. They were indeed Order troops, still dressed in grey, all back to wearing their masks. This time probably due to the frozen air more than anything else. Some of them, however, were wearing a patch on their right arms which read "Centurion" in Latin, one of the few words Boris remembered from his short time studying the ancient language.

These were probably some kind of elite group, but from what Boris had seen so far, most of The Order's soldiers, even their so-called elites, were still inferior to even standard pre-war soldiers. He did give them credit for having mobilized so quickly, but that meant they had very little time for training. Just because The Order had lots of money and resources didn't mean they could train their soldiers in a short period of time, and that was one of their fatal flaws.

Boris finished lining up a target, his crosshair right over the head of one of the centurions. "FIRE!" He shouted. He pulled the trigger of his weapon, and the man he was aiming at dropped to the ground, dead instantly. His fighters were firing at all parts of the ship; several shot at the captain's bridge, some shot below the water line, possibly trying to create enough small holes to sink the massive ship. Others just shot into the top deck, trying to kill the crew members.

Boris lined up another shot, aiming at the chest of one of The Order's Centurions. He then saw a shot hit him. But the bullet struck his armor and likely bounced off. The centurion stumbled back, yet the bullet didn't go through. He wasn't a huge man, but he was carrying a light machine gun, and managed to keep firing it. Boris figured he was first shot by an assault rifle caliber, so maybe his Dragunov could punch through.

He squeezed the trigger, and the bullet flew directly into the armor. It went in, the bullet didn't bounce off this time, but the man kept standing. The centurion reached into a container strapped to his leg and pulled out a syringe, which he quickly injected into his arm. He then dropped the syringe and kept firing, though he got a bit lower to the ground before he did. Boris looked behind him, and the bullet hadn't passed through. Somehow, this average-sized man just tanked a very powerful shot without going down.

Boris could only have guessed the syringe contained a pain-killing drug, which must have been enough to keep him going. Boris lined up another shot, and when he squeezed the trigger this time the shot ripped through the man's neck, and he started choking and bleeding heavily as he slumped to the ground.

Boris then shouted out, "The Elite soldiers have body armor!" He figured most already knew this, but it was worth making sure everyone was aware. He looked over to his side, and saw Werner, Volodya, Safiri, and several other of the Prospects fighting beside him; on the other side were Arkady, Zhenya, Jeung, and Dmitry. As Boris turned to look at those friends on the right, he saw Arkady take a shot to the chest. In slow motion, it seemed, Arkady fell as blood shot out from his back and the bullet that hit him crashed into the wall behind him. Dmitry dropped as well, but not because he was hit. He tried to tend to Arkady, but it was obvious he had died within seconds. Behind Dmitry, someone else fell, an American soldier, and Dmitry then turned and went over to them.

Boris turned back to face The Order and fired a few more times. It seemed as if no dent could be made in the Order's numbers at all. He looked up towards the captain's bridge, and saw a standard soldier trying to control the ship. Boris shot him in the stomach, causing the soldier to jerk the ship, which had been a bit ahead and to the right of Boris' ship to the left.

Shit.

Boris had hoped he'd turn right, as then they'd begin to drift off in the wrong direction, but now they were starting to turn directly towards the front of Boris and his ship. However, instead of continuing forward, the ship stopped dead, and Boris' ship began to catch up. Once they were almost even, the enemy ship started off again. Boris looked back to the captain's bridge, and the person he saw triggered a flashback to a few weeks before to seeing a video of one of the Big Three Order leaders. Boris, with a complete lack of patience, shot at the figure, and his bullet ripped into their arm. Not a miss, but not a good hit either. The figure stumbled out of the way and Boris cursed himself for not waiting for a better shot.

It appeared that the figure was the head of Defense and Expansion. Boris couldn't remember if he had been given a name or not. He only remembered a bit about what he'd seen, but he recognized the buzz cut and athletic build. It couldn't be anyone else.

The gunfight continued. The Order's casualties were higher, than they had been before, but Boris realized their ship was starting to fall behind now, probably slowed down even more by damage from the gunfire. But their overriding purpose was to get to Svalbard; if they made it there first they might have enough time to prepare a defense.

The two ships had been close enough that using the Dragunov became impractical, so Boris showered The Order with assault rifle shots as everyone else had been doing, and the deck of the other ship was covered in bullet holes and the dead. The Order had never managed to get an organized defense, so most of those who'd died had been hit where they stood at the beginning of the attack. As more time passed, The Order began to retreat to the lower decks. It was likely they still had a large percentage of their soldiers, but they must have finally realized that Boris' men were ready to shoot at the next person to try to scramble up onto the deck, so they didn't have the time to reorganize. Boris considered jumping ship with a few of his best to try to clear out their ship, but at such close range, personal skill matters much less; it's just who can react quicker.

Eventually, the entire top deck of The Order's ship was soaked in blood and covered with the bodies of at least forty of their soldiers, a few of which were their Centurions. Such a massive ship likely held a few hundred, but they still had inflicted heavy damage both to their combatants the ship; if they were lucky it would sink before it reached Svalbard.

As Boris' ship passed theirs, and they slowly faded into the fog, Boris watched through his scope at The Order's soldiers who had returned upside. Some of them, not in uniform, were clearing the deck of the bodies, dumping them into the ocean. Boris didn't order anyone to fire on them, as provoking more conflict was likely not a good idea at this time.

Boris eventually made his way back up to the bridge. The window looking out over the deck was shattered, pieces of broken glass littering the floor, but there stood Petya, relatively unharmed minus a few scratches, only bleeding visibly from one across his brow.

"Don't worry about me. I can captain a bit longer. Check on your men," he said, and Boris complied.

Boris made his way down to the deck, and in the center all of the dead had been gathered.

There were nine, in total. One of them a Prospect Boris didn't know by name, Spanish, if he remembered correctly; two American and two Russian soldiers; three soldiers either from Vasiliy, Józef, or Nikita's groups, including a very short man, a fit woman, and one who'd already been covered up. The last one was Arkady. Out of all of those he'd chosen, Arkady was the least talkative, and the one Boris felt he'd known the least. But when he'd initially recruited him, there was something about him that told Boris he'd be a good soldier, that he'd be brave. Boris was right, but now he wondered if he should have chosen someone else because Arkady's appearance of bravery and strength brought him here, got him killed.

Boris stood over the dead, all now covered in a large sheet, and took the opportunity to speak about those who'd died.

"Today, we lost a number of good people. We have lost many in the past. Some very close to everyone, others that perhaps no one even knew. However, all of them went down bravely, continuing on to the best of their ability. Before today, our group has been in perpetual motion; we didn't have the time nor option to slow down. If we had slowed, then by now The Order may have made it to Svalbard and taken everything we've tried so hard to acquire. However, today, we have the chance to stop and remember those who have been lost throughout this journey. Everyone here knew and still knows the risks we have taken and will face in the near future…" -Boris began to pace around the ship, looking everyone in the eyes as he passed them. "I greatly appreciate all the dedication I have seen from you all. Maybe you had nothing to lose, maybe this is what you saw as a noble cause, but in the end, it is no matter. You are still here, alive, and now we remember those who are no longer here, or alive. And I cannot guarantee nor say that everyone remaining will live and return to safety. Some of us, and I am not exempt, may die, but if we do, we will have done so for the common good."

With this, Boris stood in line with some others, all armed with the weapon of one of the fighters, Boris armed with Arkady's weapon, an SR3M "Whirlwind" assault rifle. Along the line there were two AK-74Ms, two M4s, a Canadian C7E, and three Kalashnikovs of various models. The bodies were all moved to the edge of the ship, and as each would be put to rest in the deep, the person with the corresponding weapon would fire it into the sky.

Arkady was last, and just before his internment at sea, as Boris examined his weapon more carefully, he noticed a small picture taped on the left side of the rifle; it was of a small child, maybe three or four. It looked like an old photo, the girl in the picture having Arkady's eyes. She must have been his daughter.

Boris shook his head quickly, not allowing himself to feel any of the emotion that might try to break through his flat expression, before continuing on with the ceremony. He then watched as Arkady was lowered into the water by a winch, before drifting down, and out of sight.

When Boris made it back to the captain's bridge, it was dark. Boris could tell that Petya was starting to wear down. Boris then called over the loudspeaker for a volunteer to pilot the ship for the night; lo and behold little Yevgeny showed up a few minutes later.

Boris had no intention on denying him what he was sure could have been his dream, but jokingly said, "I'm not sure I want a fifteen-year-old piloting my ship." Yevgeny's face hardened, and he said, "I turned sixteen a few days ago!" Boris laughed, and sat down with Yevgeny, explaining the basics of how to pilot the ship.

efore Boris retreated into his quarters, he called out to Yevgeny. "And don't get us shipwrecked! If you do, I'll… well, I won't be able to do much, because we'll be at the bottom of the ocean!"

Boris fell asleep fairly quickly that day. Seeing Yevgeny alive with his enthusiasm intact, made the day more bearable despite the losses and deaths.

CHAPTER 37

When Boris woke up the next morning, he found Yevgeny still sitting at the wheel, awake, but visibly tired. "You are relieved of duty, comrade," he told him.

Yevgeny nodded quickly and rushed downstairs, probably to get some sleep. Boris returned to the captain's bridge, and for the first time noticed the cold air blowing through the huge hole where the window used to be. He put his Balaclava and helmet back on--a good decision, as he began to notice his breath was visible in the air.

Then, after another hour of captaining, Boris suddenly heard Nikita shout from somewhere towards the front of the ship, "Land ho!"

Boris looked out over to the horizon, and there it was, only barely visible; a jagged island, right in front of them. A glacier was off to the west, showing how far north they truly were. The thermostat on the bridge registered twelve degrees below zero. Soon the cold that Boris first felt on his face started biting into his hands and feet, and he returned to his quarters to retrieve some better winter gear, including a torn white sheet improvised by Vasiliy the previous day for light camouflage. It fit over the uniform in one large drape, covering up the green print on his uniform. It wasn't perfect, but now it was a lot less likely he'd be visible. When Boris went below deck to retrieve some food, only about ten kilometers out from the island, he found Vasiliy, Yevgeny, Elena, and even Roman, surprisingly, working on cutting holes in drapes of white cloth and fitting them around people, While the ship they were on had only one or two containers with usable food, it did have lots of miscellaneous resources that could be used for all sorts of things.

Boris ended up watching Vasiliy and his group's process of making the improvised camouflage for everyone. Then out of nowhere, Werner, who'd just gotten his, said, "Couldn't you cut this into thinner strips we could wrap around our heads?" He gestured over to Boris, still wearing his helmet, as green as the uniform he'd already covered up, and then continued, "Because the way it is now, the enemy will simply be able to target our heads more easily."

Vasiliy looked at Boris, then at Elena and the others working with him, and nodded. "If you start working on it, it can happen." In the end Boris got roped into it, and there were about twenty people working on making both the body and face camo out of the sheets. By the time they'd arrived at the island, everyone was suited up.

Boris had to remove his helmet, but he let his balaclava remain, as it provided valuable warmth for his head and face. When he was up on the deck as the ship was coming very near the island, he looked over a few of his hundred plus fighters, all now as white as ghosts. When he thought about it, the outfit looked somewhat look like ghosts that American children would dress as for their Halloween, except with guns.

The ship weighed anchor about eighty meters from land, as the water was too shallow beyond that. Boris decided to be the first, followed by one of Józef's men, a stocky man with glasses who apparently had been an engineer for the Ukrainian military back in the day. He held the explosives they would use to get inside the expansive vault.

Boris got out from the bottom level of the ship and stepped into the water. It was cold; the type of cold so frigid that it burned, but there was no going back now. He sloshed his way through the water, making his way to the shoreline while the Ukrainian followed behind him, albeit at a somewhat lower speed.

When Boris made it to the icy shore, his legs from the knee down were soaked. He knew this could cause frostbite if he wasn't careful, but surely there would be some sort of heating in the vault.

Boris rushed up the slight incline, and immediately began looking for the entrance. He knew it was there, on this side of the island, but he didn't know what he was looking for, or if the entrance was buried behind a wall of snow and ice. If that was the case, they'd be there for quite a while.

As he began looking, the stocky man caught up, attempting to catch his breath, before he took out a spade and began scraping some of the snow away from the giant wall piled up on the side of the island.

Shortly after, several others followed behind, in the order of Vasiliy, Nikita, Jackson, and Gramza in the first wave.

They spread out and began searching. Soon more came, and before too long there were about fifty people spread out, digging through different parts of the mountain. Thirty minutes later, Jeung shouted out, "I've hit something metal!" and everyone rushed over to him, at least once they could distinguish where he was in the sea of white. As it turned out, the cloth drapes had made excellent camouflage.

The group gathered around the location that Jeung had indicated, and the Ukrainian man scraped away some of the snow, revealing the door. It was sealed shut, and it was clear they had no intention of just "letting people in." There was no doubt a *correct* way to do it, which was likely quite different from the way they were about to gain entry, but hopefully that wouldn't matter.

However, there could also be some sort of security system somewhere…

This thought, however, was interrupted when the Ukrainian shouted at everybody to stand back, and Boris was snapped back into reality and dived into the snow. A second later, the bunker blew, and an entrance was blown into the structure. Boris stood to the side of the entrance, and then Gramza and Yevgeny were drawn inside. Boris heard the sound of something turning and he yanked Yevgeny outside of the bunker. In the next split second many shots were heard, and Gramza stumbled backward, out of the bunker, hit multiple times in the chest.

Gramza sputtered out his last words, just before hitting the ground; "Holy... shit..."

Dmitry dragged Gramza off and started trying to resuscitate and bandage him. Boris had seen this routine enough times to know that it was only symbolic at this stage; Gramza was gone. Boris looked back over to Yevgeny, who he was still holding away from the entrance, and Boris could see in Yevgeny's eyes that he was afraid, but grateful.

"Eventually, you get a sense for this sort of thing. I guess yours is still developing," Boris said gruffly. He couldn't afford to lose anyone else. Now he needed a plan for how he was going to get rid of whatever had just shot at them.

Boris got to the edge of the bunker's entrance. He peeked his head out for a second to see if he could catch a glimpse of whatever the deadly threat was. It likely wasn't a person but he knew that he had to be very careful disengaging whatever it was. What he saw were several machine guns, designed similar to a turret, that were projected from the ceiling of the building. Surprisingly, two out of the three had been destroyed. The remaining one didn't look armored, so maybe it wouldn't take that much to disable it. He slowly brought up his pistol, the weapon that was easiest to get around the corner while exposing as little of himself as possible and positioned the barrel carefully just around the corner. Even though he wasn't looking at his target now, he adjusted the aim a bit. Then he fired, and heard some sparking alongside the gunshot.

Boris dared another glance, and saw that the turret was drooping down, sparks bursting out of it; out of commission, permanently.

Boris then turned the corner, and was quickly followed by Jeung, Nikita, and Zhenya, who'd initially almost gone in right behind

Gramza.

Boris scanned the hallway they were in, and there didn't appear to be any other defenses. Maybe that would be it. Now it was time to see if they could turn the power on; his legs were starting to feel numb, definitely not a good sign.

Boris walked over to a wall, where there were markers pointing to the locations of different sections of the building. He dusted off some of the ice frozen onto one of them, and it read, "Generators." This was probably the right direction.

Boris then began to follow the snaking hallway, trying to not let the ominous silence get to him. There was nothing, no sound.

The others who had followed him split up and went on separate paths. There were no other gunshots as time passed. Boris got up to the door in which the generators likely were located. If it was possible, he'd try to start them up. Hopefully that wouldn't activate any more defenses.

He kicked the door down and did a clean sweep of the room. He didn't expect to find any humans, but there could still be some automated defense mechanisms that could attack him which weren't reliant on the generator's power, like the turrets at the entrance.

There was nothing; it was empty. But he did find the generators. They were old, and huge. Now he just had to find a way to start them. There seemed to be some kind of control panel centered behind all of them. Boris walked over to it and tried to contact some of the others through his walkie talkie; but the signal was jammed. If anything started happening outside or in other places he hoped he could hear it.

The control panel was relatively simple. There were two buttons under a glass panel covering it--a green one, presumably to turn on the power, and a red one, presumably to turn it off. There was a slot for a key next to the panel, and Boris assumed that was a form of security.

Now standing, with his legs still freezing, although not as much as it was significantly warmer inside, he had to think of how he would deal with this. He had several solutions he could try, all of them relatively simple, but he couldn't be sure about their ramifications.

For one thing, he could simply search for the key, but with The Order not that far behind he may not have enough time. He could try to pick the lock, but if he did something wrong, that could alert some other component of the security system. His other option was simply to bash open the panel and press the button. If anything was to cause a reaction from the security system, it would be this, but time was currently not Boris' friend.

So, Boris raised his rifle, the stock facing down, and crushed the glass cover with a mighty swing. Without hesitating, he smashed the green button with his full fist, the broken glass creating small lacerations in his hand, but in the biting cold he felt nothing.

The generators roared to life, lights began to turn on, and Boris instantly felt a wave of semi-warm air. He then began to search for more signs, as they were now beginning to thaw. Before he could find one pointing to a central HQ, he heard Zhenya call out, "Boris! Over here!"

Boris rushed through two doorways and a hall to find Zhenya, trapped between two walls of laser beams. "What do I do!?" he asked, the anxiety in his voice apparent over the buzz of the lasers. The sign next to the small section of hall he was in read, "Control Room."

"Don't move. Touch one of those lasers and I'll shoot you," Boris exclaimed. It *was* somewhat redundant, as the lasers were probably connected to explosives, but the point got across very effectively. Zhenya didn't move at all.

Boris looked to see where the lasers were coming from. He quickly discovered that the light originated from small cracks in the wall. Boris thought for a second. That meant that the wall in between the location of the bombs and where he was now was quite thin… probably thin enough to shoot through. Now the only problem was shooting through the wall could detonate the explosives contained beyond it or not. He then reasoned that he was going to have to guess where to shoot to avoid setting off the detonator within the bomb. A small section, for sure, but the device itself could be small. He quickly assessed that it wouldn't be towards the back of the explosive since it would have to be close to the sensor. *Probably.*

Boris first called to Zhenya. "If something explodes, sorry. Don't move. I'm going to try to shoot it and disarm it."

"Are you insane!?" Zhenya shouted back.

"Probably. Hey, if it explodes, we both die. So, it's not like I'm making you an expendable factor here."

Zhenya didn't say anything, and Boris first aimed about as far from the sensor as he reasoned it could be. He shot once, aligned with one of the sensors, and the bullet passed right through, hitting nothing. He could see a faint glow from the other side of the wall, but a single bullet hole was too small for him to be able to discern anything. He shifted his aim a bit to the right, fired, fired again, and then once more.

He took a deep breath, holding his weapon as steadily as he could, and fired still again. He heard light sparking after the sound of the gunshot stopped resonating. He didn't see the glow anymore. Boris turned into the hallway to see that the lasers closest to him had been deactivated. As soon as he processed this, Zhenya sprinted out of the hall and stood behind Boris. Boris looked at him, shrugged, and threw an empty can he had with him into the second laser set.

BOOM!

The bombs went off, and, conveniently enough, the explosives had blown the door to the central room open. Whether this was actually supposed to happen, or if it would have been any real trouble to open the door, were completely debatable. What mattered was it seemed the last trap had been "disarmed" and Boris could enter the control room. The door that was blown open led into a staircase that spiraled down. When Boris made it to the bottom, Zhenya behind him, with the others rushing along with them him, likely because they had heard the explosion, he saw what he'd been searching for this entire time--a massive conservatory filled with plants.

This, of course, wasn't what Boris would be taking with him, at least not the plants themselves. When they'd finished dealing with The Order here, they would deconstruct some of the heating appliances so the seedlings wouldn't have to deal with the shitty weather outside but could instead grow in the Metro.

Finally, Nikita had caught up to Boris, and shouted "ORDER TROOPS ONLY A FEW HUNDRED METERS FROM THE ISLAND! BORIS! GET THE HELL UP HERE!"

CHAPTER 38

Boris snapped out of his premonitions of the future and turned to run back up the stairs and out of the bunker. The Order's container ship had almost made it to the island. Boris looked around him and had a somewhat difficult time seeing individual soldiers on the ground, though their weapons were generally easy to see. The camouflage appeared to be effective.

Boris got himself a reasonable distance from the entrance to the bunker and pulled out his Dragunov rifle. He sighted in on the front of the ship, where he saw the leader of the whatever-the-hell-it-was division, and deeply considered attempting to shoot him on the spot. He probably could, he probably *should*, but the sportsman in him wanted to give him a fair chance, so he held off. Besides, he planned on waiting to have a greater impact on the enemy.

Through his radio he directed everyone to wait for his signal to fire. At closer ranges their weapons and shapes could be distinguishable, and the more Order troops on the island when they ambushed them, the better it would be.

So, they waited.

And they waited.

They waited a bit longer.

And then there they were. The Order began unloading troops from their ship, while several were lined up along the side of it, aiming at Boris' vessel. Boris urged his men not to fire at the ship, at least not yet. If they could, they'd incapacitate it but that was not the directive; the number one priority was making sure they weren't capable of interfering with them getting what they needed, whether The Order's troops had to be chased off... or utterly destroyed.

Boris shifted his view to those exiting the ship. Surprisingly, at the front of their group stood the leader of Defense and Expansion, dressed in grey, with a peaked cap. Boris likened him to a German Officer from the Second World War. Boris thought back to a book he'd read, or maybe it was the movie adaptation evoking that image. He then messed with the frequency on his radio for a minute, until he found the one that The Order was using.

"Greetings Major Koenig. For now, I'll introduce myself as Vasiliy Zaitsev. And at this moment I'm capable of putting a bullet between your eyes."

In a strong, cold German accent, Boris heard the response. "There will be no miracle for you here. You won't shoot me. You have a sense of honor. A weakness we both share. I know your troops are hiding in the snow. However, your forces are halved at best. You put more value into the safety of your vessel. I have roughly 80% of my troops, and my full unit of Centurions. Many of my soldiers are no better than peasants in terms of soldiering, but abundant resources have their advantages. Many of my soldiers have thermal optics and can see your men spread out under those tarps, thinking they have the drop on us. Call them out of hiding. The two of us will settle this like men. This location is the source of *your* goal, and *my* goal. So, reveal yourself, *Zaitsev.*"

Boris's grip on the trigger of his rifle tightened, now centered over the Leader's heart. But he looked into his eyes, and saw the man, looking directly at him, smirking. If Boris shot right now this conversation would haunt him. This man was too wise, and potentially useful, simply to be gunned down. Boris stood up and slung his rifle across his back. He drew his pistol and his knife, then marched to face his enemy. As he did so, he removed his balaclava, exposing his face to the below-zero temperatures. His breath was visible in the air as vapor, and he could feel the cold biting into his flesh.

"STAND, COMRADES!" he shouted. Over his radio, he heard Nikita's voice. "Surely, we aren't surrendering, Boris?"

Boris responded, "No. Quite the opposite. It's just that a decision has been made between me and their leader. It seems we may engage in some kind of duel. Don't take your gun off their men though, not for a second."

Boris then saw Nikita and those others he presumed had heard him stand, rising out of the snow in front of the entrance to the base like guardians rising to defend an ancient temple.

Several paces later, Boris met the enemy commander in the middle. They were of similar height and build.

"I see you've already come prepared. So, what shall it be? Shall we duel it out as the gentlemen of old with our sidearms? Or would you prefer a more aggressive approach with your blade?"

Boris weighed his options. There was definitely an incorrect answer here. Boris sized the man up; he was already armed with a Swiss pistol in one hand. Boris then noticed a fairly large blade sheathed on his hip, about the size of a small machete. Obviously, the incorrect answer was to fight with the blade.

"I'd rather you not bleed on my uniform. Let us settle this like gentlemen." Boris tossed his blade to the ground, where it stuck into the snow. He then removed his body armor as well.

"Wise choice," the German said. He drew his blade and threw it similarly to his side, while also discarding a type of body armor. "But we may turn to these if we manage to run out of ammunition… though that surely will not occur."

Boris nodded, and drew back the slide on his old pistol. He was also at a disadvantage here. The pistol his opponent was armed with, a SIG P226, was a modern handgun designed for use by Special Forces units and high maintenance, high caliber security forces. The weapon had a capacity of around 16 rounds, if he wasn't mistaken.

Boris, in comparison, had an old military surplus pistol with 8 rounds. But he had two things in his favor. For one, this pistol was designed for this sort of environment; the round it fired perfect for penetrating winter coats. But more importantly, this was his father's pistol, and his fathers before him. This pistol kept his grandfather alive throughout the now second-deadliest war in human history. It would carry Boris through the aftermath of this one.

Boris looked into the sky and felt something pass through him. From the heavens his grandfather watched him. He will be made proud.

Boris looked back to face his opponent. "A Tokarev? Interesting. A shame I'll never hear the story of how you got it."

That's true, but not in the way you think, Boris thought.

He lined up, back-to-back, against his opponent. A Centurion on one side, Petya on the other.

"TWENTY PACES! TURN, AND FIRE ON YOUR OPPONENT!" Petya thundered.

"BEGIN!" He shouted.

"ONE! TWO! THREE! FOUR!" Petya continued counting out the paces. Boris held his pistol tightly in his hand as he approached twenty. With every pace his heart beat twice as fast. But on count eighteen, a strange calmness washed over Boris. *I have nothing to fear.*

"TWENTY! FIRE!" Petya roared.

The next second happened in slow motion, as moments of such high adrenaline always seemed to.

Boris spun around, fully aware of his surroundings; the crunch of the snow under his boot; the frigid air biting into his flesh once more; his finger, already halfway through pulling the trigger. His weapon centered on his opponent almost immediately. Boris fired once, and then all was silent.

The next few seconds were nothing but a vacuum. Boris fired several more times and saw blood spurt from his enemy in more than one place. But then the sound came back, and he fell to the ground. The reverberations of the gunshots were still sounding, and Boris found himself on his knees. He looked down at his chest. He'd been hit, exactly once. Blood slowly trickled out of the wound. He used his arms to try to stand himself back up and felt a burning across his left arm. He'd been grazed there.

Boris had no idea how he had the strength to stand; maybe because his opponent's bullets were less effective penetrating clothing than his? The SIG fired a 9-millimeter, a fat and slow cartridge in comparison to Boris' 7.62-millimeter.

But stand he could, and he walked over to his opponent. As he stood over him, he saw that he'd been hit two times. Once in the torso, once in the upper right bicep.

The man was still smiling, though he coughed up a small bit of blood. "You're a good shot," he said.

Boris nodded gratefully, then made a decision he never would have expected of himself. "Dmitry. Tend to this man. See that he lives, if at all possible."

Boris looked over to the man, shrugged, and said "I guess you have to break the honor code eventually." Boris knew that generally, if one is down he is to accept it and die, but Boris thought he could get more out of this intriguing man, or at least learn more information about The Order in general. Either way, he was to live… for now.

Dmitry began to drag the man away, and The Order soldiers that weren't wearing their masks stared blankly. The tension in the area escalated. Boris backed up to face his group and reached down to his canteen.

There was a bullet lodged in it. It had penetrated his skin, just slightly, causing only light bleeding. The chances of this were incredibly low, but evidently Boris wasn't yet destined to take a serious hit… though, granted, his wound did hurt a great deal.

Boris was now alongside his men, and some from both sides were beginning to arm themselves; loading their weapons and making other prep. Petya came to check on Boris, and he shrugged it all off, though he showed what had saved him and caused all of the remainder of his vodka to leak out.

But then, out of nowhere, one of the people on The Order's side shouted, "What are you waiting for! They took the Head of Defense and Expansion! We must retrieve him! For The Order!"

Boris was taken off guard but shouted for his group to return fire. Because of the close range, the battle quickly became a melee. Unfortunately for the soldiers of The Order, they weren't armed with knives and so were forced to use their weapons as blunt clubs against Boris' troops, who fought much more capably. After The Order's soldiers realized their ineffectiveness at close range, they tried backing up. But they were under severe fire and had nowhere to go.   Within the next few minutes The Order's botched assault had mostly been repelled, and one of the Centurions called for a retreat; about half of those remaining stayed with him while the others ran back to their ship.

Boris helped to finish off those who continued to fight, their total lack of organization making them very ineffective.

Once the gunfire ceased, Dmitry ran up to Boris. He had some blood on his hands, as he reported the Head's condition. "He's alive, sir. You got about as close to killing him *without* killing him as you could have done. Kindly do not do that with one of my patients again."

Boris nodded, and then descended back down into the bunker. When he got back into the central room, he found Nikita, Zhenya, and Jeung already working to deconstruct some of the seedling equipment. Boris took a duffel bag left in that room and entered a large warehouse-like room containing the seeds for all of the plants in the world… It was spectacular in scale, but luckily, they were divided into separate small containers so gathering them wasn't hard.

Boris gathered the seeds of plants he thought would be useful, things such as potatoes, carrots, all kinds of vegetables, though with no careful thought, as he wasn't a botanist. He likened this to some sort of heist, but what he was taking was much lighter and not remotely shiny.

After a while longer of selectively choosing plant seeds to bring back, he exited the room. He saw that the other three had collected most of the equipment needed to help grow the plants--artificial lights, heat lamps, etc. Zhenya had several large bags of soil over his shoulder, and various other things that, although small, would help regenerate some form of agriculture, to fulfill the original plan.

Soon, a large amount had been collected, and Boris exited the bunker, where five more replaced him to help gather the remaining containers and other resources. There was no point in leaving much, so they planned to loot the place dry; that way none of it could get into The Order's hands.

Boris began the trek back to the ship with Zhenya, Jeung, Nikita, and Vasiliy.

CHAPTER 39

"So, this is what we came for, all of what we'd been chasing after this entire time?" Jeung asked.

"Well... Yes, it is. This was the goal, and now we can give Moscow a stable food source. We obviously haven't been there to experience it, but once the food stocks run out I fear what people will do to one another."

Jeung nodded. "I knew hunger back in Korea, that's why I came to Moscow. Interesting that the hunger followed..."

"How... was your life in Korea?" Boris asked him.

"I lived in one of the poorer neighborhoods of Pusan for most of my life. For many years, I had run-ins with gangs. It's how I became proficient at hand-to-hand fighting. There never was space for a gun in the alleyways and corridors."

Boris tried to remember what Jeung had initially told him when they'd first met, and this did fill a few gaps. It was strange he'd known him for so long now but even at this moment still there were many things he did not know.

Within the next few minutes they'd made it back to the ship and were able to store the equipment in the brig. Boris looked out over the bow of his ship after he'd made it to the main deck and watched as the groups of five entered and exited the bunker, carrying all manner of things. Within the hour, the last group left and entered the ship.

Boris then turned on his heel and went to the other side of the ship, where the head of Defense and Expansion was being held, both tied down and being treated at the same time.

He was very much conscious, and it appeared Dmitry had already extracted the bullets from him and was now focused on stopping the bleeding while also making sure that he was still secure.

Boris squatted next to the man and started asking him questions. "So, how about a name, you have one?" he asked first.

"Do you expect me to talk? To say anything? What would I have to gain from that?" he responded.

"Well, the simplest answer is that given your organization's immorality throughout most of its existence, I nor anyone else here would lose much sleep if we threw you off the boat, or simply marooned you here. So, you can decide not to talk and die, or you can give us what we want, and you will maybe not die," Boris responded, cocking his head and smirking with his last remark.

"Obviously this is why you didn't kill me in our duel, though honor dictates you should have… but fine, I'll oblige your first question for now. Paulus. Indeed, the same name as the general who commanded those in Stalingrad… though no direct relation."

"Interesting. I might as well give you a name as well. Kasyanov. Indeed, the same name as the soldier who burned down your company's headquarters in Riyadh… though the name is the same because I *am* that soldier."

"It couldn't be anyone else could it? A shame I was never there in person, I never dealt with Riyadh, but I did hear the story of how it burned."

"I'm quite the legend then, eh?"

"Well, the never-captured half of a pair of Russians who'd been harassing a major military complex for months before burning it to the ground does become quite a concern for the company running the complex."

"So, then, to the questions I originally intended on asking. How exactly was it that you came to join this… company?"

"Have you ever heard the saying, 'All wars are fought for money?' It's the words of Socrates, and he was correct. I was a soldier once, but I was not getting any of the real money at stake in the wars I fought. There wasn't even a war; so, I decided rather than waiting for one, I'd go to a group that could start one and advance so far in that group that I could leave the fighting and dying to others, while taking the profit for myself. The way I saw the moral dimension of my oversight of those fighting and dying is that it was their inability to understand this truth that got them killed to begin with."

Paulus paused for a moment, and looked off into the distance, into the horizon, before returning his view to Boris, his gaze as icy as the arctic waters.

"And being part of a company, our organization had much less of the triviality than nations have; we have no citizens, only employees. No innocents to protect, only those fighting and those commanding those who fight. And for the cost... well, as long as we kept our wars confidential to the public and a fear in the minds of those we dealt with being at our mercy, there was never a lack of profit. And to quote more from history, 'To wage war, you need first of all money, second, you need money, and third, you also need money', those being the words of one Prince Montecuccoli."

"So, if to wage war all it required was money, why are your soldiers so ill-trained in comparison to mine? Many aren't military, though admittedly many are. What made your soldiers ineffective in the Pan-Arab war, and what makes them ineffective now?" asked Boris.

Paulus continued, "It's simply a balance of numbers and security. Numbers were never a problem; I'll get to that later. Security was the main concern, of course. I'll give you one more piece of rhetoric, but in my own words... 'The most powerful truth a superior can tell a subordinate... is a lie.' The Overseer is the superior to all of those subordinates, and he, indeed, hasn't done anything but lie to them. Do you really think that the average soldier of our company knows what he's doing? I won't deny whatsoever that our actions are directly harmful to the average person. Our objective simply has been to expand our power until there was no other competing force and we could then run the world our way... but do you think that's what our soldiers think they fight for? Of course, it isn't. Why not? Because they *don't think.*"

Paulus sat silently for a minute to allow his words to sink in and gather their full effect before he continued.

"They don't need to think to do what we want; having our men think is directly counter-productive, according to the Overseer, as then they would realize we've been lying to them this whole time and would turn on us--and there goes our army. So, we take that aspect out of it; we think for them. They are happy and are constantly fed the 'answers' to their questions. Therefore, we have a completely obedient fighting force, and, besides, the state the world is in now, it isn't hard to recruit the many without masters. Take those Middle Eastern soldiers that invaded France. Along with us encouraging that invasion, the estranged soldiers remaining there after the bombs dropped have made up a significant portion of our forces for some time now. Many have indeed slipped through the cracks; the smart ones from all of the groups we draw from do. They are a good example of how we can afford to throw away our soldiers."

Dmitry, who'd still been treating his wounds, at these last words, stood up and spat on the floor in front of Paulus, the most expressive thing he'd ever done, a quite powerful act at that. Dmitry then composed himself and walked elsewhere in the ship to tend to a few other wounded troops.

"And of course, the other reason is that your group of fighters has really been the only obstacle to our expansion. At first, we didn't think we'd need a very strong or elite army, just one that looked intimidating and had just enough bite to keep people in check. Cities fell like dominoes once the bombs dropped. It was really much easier than expected. We let the armies destroy each other;

then we dropped the first bomb, and everyone panicked because they didn't know who did what. Out of the ruins we emerged and simply walked into Europe's biggest cities. Even in Asia and America, where our other enterprises were, our forces simply marched into cities and took them, all of the surviving population simply having to accept our rule, while those surviving outside of cities were not significant enough in numbers nor equipment to truly be a threat."

Paulus cleared his throat, expecting a reply from Boris, but Boris instead asked a question to keep him talking.

"You do openly acknowledge all of the wrongdoing of the Overseer, so what's kept you in a position like this? I wouldn't even be surprised if you betrayed him and simply took his place rather than simply leave."

Paulus responded, "It's the equivalent of being the president of a country. A very small, poor, insignificant country. Everyone under its rule is miserable, but your job is to manage them, and your life is, if not easier or better, much safer and more profitable. So, I could be leader, or I could be in exile. However, if it hasn't occurred to you already, I am in practical terms impartial to who wins in the end, so I haven't been trying very hard to kill you, only to find you."

Paulus stared deeply into Boris's eyes, as if confirming what he'd found in the person who'd been causing his organization so much trouble for the past months, before he began talking again, although on a somewhat unrelated subject.

"And I'm sure you want an update of how things now are in the world. Lucky you, I'm one of the only people who knows. So, we'll go by continent. We'll start off easy at Antarctica. Some scientists were there when the bombs dropped. They probably aren't there anymore. South America, then. Unfortunately for South America, drug cartels don't care about global thermonuclear war, so it's divided up between what remains of the cartels, which in most cases have become minor feudal dictatorships, against the pockets of regular people fighting them. We've yet to set foot there, and we don't plan to. South America Is a very hungry lion's den, as neither side would take kindly to us and we needn't give them anything to unite against."

And in those sentences Boris learned the fate of hundreds of millions of people, an imperceptible number that somehow didn't faze him, despite his sympathy for those suffering.

"Now for Africa, unfortunately in similar condition to South America. Small warlords run small states while others fight them in perpetual battle. They weren't as affected by the wars directly, but instant loss of Western support for their countries and trade left the nations to fight each other until the nations split, and now those split-off factions fight one another."

Another billion-people's story told, yet still nothing that can be done for them. Especially for those already dead; though who had it worse, Boris wasn't sure.

"As for Asia, it's been in a similar situation to Europe. However, the nuclear weapons weren't the direct killers, starvation was. In the massively populated countries, there was no longer a system to support the huge numbers of people. Stocks of food ran out quickly, and then people either began to fight for the food sources or try to join up with those who would fight for them. Our presence there has been negated by the sheer number of people to deal with, and the fact those people have been less than welcoming to our advances."

This was not a billion people, but several billion. Reduced immensely as the rest of the world has, once again something Boris was powerless to help.

"Second to last, North America, though mostly the United States is of concern. Surprisingly, or maybe unsurprisingly, the number of armed Americans and those who'd prepared for things like this led to unusually high survival rates. The United States now exists more as a loosely connected network of communities that are constantly harassed by bands of those seeking to steal from them. Lots of the urban Northeast is still in our control, but the further south and west we go the more bands of armed rebels we find and fight, making our progress very slow. Honestly speaking, it's just a matter of time before they pull themselves together and push us out. That's not me being defeatist; it's just what's going to happen."

Boris was less surprised here. America was a very unique place, and he wasn't surprised that it managed to hold together. They were once his enemy, but only in terms of his duty. America was truly an incredible nation, managing to withstand even the deadliest of wars, even in its current weakened state it. Maybe, one day, he could go see the Statue of Liberty, the Empire State Building, and all of those famous landmarks he'd heard so much about on the internet and on postcards.

"Now, of course, Europe... I'm sure you've heard many stories about it. A unique case, really. As you know, our presence was strongest here. Yet our inability to pin down your group of fighters has been our downfall and is obviously why I am in your capture now. What you haven't heard are the stories of those still fighting. Those you've spoken to have only seen what you have. After you broke up that fight in Smolensk, on the one front of the war that was still being fought, you managed to get the soldiers to cross lines and shake hands. Together they then turned to fight us as we approached. Since that turning point, we've never made it into your motherland, and have been steadily getting pushed back this whole time."

Boris felt the greatest impact with this news. His actions early really *did* stop a war, albeit only to fight another...

"And of course, what you've probably realized is the reason we've been unable to crush you is because there's been a war going on for the past months, one you've conveniently run straight through and past. Our soldiers, as many as we have, are, as you know, of low quality, so at the rate we must replenish them we cannot afford to break any off to crush you, or we'd face a total breakthrough. So, without realizing it, your men deciding to cross that battle line fucked up everything. If it hadn't happened, you'd likely have been dead a long time ago, and we'd have had a chance to recover. This would be especially true if I'd managed to convince the Overseer to kill you, though he thought you were too useful to destroy. Your damage had already been done, but those soldiers you turned on us wouldn't suspect anything, and we'd be able to hide out until we could rise again. But no, now you're coming for us. You're coming for us because of your incredible success and our incredible failure, and that's the simple fact. The entire reason I've been so talkative is because I've known for the past few weeks that we are doomed… it's just that *you* didn't know we were doomed."

Boris was absolutely stunned, his heart racing and his skin breaking into a cold sweat. So much has been going on all around him, and he never knew, never had the slightest inclination that his selfless, though rash and impulsive actions were what had gotten him this far, that he'd practically stumbled to success, and that it would likely be told as a hero's tale, him being portrayed as a warrior and tactician twice of what he probably was. Boris looked into the sky, and he knew that there was no other word but--destiny. The one created for him to fulfill. It mattered not whether he knew the impact of his actions, but they had consequences that had ultimately saved Europe and the world, through one small act of mercy.

In the end, through all of the killing, it wasn't the enemies he'd killed, all of The Order's plans he'd foiled, all the times he'd fooled his opponents, even his capturing of Paulus here, were very small in the face of the impact of one pure and good act he'd made.

"I'd like to give you an offer, Paulus," Boris stated, trying not to show his anxious state.

"You do now?" Paulus responded, obviously taken aback.

"You've told me more than I could have asked for, and you've been brutally honest. I know you've been truthful as every time you've spoken, your gaze never wavered; your voice stable. I know what you say is true and you cannot deny it, cannot confuse me. So here I'm offering you not money, fame, or fortune, but a chance to make up for what you have done. Maybe you have regrets and maybe you don't, but you can easily be beneficial to us. I'm not going to simply free you, not yet, but when the time comes."

Paulus responded, "You're as insane as the Overseer said you were. But I can see you mean what you say, and to be honest I'm surprised you haven't thrown me overboard by now. I expected that because I supposed you were simple-minded, a barbarian who solved his problems only with brute force. But as I've studied you, I've grown to admire the tact and intelligence you've shown, whether or not you believe you possess it. You are far worthier a leader than the Overseer ever was… he's a sad, unfulfilled man. You have spirit, and you have a purpose. So, I accept your offer, Mr. Kasyanov."

Boris simply nodded, turned on his heel, and retreated back to the bridge. On his way up, he saw Petya on his way from the bridge, who waved as he passed.

CHAPTER 40

B oris entered the bridge. Elena was sitting in one of the chairs and she gave him a small smile. "So, what did you get out of that guy?" she asked.

Boris closed the door behind him and took his own seat in front of Elena, shifting slightly before he began speaking. "Well, I found out many things… the inner workings of The Order, how they get all of their soldiers, what's been going on in the rest of the world… basically the answers to most of the questions I've had for a long time."

Elena nodded, and asked him to elaborate.

Boris then proceeded to tell Paulus' story, about his indifference to everything he was a part of, and about the fate of the rest of the population of the planet. Then he stopped to find a way to tell her about the forces that had been pushing The Order back.

"Elena," he said.

"Boris?" she responded, confused as why he'd changed his tone.

"Do you remember when we met those American soldiers, and one of them stopped that fight, and you saved my life?" he asked.

"Well, of course. That was one of the greatest things I've ever witnessed in my entire life," she said.

"Well, according to Paulus, the news of that spread north and south across the front, and all of the armies continuing to fight each other with none gaining anything, instead joined together and started fighting The Order. It's the reason that we've practically been able to cruise through Europe. Almost all of their forces are concentrated attempting to hold the line, and therefore they've decided to try to brush us off, not realizing how much we were achieving. If he's right, it's now too late for them to do anything but hope we fail in the inevitable second battle in Berlin."

Elena took several minutes to sit quietly and mull over the information. It really was a lot to take in, to realize what Boris had said, that everything they'd done in the past weeks and months was made possible by that one action. If not for that, the sheer number of The Order's forces, as was evident when Boris was captured, would have crushed them all.

"That's... incredible. Something told me that there was going to be a greater effect from that action than what we had seen. But now what we must do is finish this. We have to finish it all, and then finally go back home."

"And that's exactly what we are doing. In a few days we'll be back in Denmark, and then... well... it's the last battle."

"Yeah, it is. But what then?' She asked.

"Well..." Boris's mind froze for a second, as he tried to think of a good response. "We'll figure out what we do. Whatever it is... I want to do it with you. That's all."

"I... yeah. I don't know what we'll do either, but it can't be without you."

Boris smiled lightly, his face certainly giving away his relief. Elena had never been able to be his main focus, there was always the mission, but there was a connection, and when he returned home, she could, just maybe, become his new focus, and maybe his life.

"If you don't want to sleep below deck... you can take the captain's bed. There's a nice recliner in that room I wouldn't mind sleeping in. The captain must have been a rather short man, as the bed is a single and quite small, but it should be fine."

Elena smiled, and at first insisted Boris keep it before giving in to his refusing to sleep in the bed. Whether she would or not, as

286   JAKE BARATKA

it was indeed too short for him.

They sailed for the rest of the day. When the sun set and Petya came back up to take over the wheel for the night, Boris did as he said, and slept in the chair. In the end, he surprisingly slept better than he had for several days.

The next day he awoke, and got back to captaining, with Elena by his side the whole day, as they made idle conversation. Nothing too exciting, but it passed the time. At around 16:00, late in the afternoon, Dmitry entered the captain's bridge, obviously less than pleased with something. "Why are we keeping this rat alive?" he asked as soon as he'd stepped into the captain's bridge.

Boris made a face and gestured with his hand, saying "We may not be for long. We can make some use of him when we're in Berlin. His knowledge of their headquarters could help us greatly. Whether or not we shoot him after that is up in the air."

Boris noted in the back of his mind he may have to keep up with this half-lie, as while he was telling the truth in saying he could very easily end up shooting Paulus, he lied in implying it was at all likely to happen. Given how cooperative Paulus had been, he'd already given up so much of the advantage he would have needed had he intended to escape that there was no practical reason to seriously distrust Paulus's word.

Dmitry seemed satisfied with the answer. As he left, Elena gave Boris a look, and he returned it with one that he hoped expressed he'd indeed partly lied to him. The issue wasn't pressed any further, and the rest of the day was relatively peaceful.

Boris went to sleep once again in the reclining chair, awoke, and then captained for the rest of that day, the day after it, and into the last day with no real issue. He had several conversations with the others, but ultimately it was a far more pleasant return trip than the going trip.

Towards the end of that last day, they dropped anchor in the Danish port, and slept one more night in the ship, before the process of "unpacking" began, the people gathering their supplies and moving them into the trucks which, surprisingly, were still there, though--granted--the city was virtually abandoned... except for one.

Another surprising thing was that the trucks hadn't been stolen by the two they'd met when they originally got to the port, and that they were actually waiting for them when they arrived. They did as they promised and offered them the vegetables that had already been planted and grown. And, at Yevgeny's request, they also offered them to join them on the trip back to Moscow, as there was nothing left for them there. They accepted, though Boris made them promise to stay out of any of the battles they got into. He could bear the loss of soldiers under his command, but not children.

By noon, the rest of the supplies had been loaded onto the trucks, and they began driving back the way they'd come, with Boris once again driving for a good deal of the trip. When they passed by the area where the warhead was, Boris decided to peel his truck out of the group to investigate, and, indeed, it was nearly a ghost town. He pushed the place out of his mind and rejoined the group.

CHAPTER 41

Towards the end of the trip, he didn't drive at all, as he knew he would need to have as much energy as possible, because he'd be commanding one of the most important operations of his entire escapade--finally driving a stake into The Order's heart.

In the same amount of time it took them to leave the city, they returned. First, they tried to meet up with the rebels. When they did, they got some shocking news about the progress of the armies that had been pushing The Order back.

As it turned out, they were almost at the gates of Berlin, but a few miles from where Boris and his group were now. They'd been pressing especially hard against The Order's line to try to assist in Berlin once they'd heard of Boris' plan.

This, as Boris found out, was due to Ischez, who'd taken the truck and driven to the Allied lines to explain the situation, before returning to Berlin to continue the guerilla war against The Order.

Once Boris and his fighters were welcomed back into the Headquarters of the German Partisans, he immediately began searching for Ischez. When he found him, he looked a lot more beat up than he had before, with bandages around his arms and torso. He said he'd been shot a few times, as well as having to escape and hide in less than ideal positions, leading to his current condition. Dmitry took him aside and examined him to make sure he hadn't caught anything. Despite his physical injuries, he appeared mostly unafflicted.

Marvin, Otto's old friend, also seemed to be holding up reasonably well considering his situation and what he'd done. It clearly had been an accident. And, anybody would have done the same thing in his situation, but it didn't really change the weight what had happened.

The Partisans looked a bit more disheveled than they had when Boris last saw them, likely due to the added pressure from The Order, with the majority of their reinforcements now fighting in the area, but they didn't show any signs of wavering or defeatism.

After some discussion about the logistics of the situation with Hans, Boris decided that the plan most likely to yield success would be to wait for the other soldiers to arrive in Berlin first, while Boris' group and the Partisans constricted The Order, attempting to weaken them as much as possible before the arrival of their reinforcements.

So, with that, Boris' group spent the rest of the day around the area, however on alert as if The Order would ambush the group at any moment and attempt one last time to destroy them without fighting on their own ground. This was right after they'd arrived and still weren't particularly organized.

There didn't appear to be any aggressive action from The Order, and the rest of the day was quite peaceful. Most of Boris' men ended up spending the night in an abandoned building across the street from the rebel headquarters, with guards in rotating shifts to ensure that if nothing else, the supplies in their trucks wouldn't be stolen or attacked.

The next day, Boris got up to the sound of gunfire and explosions. He stood up as quickly as he could, picked up his weapon, and leaned out the window, looking for the source of the noise. He couldn't see anything, but people were rushing down the halls descending the stairs, so he knew that everyone was on alert.

By the time Boris got out to the front of the building, many of his own fighters and a good number of the Partisans were already gathered.

After several minutes of tense waiting, with gunfire still going off to the East, Boris assumed that this meant the battle had almost reached them. Within an hour of that, everyone's radios activated, and a message was broadcast.

"THIS IS CAPTAIN SENAVIYEV OF THE RUSSIAN ARMY!" Another voice cut in temporarily, with an American accent, "AND THIS IS COLONEL MORGAN OF THE AMERICAN-NATO ARMED FORCE!"

Senaviyev, of course--he's still alive. Boris thought back to his old captain, who'd apparently been nicknamed "The Roach" because it seemed he couldn't be killed. He'd lost an eye and several fingers, as well as reportedly having been shot several times, but he was still in the military and apparently commanding the Russian section of the armies allied against The Order.

The next part of the announcement was delivered in several languages, Morgan going first in English, Senaviyev in Russian, and an interpreter in German. The message itself was direct.

"ALL SOLDIERS OR WORKERS FIGHTING FOR THE ORDER ARE TO SURRENDER THEMSELVES UNCONDITIONALLY OR BE SHOT. IF THERE ARE ANY PARTISAN FORCES OR THOSE UNDER THE COMMAND OF ONE BORIS KASYANOV, YOU ARE ENCOURAGED TO CONTINUE THE FIGHT, AND WE WILL BE WITH YOU SHORTLY."

What element of surprise Boris may have had about his return to Berlin was blown. But at this point it didn't matter. Boris and his soldiers began to assemble into the trucks with the Partisans either joining them or going right behind them, and Boris began driving just as, through his mirror, he saw some Order soldiers retreating onto the streets.

The Order's headquarters took longer to get to than before as apparently the city had been hit a few times from the air or by artillery, so some of the roads were damaged, but none so greatly that the damaged areas couldn't be circumvented.

Once they arrived where they had stopped before on their first trip to The Order's HQ, the masses of fighters began to pile out of the trucks, with Boris watching over them as they did. Józef was once again in the front of it despite his injuries, as was Elena.

Boris stepped out of his vehicle, this time ready to be on the frontline of the fight. He looked behind him and saw a lone BTR armored vehicle driving up to him followed by an American armored car.

Within the minute they parked, soldiers had emptied out of them, looking as worn as Boris and his men did. However, one person who looked the same was Captain Senaviyev.

"Kasyanov. Last time I saw you, you were late, and I made you do 50 pushups, I believe. Between then and now you have created a chain reaction that is going to rebuild Europe. I will be honest with you, I am impressed." Boris could tell by looking into his old officer's eyes, still wearing his old red beret, however hard his face still was, that he meant what he was saying.

Boris nodded, and thanked him, "*Spasibo, Tovarisch Komandir.*"

Boris glanced over to the American commander, who looked similar to Senaviyev, very gruff, wearing Aviator glasses.

He walked up to Boris and stuck out his hand before giving a firm handshake. "I'm Colonel Morgan, Mr. Kasyanov, and I've heard of your exploits. It's an honor to meet you, and I'm personally ready to kick the remainder of The Order's ass."

Boris stifled a laugh, and resisted the temptation to say something along the lines of "yee-haw," but instead he said "Yes, let's, how you say, kick ass and chew gum?" Boris thickened his own accent slightly for a slight comedic effect, and Morgan chuckled a bit. Boris looked past him, and saw rows of armored vehicles, tanks, and soldiers marching over to where he and his men were gathered.

There were troops from all over the world--Americans and Russians, of course as well as the British, French, Spanish, Germans, Italians, all of the western NATO countries, even

Scandinavian countries like Finland and Sweden, and others from overseas such as the Canadians and Australians.

Most surprising of all were the Middle Eastern soldiers of the Pan-Arab alliance, who seemed to be as tightly knit with the Europeans as they were with each other. One of their soldiers, wearing an Iranian flag on his sleeve, saluted Boris. Boris returned the gesture, and turned, with the armies of many countries behind him.

Boris heard many languages being spoken, and several he could tell were prayers, others joking, some still talking about what the soldiers would do once this last battle was done.

Some of those from overseas countries seemed to stay silent, perhaps thinking they were trapped in Europe. So Boris walked over to where some Americans, Canadians, and Australians were gathered, and told them of the container ship port in Denmark. As he did, he saw the hope in their eyes return as they realized they'd have a chance of returning home.

Boris then returned to his own line, where a Russian T-14 Armata tank stood. Boris climbed onto the beast and saluted one of the crew inside of it. As he did, Senaviyev approached him, and said, "We had to stretch our lines pretty thin to get this far forward in time. We must destroy this HQ as quickly as we can; we know they are keeping a significant number of prisoners, many of whom we may be able to rehabilitate from brainwashing. So, unfortunately our armored vehicles must be relegated to defending our perimeter to avoid collateral; the attack must be done on foot."

Boris nodded, and got off the tank, having enjoyed his few seconds of standing on the mighty vehicle. Though he didn't know it, Daniel was somewhere in the area. Perhaps he would finally be able to find him; as well as Dr. Ward and Zakhar, two people he would dearly like to rescue. Besides, he needed to have one last talk with the Overseer.

Boris got to the ground, and was handed a megaphone by

Morgan, who told him to give a speech. Boris stood for a second, trying to formulate where to start, before it sort of came to him. As he looked into the lines, he saw Nikita, Vasiliy, Józef, Elena, and everyone else, including Paulus who he'd be keeping close for the sake of navigation through the HQ.

"MY FRIENDS! THIS IS THE FINAL HOUR OF THE FINAL BATTLE! IT'S ALL OVER AFTER THIS! THE FINAL STRETCH! WE WILL ALL GO DOWN IN HISTORY AS THOSE WHO SAVED THE WORLD FROM THE ORDER! I SHALL WASTE NO MORE TIME WITH THIS, BUT MAY GOD LET US WIN OUR FINAL BATTLE! FOR HUMANITY!"

"FOR HUMANITY!" rang out throughout the lines. Enthusiastic cheering continued for a few solid minutes, before Senaviyev and Morgan both shouted "ONWARD!" and they all began to advance towards The Order HQ, in unison.

CHAPTER 42

As Boris marched on, he noticed a familiar tune begin to rise up from the Russian parts of the line.

"...*Vstavay na smertny boy! S'fashitskiy siloy tyomnoyu, s proklatoyu ordoy. (Arise for a fight to the death against the dark fascist forces, against the cursed hordes.)* "

It was an old Soviet tune, called "The Sacred War" written during World War Two to inspire the troops. It became their marching cry for victory, as it fit well here. Boris joined in the chorus.

"*Pust Yarost Blagorodnaya, Vskipayet, kak volna! Idyot Voyna narodnaya, Svyechenaya Voyna! (Let Noble Wrath Boil over like a wave! This is the people's war, a sacred war!)*

From the American lines, My Country 'Tis of Thee, rang out. Every group sang a patriotic song from their nation to pass the time as they approached the HQ. Once they were close and could see the building, the singing died down and the soldiers began to raise their weapons. It was surprisingly quiet as they approached. Some broke off and went into the forests around the HQ.

Boris separated into a group with the old Big Four, including Nikita, Vasiliy, and Józef. There were a few others, such as Jeung, Petya, Elena, and Gill on one side with Safiri, Volodya, Olivia, and Kakko on his other side.

Once they were all in position, they waited. They didn't want to be ambushed as soon as they moved. Now that they'd stopped, with their momentum gone, contemplating their next move was extremely stressful.

Then, from the building itself, an announcement rang out; it was the Overseer. "Attention to all of those currently outside the Complex of my Order. I'm going to tell you something that I'm *sure* Kasyanov and his group already know. Our Order has been equipped with nuclear weapons for decades. The war that started had nothing to do with us, but the bombs that were dropped did, as a means to bring fire to the world so that it could be reunited under one banner; the one of our righteous Order. If you tear us down now, there may never be a truly united humanity. Through suffering and work I united those under my guidance. However, I may be left with no choice but to detonate the on-site nuclear device, which would kill all of you, all of my followers, and all of the Partisan Germans. Your line will shatter, and those who have been fighting so long will be crushed by my mighty soldiers. Step forward and bring nuclear fire back into the world. Turn, and leave."

Senaviyev came on over the radio. "He's bluffing. It simply is not possible."

Boris responded, saying "It's true. I saw an undetonated bomb in Denmark. The Order did drop the bombs. However, there is no guarantee they have anything left here, and if we send a small group in we may be able to take care of them. We cannot leave, nor can we give up now."

Senaviyev responded, "Indeed, we shall not give up. Take some men into whatever entrance you can find."

Boris went over the radio again and announced who he was taking. "Nikita, Vasiliy, Petya, Jeung, Volodya, Safiri, Olivia, Werner, five volunteers from the allied soldiers, and Paulus. Come to me, and we'll find a way in."

Given that most of those people were close to Boris already, they were able to gather very quickly. Once they did, Boris turned to Paulus and said, "So, what's the plan? And do they actually have a nuclear device?"

Paulus thought for a second. "Well… I'm going to answer your second question first. Yes, they have a nuclear device, but he isn't going to use it. Mostly because I am here, and you are here. If *we* hadn't made it here, they likely would. But the Overseer is very…

thematic, he would want a dramatic last battle. However, if we just send everybody in and he thought it likely he'd be killed by a random soldier, he probably would, but he'd enjoy fighting a small group... and in that event, his narcissism would keep him from pressing the button. As for getting in, we could simply march into the first building and shoot it up, but there isn't a point to that. The standing building is all logistics and communication, not something we are concerned with here. Most of the HQ is a few meters underground, but the doors where you all exited the complex from for the Test...if we could get them open, we could pretty easily get inside and work our way in."

Boris nodded to the affirmative. He saw it as fitting, as he would be re-entering the Order's HQ from where he last exited it.

Boris and the small group began to circle around the buildings at a generous distance, with Paulus leading the way, staying a few meters ahead of the rest. Once they'd rotated around to the side where the entrance should be, Boris noticed they were even further from the buildings than they had been before. But then he noticed it--a rise and then drop in the land. When they were properly facing it, the doors were clearly visible, grey as steel. It was far enough from the road and everything else that it wouldn't have caused a lot of suspicion, and if it had, well, anyone who'd tried to enter before likely didn't face a pleasant fate.

They approached the doors, and Boris called Volodya over, who'd gotten an RPG from one of the Russian soldiers. Given they didn't have many options nor time, it was their best method of getting in. The group backed up a good distance from the doors, and Volodya aimed the rocket launcher before he pulled the trigger. The rocket crashed into the doors, blowing them open and off the hinges.

Volodya was the first to get back up, and Boris soon followed. They approached the doors, and an alarm went off, originating from a wall unit, which Jeung shot and disabled within a few seconds. A good idea, as the sound would have been distracting. There would probably be more of those units but for now, at least, the alarm was delayed.

Directly behind the doors was a long corridor, sloping down into the ground, wide enough to fit two vehicles. At the end there was a large warehouse-type garage where several of the trucks and jeeps Boris had seen before were parked. Supervision was low, surprisingly, and there were only a few workers who surrendered quickly or ran away, either back behind them and into the outside or deeper into the facility.

The group fanned out, searching for anything like a map or visual indicators to send them in the right direction. The primary goal was to kill or capture the Overseer.

Within the first minute, Werner found a sign over a doorway which read, "Agriculture and Industry Section." This likely was where the third Order leader was, the one that Boris had yet to have any contact with. Considering their high-ranking position, it was probably best to take them out. However, he couldn't distract himself from the primary goal of getting to the Overseer.

"Werner, Jeung, Olivia, go down this corridor and kill or capture the Order's Head of Agriculture and Industry. They've proven the most elusive, but it's unlikely they will pose much of a threat considering their civilian role," Boris said. The five split off and went down that hall, leaving only Boris, Nikita, Vasiliy, and Paulus.

Boris turned to Paulus and asked, "Okay then. Now where do we go? The rest of the corridors are unmarked."

Paulus turned back to him, then looked toward one of the corridors and turned into it. Boris, at this moment, realized that Paulus was unarmed, and mulled over giving him a weapon. He indeed could get one, then turn and kill Boris, but that wouldn't serve any purpose. He seemed like too much of a realist to think that doing so would help The Order survive the battle, assuming he still had any loyalty to it by then.

Boris shouted out to Paulus, and tossed him his pistol, the very one he'd shot him with earlier. He didn't give him any spare ammo, so he only had the eight rounds that fit in the magazine. Enough for him to be somewhat capable of defending himself.

They continued down the corridor, with Paulus directing them into the greater part of the base. It was distinguishable because it had different lighting and better quality construction. The dim industrial lighting and concrete walls were replaced by the sterile white light and walls Boris had gotten used to during his time spent as a Prospect in training.

As soon as they crossed this barrier, another alarm sounded, and footsteps started thundering down the corridor. Nothing was visible yet, but Boris and the others crouched down and aimed their weapons into the hall.

Then the buzzing white light shut off and was replaced with blood red that illuminated the halls; it became noticeably darker, though visibility was still clear enough.

The first Order soldiers then ran into their corridor, shooting continuously toward Boris' men. Despite their inaccuracy resulting from having had minimal training, Boris then ordered his comrades into a side room, without time to scope it out. When he entered, he saw it was a massive armory, containing what he'd seen in other armories, and more. Boris felt no need for another weapon, but instead searched for ammo, and ammo he found in the form of large, 80-round drums in the same caliber as his AK-74M. This provided a massive advantage over the 30-round magazines he'd been using up until then. He took several of them, and distributed them to Nikita, Volodya, and Safiri, who were also using the same or similar models of weapon.

Boris stashed some more ammo in his pack and then turned back to face the door, The Order now directly behind it. They were likely to shoot the locking mechanism then bust it down. Boris took cover next to the door, and after a few shots were heard, there was a huge *CRASH!* as the door burst open. Outside it stood a massive man sporting the Centurion colors. He was also identifiable as a Centurion by his heavy body armor, a full-face shield that appeared to be based on an old Soviet design, and most surprisingly, a rotary cannon… otherwise known as a minigun. He dropped the sledgehammer he'd used to get in, and lit up the room, warping and bending all sorts of equipment as well as causing ricochets throughout. The barrel of his weapon was a fiery red as he dropped his minigun to reveal he was also sporting an automatic shotgun.

Boris dared a quick glance over to his comrades and saw Safiri clutching a bleeding wound in his leg. Volodya was preparing bandages, and they seemed to be behind safe cover. Nikita and Vasiliy were debating something behind an ammo crate, and Paulus was waiting around a corner with Boris' Tokarev aimed right where the Order soldier's head would be. Petya was in a precarious position, behind a thin wooden wall, but looking for another opportunity to move. The volunteers had stayed outside the room, and had sprinted into another room, all except one, a New Zealander, identified by the flag on his uniform.

Boris had to refocus on the "elephant" in the room, the elephant-sized man. The armory itself was large, and it would take the armored man a while to patrol through it all given the weight he was carrying. The Centurion fired indiscriminately through thin walls and barriers, hoping to hit those behind.

He was approaching where Volodya and Safiri were, and the two of them fired a few shots into the rear plates of the Centurion's armor. One hit in between, and Boris saw a small spurt of blood come from his side. The man did what Boris had seen the Centurions do before, inject himself with what looked like a form of steroid or morphine before continuing to fight, not seeming to notice the wound any further, despite the fact it was still bleeding. Boris, who had to shift his position to keep out of view, saw that the behemoth was right upon Volodya and Safiri.

Boris couldn't help but watch as Volodya finish bandaging Safiri, before turning to face the Centurion. The armored man fired a few shots in his direction, which all missed. Volodya looked around him, then at Safiri, before making a decision.

Volodya ran out of cover, spraying his weapon towards the armored man before trying to make it to cover again; several shots were fired at him, and he angled around to face the armored man, allowing Boris to get a better look at his comrade. Blood was spreading in several places across his body. However, Volodya seemed to be running on adrenaline. Boris risked another burst of fire at the armored man, as did a few others throughout the room, but most of the shots bounced off.

A few other Order soldiers entered the armory, and Volodya quickly turned, shooting them all down in no more than three seconds. As they collapsed to the ground, he noticed the armored Centurion turn to face Safiri's position again. Volodya, who was now bleeding more, jumped out of cover with a knife and ran towards the Centurion, just out of his sight. Boris tried to relocate, getting around a column in the room to see Volodya jab a knife into the armored man's neck. Blood spurted out of that new wound immediately; quickly and the armored man couldn't save himself from this injury. Boris was about to fire another burst to finish him off when one last, deafening blast from the shotgun sounded out. Boris leaped out from his own cover to see the Centurion drop his shotgun, the barrel smoking, and rip the knife out of his neck, possibly as a last sign of defiance, before crashing to the ground with a mighty thud. Then he saw Volodya, stumbling backwards. He sprinted over to him, as did the rest, with a few going a bit further towards the door to await the approach of other soldiers. Boris and Safiri both crouched down to face Volodya, now laying on the ground, his chest a bloody mess with blood beginning to pool under him.

"Shame I couldn't... make it through this last battle. I guess I got to be the hero, though..." he coughed roughly, and spat up a bit of blood. "I may not have made it... but you will make it... win, for everyone. But now I'm called... to be with God. See you above, brothers..." He ripped off the necklace he was wearing, with the cross on it, identical to one Safiri had, and shoved it in

Boris's direction; it was bloody, but still shined. "For luck…" He said, and Boris took it before his arm went limp and he breathed his last.

Boris lowered his head and said a silent prayer, Volodya's cross clenched in his hand; the first of any kind he'd had in years. Ever since Zakhar… he didn't think there was any good in the world, then the war… but the genuine goodness in this man who'd just died, and what Boris now had to live and fight for, changed something in him. There was a sort of switch, which flipped.

The supposed death of one man removing his faith, and the true death of another putting him back in--how ironic.

Boris looked up to Safiri. Safiri was silent, and a single tear was shed from his eye, and spoke quietly, "Le'ăhuni dehina," In his native Amharic.

He and Boris stood up and turned to the armory exit. He walked through the exit, and there weren't any Order reinforcements directly on them at that moment. Boris looked into the other room the volunteers ran into, and three of them came out. Now there were four volunteers left, and one of them, an Italian, said "Lyman was the one killed." As he walked past Boris, continuing down the hall.

Boris turned and followed him, with the rest directly behind him. They continued down the hall, sweeping and clearing the rooms they passed, mostly empty barracks and sleeping quarters. Then, a few minutes later, they used the armored man's dropped sledgehammer to bust open a door which led to a wide, downward stairway to the auditorium that Boris had walked through just before the Test. As soon as the doors swung open, several Order soldiers began shooting at them. Boris backed away from the door quickly, shutting one of the two doors behind him. The rest backed away from the doors, while the New Zealander threw a hand grenade into the auditorium. A few seconds later, an explosion echoed. Then, Boris and the New Zealander peaked out, and saw the grenade had killed a few Order soldiers, but there were several still in the room who fired a few more shots. The group was bunched up toward the doors, and they didn't have any good ideas. At least, not until Nikita commented.

"Hey… about that minigun…" he said, looking over to Boris. Boris thought about it for a second, knowing instantly what Nikita was suggesting, and for a lack of better ideas, he nodded quickly and sent Nikita off to retrieve the weapon.

A few minutes later, Nikita returned, lugging the massive machine of death over to the once-again closed doors. "It's surprisingly lightweight." He said. It was still obviously very heavy, but generally speaking, weapons like that weren't man-portable, so some advancements had been made by The Order in this case.

Boris now needed a plan If Nikita simply ran out there, he would be cut down before he could train his weapon on anybody. So, the best idea was to give him cover fire and hope he could first get down into the central area

"I and a few others will give you cover fire. Jeung, Olivia, go with him."

The group reorganized to try to shove the doors open again. The additional force swung the doors open and everyone began firing at once. Boris only saw one Order soldier, who was cut down by his and others' fire within the first few seconds. After adding the drum magazines he was able to keep up the fire for longer than usual. He ran out of ammo with his first of the three drums. Looking up while he prepared the next one, he saw that much the room had already been shot up. Nikita, the New Zealander, and Petya made it down to the central section while Nikita was tearing through the seating of the right flank. At the same time, Boris and the others trained their sights on other entrances to the auditorium. Many of The Order's soldiers poured in, but they didn't have the reaction time required to save themselves from the overwhelming volume of fire. They couldn't have managed this even had they been well trained, which of course, was not the case.

Then, the tide changed when two more minigun-armed Centurions entered the building, wearing even more heavy armor. They both took at least a dozen shots before they could begin returning fire. Boris knew instantly he could either stay at the doors or make his way down and try to outflank the armored men. He chose the second, and sprinted down, followed by the Italian volunteer and Vasiliy. Boris made it down first, followed by Vasiliy, and Boris looked back for the Italian, but he'd been shot many times, his limp body falling down the stairs, bleeding heavily.

"*Shit!*" Boris shouted, his voice drowned out over the sounds of the gunfire. He looked up over the seating and desks and saw both of the heavily armored brutes. They'd been shot several times, but both had already injected themselves with the "hyper-morphine" or whatever it was. Boris pulled out a grenade, one of a few he'd gotten from the armory, and pulled the pin, waiting a second before throwing it at one of the Centurions, hoping that it would do some damage. He expected most of the shrapnel would hit and bounce off the armor, but some would make it through the cracks and the force of the explosion itself could throw them off or even damage their weapons.

Boris waited, and the explosion came. He dared a glance over the deck he was behind, and saw the armored man had fallen over, and was having a less-than-elegant time trying to get back up, but get back up he did, though his armor was scorched, his weapon was destroyed, and he was bleeding more than he had been before. Boris fired his weapon a few more times, and he could feel his second ammo drum was getting close to empty based on its weight.

The shots still didn't seem to faze the man, even after he took a few other hits from another direction. However, he was slowing down, and his blood loss was increasing. Along with that, he was now unarmed, having lost his minigun, which took him a second to realize. He then sealed his fate by running at two people,

Jeung and Petya, who shot him several times before he got close, at least one of which got through as the man dropped before he got to them, stumbling and crashing to the ground.

Petya and the New Zealander looked at each other, both seeming to be surprised that they brought him down, before drawing their attention to the last Centurion.

Boris looked up to spot the man, who was still sporadically firing his minigun. Boris could see that the barrels of his weapon were turning a burning shade of orange, so he was apparently doing this to keep the weapon from *melting*. However, this low fire-rate and the fact Nikita hadn't yet fired enough to overheat his own weapon meant he was able to pepper the armored man with blasts from his minigun, forcing the armored man to keep his head down, making it difficult for him to fire back to begin with.

Boris looked over to Nikita, who fired a few more bursts before the barrels just started to spin, indicating there were no more bullets left. Nikita tossed the weapon to the side and drew his rifle again, firing a few more shots over the enemy's head.

Boris looked back towards the armored monster, and saw he'd given up on the minigun and had drawn a shotgun similar to that of his comrade in the armory. Boris took the opportunity to make his way around the man, who was now doing as Nikita had been, firing in the general direction of his enemies to keep their heads down. However, as his helmet limited his view, he seemed to lack a good sense of spatial awareness, allowing Boris to get ever closer.

Boris was within a few meters, moving between the splintered desks until he got closer to the armored man, and took out his knife. He wasn't going to let what happened to Volodya happen to him. This was *for* Volodya.

Boris leapt out from the desk and first knocked the shotgun out of the man's hand before jamming his knife into the monster's neck, tearing it out a second later. Boris looked into the man's eyes as he died, wild, unfocused. Whatever drugs he'd been using must have been made of some wicked stuff. However, nothing in them could protect him from his neck being ripped open.

After the armored man crashed to the ground, the group then met up in the center, turning to shoot the occasional straggler once or twice.

Boris noticed one of the other volunteers was gone, leaving only the New Zealander, a Norwegian, and an Austrian.

Boris turned to them, all very young except for the New Zealander, who seemed to be in his late thirties, and said, "Unless you want to end up like the rest, you have to stay with us. Follow close."

The Austrian and Norwegian nodded while the New Zealander began to follow Vasiliy, already making his way up to the other side with Safiri limp-walking behind him.

Boris followed them but turned around when he heard some people sprinting from behind him, who turned out to be Jeung, Olivia, Werner, and… Daniel. Werner had some blood on his face, but it evidently wasn't his.

Before asking about that, Boris looked over to Daniel, who seemed to be severely injured. He had cuts all over his arms and face and was missing a finger. Boris didn't say anything, as no words came, but Daniel spoke instead, saying "They didn't break me. If they had, they probably would have beaten you to Svalbard. They *were* actually gonna kill me pretty soon. There's not much to say right now, but thanks." Boris was astounded at the return of his long absent comrade so suddenly, but there was no time to discuss it now. He then turned his attention to Werner.

Because Boris was looking directly at him, Werner was quick to explain the blood on his face. "We got to their area, that the Order's Head of Development was located, and we entered her office. She only had two guards which we disposed of with ease. However, once we'd entered the room, she said "It appears we have lost. Farewell, Ladies and Gentlemen." And… well, she shot herself in the head. We couldn't get anything out of her and there was really nothing of use to do."

Olivia looked around with a quizzical look on her face. "Where's… Volodya?"

Safiri looked back for a split second at hearing his friend's name but returned to moving a bit ahead with Vasiliy.

"Volodya… died heroically. Saved our lives. He did the VDV, the motherland, and all of us proud," Boris said stoically, avoiding dwelling on the topic.

Olivia nodded solemnly before turning to go with Vasiliy and the rest. Boris jogged to catch back up to Vasiliy, who in his own mind probably had the entire complex marked for obliteration. Boris looked at him and noticed his hair was grayer than it had been before. Understandable, but apparently there was more going on with him than he'd ever let on.

Boris said, "So, we've almost made it Vasiliy. This is our finest hour!" Vasiliy's expression, stone-cold before lightening a bit, said, "Indeed it is, Boris. Indeed, it is."

Paulus, who'd been a meter or so behind Boris spoke up and commented "If the Overseer really *does* have one of the warheads active, it's pretty close to here. A minor diversion."--They walked a few more steps- "Turn left here," he said.

Boris did so, and they were brought into another large room similar to the auditorium, except it had a massive metal ceiling that looked as if it opened with several empty missile bays.

"Yes, yes, I know, we launched the bombs, you already knew this. Don't get mad at me. I had nothing to do with it, and if we weren't the ones who did, some country would have. Anyway, whichever of these missile bays isn't empty is obviously the one," Paulus added.

Boris nodded, but then as soon as they walked into the room an alarm sounded, and several squads of Order soldiers flooded in from the other side.

Boris opened fire quickly, and depleted the ammo in his last drum, dropping it to the ground and replacing it with a standard magazine, thankful for the relief in weight. The Order soldiers here weren't uniformed, and lacked masks, which had always had a dehumanizing effect. This made fighting them now more mentally impactful. However, there was nothing to be done. If they were devoted enough to fight such a desperate battle they wouldn't be turned back.

As the last one dropped, Boris looked behind him and noticed that one of the other volunteers was gone, the Austrian. *Damn, and he was closest to home out of the three as well.* That was all Boris had the time to give him in terms of sympathy for then.

Within a few minutes, Petya called out, "This must be the one, Boris!"

Boris immediately rushed over to Petya, and looked at the silo; indeed, it wasn't empty. One of the panels was open and blinking. Werner walked over and said, "Let me take care of this. I was on a bomb squad."

How much do I not know about him!? Boris thought.

Werner was done in a few minutes, and he said, "Defused. You might as well call your captain and tell him he can begin the attack; by the time they would get to wherever the Overseer is we'll likely be long done with him anyway."

Boris nodded, and Paulus said, "Indeed we will be. A few more halls and several more guards thrown at us and we'll be at his office. He's unlikely to do what the Head of Development did."

Before Boris did so, he looked over to Petya, and patted him on the back. He noticed that Petya looked sickly, and it must have showed. "Heh," Petya said. "I guess you noticed it. Writing isn't the only reason I left my village, you know... I also had another reason."

"You were sick," said Boris, not believing it.

"Yes. Pancreatic cancer. I never did get treated, not in a permanent way. This isn't an opportune time, Boris, but I want you to know what I'm going to do. I'm not going to die like a dud laying in the back of a truck on the way home. Let me soften up the Overseer's guards before you get there. Make it easier for you." Petya gave a genuine smile, and Boris still couldn't believe it.

"But, Petya…" Boris trailed off. He couldn't take it away from him, it's how he'd want to go in the situation. Instead he cut back in, with "good luck, Uncle Petya."

Petya rested his hand on Boris's soldier, and said "I'll be with you, from above, Nephew." And he smiled one more time before marching to the front of the group.

They then advanced out of the room, and Boris contacted Senaviyev through his radio, trying not to let his emotion show. "The device is defused. Despite the unlikelihood of him using it… commence attack." Senaviyev wasted no time, said "Copy." Boris then began feeling vibrations from above resonating due to the volume of fire they released.

Boris stood at the head of the group next to Petya, with Vasiliy and Nikita behind him. They arrived at a door, not the last one, however.

"This is the second to last door," Said Petya. "After this one, the next will take you right there, where I can guarantee the Overseer will be."

Boris looked over to Petya, who smiled one last time, before opening the door and closing it behind him. A few seconds passed several gunshots rang out, including a few hitting the door. The fighting went on for a few minutes, and every nerve, every cell in Boris's body screamed at him to intervene and save Petya, but he knew this is what he wanted. He instead stood in front of the doors, blocking them, not saying anything while the others just stared at him.

After the last shot was fired, Boris quickly explained: "He was dying. He wanted to go out fighting. I wasn't going to take that from him."

Boris kicked open the door and shredded the few remaining guards, both Centurions, with clean headshots. He found nearly a dozen Order bodies laying strewn in the hallway, with Petya laying against a wall, stained with his blood.

He was dead, no doubt, but he did what he wanted; he went out fighting. Boris noticed in one hand he was clutching his journal. He picked it up and read, scrawled on the first page; "To Boris. You've done everything and more I could ever have wished of myself, or anyone. This may be the last you'll hear of me, but I will watch over you always. *Petya.*"

Boris clutched it to his chest and put it in his pocket.

Nikita and Vasiliy walked up to him. "He was a good man," said Nikita. "They don't make people like him anymore," Vasiliy said quietly.

Boris turned to those behind him, and Daniel motioned for him to move towards the door. *This is for you three. This was your mission.* He seemed to be saying. Despite all he'd gone through, he wanted to leave this to them. Boris looked at Nikita and Vasiliy, and they all nodded.

The three of them marched up to the door, and Boris kicked it open, and as soon as they stepped in, all of the lights shut off. Three shots sounded, and the light returned abruptly.

CHAPTER 43

B oris knew he wasn't the one who was shot.

On one side lay Vasiliy, a bullet in his head and in his chest. On the other side lay Nikita, writhing in agony from a shot to his gut. All Boris could do was shift his gaze between the two, Vasiliy's face frozen in a steadfast gaze, Nikita beginning to bleed heavily.

Boris then suddenly looked up, seeing the Overseer on the other end of a handgun, the barrel still smoking, an expression of victory written on his face even in his greatest defeat.

The Overseer kept his weapon aimed at Nikita's head while he began to speak.

"You have taken everything from me. My credibility, my soldiers, my money, my few friends…"

Paulus burst into the room, but the Overseer was too quick, and he was downed as well. "You… Sadistic… Bastard… he said, fighting for every breath. The Overseer slowly turned his aim toward Paulus, whose last words were "See… you… in… Hell…" Before the Overseer pulled the trigger, his bullet crashing into Paulus's skull, killing him instantly.

"I always was the better shot…" The Overseer said smugly. "Bet you didn't expect that. Now… where were we? Ah, yes. You took everything, including him. You just made me shoot my best friend. My wife, as well, if you'd never pieced it together, a few minutes ago in her office… So… I'm not going to kill you. No. You are going to live with everything I have now done to you, and whatever happens to you will be brought upon you by yourself. Goodbye." The Overseer placed his weapon to his jaw, in a manner similar to how Werner described the Overseer's wife doing it.

"Not this time," Boris said. He drew his pistol and shot the Overseer's hand, forcing him to drop his weapon. Boris marched over to the sidearm and threw it against the wall.

"What, do you think you're going to 'bring me to justice'?" the Overseer balked.

"No. I'm not an idiot. But I do believe in retribution. I may have more pain to live with than most, all due to you, but I have gained one important thing from you, and that is purpose. I ended your cruel despotism. I have a reason to live my life now. You may take my friends from me physically, but those who died are still with me and those living can have better lives now. I'd let you live for you to repent your own sins, but I can't risk leaving a *parasite* like you alive." Boris then rose his weapon and aimed it at the Overseer's heart.

The Overseer scoffed. "You won't do it. The hero never kills an unarmed man." And his smile returned.

"Maybe that's true… But I'm no hero." Boris pulled the trigger. The bullet crashed into the Overseer's heart, and he could do nothing but stare at Boris as he slumped over in his chair, clinging onto his last shreds of life. "I'm just what you deserved," Boris finished, as the Overseer's last moments passed, his corpse falling from his chair.

Nikita, behind Boris, coughed. "I wish I could have gotten a shot at that bastard. Can you help me up?"

Boris turned and helped Nikita to his feet and wrapped bandages around his wound. They'd work for now.

As Boris began making his way back to the group, one of the walls in the Overseer's office splintered apart. On the other side was the Ukrainian demolition man and Captain Senaviyev.

Boris turned abruptly, and quickly saluted his old captain, his hand still shaking from the events of the past minutes.

"I see you beat us to him. I guess this is the bastard we've been chasing this whole time." Senaviyev looked over to Vasiliy and Paulus. He stuttered for a second, before saying "I see… you've lost some good men. Here, my medic will take care of this one," he said, gesturing to Nikita, and a Russian medic rushed over to him and took him behind Senaviyev.

Boris looked back to Vasiliy and Paulus, crushed by the losses he'd just suffered.

"I think that one has something sticking out of his pocket," Senaviyev said, gesturing to Vasiliy.

Boris looked over to Vasiliy and saw something, as well. He crouched down and pulled out what turned out to be a photo. It was somewhat old, with a picture of a much younger Vasiliy, who was holding the camera, pointed at him and two girls.

On the back was written *"Anastasiya with Cousin Elena, 2005."*

Cousin Elena!?

The girl in the picture, Elena, couldn't have been anyone else. This whole time, Vasiliy was her uncle… How did he never know? He'd have to ask Elena.

But before Boris left Vasiliy's body, Boris said in a quiet voice, "They don't make people like you anymore, either, my friend."

"Excuse me, captain," Boris said with as much composure as he could muster, before following the path they'd taken to the Overseer's office, over bodies, mostly of Order soldiers, until he got to the surface where the forest and plains had been replaced by a scorched battlefield.

"Elena!" He shouted out. He turned and saw her running towards him, and they met in a tight embrace. "You're okay! You made it," she said.

Boris couldn't focus at all on the carnage around him, only on Elena. He nearly forgot the photograph, but it wrestled into his mind, and he whipped it out of his pocket.

"You... were Vasiliy's niece?" He asked.

"Uh... yeah. I was best friends with his daughter, my cousin, until 2006... his wife and my cousin died in a car crash... He disappeared from our family after that. I didn't even realize it was him until a few days or so ago... but I couldn't bring it up, we were so close to the end. Maybe we can reconcile now! Where is he?" she asked, in the last words the stress in her voice increased exponentially.

"I... He... Vasiliy... is gone. As are Petya, and Paulus, and Volodya. Nikita was gravely wounded."

Elena looked crushed. "You mean...?"

"Yes... but the Overseer is gone, and Vasiliy's at peace... with his family now. As are the others... and... well, it's over now, Elena. *It's over.*" Boris said, his voice trembling as he neared the end of those words.

Boris and Elena met again in a tear-filled embrace, and stayed there for several minutes, before they met up with Boris' men, the soldiers, and the Partisans.

Boris was prompted again to make a speech, now they'd won. He stood up on a few piled-up cinder blocks before speaking. He looked out over the battlefield, where the dead were scattered all over. Some were already being covered in white sheets. He looked to the crowd, and saw his men, the soldiers, the Partisans, and even Zakhar and Dr. Ward, both alive, before speaking. "Attention, everyone. It's over. We... have won." He got out of the way first. All of them cheered, and he continued. "And we lost many brave and good people in this final battle... but now, finally, and for the last time, we have won. There will be no more fighting. But with that, there is nothing else to say."

Everyone cheered loudly, the echoes likely traveling through the forests and cities, rivers and plains, to Moscow and across the English Channel, it was over. People embraced, hugged and cried, many broke out into song, singing their national anthems, folk songs, all of it with more vigor than they'd ever done before.

When the celebrations were over, the rations from Svalbard were split up between the members from each country, and people began to split off into groups. Most of the soldiers congregated with their fellow countrymen to return home. Ischez, who was still alive somehow, was organizing those who would go to Denmark to take the cargo ships to their respective countries. Those travelling by land took Order trucks. Others became scouts to spread the news of victory, while the remainder stayed with Boris.

Before anyone left, Boris said his goodbyes to those he'd likely never see again, who were returning to their own countries. The New Zealander, the Norwegian, Gill, Henderson, Ischez even, he could part with as equals, as well as all of the rest who planned on leaving--including Werner, Kakko, and most of the other Prospects. All except Olivia, who apparently had nothing left to go back to. All of the American soldiers as well, including Jackson, that soldier he'd met with who made it all possible. "See you later, my friend," he said to Jackson, who responded, "Yeah, see you brother." They shook hands and parted, with Jackson leading the rest of Boris' American soldiers off to return home.

In the end it was Boris, the Russians, and his men with some scattered others who apparently had nothing left to return to. By the time they were among the only ones remaining, it had been about two days, and finally it was time to head home.

All of those with Boris gathered into The Order's trucks, the Russian armored vehicles, and everything else they could find. Boris, just before entering the truck to leave, looked out to the last ones still there, the battle-hardened Partisans of Berlin. He went out to Marvin and to Hans, said his goodbyes, and in the loudest voice he could muster, "In the words of John F. Kennedy... Ich Bein Ein Berliner!" The Partisans cheered, and Boris waved, before getting into the truck and beginning to drive.

Nikita was in the back of his truck, and one of the Russian

medics, as well as Dmitry and Dr. Ward, were still operating on him. Boris drove to distract himself from the prospect of losing another of his friends.

However, his oldest friend was now in front with him. Zakhar.

They talked as they drove, as it would be a long several weeks. Zakhar told about how he'd done what he could to sabotage The Order's alarm systems for when Boris would inevitably arrive, explaining his ability to travel through much of the base with less interference than expected, and about how he and Dr. Ward had a well-established escape plan ready with some of the other non-brainwashed Order people willing to defect. Apparently, as Boris entered, they were able to sneak out behind them from a door they hadn't seen.

Up in front was also Daniel, who was slightly less talkative and was only there for the last half of the trip, as his injuries had to be treated, but he said that there was nothing for him back in America; that he'd stay in Moscow. Apparently, he'd been held as The Order was too busy to decide what else to do with him, and this had simply been his life for weeks and weeks. Fortunately, he seemed to be making a recovery.

Boris thought Zakhar's actions had been quite clever, and they got to talking about old times, and about what they'd do once they got back. It passed the time well, and it eased Boris' mind greatly to still at least have Zakhar, and then, hopefully, Nikita.

After over a week of driving, they were once again on the outskirts of Moscow, Boris' home. He recognized it as he drove in from the roads he'd last left from so long ago, especially the base they'd defended so adamantly for so many weeks. One of the first things he noticed was that there were now people outside on the streets. Some still wore gas masks, but not all. And they weren't destitute, they were alive, if hungry looking… and that was a problem Boris had just arrived to solve.

The groups piled out of the trucks, and they were greeted warmly by the citizens of Moscow, and the Metro. Boris turned to the back, and helped Nikita stand, and began walking him over to the entrance of the Metro.

Boris was focused on the entrance, but he looked to Nikita, and saw his focus was elsewhere, on a woman about his age, wandering the streets, her head down.

"ANYA!" he shouted.

The young women looked up, and her dreary expression lit up instantly. "NIKITA!" she shouted back. She ran over to him, and Nikita broke away to limp over to his love.

The two of them met in a tearful embrace similar to that of the one between Boris and Elena. Elena herself had shown up behind Boris, and she put her arm on his shoulder. "Looks like he's definitely getting a hero's welcome," she laughed.

Boris couldn't help but smile. Nikita never seemed happier. He watched as they talked and unloaded supplies off the trucks before descending into the Metro. Boris looked around at everyone else, and even caught Zakhar and Olivia hovering quite close to each other.

Boris and Elena then got to work unloading supplies and distributing them throughout the Metro, which had become much more peaceful since Boris had completed his work. The fringe elements such as the fascists being wiped out, the Metro had evolved into a loose confederation, as over time everyone realized they'd have to work together to survive. With the supplies Boris and his group had brought they began to grow exponentially, and the great city of Moscow was inhabited once again.

One morning at daybreak, a year after the day of their return, Boris and Elena left the Metro to stand at the end of the city and look out West, where they'd spent so much time and done so many things, and back into Moscow where vehicles were still parked, others by then being driven around the city.

"I can't believe," Boris began, "that we really did it."

"Whether you believe it or not… we did, and now we have the reward for all that's been done. We must enjoy it… you won… you played Armageddon in a game of chess and you got the checkmate."

"I guess… I never expected the aftermath to have any… hope."

"The sun always rises again," Elena said.

And it did. Boris looked east, and saw the sun, now perfectly visible through the buildings, begin to rise once again in the sky.

EPILOGUE

Boris and Elena lived out the rest of their days in Moscow, eventually residing in a building with a few of their old friends, including Nikita and his new wife Anya. They had kids after a few years, and Boris told his stories to them. However, there were always the parts he left out, that he thought were best not told. But, they weren't the only stories his children and the other children who visited him heard. Some came from the book of an old man named Petya, who'd always turned the darkest of situations into exemplars of hope and courage. And Vasiliy lived in his and Elena's hearts, never to be forgotten, his impact permanent. Boris indeed had lost a lot, but he'd gained so much, and because of him the world was born anew.

Nikita and Anya lived in the same building as Boris and Elena, and had kids of their own, the oldest of which would head expeditions to European cities to re-establish contact and even trade between them. With The Order gone, the only antagonists were the occasional bandits and other criminals, who could never truly be completely eradicated.

Nikita recovered from his injuries, and he and Anya spent the rest of their days happily. He and Boris joint-led the Moscow division of United Europe, the new confederation created in the decades after their adventure that sought to unite the continent, maybe eventually the world under peace and freedom.

Zhenya and Yevgeny, the two youngest of the group, despite not having been particularly active in the last battles, as most of the professional soldiers refused to let those so young fight, still had excellent stories and were able to grow up and find relationships of their own, as well as helping Nikita's eldest son in his expeditions.

Jeung spent most of his life helping the poorest of the Metro, and one of them, another Korean, one who'd escaped from the North, ended up becoming his wife. His life was fulfilled, but he never forgot his harrowing experiences and visited Boris regularly.

Józef, kept out of the last battle because of his injuries, eventually got used to his life without his arm and a permanently damaged leg. He also eventually met a woman who was perfect for him. He wrote memoirs of his experiences and took great joy and pride in telling young children the stories of how he'd planned out the whole expedition, however never giving himself enough credit for the impact he had. He was the one who ended up turning The Order into an old monster story. 'Be good, or The Order will kidnap and brainwash you!' he'd say to misbehaving kids.

Safiri, the Ethiopian VDV soldier, fit well in the Moscow metro system. He worked often with Jeung and was one of the first to venture back out into Europe, helping to bring refugees back to Moscow, including a Turkish woman who eventually became his wife. He always kept a part of Volodya with him, and never forgot his best friend, often thinking of him and the incredible sacrifice he'd made.

Roman, Vasiliy's strongman, ended up helping to fix cars and other modes of transportation to help the citizens of Moscow regain mobility. He even created a school to teach young men and women his skills, which included interrogation, and bartering effectively for good prices.

Zakhar and Olivia ended up getting together and remaining as a couple in a relatively peaceful relationship for many years ahead, never losing hope and always doing what they could to help those around them-- in other words working together for the benefit of others, a spirit they kept up throughout their lives.

Daniel, once he made it to Moscow, took a reasonably long time to adjust to the new life, as he'd known nothing but The Order's complex for so long. However, he did eventually return to reality and made a decent living in Moscow, recovering from his injuries in full, despite never getting rid of his scar. He enjoyed hanging with Józef, as he could tell his stories about being captured by The Order to add some flavor to Józef's stories.

Those who had to travel overseas generally made it back to, their countries of origin. With the supplies they'd gotten from the expedition, they were able to speed up the recovery of their respective parts of the world, particularly in places like Britain, with those like Ischez and Gill proving to be strong leaders who helped their nations recover faster than they would have without them. Most of the Americans landed in New York, near The Order's HQ in America, where there was already a militia of Americans fighting them. It took a week and there were many losses, but eventually the enemy was brought down, and the supplies Jackson and his soldiers brought helped restore America.

The Partisans began to slowly rebuild Berlin, one of the most damaged cities. They scavenged from the Order's HQ, sending much of the equipment to Moscow, as they had no use for it. Then they began to piece their city together, while maintaining regular contact with Moscow, as well as the other cities that were returning to life, such as Warsaw, Minsk, and London.

Over time, the world began to piece itself back together. Those from the expedition would continue to explore the world and attempt to help those they came across. The first areas to completely come back were primarily the European and American cities. Asia, South America, and Africa came back slowly, as others began to travel to them with aid. In the coming decades and centuries, the world would never again know a new World War.

ACKNOWLEDGEMENTS

Well, before I start, the first person I'd like to thank is you, reading this book right now. If you are reading this, that means I've accomplished part of my dream.

For the real acknowledgements, it would be wrong to thank anyone first who wasn't you, Olivia. Without you, there's no way would I have had the motivation or ideas to continue this pet project of mine. Your illustrations of the characters, constant encouragement, and dedication to the project are a major reason why this whole project exists!

Next would have to be Nathan, the second person to read through this book, and my pro grammar checker. Your job maybe wasn't glamorous, but it was very important, and you did a good job at it.

And great thanks to my Lit Comp teacher, Mr. Greg Koch. I started the book during some free time in your classroom, and your constant encouragement of my project has been a great help and is appreciated more than you could ever know! Now you can brag to your new students one of your past ones published a novel!

Now for the obligatory Mom and Dad acknowledgement. You guys have always supported me no matter what I've been doing, and this book has been no exception! You guys are awesome, and I could never have asked for better parents.

I also want to thank my good friends who listened to me ramble on about how excited I was about publishing this book throughout this whole process. Thank you to Caden, Connor, J'knox, my girlfriend Harley, and the countless other people who have supported my project in one way or another.

Now, back to you, the reader. I cannot express how much you've done for me just by picking up this book and deciding to read it. You have fulfilled one of my absolute greatest dreams, and if this all went how I hope it would, then it's just the start of what is to come, and I will be writing and publishing more before you know it.

Until next time!

ABOUT THE AUTHOR

Jake Baratka is currently a high school student and continues to write stories on a variety of topics, from Sci-Fi to Medieval Fantasy. He also runs a YouTube channel called Tsar Andrei, another avocation he greatly enjoys.

CPSIA information can be obtained
at www.ICGtesting.com
Printed in the USA
LVHW021337070820
662628LV00020B/2495